HARDEN

LEE HARDEN SERIES

BOOK 1

D. J. MOLLES

Text copyright © 2018 D.J. Molles

ISBN-13: 978-0-692-17656-6

For those who have looked into the woods,
But decided that they have promises to keep,
And miles to go before they sleep.

FOUR YEARS AGO...

IT WAS THE DAMN BETTA FISH.

The betta fish was the reason for the end of the last meaningful relationship that Lee Harden would have before the world went to shit.

Of course, no end of a relationship is ever quite that simple.

But you could say that the betta fish was the beginning of the end.

Her name was Deana. They'd been dating for about a year at that point. Lee's overseas deployments were behind him, and he was fresh out of the long and strange training protocol of Project Hometown when he met her.

They'd tapped him to be a "Coordinator" for Project Hometown because he had no one in his life. No siblings. No close relatives. His parents had died in a car accident in the last few months of his last deployment.

Project Hometown was a government initiative under the loose umbrella of the Department of the Army. *Subvenire Refectus* was their motto: Rescue and Rebuild. It was essentially a last-ditch contingency plan for any event that might lead to the fall of American society.

Nuclear events.

Invasion.

Any other shit that the Washington Worry-Warts dreamed up.

There was a Coordinator in each state, and they lived a quiet life of secrets, in a house that had been designed over top of a bunker. A bunker that the Coordinators referred to as The Hole, in the same spirit that a lifer in an old prison farm might refer to the punishment of solitary confinement.

Which is, in fact, what it was.

At first glance, it was just as comfortable as a nicely-appointed apartment. But no amount of trappings and trimmings could make a man long forget that what he really needs is sunlight, freedom, and human interaction.

Even people that hate people still miss them when they're gone.

Anytime the Washington Worry-Warts came up with something that could possibly destroy American society, Lee would go down into The Hole and he would wait there for the all-clear. It never turned into anything. Until it did. But that's a different story.

It was a lonely life.

So he'd met Deana, and they'd dated. She was understanding of his job, which required long absences in which he was in The Hole and not allowed any contact with the outside world. She didn't *know* that he was in The Hole. He told her that he was on "business for the government" and she was smart enough not to ask questions.

"The Betta Fish Incident," as he came to call it in his mind, occurred on a rainy December 31st, when he was picking Deana up from her job as a paralegal, heading to a New Year's Eve party.

Deana was shuffling paperwork. Sending the year's last few emails. She was auburn-haired, and tall, but not lanky. Filled out. In a sort of warrior-princess way. That was okay. Lee was 6'3" and had a perennial soft spot for women of a healthy size.

She had already changed from her business attire into a silvery party dress that highlighted her sporting dimensions. Lee thought that he might be underdressed in his jeans and black button-down, but at the same time, he didn't care.

It was dark, and through the windows of the office that Deana shared with several other paralegals, the world beyond was slick and black and shimmering with streetlights and stoplights.

Standing at the side of her desk as she finished up, Lee spotted a flash of purple and blue inside the clear vase on Deana's desk.

He leaned down to look in at the small creature inside the fish bowl. "What's this?"

"Betta fish," Deana said, in a manner that suggested the fish was a pothole in the otherwise smooth boulevard of her daily life. "It was a white elephant gift from the Christmas party."

Lee knew it was a betta fish. Also known as a Siamese fighting fish. He knew you couldn't put two of them together because they'd fight and kill each other. He appreciated that about them.

He put his index finger gently up to the cold, glass fish bowl.

The creature inside bristled at this intrusion, puffing out its gills to make it look bigger, flashing its colorful fanlike tail. Ready to fight.

Lee traced his finger across the glass, and the betta fish tracked with it.

When he withdrew his finger, the fish looked almost disappointed. Here, it had geared up for a big fight and nothing had happened.

Lee knew the feeling.

"That's probably the most excitement he's had all week," Deana observed with a smile. "I sometimes forget he's there."

Lee didn't respond. He was looking at the fish and, stupidly, starting to feel pity for the dumb thing.

"You ever feel bad for it?" Lee asked her.

Deana clicked around on her computer. Closing windows. Distracted. "Why's that?"

"It just sits there. In a fucking bowl. Day after day. Staring at your desk."

Deana pulled herself away from her computer. Looked at the fish. Then raised an eyebrow at Lee. "I think the fish will be okay."

"How long do they live?"

Deana sighed, like she had researched the answer and didn't care for it. "Up to three years. You see why it was the gift that no one wanted."

"So for the next three years, it's just going to sit there, bored out of its mind. Yearning to fight in the ponds of Siam."

Deana snickered at the glimmer of humor. "I think he'll be okay," she repeated.

"What if it's driving him nuts? Like being in solitary confinement."

"He seems to be handling it well."

"Maybe he's just stoic."

Deana stood up and grabbed her purse off the desk. "Maybe you think too much, Lee."

Then she slipped her arm in his and they left the office. Deana turned the lights out as she went, plunging the room into darkness where the little creature would float aimlessly.

They went on to the party.

Lee was surrounded by Deana's friends. He cracked jokes. Made them laugh. But he didn't really know them. And they didn't really know him. They were not really *his* friends.

He couldn't stop thinking about that stupid fish after that. And the idea had become planted in his mind now, the idea of sitting in a fish bowl in the darkness, completely alone, bred to fight, and yet never fighting.

If Deana couldn't understand something as simple as that fish, how the hell was she going to understand him?

It was a silly thought. Ridiculous.

But it germinated and grew.

Lee and Deana eventually parted ways, but it was amiable.

They kept up with occasional texts, phone calls, or messages on social media. Just checking in. Yes, things are fine. Glad to hear it. Blah blah.

Six months after they had parted, Lee was sent into The Hole because a certain bacteria called Febrile Urocanic Reactive Yersinia was eating away at people's frontal lobes and turning them incredibly violent.

The Washington Worry-Warts did their job of worrying, concerned that containment efforts might fail.

Lee did his job and went down into his fishbowl to wait for the all-clear.

It never came.

IN THE PRESENT

ONE

MOVE OUT AND DRAW FIRE

WE ARE BORN SURROUNDED.

That's what he was thinking as his blood-oxygen level reached its terminal low point. Like a seemingly purposeless flash of clarity in the midst of a drug-induced haze.

We are born surrounded, and spend our lives fighting to the death.

Then his heart stopped.

—

Mid-clavicular line.

This was the mental Mobius strip that looped through Julia's mind.

Second intercostal space. Mid-clavicular line.

A green chemlight jittered from a strap on her shoulder. It was the only light she had to work with. And it wasn't much. She could see the chest. The ribs. The hair. The blood. Everything else around her faded into darkness.

"Is he breathing?" A voice called out.

Julia glanced up from her fevered work.

At the window to the apartment, Julia could barely see the shadow of Brian Tomlin, looking at her over the stock of his rifle.

Abe Darabie stopped pumping chest compressions. Gasped for air. "Just watch the fucking road, goddammit!"

Julia snapped back to Abe. "Don't fucking stop!" she barked at him, and then she turned back to the inert form of Lee Harden, lying on his back, having taken his last breaths three minutes prior.

Lee's long, lanky body began to move limply as Abe grunted and continued with the chest compressions. Continued trying to keep that heart beating.

But starting the heart wasn't going to do them any good if Julia couldn't re-inflate Lee's lung.

She pulled the cap off a decompression needle with her teeth, then spat it off to the side. The 14-gauge needle glinted in the low, green light.

She held it in her right hand, and with her left hand, she rammed her fingers hard into Lee's left pectoral.

Her fingers slid across his blood-slick skin. She pressed them harder to get some traction. She felt the bony protuberance of one of his topmost ribs. She pulled her finger down. Felt the hollow between the ribs.

Second intercostal space. Mid-clavicular line.

She found the second space between the ribs. Leaned in close. Close enough to smell him. The smell she knew very well. Sweat. Body odor. The metallic tang of blood. The heavy chemical scent of gunsmoke.

The chest was jumping with Abe's compressions.

The needle in her hand trembled, inches from the skin.

"You need me to stop?" Abe gasped out.

"No," Julia said, frowning with the focus of someone disarming a bomb. "Don't stop."

She had the space marked by her left index finger. She pushed the thick needle into Lee's skin, just below that finger, until it hit the rib beneath that space. Then she angled it, guided it up. She felt the tip of it threading along the top of that rib, right into the space between.

Slight resistance as it poked against the pleural cavity.

Then give, as it penetrated.

Hope, fleeting.

She fed it in a little further.

He's dead.

Errant thought.

Her fingers were shaking badly. She got the catheter off the needle. Pulled the needle out.

"Keep going." She pointed to the mop of brown hair to her right. "Nate, breathe him!"

Nate looked terrified, but shoved the CPR mask down over Lee's face and started pumping the bag. Pressure now, filling Lee's throat and lungs. Moving things around.

Black blood trickled out of the corner of Lee's mouth.

"Oh, Jesus, shit!" Nate cried out. "He's bleeding out of his mouth! What do I do?"

"Just keep going," Julia commanded.

She hunched further over Lee's form, to the hole in his chest. An occlusive bandage had already been stuck to it. The hole was no longer visible behind a thin layer of bright, arterial blood. The one-way valve at the bottom corner of the dressing started to leak more of that bright blood.

Julia was nodding. "Keep going."

Come on, Lee. Come on…

Blood exiting the pleural cavity. The lung re-inflating.

Didn't mean Lee was resuscitated, but it was a step in the right direction, wasn't it?

He's dead, the cold clinician in her said. *Been dead for three minutes.*

Julia realized she was clutching the tatters of Lee's bloody combat shirt in her hands, twisting it like she might wring the death out of him and replace it with life, but all she could do was sit and hope, the cards dealt, the die cast, and hope to God they'd done enough, quick enough.

"Contact!" Tomlin called out. "Down the road!"

"Fuck!" Abe shouted at Lee's unresponsive chest, still hammering the compressions.

Tomlin and Julia's eyes connected in the dimness of their little hideout.

"They're comin'," Tomlin said.

Julia could only shake her head. "We need more time."

—

Whoever it was had sprung the ambush like an expert.

They'd hit them hard with automatic weapons, and then funneled them right into a dead end road. They'd had to abandon their two pickup trucks at a defunct and overgrown power substation, and the six of them plunged into the woods, running back east towards the town they'd just come through.

It was a tiny little burg on the eastern edge of Alabama. According to the map and the ivy-covered Lion's Club sign that they'd passed on the way in, the town was called Hurtsboro, and Brian Tomlin couldn't stop thinking, *how fucking appropriate.*

They had tried to set up a hasty counter-ambush, but whoever it was had only surrounded them again.

That was when Lee had been shot in the chest.

He'd stayed on his feet over the course of another quarter mile of fighting retreat, but had collapsed in the courtyard of a small apartment complex. Which was where they were currently hiding.

In the dismal dark inside that apartment, Tomlin and Carl Gilliard held coverage on the front windows, as Julia tried to fix Lee.

It wasn't going well.

It was there, crouched at the window, that Tomlin saw moonlight glint off the cab of an SUV, about two hundred yards down the road from the apartment. Headlights off, creeping towards them.

"Contact!" Tomlin called out. "Down the road!"

Beside him, at an adjacent window, Carl sank down onto one knee and got behind the optic of his rifle. "I got 'em."

Tomlin looked back over his shoulder. Lee was on the ground, limp, mouth hanging open, eyes closed, and in the glow of Julia's green chemlight, he looked like a cadaver.

Oh Jesus, Lee, Tomlin felt his chest tighten.

Julia glanced up from her work and her eyes hit Tomlin's. Her usual clinical detachment had fled from her face. She was not able to distance herself from this one. She looked terrified.

"They're comin'," Tomlin reiterated.

Julia shook her head at him. "We need more time."

Beside him, Carl raised his voice. "Julia, you need to stuff that chemlight somewhere. They're gonna see the glow."

Julia seized the chemlight that hung from a bit of strapping on the shoulder of her chest rig, and stuffed it behind her magazines. "I've got the decomp needle in," she said. "But we need more time on CPR or his blood pressure's gonna bottom out. We gotta give him more time."

Carl didn't take his eyes from the scope of his AR-10 rifle. "Jules, I got two bad-guy-trucks rolling slow up the road, accompanied by about ten motherfuckers on foot. So, you need to take a good honest look right now and tell me whether Lee can be saved."

"I don't…I don't know, Carl."

"Is he fucking dead?" Carl demanded.

"I don't fucking know!"

Carl let out a low growl. "Motherfuck." Then, to Tomlin, he said, "Alright, Brian. We gotta give them some time."

Tomlin turned back to the window. Back over his rifle. His cheek against the buttstock. The same spot where his stubbled face had abraded the rifle's paint job back down to the original black.

Out beyond, the trucks had crept closer.

They weren't just letting them go. They were pursuing them.

Who the fuck was it? Was it some of President Briggs's troops from Greeley, Colorado? That didn't seem right. From the glimpses that Tomlin had seen, most of their attackers were wearing civilian clothes.

Beside the vehicle, ten or so hostiles on foot were fanning out, several on either side of the road, and some of them had disappeared into the trees. It looked to Tomlin like they were trying to surround the apartment complex.

"We'll give him another couple of minutes, okay?" Julia called out, her voice on the ragged edge of desperation. "Just another couple of minutes."

"Alright, listen up," Carl called out. "Hostiles are a hundred yards down the road, moving to encircle this complex. Me and Tomlin are gonna run out, guns blazing, and hole up in the apartment directly across the courtyard here. We'll keep those motherfuckers off your back for as long as we possibly can. Julia, the second you get a fucking pulse back, you take him and get the fuck out the back, do you hear me?"

"I hear you."

Carl shifted in place, cast a glance over at Tomlin. "Alright buddy, it's you and me. You ready for this?"

All they had to do was run across thirty yards of parking lot, to the apartments on the other side.

They were a long way from home, and they had no QRF to come and save them. They had no safe place to retreat to. It was up to Tomlin and Carl to break inertia and give the rest of them a chance.

Move out and draw fire.

Tomlin nodded, despite a grip of fear that squeezed cold sweat from his brow. "Let's fuckin' do it."

Carl shoved himself off the window and went to the door. It was closed, but not latched. The frame around the door had been destroyed when they'd kicked it in. Carl put his left hand on the doorknob and held his heavy rifle with the other hand. "Let's stay tight, okay?"

"Okay. It's on you."

Carl yanked the door open, let it bang off the stopper, and then sprinted out into the night with Tomlin close on his heels.

TWO

LAST STAND

THE SWEAT WAS POURING down Abe's dark face, getting in his eyes, and tickling through his beard. But he didn't dare take his hands off of Lee's chest. He didn't dare stop the chest compressions, even though his core felt like it was splitting from lactic acid, and his triceps were cramping.

Everything else had become peripheral—their desperate mission into Alabama, the fact that they had no clue who the hell had attacked them, and the fact that all this gunfire was sure to attract primals. Abe's only concern in the world was trying to keep Lee's blood pressure high enough to stave off brain death.

At the front door, Carl and Tomlin disappeared into the darkness, like the night had swallowed them.

A second or two after they'd gone out, the night exploded into chaos. He heard Carl's .308 rifle pound out a few rounds, but then it was all lost in the din of hectic return fire and the screaming of men that Abe prayed wasn't Carl or Tomlin.

A round smacked through the window, whining over Abe's head and smashing something in the kitchen.

Julia ducked down over Lee's body, her hands on his carotid, trying to feel for that pulse.

"Come on, Lee," she pleaded, quiet as a prayer for the dead.

"Come on," Abe gasped as he pumped Lee's chest, feeling that horrible wall approaching him where he knew that his body was going to give out. He just had to keep going a little further… "Come on!" *Pump. Pump. Pump.* "Come on!"

"Wait! Stop!" Julia commanded.

Abe nearly collapsed, sucking wind.

Outside, the gunfire continued, nonstop.

But it wasn't directed at them anymore.

Julia swept her hand up, pushing the mask and Nate's hands out of the way to uncover Lee's mouth. She hovered there for a moment, staring, her cheek close to his lips, her fingers still pressed against his throat.

Then she nodded and bolted upright. "He's got a pulse! Let's go!"

Julia rammed whatever she could grab into her medical pack and zipped it closed in one motion, then hauled it onto her back, leaving behind a disaster area of medical detritus and sterile wrappings.

Abe staggered to his feet, still barely able to catch enough breath. He bent to grab one of Lee's arms, but Julia had the common sense to see that he was physically spent from nearly five straight minutes of doing chest compressions. She slapped his shoulder.

"You cover us," she said. "Me and Nate'll carry him."

Abe nodded and grabbed his rifle from where he'd slung it off to his left side. It felt treacherously heavy. He pulled it into his shoulder and raised it, and felt his shoulders twist at such a minor strain.

Breathe, he ordered himself. *Get your heart rate down.*

Nate and Julia each grabbed one of Lee's arms, and started hauling him back into the apartment towards the back door. Abe plunged ahead of them, fumbling through the dark.

He registered the stale smell of old death, leaking through the stink of his own sweat. By gradations of shadows, he picked out what could have been the long-ago-rotted body of the apartment's previous tenant—now just a jumble of clothing and bones, huddled by the back door.

He kicked a desiccated limb out of the path of the door. It sounded like dry wood wrapped in plastic. Abe's hands scrambled over the locks on the backdoor, undid the deadbolt and threw the door open.

Fresh, night air washed over him.

He punched through the door with his rifle at a high-ready, then cleared right, then left.

"Clear!"

Nate and Julia dragged Lee's body out of the apartment.

Straight ahead, trees huddled in darkness.

To their right, the road.

Behind them, the rattle of gunfire—which hopefully meant that Carl and Tomlin were still alive and fighting.

They plunged straight ahead, into the trees, Abe leading them. Branches and leaves reared up through the gloom at him, lashing his face.

The stand of trees was thin. About fifty yards through it, they stumbled back out into the open again. Overgrown grass and weeds that grabbed at his tired feet.

"We need to get indoors," Julia puffed, her face showing strain as she looked around them. A vein visibly standing out on her forehead, even in the darkness.

There was no shelter on their side of the road. Everything was across the street.

"Primals," Nate whispered between gulps of air, spittle from desperate breathing wetting his lower lip and chin. "They're gonna be attracted to the gunfire."

"I know," Abe growled.

Nate was right. The primals were going to show up. They always did. Like carrion birds, they were attuned to human conflict because they knew that meat would be left behind.

Abe took a big breath. "Alright." He pointed across the road. "We're going straight across. The quicker we move, the faster we're out of sight. Let me sub in with one of you."

Julia clung stubbornly to Lee's arm, but Nate nodded quickly, looking exhausted.

Abe slung his rifle and shouldered Nate out of position, taking Lee's limp right arm. "Get on point, Nate. Lead us across the road."

Nate gulped a few breaths, then shouldered his own rifle with exhaustion-clumsy hands and directed his muzzle down the street, where the gunfight was still raging. "Alright," he mumbled. "Moving."

He sprinted across the street.

Got to the ditch on the other side. Went down on a knee and covered the road.

Abe gave him a three-count, waiting for him to open fire, but Nate held steady.

"Okay, Jules, let's move."

They hauled Lee across the street, the unconscious man's boot heels scraping on the concrete. Abe's slung rifle jumped around and jabbed at his side.

Halfway across the street the sound of the gunfire changed from the *pop-pop-pop* of someone shooting at someone else, to the very distinct *snap-buzz* of incoming fire.

Abe grit his teeth and tried to pull faster.

He made it another two steps before something smacked his right calf.

"Shit!" was all he managed.

They tumbled into the ditch, Abe falling first as his leg collapsed under him, then Lee on top of him, and Julia on top of Lee.

"Contact!" Nate yelled, and opened up with his rifle.

Abe writhed out from under the tangle of bodies. For a moment, Lee's face was pressed against his. Julia was shouting at him, trying to figure out what had gone wrong.

"Move!" Nate was yelling at them as he fired. "Get to cover!"

Julia was already up on her feet again, tugging at Lee's left arm as Abe struggled up, the pain in his calf lancing all the way up his body, tingling in his lower back.

But he could move. He *had* to move.

He got ahold of Lee's right arm again and he and Julia started pulling for the first piece of cover in front of them—a long, squat, steel building.

Abe and Julia made it to the corner of the building. Abe staggered to a stop, still clinging to Lee's arm, readjusting his sweating, loosening grip. He registered that Nate wasn't firing anymore. He looked behind him to see if Nate was running for cover, and saw Nate simply lying there, face-first in the dirt.

"Nate!" Abe yelled.

No response.

A flurry of four or five rounds hit Nate's body and twitched it about, puffing little clouds of blood and dust into the moonlight.

Abe almost called out to Nate again, though he couldn't figure out why.

Julia was already pulling them on again.

"Come on," she belted out between haggard gulps of air. "We gotta keep moving!"

—

"That's it," Carl called out, as the slide on his pistol locked back. "Empty."

Carl pulled back behind the kitchen counter of the apartment. Their last little redoubt.

Tomlin sat there, shoulder to shoulder with Carl in the darkness, and they both stared at the empty pistol as though it were all a cosmic joke.

Their rifles were already empty, laying useless at their sides. The ground around them was littered with brass and all the empty magazines that they'd already used up.

Around them, the night huddled, black as the pit, and their vision was speckled with the ghostly after-images of their own muzzle flashes.

"Well, shit," Tomlin said.

Carl nodded, dropped his hand holding the empty pistol to his side.

The return gunfire from outside of the apartment had now slowed to trickle. Just random potshots. After another few seconds, it stopped altogether.

There were some shouts from outside. Neither Tomlin nor Carl could tell what they were saying. Their eardrums were destroyed at this point. They'd shot about two hundred rounds in that small, enclosed space. The world was humming, and even each other's voices, a foot away, were hard to hear.

Gunsmoke filled the kitchen like a low-hanging bank of fog.

Tomlin could taste it on his tongue. Sharp and metallic.

He cleared his throat and spat. "They always say not to shoot in unventilated areas. We probably have lead poisoning or something."

Carl puffed out a breath. "You know, that's something I always liked about you, Brian. You always kept it lighthearted."

"Yeah?" Tomlin felt sick to his stomach. If his hands weren't clenched, they would've been shaking. "Shit, Carl. I never even realized you had a sense of humor."

"Well…" Carl released the slide on his pistol and slid it back into its holster. "Don't tell anyone."

Someone shouted at them from somewhere in the apartment. Incoherent syllables.

"The fuck did he say?" Tomlin asked.

Carl just shook his head.

More shouting. Then the shouting stopped.

"You think we gave them enough time to get away?" Tomlin asked.

Carl shrugged. "We did the best we could." He raised his left fist to Tomlin. "It's been good workin' with you, sir."

Tomlin bumped his fist to Carl's. "Yeah. Knives?"

"Might as well."

Both of them were reaching for their knives when a shape loomed in the kitchen window. The glass was already broken from a multitude of gunshots. A rifle barrel jammed its way through and Carl and Tomlin froze.

"Don't you fuckin' move!" the shadowy figure screeched at them. "Don't you fuckin' move or I'll kill both of you, I swear to God! Hey! Hey, I got 'em! I got 'em in the kitchen! They're in the kitchen!"

Tomlin sat there, staring up at the dark figure.

There came a point where even a professional warfighter must admit that his opponent has gotten the drop on them. And in that moment, you know that any gesture you make will leave you dead, and that will be that. The guy that kills you likely won't be terribly impressed by you trying to make a last-ditch move.

Tomlin also knew that sometimes, if you're patient, an opportunity will open up for you, and you'll have a far better chance than you did if you simply tried to kamikaze your way out.

All of this occurred to Tomlin in the second or so of him staring up into the muzzle of that rifle.

"Put your hands up!" the man in the window was screaming. "Hands up! Hands up!"

Slowly, Tomlin and Carl both raised their hands.

The kitchen abruptly filled with bodies. Boots squeaking on linoleum. Men shouting. Grabbing them. Punching them. Kicking them.

A buttstock to the side of his face made Tomlin's world turn to stars.

A second blow knocked him out completely.

—

The primals were coming.

Abe and Julia pulled Lee's body through the ink-dipped ghost town of Hurtsboro.

The gunfire in the distance had gone silent moments ago. But another sound had replaced it.

Some people called it a howl, but Julia had never thought it sounded like a howl. It was more like a scream. It was the raging, aggressive animal that abides deep down in all human beings. After the FURY bacterium ate away their frontal lobe, the primal animal was all that remained.

"We need to get inside," Abe said.

They stumbled up to the basement door of a split-level house. It was nearly covered by a shrub that had grown up to monstrous proportions.

Abe collapsed against the brick wall of the house, breathing hard, trying to rest his wounded leg. Sweat poured down his face. Pain evident in his features.

"I'll clear it," Julia said.

She left Abe holding onto Lee. She tested the door, found it unlocked.

She slipped in. Her eyes were already adjusted to the dark, and she didn't bother with her weaponlight. She cleared the basement area with the economical movement of something practiced thousands of times. It smelled musty, but there was no stench of piss and shit, which meant that they hadn't stumbled into a primal den.

Small miracles.

She went back out and helped Abe pull Lee into the basement.

She closed and locked the door as Abe laid Lee out on the hard floor—concrete with a thin layer of industrial carpeting tiles. Then Abe collapsed on the floor beside him and began to address his own leg wound.

Julia would help him in a moment. "I need to clear the upstairs," she said, her voice low.

Abe nodded.

She dropped her medical pack, her lower back screaming with relief. She went up the basement stairwell, like a burglar invading an occupied dwelling. She listened to the house, and it was silent, but out beyond the walls, she could hear them. Drawing closer.

They were going to feed on the dead.

They're going to feed on Nate.

And what about Carl and Tomlin?

No. Don't think about it.

Up the stairs.

The middle level was a kitchen and a living room. The top level was bedrooms.

The house was empty. Quiet. Abandoned. Whoever had lived here had not mounted a defense when the infection had stricken the world. They'd probably evacuated. Died in some FEMA camp somewhere. Probably died wishing they'd just stayed here in this house.

Back down to the mid-level, Julia went to the kitchen and grabbed wooden chairs from around the small, dining room table. She propped one up under the doorknob of the kitchen door, then the front door. Then she took one downstairs and propped it up under the basement door.

It was just a stopgap.

If the primals wanted to get in this house, they would get in.

If they wanted to feed on Julia and Abe and Lee, they would.

Julia and Abe would take several of them down, but the primals would eventually rip them apart.

They could only hope that they would be ignored.

In that basement, as the shrieks and calls of the creatures without sounded closer and closer, Julia didn't dare use her flashlight. She didn't even dare use the chemlight. So she worked in darkness, and in silence, trying to stop Abe's bleeding, and trying to keep Lee alive, and wondering for the first time since the ambush had been sprung on them, *How the fuck did all of this go so bad?*

THE PREVIOUS WEEK

THREE

FIELD 29

LEE STEPPED OUT OF the pickup truck.

The sandy loam shifted slightly under his feet.

The type of soil that didn't grow things willingly. It had to be coaxed. Anything worthwhile had to be pried from it like a gold coin from the purse of a miser.

He stood to the passenger's side of the truck with the door still hanging open. It was a late model F-150 that had once been white. Now caked with two years' worth of mud and dust. Mismatched offroad tires. A battered brushguard on the front.

Lee's rifle was at rest, muzzle pointing at the ground, but his hand still held the grip, finger poised outside the trigger guard.

Behind him, another truck, identical to the one he'd just exited.

This was his team:

Abe and Tomlin beside him.

Carl, Nate, and Julia in the truck behind.

Not sure what they'd find at Field 29, they were all in full battle rattle. Some of them in jeans. Some in fatigues. But all of them wearing their plate carriers, and all of them strapped with a rifle and a pistol, and extra mags for both.

M4's mostly, with the exception of Carl, who'd gone with his scoped AR-10 in case they needed any long-range capabilities.

Helmets were kept stowed. It didn't look like they were going to need them: what they were going up against didn't shoot bullets—it went for the jugular.

The two pickups idled in the still morning air.

The road beneath them was hard-packed sand that cut through a forest of pines. Straight ahead, the pines cleared out, and a huge field lay there, the dirt heavily tilled and brown amongst the live-wire green of a newly-born spring.

In the middle of the field, frozen in its work, a large red tractor, towing behind it a gang of disc plows.

Further back in the field, a command trailer, still attached to the Heavy Expanded Mobility Tactical Truck that had towed it there.

To the right-hand side of the road, just inside the field, a smaller tractor sat, with an auger half-plunged into the ground. A bundle of heavy-duty fence posts sat beside this tractor. A spool of electric wire sat unused beside the rest of these supplies.

The fencing had barely been started.

Lee bit his lip hard, and felt his heart sink, pulling his insides taut.

What were they thinking?

They should've known better than to run the plow tractor before the fencing was up.

But he knew what they'd been thinking.

They'd been thinking that they had to hurry. That time was of the essence. That there were thousands of people in the Fort Bragg Safe Zone, and beyond that, the entire United Eastern States, that were on the verge of running out of food.

And of course, they'd probably also been thinking that their protective detail would be enough. That if the primals came, all the workers and the protective detail could simply pile into the command trailer on the HEMTT and wait them out until the QRF arrived.

But sometimes Quick Reaction Forces weren't as quick as you needed them to be.

Lee felt guilt creep up on him but spurned it away.

We got here as quick as we could.

A few gnats had already managed to scent him out. They hovered around his eyes and ears, and he waved them off. The spring sunshine was just now cresting the trees and warming the cool shadows that the night had left. The gnats seemed to like this intermediate temperature.

Lee snapped the fingers of his left hand, and glanced into the truck.

From between the two front seats a head protruded. Long, wolf-like snout. Pointed ears swiveling in his direction. Golden eyes locked in with intensity.

"Deuce," Lee said, quietly. "Come."

The dog needed no further encouragement. It was a nervy dog by nature, and sought to stick to Lee's side whenever possible. Deuce scrambled out. Hit the ground at a trot, then cut a wide circle around Lee, with his nose in the air.

The golden eyes looked everywhere. In the woods. Towards the field. Towards the tractors and their implements sitting lifelessly in the dirt. And always, every couple of seconds, a glance up at Lee, as though Deuce were using Lee's face as a gauge for whether or not he was operating correctly.

After a few more circles, Deuce plastered his side to Lee's leg and let out a tiny chuff.

"Nothing?" Lee kept his eyes up. Scanning the fields, although he felt some of the tension ebb from him. If Deuce wasn't growling, then there likely wasn't any infected nearby.

However, they moved fast. Very fast. You might think you were safe, but that could change very quickly.

Lee made it a point never to let himself feel safe.

He gently closed the door to the truck, then looked through the open window.

Tomlin in the driver's seat. The usual glint of mischief in his eyes had become an intense hyper-focus. His normally good-humored face was pinched down, his lips tight.

Abe sat on the rear bench seat. His dark, serious gaze scrutinizing everything, as though that rock over there, or that tree, might suddenly come to life and threaten them.

"Alright," Lee said. "I'm gonna walk you in. Go slow. Stay frosty."

Lee glanced behind him, raised a hand and twirled his index finger in the air once—*we're rolling.*

Then he started walking.

Deuce trotted alongside him.

The trucks rolled, their tires making slow and constant crunching noises on the dirt beneath them.

The sun was warming the back of his neck. The smell of morning dew rising. Sand. Pine needles. Freshly turned dirt.

Somewhere off to his right, a crow cawed obnoxiously, and took to the air. Its argumentative voice faded with distance.

Lee snugged up into his rifle. Raised the muzzle as he walked.

Around them the trees stretched out. Still and silent.

He stopped first at the tractor that had been drilling post holes. He surveyed the scene from a few paces off, taking in the details. They'd drilled maybe a dozen post holes along the wood line. They'd managed to erect a few of the steel, ten-foot posts. But they hadn't put up any of the chain link, or the high voltage wires.

He heard footsteps behind him and turned with a jerk.

Julia had exited her truck and was approaching him with her usual soft stride.

"Relax," she said, though it was almost tongue-in-cheek.

No one was relaxed. Especially not outside the Safe Zone.

"You just can never stay in the truck," Lee mumbled.

Julia shrugged.

She liked to do her own thing. She was about as bullheaded as Lee himself. They got along well. Except for when they didn't, which was usually when their bullheadedness clashed.

Deuce sauntered over to the tractor with the auger attached and gave it a once over with his nose. He found something interesting on the ground and spent some time inhaling it fervently, then lost interest and moved on.

He still had not growled.

"Look like primals to you?" Julia asked.

"That would be my guess."

Julia's restless gaze had wandered on from the abandoned fencing operation. Out across the half-tilled fields. To the trailer and HEMTT. She nodded towards it. "There's your last stand."

Lee followed her gaze. Closer now to the trailer, he saw some details he hadn't seen earlier. There was a peppering of bullet holes in the metal siding. Likely bullets that had been shot from inside out. Shooting at the creatures that had surrounded them.

"Alright," Lee said. "Let's move it in."

They started walking again. Rifles up higher now.

The two pickup trucks trundled alongside them.

Deuce took a hurried piss on the side of the tractor's tire and trotted to catch up with Lee and Julia.

As they drew closer to the trailer, the scene began to clarify.

A patch of blood here.

Drag marks in the dirt over there.

Footprints—both bare, and booted.

A rifle lying dropped and abandoned in a clump of weeds. Brass casings all around it. The bolt locked back on an emptied magazine.

A hand.

A foot.

The workers sent to secure this little field of agriculture had attracted the wrong attention. And they hadn't had the fence up. The primals had come, probably from many different directions. Picked away at the workers and their protection detail.

And it hadn't taken them long, either. The protective detail had only had the chance to get out one radio transmission:

"QRF!" the man had screamed. *"QRF now!"*

Lee and his team had immediately dispatched from the Fort Bragg Safe Zone, twenty miles away, and they had hauled as fast as they possibly could over roads that were washed out, potholed, and obstructed by fallen trees. But not fast enough.

Deuce growled.

Lee stopped dead in his tracks.

He was about ten yards from the trailer now.

He glanced down at Deuce. The dog was stock-still next to his leg, his tail low and stiff, his body tense. He issued a long, protracted rumble in his chest that ended in a chuff. Ears completely forward. Locked onto that trailer.

Lee looked at the closed trailer door. The siding.

Bloody smears around the door.

Whoever the primals had caught inside the trailer, they'd dragged them back out the front door. And whoever that had been, they'd been alive and struggling when it had happened.

Behind Lee, the trucks rolled to a gentle stop, and a few doors creaked open. The team was well-versed with Deuce's alerts. They didn't need to ask what was going on.

Carl and Tomlin flanked around Lee, moving with softly rolling footfalls towards the command trailer, their rifles trained on the door. They stopped, a pace or so away.

Lee leaned down and gave Deuce a scratch behind the ears. "Good boy," he whispered, then put that same hand on Deuce's grumbling chest and gave it a gentle press. "Ssh," Lee said.

It was a new command that Lee was working on. And it didn't always work.

Deuce kept growling at the trailer, louder now, getting to that point where it sounded like he might start barking.

"I hear you," Lee hissed at the dog. "But you need to *ssh*."

Another press on the dog's chest.

Deuce glanced at him. Then took a half step backwards and was silent.

"Good boy," Lee mumbled, bringing his rifle back up to the door of the trailer.

He approached, Julia right behind him.

Nate and Abe stayed behind the wheels of the running trucks, ready to go into escape maneuvers at a moment's notice.

Lee pulled up to the right of the door, sidled up close to Carl's tall form. The sun was shining off of Carl's sweating, prematurely-bald scalp. He blinked as a drop of it got into his eye. Glanced at Lee with eyes as still and cold as a deeply frozen lake.

"You hear anything?" Lee breathed.

Carl nodded once. Pulled his lips back and gave two deliberate chomps of his teeth.

The gesture was disturbing, but its meaning was clear.

Feeding.

Lee caught Julia's gaze, then nodded towards the door.

Julia pulled her rifle up into a high-ready and side-stepped to the left of the door, her hand hovering over the doorknob. Then she looked at Lee.

He squared himself to the door.

Rifle up. Looking over the top of his sights.

Julia's fingers touched the knob. Squeezed. Gently turned.

From inside, there was the sudden sound of something thrashing.

A wet, throaty bark.

Julia thrust the door open.

Lee punched the entry hard, flowing into the room as the door opened. He shouldered the door onto its stopper, and for a moment thought there might be something behind it. But the second he'd taken a single step into the room, he caught a flash of pale flesh in his left periphery.

A blur of movement.

A high-pitched screech.

Lee pivoted deftly on his right foot, eyes already in his optic by the time he faced left.

Jaws. Teeth. Claws.

Lee fired five rounds, backpedaling. His back hit the wall behind him.

The thing hit the ground.

Lurched. Trembled. Then rolled onto its back with a groan that turned into a gurgle, and then it was still.

Lee's heart hammered on the inside of his chest, worked its way up his throat, started pounding in his head. He consciously removed his finger from the trigger. Then lowered the muzzle a few inches.

"Fuck," his voice shook.

"You good?"

Lee jerked.

Julia was standing in the door to his left, but she wasn't looking at him. She, and her rifle, were addressed towards the thing on the floor.

Lee let his eyes take in the entirety of the trailer for the first time.

It was a small area. Metal cabinets on the walls. Two rolling chairs, both upended.

Blood on the walls.

On the floors.

Brass.

Bullet holes.

Through the stink of spent gunpowder, Lee caught a heavy whiff of blood and bowels.

Julia edged forward, towards the tangle of strangely-shaped limbs on the ground in front of them. Lee stepped forward with her.

The thought crossed his mind to give it a security round, but he knew it was dead. Knew it by the worm of brain matter that was actively oozing out of a hole in its head. Curling, like pus out of a cist.

"Got one," Julia called to Carl and Tomlin outside. Rote. Mechanical. "Dead."

From outside the trailer, Carl called out: "Primal?"

"Yeah," Lee answered. He frowned as he lowered his rifle, standing over the body on the floor.

It wasn't human. Not in the strictest sense.

Some bastardized version of it, though. The basics were there. It had two arms and two legs and a torso and a chest and a head. It had five fingers on each hand. Eyes and ears and mouth and nose.

Head, shoulders, knees and toes.

Yeah, all the basics were there.

But could you really call them fingers? Or were they claws?

Could you really call it a nose? Or was it a snout?

Mouth too large to be normal. Gaping open.

Lee twisted his head as he looked down at it.

Strange.

Not many teeth.

The ones that were there were small. Like toddler's teeth.

In fact, the whole fucking body was small, wasn't it?

Small and pale and scrawny.

Naked.

Female.

"Fuck me running," Julia breathed.

Lee swallowed and felt it go down hard, like taking a large pill on a dry throat. He looked at the wide, open mouth. The slick blood around it. The bits of gristle still stuck between the thing's smallish teeth. Then his gaze tracked to the corner of the room where the primal had come from.

A bloody pile of rags and limbs and intestines. A bare ribcage evident, poking up through a tattered green jacket stained with red.

"Carl," Lee called.

Carl stepped into the trailer. He stood at the door and looked at Lee, then down at the body on the floor. He tilted his head, just like Lee had. Like a dog hearing a confusing noise. Then he stepped forward. Stood between Lee and Julia.

He reached out with the toe of his boot and turned the head so that he could see it better. The shape and dimensions of the face. The small teeth. The bare gums where molars should have been.

"Another one of the juveniles?" he suggested.

"So it's true," Julia said.

"I didn't doubt it."

"First time I've seen one up close."

Lee shifted his feet. "We should take it with us."

Carl frowned. "Why?"

"I wanna know how old it is."

"You want Doc Trent to take a look?"

Lee nodded.

"The fuck you think a general practitioner's gonna do?"

"Teeth. Bones. I dunno." Lee shrugged. "He can make a better guess than me."

"What's your guess?"

Lee looked down at the body and tried to equate it to a human child, but it wasn't a fair comparison. "No clue," Lee decided. "That's why I want Trent to take a look."

Lee switched the sling on his rifle from a single point to a two point, and then shoved it off to his side where it wouldn't be in the way. He knelt to grab the corpse's filthy feet. It stank like a wild animal. "Come on. Grab the other end."

He had the fleeting thought that maybe ignorance was bliss.

But they were already carrying the body out.

FOUR

THE UNION

MARIE STOOD AT THE Fort Bragg food distribution center, watching the lines of people like you might watch a kettle start to simmer.

The woman at the lead of the queue had an expression on her face like she'd just been sold a dog turd disguised as a chocolate bar, and her voice was starting to rise.

And the young woman on the other side of the table—the poor, hapless worker trying to hand this bitch a box full of rations—was trying to speak, but was losing the volume battle.

The "food distribution center" was a really fancy name for what was essentially a few battered folding tables set up next to a flatbed truck with two hundred ration boxes stacked on it. The ration boxes themselves were a mix of cardboard crates and plastic laundry baskets that had been re-used God-knew how many times. Most of them were held together with duct tape.

The whole setup was positioned in a parking lot outside of an activity center on the base. It'd been a cool night, but it was promising to be the warmest day of the year so far. Marie thought that maybe they should've set it up on the north side of the building, which was still in shade. They were on the southern side, and the sun was warming the concrete, and perhaps heating people's tempers as well.

Marie looked sidelong at Mitch, who stood to her right, and back a pace or two.

He caught her looking at him and gave her a quirk of one of his bushy, chestnut eyebrows.

Marie shook her head, knowing that if Mitch and his team got involved it was only going to make things worse.

His team was in plain clothes today, but you could see the soft-armor that they wore beneath their shirts, and they still had their rifles, although they kept them slung on their sides.

Ostensibly, they were there to keep the peace. Food was the flashpoint that certain people were using to rile up dissension in Fort Bragg.

But Marie knew that what Mitch really wanted was to identify the "agitators."

Or "Lincolnists," as the agitators had titled themselves.

Marie stepped up to the side of her worker, took the box the girl was holding and set it down. She didn't give the contents of the box a glance. She knew what was in it, because she'd been up all night filling it, and hundreds of others just like it.

Instead, she directed herself to the woman across the table.

She was a tall woman, where Marie was short, so that Marie found herself looking up at her. The woman had short brown hair pulled back by a headband, so that it created an unfortunate, dirty halo that framed her severe features. Features made worse by the anger scribbled all over them.

"Is there a problem I can help you with?" Marie said, as diplomatically as she could manage.

"I don't know if you can help me," the woman spat, her halo of hair trembling as she spoke. "Can you give me some real fucking milk? Last week we had real milk."

"Last week there was enough for everybody to get real milk. We hope that there will be enough to do that again next week." And then, because she couldn't help herself, Marie said, "I can't make the cows lactate any faster."

The woman pulled back like she'd smelled shit. "Oh. Nice. Now you're gonna get smart with me. What is it? Marie, right?"

"Yes, ma'am, that's my name."

"Well I got a three-year-old at home. And she won't drink this stuff!"

From a few people back, a man leaned out and hollered, "Mine won't either! I got the same damn problem! Can't you let the people with the kids have the real milk?"

Marie held out a hand. "We haven't worked out a fair way to do that just yet—"

"That's not my problem," the woman across from her said. "That's *your* problem. You're the one that's supposed to have all this shit figured out."

Anger was starting to flush Marie's cheeks. "Ma'am, I'll do my best to work that out moving forward. But for *right now*, these are the boxes that we've been able to put together."

The woman, who was beyond being placated, shoved her hands into the box and batted around a handful of green packages like they were trash. "And these! These fucking MRE's! They gave my five year old constipation for *three days*!"

Another chorus of agreements from the line of people.

Marie blinked rapidly.

She couldn't believe her ears.

Two years ago, she'd slapped a one-cup scoop of rice and beans in a coffee can and people thanked her for it. She remembered her heart breaking to be thanked for so little. She remembered the faces of those people as they looked at the tiny amount of food they had and tried to figure out how they were going to divvy it up amongst their family.

Had this woman never been in straits so dire?

Or had she simply forgotten already?

And did she not know that those times were coming again?

"I'm sorry," Marie snapped. "But do you have any fucking clue what's going on out there?"

"Oh, now you're gonna cuss at me?"

"Yeah, I'm gonna fucking cuss at you. You been cussing at me and my people for the last five fucking minutes, so why don't you just think about the people that are outside the Safe Zone right now, risking their lives to grow enough food that we don't starve. Do you not realize that in two months, you might have nothing?"

The woman wasn't impressed. If anything, she was getting madder.

She thrust a finger at Marie's face. "We wouldn't even *be* in this position if you and your bullshit secession hadn't happened!"

The crowd rumbled its assent at that, and the woman heard it, and then she turned to the people in line behind her, now addressing them with an orator's bravado. "We could all be safe with President Briggs right now! I bet they have plenty to eat in Colorado! Because they have a *real* government to take care of them! They have a *real* president!"

Marie had run out of words. She was so flabbergasted by what was happening right in front of her face, she could only stand there, on the ragged edge of giving this woman an uppercut and letting her eat a few of her teeth to see if that didn't curb her appetite...

The woman turned, amid the bolstering cries of her peers behind her. She slapped the folding table. "I wanna know what Angela's family eats!"

Several others called out that they wanted to know too.

"I heard her family eats whatever she wants! I hear that she and her cronies get first pick, while the rest of us get whatever's left over!"

"That's a bullshit rumor," Marie growled.

"Yeah?" The woman leered at her. "Maybe you're one of those cronies. I wanna talk to Angela! Right fucking now!"

"No—"

"If she wants my family to eat this shit, I want her to come down here, look me in my face, and tell me that she's eating the same thing!"

A roar of approval this time. More than just a dozen people.

"We're all eating the same thing!" Marie belted out. "If you don't want the box, then get the hell outta the way and let someone else take it that is happy to have it!"

"I'm not fuckin' moving!" the woman declared.

Out of the corner of Marie's eyes, she saw two of Mitch's team start to move in.

But then four more people came rushing forward out of the line and planted themselves next to the woman with the dirt-colored halo of hair. Then a few more. And a few more. Until there were nearly a dozen standing there, all saying that they weren't moving until Angela came down and talked to them directly.

They started to link arms.

Marie turned to Mitch and gave him a sharp *stand-down* gesture.

Mitch waved his guys off. They retreated a couple steps, but kept a close eye on the group of people now standing one table's-width away from Marie.

Marie threw up her hands and leaned over to Mitch. "Fuck it," she said. "Get on the horn and tell the Support Center we got a problem and they want to talk to Angela."

—

Angela stood in front of the desk in her office. She leaned back on it. Felt the molded, wooden edge of it. Tapped her fingertips on the lacquered wood. They didn't make clicking noises. Just dull *thumps*. Because Angela didn't have fingernails to speak of.

Even if she didn't chew them off all the time, she would keep them short.

She did not dress for her office.

She wore jeans and a button-up shirt. Boots on her feet. Curly blonde hair pulled into a plain pony tail. Her advisors all agreed that she should look more *presidential*, seeing as how the plaque on her desk said *President Angela Houston.*

But she refused.

What was she going to do? Wear a pants suit? Cut her hair into a conservative bob? Put on panty hose and business-style pumps?

Fuck that.

The mantle of leadership was not just a yoke on her shoulders. It was a millstone around her neck. She didn't want this office. But it had been given to her nonetheless. She craved the end of this year, because the end of this year would bring about the end of her first term as the elected leader of the fledgling United Eastern States.

First and *only* term, if God had an ounce of mercy in him.

She didn't see how she could possibly be re-elected.

The populace was not that stupid.

It was not that she had intentionally sabotaged them. Her desperation to be free of this leadership position didn't extend to her putting everyone else in jeopardy.

No, she'd done her level best. She'd done *more* than her best. She'd gone long days without sleep. She'd dug post holes with the work parties, and erected fences and planted seeds and herded cattle. Then she'd turned around and parlayed peace between warring parties and convinced fractious loners to become allies. She'd given every bit of herself to try to make things work.

But…

It wasn't enough.

The man standing in front of her shifted his feet.

Angela realized that she'd been silently marooned in her thoughts for nearly a minute. She looked up at the man. He was tall and rangy. A good looking guy, but in a humble sort of way. He looked like a farmhand. Which was fitting, seeing as how he was her Director of Agriculture.

Jesus. Such lofty names.

The pomp and circumstance was necessary to secure people's faith in their new government. She understood that. But every once in a while it seemed absolutely ridiculous, like they were kids in a treehouse, playing at being adults.

"Sorry, Jeff," Angela said, standing erect again, as though she didn't feel like there were a thousand pounds on her back. "I was just considering the options."

"Right." Jeff nodded. He seemed almost relieved to see Angela stand fully upright again. As though he'd been concerned that she'd been crushed by the bad news. "Look…" his eyes flitted to the rug beneath their feet. "…I know that you haven't had it easy lately."

Angela forced a smile and gestured to the office around her, which was a far cry from the cold dungeon of the Camp Ryder office where her journey had begun. The Camp Ryder office had been a concrete and tile cube. This office had a nice green rug and hardwood floors and paint on the walls. Camp Ryder had been industrial steel and one small portal, like a prison cell. This office had a wooden desk and upholstered chairs and windows to let in natural light.

She was living in comparative luxury.

"Don't worry about me, Jeff," Angela said. "I'm just the figurehead. You guys are the ones that this shit is hitting. Pardon my language."

"That's very humble of you to say, ma'am. But we're all in this together." He smiled. Then let it fall. "I know you feel the weight of it. Just like I do."

They sat there, staring at each other.

And, dammit, Angela was suddenly on the verge of tears, like the weight of the pressure was condensing them out of her. She wanted to collapse into one of the chairs that surrounded the rug. Or curl up in a fetal position. Or grab a hold of Jeff and hug him. Cry into his shoulder.

So weak…

Instead, she took a breath. Smiled as warmly as she was capable of, and nodded to him. "Thank you. We will see what we can do."

"That's all we can ask."

And with that, Jeff turned and exited the office.

Angela watched him go, feeling the corners of her mouth melt out of that smile and stiffen like cold, hardening wax, into a grimace. It was only as Jeff reached the door to the office and went through it that Angela realized that her assistant was standing there.

Angela raised her eyebrows. "Yes, Claire?"

Claire Staley stepped forward. Green eyes level and evaluating. "Captain Harden radioed in about ten minutes ago, but you were in the meeting."

Angela felt her gut twist up all over again. "Field Twenty-Nine?" she asked with an inward cringe.

Claire watched her for a second or two, then shook her head. "Negative, ma'am. No survivors."

The room was still. For four steady beats of Angela's heart. She didn't breathe. Didn't react. Neither did Claire. Both women just standing there facing each other.

Finally: "Okay. Thank you, Claire."

Over the top of Claire's head, one of Angela's bodyguards loomed. His finger was pressed to his ear piece, as though he were listening to a garbled transmission. But he was looking at her with urgency in his eyes.

"Ma'am, you're being requested down at the food distribution," he said. "It just came over the radio."

Angela's already pensive demeanor fell even further. "Oh, Jesus. Is it the Lincolnists again?"

The bodyguard, Kurt, shrugged. "I don't know, ma'am. But it's Marie that's asking for you."

—

Angela descended the stairwell from the top level of what had once been the Fort Bragg Soldier Support Center. It was now...offices.

What the hell else would she call it? It was nothing like a government building, with an orderly conglomeration of "this person in this room, and this group of people on this floor." It was much more slapdash than that. It was simply a place for people who needed a place, of which Angela had the nicest place, because the tag on her desk said "president."

Kids playing in a tree house.

In front of and behind her paced her two bodyguards.

No dress uniforms and salutes here. They all kept it pretty casual. Kurt and Anthony wore their regular operational gear, although they typically eschewed the helmets, and Angela didn't blame them. When they'd first been assigned to her, she'd had trouble telling them apart. They were both medium-height and brown haired, with remarkably unremarkable faces, and the rank of sergeant.

Luckily, they wore their name tapes on their plate carriers.

Anthony was "MIZZUTTI".

Kurt was "BARSCH".

An additional identifier for Angela was that Anthony was typically dour and didn't say much, and Kurt was generally smiley and exchanged pleasantries with her. From a distance, it was helpful that Kurt had painted his rifle tan, and Anthony chose to leave his black.

Anthony led them, and Kurt took up the rear.

They reached the bottom of the stairs and stepped through the door, Anthony holding it for Angela while keeping his eyes outward-oriented with that grim, suspicious expression of his.

"Your meeting go okay?" Kurt offered as he took Anthony's spot holding the door for her.

Angela's mind was lost in thought.

She blinked as she walked, glanced over her shoulder. "I'm sorry, what was that?"

Kurt nodded at Angela. "Wasn't tryin' to pry. You just seem a little tense, that's all."

A noise like a subtle groan came from Anthony. Like Kurt's small talk was testing the structural integrity of his patience.

Angela walked through the foyer of the Support Center and towards the front doors. "I'm fine, thank you for asking." She realized it came out very stiff, though she did actually appreciate Kurt's concern.

She decided to give Kurt something for his efforts. "It was just more bad news. And we've got enough of that already, don't we?"

"Yeah, we sure do." Kurt nodded ahead. "The car's pulling around for you now."

Angela slowed her pace, thinking about what Jeff had told her and swallowing it down. *We don't have enough.* "No, actually. I think we should just walk. If it's okay with you two."

Anthony reached the front doors of the building and pulled one open for her. "Fine by us, ma'am."

She heard Kurt's voice, speaking through his radio on the command net: "Diamondback One to command. We're going to be on foot towards the food distribution."

Diamondback.

That was her.

A dangerous sounding codename for a housewife who didn't know what the fuck she was doing. But it had been chosen for her. A vague reference to the Gadsden flag. A subtle warning that she often feared she didn't have the teeth for.

She stepped out into bright, late-morning sunshine. It was early April, and beginning to hint at spring. The nights stayed cold, as well as the mornings. It had been cold when she'd arrived. But already the sun was warming things up.

Warming the earth.

Getting it ready for planting.

If only we had enough to actually plant.

To her left, the dusty black Tahoe that ferried her around the base was pulling up. Kurt stepped forward and waved it off. The passenger's side window came down as the SUV stopped at the sidewalk.

Kurt hollered at the driver, "She's gonna walk."

The driver responded something that she couldn't hear.

She stepped out from under the shadow of the building she'd just come from and enjoyed the warmth of the sun on her face.

Something on the third floor of the middle school across the way twinkled in the sun.

She didn't pay it any mind.

Anthony shuffled to get in front of her. They always liked to have one in front and one behind.

The next few seconds were very odd.

She felt something hard hit her waist, just above her hip. And she thought for a second that Kurt had grabbed her, but then it didn't quite feel like someone's hands, it was something else, something she'd never experienced before, and why in the hell would anyone grab her that hard anyway?

And when she turned to look at Kurt, he was two paces behind her.

As she turned, her core suddenly spasmed, and the strength went abruptly and mysteriously out of her legs, and she toppled, barely catching herself with her arms and wondering what the fuck had just hit her...

All of this in a bare instant.

And in the next instant, the rumble of a rifle report, and she knew what had hit her.

I've been shot.

FIVE

DIAMONDBACK ACTUAL

By Mitch's best estimate, the crowd at the food distribution point was now split right down the middle.

Half of them were bolstering the angry woman that had started the problems in the first place. The second half were yelling at the first half, telling them to get out of the way and quit holding up the line.

Marie was trying to tell everyone to calm down, and that Angela was on her way to speak to them. Behind Marie, her two helpers stood, a young girl and a middle-aged guy, and they looked supremely uncomfortable with being caught in the middle of this.

Mitch was busy scanning the crowd for faces he might recognize. People that he knew were involved with the Lincolnists. He was looking for one face in particular: Elsie Foster, their leader.

So far, she'd made herself scarce.

His two 82nd Airborne boys, Logan and Blake, were flanking him on either side, several paces out. Further towards the rear of the crowd, he saw his two Delta teammates, Rudy and Morrow, hanging around semi-casually. Not exactly brandishing their rifles, but holding them in a loose port position.

Amid the tumult of angry proclamations from both sides, Mitch heard a distinct *pop*.

He twitched. Turned to his left, where he thought the sound had come from.

The crowd hadn't reacted to it, they were still focused on bitching at each other.

But Blake was peering off towards the middle school grounds. He turned back to Mitch and frowned. "Did you—"

Pop-pop-pop

This time there was no denying what it was.

Not everyone reacted, but enough of the crowd heard it and went silent that the overall volume dropped a few decibels.

Mitch grabbed his radio PTT. "Mitch to command, we just heard something like gunshots coming from the area of the middle school…" *Jesus, someone wouldn't do that, would they? Not here! Not now!* "Can you advise?"

Another flurry of gunshots. And then an answering rattle of fully-automatic fire.

The crowd had now forgotten that they were about to start choking each other. The tone had turned abruptly from anger to fear.

At the edges of the crowd, Rudy and Morrow were already jogging in Mitch's direction.

Logan appeared at his elbow. "That's fuckin' gunfire, for sure."

"Yeah, I know it's gunfire." Mitch started to move in that direction.

Then his earpiece crackled, and the voice of the Watch Commander came over. "Command to Mitch, I've got word that Diamondback One is taking fire. Be advised, they're saying Diamondback Actual is down. Diamondback Actual is down."

—

It's just the stomach.
Just the stomach.
I'm still alive.

The world swirled. Went topsy-turvy. Pitched and yawed.

Angela found herself on her hands and knees, trying to get back to her feet, but she felt like she was on the center of a whirling dervish and she didn't trust her balance.

She heard rifle fire.

Some close, some far away.

She saw her hands on the blacktop, crawling. Shuffling knees. A burdensome, pregnant pain in her belly, like the first contractions before labor.

You're not dead. You're still moving.
Is this really happening?

It was so monumentally unbelievable...

Something hit the concrete very close to her.

She turned and saw the crater that it had left, a little cloud of concrete dust hanging in the air like a smoke plume over an active volcano.

Shit. They're still shooting at me.

But it did her a favor. Focusing on that little pockmark in the concrete gave her a center to her reeling universe and it shut the whirling dervish down long enough for her to stagger to her feet.

Her eyes came up.

Kurt was reaching for her with one hand, the other holding up his rifle, the muzzle slamming away, spitting fire, brass hurtling out the ejection port.

There was the roar of an engine.

She saw a black blur out of the corner of her eye, coming in fast. The black Tahoe screeched to a stop behind her, its engine block positioned to provide her with cover.

Kurt grabbed her by the back of the neck and shoved her down behind the front wheel of the Tahoe. "Keep your head down!" His thighs pressed her hunched form against the tire, the heat of the engine like a hot blanket over her face.

He fired rapidly over her head and shouted, "Peel! Peel! Peel!"

I need a fucking gun, Angela thought.

The pain in her belly was now knocking on the door of agony.

Boots on the ground.

Anthony skidded around the front of the truck while Kurt laid cover fire for him. He slid, his knee pads scraping. Came up squatting back on his knees and heels.

"Get her back in the building!" Anthony bellowed.

Something hit the truck. A hard, metal-on-metal *thwack!*

"Shit!" Kurt ducked below the engine block.

"What about the truck?" Angela managed.

"He's dead," Anthony replied. "Now move!"

Kurt hauled her onto her feet and half-dragged, half-pushed her to the doors of the Support Center.

He's dead, rang in her ears like a language she didn't understand—until she looked over her shoulder and saw the silhouetted shape of the driver of the Tahoe slumped against the wheel, with ribbons and splatters of dark red across the inside of the windshield.

For you.

Because of you.

Halfway to the building, Angela's legs gave out again.

She tried to apologize to Kurt, but her breath just came out in ragged gasps. And the shame of physically failing was rapidly washed away in the thundering reality that this was real, this was actually happening, this was no waking nightmare.

This might be the end.

"Abby," she managed.

The glass doors loomed in front of her.

In their reflection, she watched as Anthony spun and ran to catch up to them. His leg went out from under him, and he staggered.

Angela meant to call his name, but what came out instead was, "Abby…"

They hit the door.

Bullets chased them. Destroyed the glass.

People were in the foyer. Civilians. Wide eyes. Half-crouched postures.

Two guards, running up with pistols drawn.

"Across the way!" Kurt shouted at them. "At the top of the school! Tell command!"

Kurt pushed her behind a large reception desk that was made of concrete and marble and pressed her down into a sitting position.

The marble felt freezing against her back. Angela realized she was shivering fiercely. Her teeth clacking together.

Kurt laid his rifle down and ripped open the IFAK he carried. He looked at the civilians crowding into the atrium area. "Get the fuck behind cover!" he shouted at them.

Angela grabbed Kurt by the shoulder. "Anthony!" she finally managed.

Kurt grabbed her arm, took it off his shoulder, and placed it over the hole in her stomach. "You first. Put pressure there."

—

They were still ten miles from the Fort Bragg Safe Zone when Carl's voice crackled in Lee's earpiece.

"Lee, something's going on at Bragg."

Lee frowned out the windshield as the dirt-and-leaf covered roadway sped by them, years of unrepaired potholes rumbling under their worn out tires.

Carl was their designated radioman who kept comms up with Fort Bragg command. The rest of them only kept the squad comms.

"Alright," Lee said, holding out any rash judgement for the moment. "What kind of something?"

"It's not super clear yet," Carl responded. "Mitch just asked about gunfire…wait, hold on…"

Lee's stomach plummeted.

Was it primals? Had the wire been breached? The high-voltage fences around the Fort Bragg Safe Zone had kept them out so far, but they were smart. Had they figured out a way in?

"Lee," Carl said, and the tone of his voice had changed to something that Lee did not like. "It's Angela. Someone shot her. They got an active shooter right now. Right outside the Support Center."

Lee thrust a finger forward and said, "Go!"

But Abe had heard the transmission and had already punched the accelerator.

—

"Patch everyone into the command net!" Mitch ordered into the radio as he sprinted across towards the middle school.

The broad side of the first building was in front of them, about a hundred yards away.

Rudy and Morrow were keeping pace behind him, heading for the left side of the school building, while Logan and Blake kicked out to the right.

"You're patched," the Watch Commander said.

"Who do I have over at the Support Center?" Mitch demanded.

"Diamondback One!" a voice came back, taut as high-tension cables. "This is Kurt Barsch. I'm in the atrium of the Support Center." He sounded breathless. "I got Diamondback Actual secured, but she is injured—I repeat Diamondback Actual is injured. Diamondback Two is down. It's just me."

"Fuck!" Mitch said to himself, and then transmitted: "Where's the shooter in relation to you right now? And how many are there?"

"Ahh…I don't know how many there are. But I saw muzzle flashes from the top of the school."

"Copy." Mitch raised his rifle along with his eyes, scanning the top of the school building. But it was immediately apparent that the shooter was on the opposite side of the building from them. "We're coming up on the east side of the middle school. I've got the team with me. We're gonna clear that school building, okay? Can you pinpoint where you saw the muzzle flashes from?"

"He's not shooting anymore. It was in the middle of the building. Maybe the fourth window in?"

Shit…

Another thought occurred to Mitch.

They returned fire.

Right at a fucking school.

"Yeah, copy," Mitch said. "Command—has the school gone into lockdown?"

"Command to Mitch, lemme confirm. Standby."

Mitch, Rudy, and Morrow hit the eastern side of the building, right at the corner. Rudy immediately covered their backs, high, addressing the windows over them, while Morrow covered their backs low.

Mitch peered around the corner with his eyes and the muzzle of his rifle.

About two hundred yards away, he could see the Support Center. The black Tahoe that drove Angela around was sitting at the front, not moving. Even from where he was he could see that the vehicle was shot up.

"Command to Mitch. School's in lockdown. Guards are moving to intercept on the third floor. That's *third floor*."

Good.

"Blake and Logan," Mitch said over the comms. "Hold that northwest corner for us. And everyone, pay the fuck attention to what you're shooting at—there's kids in there." He released the PTT and looked back over his shoulder at Rudy and Morrow. "Hey! On me!"

He went around the corner of the building, crossed the face of it at a quick pace. Windows to his right. Out of the corner of his eye he saw people in those windows. A quick glance. His eyes flicked over a kid, staring at him with terror on his face.

Mitch motioned him down, and the kid dropped onto his belly.

At the next corner, Mitch stopped. "Next side is the shooting side. There's an entrance about ten yards in from this corner. We're gonna hit that, then take the stairs up."

"Roger that," Rudy responded.

Morrow squeezed his shoulder. "On you."

Mitch turned the corner. Scanned low. Scanned high.

Mild spring air. Sunshine.

A clear and beautiful day.

The sun glinted off the windows of the school.

All except one.

Because it was busted out.

Mitch focused his rifle on that window. "Third floor! Fifth window in!"

Many of the classrooms on the third floor were not in use. Mitch hoped to God that the broken window belonged to one of those empty classrooms. Otherwise, it meant that the shooter was in there, barricaded with a bunch of kids.

The entrance to the school was right ahead of them.

It occurred to Mitch that if the school had gone into lockdown, they might have to breach that door, and they had no breaching equipment. It also occurred to him that they weren't equipped for an assault, or a standoff. It was just them, their soft armor, and their rifles.

Shoulda just watched the damn food crowd in full gear like I fucking wanted to in the first place...

A shadow in the window caught his eye.

A shape.

A man.

Mitch brought his rifle's optic up, but he didn't pull the trigger. He couldn't ID who it was—A teacher? The shooter?

Mitch heard gunshots. Muffled, because they were inside the building.

Then the shape of the man came *through* the window.

"Contact!" Rudy yelled.

But the shape of the man wasn't a threat.

He was flying out. Out into midair. Then nosing down. His legs and arms held at his sides, like he was a skydiver trying to build as much velocity as possible.

He tilted in midair.

Hit the ground, back first.

"Holy fuck," Mitch rasped, then started running. He couldn't see the body through the tall weeds around the school building. He kept his rifle up as he ran. "Watch that window!"

Had the shooter thrown someone out the window? Was the shooter still inside, still waiting to gun them down in this open space?

"Contact!" Rudy yelled again.

Mitch snapped his gaze up and saw two shapes in the window, but they were waving their hands urgently in front of their faces, palms out, the signal for "hold your fire."

"Friendly! Friendly!" they were shouting.

Back to the body on the ground.

He could see it now.

Writhing.

Still alive.

Mitch slide-tackled the body. He heard a grunt of air come out of the man. He snatched the wrists. Yanked the body harshly so it turned over, belly down. Then wrenched both arms behind the back and pinned them there with his knee.

One of the arms felt limp. Detached.

Mitch got his first solid look at the man.

Middle aged. Shaggy brown hair.

He grabbed that shaggy hair and wrenched the head back and around, heedless of any neck injuries—that was not his problem. Blood dribbled out of the man's mouth. Crushed innards. Maybe rib-punctured lungs.

"Who the fuck are you?" Mitch shouted into the man's ear.

The man's eyes stared at the ground. Blinked. Went wide. He struggled for air.

Mitch pulled a little bit of weight off the man's back to let him breathe.

The breath that the man took rattled terminally and more blood came out of his mouth. He tried to say something, but it wasn't audible.

"What? Motherfucker!" Mitch shook the man by the hair. "Who the fuck are you?"

The last bit of air came out of the man in a groan. His lips moved. Made words.

His last.

"Preserve the union," he muttered through blood.

Then died.

SIX

ABNORMALITIES

THE TWO DIRTY PICKUP trucks came screeching to a stop in front of the Soldier Support Center.

Lee jumped out of the passenger side of the lead truck, his rifle at a low ready, rapidly taking in the scene.

At the front doors, a black Tahoe listed on flat, bullet-popped tires. All the windows shattered.

Slouched behind the cover of the engine block was one of Angela's bodyguards, Anthony Mizzutti. He was conscious, but Lee saw the dark red stain that had soaked his left pants leg, and the tourniquet he'd applied on his thigh.

The glass doors to the Support Center were stitched with holes in several places. One of the big windows was broken completely, the glass littering the sidewalk in front of it.

Julia appeared beside Lee, her rifle slung, and her big medical bag on one shoulder. "Where is she?"

Lee had no clue, but he was already moving towards Anthony. He got low, unsure if there would be more incoming rounds, and sidled up next to the man.

He touched the man's left leg, felt the wetness, now lukewarm. "Is that the only wound, Anthony?"

"Yeah," he grunted through clenched teeth. "Get Angela. She's inside the atrium with Kurt."

Julia patted Lee on the shoulder. "I'll get Angela, you take care of him. Cover me."

Lee came up over the hood of the Tahoe with his rifle. Across the road stood the school. He saw men in the tall grass by the side of the building, focused on something at their feet. It looked like Mitch and his guys.

Lee panned up to the broken window directly above them. He rested his rifle on its rail and held it there with one hand while he keyed his comms with the other. He'd already patched his radio back into the command frequency. "Mitch, can you advise on the shooter? Are we still hot?"

From two hundred yards away, he watched Mitch look around. "Yeah, hold what you got. Shooter is down. I repeat, shooter is down. But we need to clear this building. Check for secondary hostiles."

"Roger that. Keep an eye out for devices too."

"Yeah. Hey, Blake and Logan, you guys copy that traffic?"

Logan's voice came back: "We copy. We're on the third floor now. Room to room. Standby for all-clear."

Lee sunk down behind the engine block again. Looked at Anthony. "What can I do for you right now?"

"Nothin'." Anthony eyed Lee, then his right shoulder. "You got some water in that Camelbak?"

Lee nodded, pulled the drinking tube from the shoulder of his rig and leaned down so that Anthony could get his lips on it. The man drank deeply for several seconds, then let the tube fall out of his mouth.

"How you feeling?" Lee asked him. "You with me?"

"Yeah, I'm with you." Anthony looked pale, but his eyes were still sharp. Focused.

Lee clipped the drinking tube back to his rig. Looked over his left shoulder. The rest of his crew had taken up positions behind the engine blocks of their two white pickups, rifles trained over the top, covering in the direction of the school.

He made eye contact with Abe. "We need to get this guy to the Med Center."

Abe nodded at him. Shifted into a sprinter's stance. "Alright, coming to you."

Lee gave him cover while he scuttled over.

"Hey!" Julia's voice from behind him. "Comin' out with one! Moving to our pickup!"

"Move!" Lee called back, still covering.

He heard the shuffling of boots behind him.

He wanted to turn and look, to see how bad it was, but he kept his attention forward.

Watch your lane. You can't do anything for Angela that Julia hasn't already done.

No one had said she was dead. That was the important part, right? And Julia wouldn't be rushing her out right now if she had died.

She's still alive, he told himself.

"Logan to command, we've cleared the third floor. No sign of an additional shooter. No sign of any booby traps. Everyone's saying it was just this one guy. We're gonna continue on, get all the rooms cleared, but I think we can downgrade a bit here."

Lee pulled his rifle off the hood of the Tahoe and slung it to his side. Abe was there beside him. "Let's both grab arms. Hobble him over to Carl's truck."

Lee got Anthony's left arm, and Abe his right. They lifted. Anthony hissed but gutted it out and they hobbled him over to Carl's truck.

As Lee passed his own truck, it roared to life. Kurt was in the driver's seat, and Julia was in the backseat, hovering over a body. In the moment that he passed the back window, Lee saw a frizz of blonde hair, and a hand that was clutching the backrest of the seat.

She's alive.

God, please let her stay that way.

—

Lee stalked into the waiting room of the Medical Center's surgical wing. Julia was waiting for him.

It was a typical hospital room. A failed attempt to be warm and inviting, but you couldn't hide the utilitarian practicality that went into everything medical. And it still smelled like a hospital.

Like latex and disinfectant.

Lee shucked his rifle off his shoulder and set it down in a chair, next to where Julia was standing. He'd already doffed the rest of his gear, and managed to shove Deuce into the front door of his house around the corner, before high-tailing it back.

Lee's voice was stone cold. "How is she?"

"She's in surgery." Julia put her hands in her pockets. "Bullet was through and through. She was conscious the entire time. I don't think it hit anything vital. But we won't know until the surgeons get in there."

"Surgeon," Lee said, emphasizing the singular aspect of it.

They only had one true surgeon. The others on the surgical staff were two registered nurses who'd worked in high-level trauma centers. They knew more than the average medical practitioner, but they were still learning.

"What about Anthony?" Julia asked.

"The nurse triaged him as secondary to Angela." Lee shook his head, wondering how Anthony felt about that. The man was a solid soldier. Lee thought that if anything, he would have insisted on it that way, even if the nurse had triaged him as primary. "They loosened the tourniquet when I was in there with him and it didn't squirt."

"That's good."

They stood in silence for a long moment. The waiting room had a single window that looked south, right at the school buildings. From their vantage point they saw the broken window on the third floor, and the tall grass underneath it that had been mashed by foot traffic.

And the body that had flown out the window.

"Who was he?"

"Some fuckin' guy." Lee rubbed the three-day growth on his cheeks that was starting to irritate him. "John Burke, apparently. Name means nothing to me. I didn't know him."

"Lincolnist?"

"Mitch said his last words were 'Preserve the union,' so that's a safe bet. Carl and Mitch and the guys are investigating it. Seeing if there's any more like him."

Julia let out a long, discontented sigh. "The fuck's wrong with these people?"

"They think we're the bad guys. They hear 'secession' and they think that history is going to find them on the wrong side of it. Like the Confederacy, I guess."

"That's bullshit. Fucking President Briggs left us all to die out here. Did they forget that?"

"We got the power plant running again," Lee said. "They've got high-voltage fences between them and the primals. They think they're out of danger now. And, yes, I think that makes them forgetful."

Julia folded her arms over her chest. "Two years ago we'd've kicked their asses out. Let the primals have them. Shit, if they want to go to Colorado so bad, why don't we just let them?"

"Angela wants to be civilized."

"Bullshit."

"Maybe." Lee compressed his lips. "But I'll tell you one thing: The second that bitch Elsie Foster fucks up—I mean, the goddamned second we get a shred of evidence linking her to these people that she claims weren't following her orders—she's gonna disappear."

Julia's nose curled. "Yeah. I wonder who all's gonna be dead by the time that happens."

Lee looked away from her. Out the window. Towards the school building. There was caution tape over the broken window now. They would board it up later. Couldn't fix it. Not like they had spare windows laying around.

"No kids got hurt," Lee changed the subject. "So that's good."

"Sure." A pause. "How'd he get into the building?"

"He was one of our electricians. Told the principal there was a drain in the power grid coming from the school."

Julia made a raspberry noise. "Fucking drain in the power grid. The fuck's that even mean?"

Lee shrugged.

He glanced sidelong at Julia.

She was watching him with sharp, searching eyes. He looked away. Restrained a grimace. Knew what was coming.

"Where's your head at?"

Lee felt his core tighten at the implications. He turned his head and met Julia's gaze. "My head's fine, Jules."

She held the eye contact, unabashed. Arched that damn eyebrow. "It's cool, Lee. I'm not the jealous type."

Lee grunted. Looked out the window again. "You act like she's my ex-wife or something."

"Yeah, well. She kinda was."

"There was never anything between us."

"Maybe not physically. But emotionally…"

Lee clenched his jaw.

Things were complicated. They'd been complicated between him and Angela. And now they were complicated between him and Julia, although you might say for the exact opposite reason.

Julia took his hand. Gave it a gentle squeeze. "Look at me."

Lee took a breath and looked at her.

Her eyes were very earnest. Not evaluating anymore. "I'm just saying…you had something with Angela. It's okay to react to her being hurt. You don't have to hide that from me. I get it."

Lee gave her hand a squeeze back. "I know you do."

Someone cleared their throat.

"Excuse me."

Lee held onto Julia's hand for a fraction of a second longer. Then he turned to the voice.

It was Doctor Trent, standing in the doorway of the waiting room.

He was an older man of middle height with a paunch that seemed to stick to him despite reduced rations. He had a crown of gray hair and horn-rimmed glasses perched on the bridge of his nose.

He nodded to them. "Captain Harden. Miss Julia. I was told that you have something for me."

Lee stared at the man, and for a moment, had no idea what he was talking about.

Then he remembered the body in the back of the truck.

The dead primal.

"Yeah," Lee said. "We'll get it. You got an autopsy room or something?"

"Aut…" Doc Trent trailed off, blinking like he wasn't quite understanding something. "Uh. Well. We don't have autopsy rooms, per se. But I'm sure I can come up with something workable."

—

"Oh, *Jesus*!" Doctor Trent exclaimed. "You can't bring that thing in here!"

It was lying face up on the stainless steel table of an unused operating room.

The harsh light from the overhead lamp made the shadows extreme.

It was a table meant for an adult. It seemed to accent the thing's small size.

It was as dead as dead could be. But Lee still felt weird standing next to it.

He remembered as a child, visiting a science museum, and in the Africa exhibit there was a stuffed male lion. He recalled looking up at the animal and knowing that it was not alive, could not hurt him, but feeling something deep inside his subconscious that wanted to run away from it.

He felt that same way now.

If Julia was perturbed by it, she kept it hidden.

"Well, it's here, Doc," Julia said. "And now you need to take a look at it."

Doc Trent had backed up a step. "Alright. Fine. I'm looking at it."

"No, I mean really *look* at it." Julia made a motion as though cutting her chest open and scooping her organs out.

Doc Trent recalled what they'd said in the waiting room. He blinked rapidly again. "You want me to autopsy this thing?" He shook his head. "We don't need an autopsy. It died of a gunshot wound to the head. That's pretty evident."

Lee cleared his throat. "We're not looking for cause of death."

Doc Trent rubbed his face. "Okay. Alright. What is it that you want?"

"I want to know how old it is," Lee said.

Doc Trent looked at the body. Then at Lee. He quirked his head, and his mouth twitched. "You're still stuck on this juvenile primal bullshit."

Lee gestured to the creature on the table. "I wouldn't call it bullshit. You can see how small it is."

"So it's a small primal."

"Look at its mouth. Look at its teeth. Look at its musculature. It's not an adult."

Julia nodded at the body. "We told you these things were out there. You didn't believe us."

Doctor Trent swiped his glasses off his face like they'd offended him. "What do you want from me, Julia? I'm a fucking doctor. I believe what I see. You guys are out there in tense situations. Sometimes tense situations cause us to see things differently than reality."

Lee watched the older doctor carefully. "You've read Jacob's notebook, haven't you?"

Doctor Trent was very still for a moment. Like he was sensing a trap.

Doctor Trent didn't care for Jacob's notebook. He didn't care for Jacob's findings. Despite the fact that Jacob had in fact been *Doctor* Jacob, a CDC microbiologist that had actually studied the infected, Trent referred to Jacob's findings as "unsubstantiated."

Unfortunately for science, Doctor Jacob was no longer living.

He was not available to defend his research.

"You know my opinion on Jacob," Doctor Trent said.

"Sure," Lee gave him a bare nod. "A quack. Someone who'd lost his mind in the chaos. Someone who was grasping at straws to explain the unexplainable. An alarmist, I think you've called him."

"What's your point?"

"My point is, did you read the notebook?"

A disgruntled huff. "Yes. I read the damn thing. Who hasn't?"

Lee watched the old general practitioner. A man of reason. A man very far out of his depth, too. "Well, for the sake of argument, let's assume that Jacob wasn't a quack. Let's assume that what he observed was true. The notes he made. All true. Just assume that for me."

Doctor Trent pursed his lips and said nothing.

"If you accept the notes as true," Lee continued. "And then you take a look at what's lying on the table in front of you…I mean, I don't think we're being crazy here, Doc. Just look at it. Don't you think it's reasonable to conclude that the infected are breeding and developing abnormally fast?"

Doctor Trent's agitation seemed to reach its peak. He crossed, then uncrossed his arms. Let them hang. Then finally clasped them together in front of him and was still. "Yes. If you take all the rest of it as fact—which I don't—then that would be a…reasonable conclusion."

Julia leaned on the table, looking at the primal's face, its glassy eyes staring dead at the ceiling. Its jaw gaping open. "More like what you'd see in the animal world," she said, almost as though speaking to herself. "Animals that have to hunt to survive don't have time to develop slowly."

Doctor Trent pursed his lips. "Humans evolved delayed development in their offspring to accommodate for our complicated social structure…" he trailed off, as though realizing he was making their point for them and he didn't like it. "But I protest your conclusions. In the strongest possible terms."

Lee nodded. "I'll be sure to pass that along."

The doctor's nose wrinkled like he'd smelled something bad. "You're going to start a panic."

"I'm going to be realistic," Lee responded. "It's my job to address threats. Just because something is bad doesn't mean we deny it until it comes back to bite us in the ass."

Doctor Trent considered both of them for a moment. "I'm not an unreasonable man, Captain Harden. But people around here don't need their hopes crushed any more than they already are. They don't need more bad news." His face became plaintive. "Promise me that you'll keep this quiet. At least until I can cut into this...this *thing* and...hopefully disprove you. No offense."

Lee raised his hands in surrender. "No offense taken. I would *love* for you to disprove me, Doc. That would make my life a helluva lot easier. But we're beyond believing in easy things. We need to see the truth and confront it for what it is."

Doctor Trent sneered down at the body, his face a splatter-painting of disgust. "Fine. Fucking *fine*. I will...look into it."

"That's all we're asking," Julia responded.

Doctor Trent had nothing else to say to them, and they had nothing else to say to him.

So Lee and Julia simply gave the thing on the table one last look, then turned, and departed the room, leaving the doctor to his disturbing task.

Walking down the brightly lit hallway, Lee felt the reality of everything begin to settle on him. Like seeing funnel clouds form in a stormy sky and knowing your home was in the path of something supernaturally destructive.

His gut felt sour. Jumpy.

His head felt heavy. The weight of everything, compressing him down.

"What do you think?" Julia asked him, earnestly curious.

Lee's voice was hollow and distant. "I think that we may have won the war against the regular infected. But I think we're losing against the primals."

SEVEN

THE GULF

ANGELA WAS IN SURGERY for three hours.

She was conscious the whole time. They didn't have an official anesthesiologist. And even if they did, they'd run out of most of their good drugs a long time ago. What they did have was a surgeon who was familiar with nerve blocks, and so that's what Angela got. Just like if she was giving birth and had asked for an epidural.

Three hours she spent staring up at the bright lights of an operating room while she felt the distant tug of things in her middle section being moved around, stitched up, put back together.

Occasionally one of the nurses, a woman a little older than Angela, with her body and head and face all covered in sea-green garments, would lean back from the curtain separating Angela from the sight of her own body.

"You okay, hon?" the nurse would ask.

"Yeah," Angela would nod, her voice faint. "Thank you."

She heard the steady blip of her own heart on the monitor that they'd hooked up to her, and she thought it was very odd that it was so even, so relaxed. She didn't know why she was so calm.

She kept thinking about that sunny parking lot. Kept picturing the little puffs of rifle shots from up on the third floor of the school. Kept thinking about the feeling of being hit in the gut with a bullet. But for some reason, it never made her pulse spike.

I'm dead inside. I can't feel anything anymore.

And she thought that maybe she was okay with that.

Because what good would it do her now? Cause her heart to race? Cause adrenaline to spike through her system? Cause her to cry out and weep?

What good did that do anybody?

Why do they want to kill me? she wondered. Detached from the issue, like she was considering someone else's life. *That won't accomplish anything for them. I guess it's just symbolic. If they kill me they'll feel like they won something.*

Well...

Sorry to disappoint.

"Almost done, Miss Houston," the nurse said.

Angela stared at the ceiling.

She thought about what Jeff—her Director of Agriculture—had told her.

Bad news on bad news.

That's what was keeping her from feeling. There was only so many times you could deal with bad news before you stopped reacting to it. Before you just shrugged when it came. You almost expected it, really.

"I need to speak to Captain Harden," Angela said.

The nurse peeked back around the curtain. "What's that, hon?"

It was difficult to speak with volume. The nerve block seemed to make it hard for her to use her diaphragm to push the words out of her, so most of what she said came out in a murmur.

She blinked a few times. Frowned. Focused on making her anesthetized body work. "I need to speak to Captain Harden."

"Okay, hon," the nurse said, slipping back behind the curtain. "Just let us finish up here."

Angela got the feeling that she was being humored.

"Hey."

"Yeah?" the nurse's head again.

Angela fixed the woman with a frown. "I'm fucking serious."

The nurse's eyes behind their protective glasses blinked a few times. "Alright," was all she said.

The last hour ticked by. They gave her the basic play-by-play. Infused it with some good-humor: "Hey, Humpty-Dumpty, we're just gonna put you back together again, and you'll be done. Just a few more stitches...you feeling okay? Alright. Great. That's great. There we go. Almost done..."

And so on and so forth.

They finished. Cleaned her up. Wheeled her from the operating room into a recovery room.

The nurse was setting up her IV stand. Her name tag dangling from her large-ish breasts.

SULLIVAN, it said.

"Now, it's gonna be best if you get some rest, Miss Houston..."

Angela cleared her throat. Already the nerve block was wearing off, and she felt a spike of pain go through her. She ignored it. "Sit me up."

"No, you need to stay lying down."

"Nurse Sullivan," Angela said, sharply. "Sit me up right now."

Nurse Sullivan gave her another long look, like she was trying to decipher how serious Angela was. How *sober* she was. "Ma'am, with all due respect, even though you're conscious doesn't mean the nerve block hasn't gotten you a bit loopy. It might be impairing your judgement."

Angela stared at the nurse for a moment. Took a ponderous breath that caused her midsection to ache. "Do you enjoy living here?"

The nurse responded with another flurry of blinks. She shifted her feet. "Of course, Miss Houston."

"And you enjoy having fences to keep you and your family from being eaten?"

No response to that one.

"And you enjoy *having* food, instead of *becoming* food?"

The nurse swallowed. Looked around, like she was searching for help, but they were alone in the room.

Angela leaned herself upward, ignoring the dull throb that it caused. "Then sit me the fuck up and get Captain Harden."

—

Lee stepped into the hospital room, alone.

The nurse had retrieved him from the waiting room with a matronly look that told him she was fetching him against her better judgement. It was rare that Angela got pushy, but Lee had seen it a few times. Because she was usually so nice, it shocked people when she put niceness aside for a moment.

Lee had never really had that problem.

Most people seemed convinced that he was a violent machine of a man. That kind of reputation was useful to him.

But perhaps he spent more hours than he wanted to admit, trying to convince himself that there was more to him than that. That there was still something kind and good inside of him. That the inner workings of his mind hadn't been completely reduced to steel and ash.

Of course, you could tell yourself all kinds of nice things about yourself.

People are best at lying to themselves. Oftentimes we are the only ones who fall for our own deceptions.

"You rang?" Lee offered up as he entered the hospital room.

Angela was sitting up in her bed, with a blanket covering her from the waist down. She was wearing one of those tie-in-the-back hospital gowns. Thin and gauzy. Her blonde pony-tail was tangled and askew. Her face was drawn and exhausted.

"Are you okay?" he asked in earnest. "How are you feeling?"

"Hm." She squinted skyward, as though she really had to think about it. "Feels…like I got shot."

Lee smirked. "Hey. Welcome to the club. You're one of us now."

Her eyes became serious. "I didn't hear about the shooter. Did they get him?"

"He got himself. Jumped out of the window."

"Did he die?"

"Not immediately. But yes."

She looked out the window of the room. Lee thought it was good that it didn't overlook the school. He watched Angela's mouth tighten down. Her eyes…they didn't narrow or squint, but there was something about them that hardened, like watching a scrim of ice rapidly form on the surface of water.

"Well," she said, quietly. "Fuck him."

"Yeah. My thoughts exactly."

She turned back to him. "Lee, we've got a problem."

We've got a million fucking problems.

He struggled not to take a big breath to steady himself against the sudden drop that he felt in his gut.

"I spoke to Jeff Teague today." Her hands found each other. Fingers knit together. "You remember him?"

"The agriculture guy."

"Yes." Her mouth opened. Closed. She appeared to consider her words carefully. "Even if we'd been able to plant in Field Twenty-Nine, we wouldn't have had the fuel necessary to harvest what we planted."

Lee frowned. "I thought we worked the numbers out. I thought we had enough in the tanks to last us through the harvest."

"Yeah, we did. But the fencing operations." She shook her head, grimaced. "It used more than we thought."

"We accounted for a fifteen percent overage."

"It used more than that." She looked away from him. Out the window again. "Some of the ground was harder than was expected. Harder for the augers to get through. It burned through a lot more fuel than we expected and we didn't catch it until it was too late."

"*Jeff* didn't catch it until it was too late."

"You can't blame him for this."

"I *am* blaming him for this. It was his fucking responsibility."

"Lee, you know as well as I do that sometimes the numbers just don't work out."

Lee bared his teeth briefly and decided to look at the blank, textured hospital wall instead of Angela. Because she was right. Sometimes this shit happened. But it couldn't have come at a worse time.

"So, what does Jeff project now?" Lee asked.

"We got enough to finish the thirty fields," Angela replied, slowly. "And we can run the planters. But then the tanks are gonna be at the dregs. Any cultivating will use the little we have left. And we won't have a goddamn drop for harvesting operations."

"What about harvesting by hand?" Lee said.

Angela nodded. "We're going to have to. But Jeff says that it won't be enough."

"What do you mean it won't be enough?" Lee found his hand rubbing at his head, his fingertips touching the scar that ran across his scalp. "You saying we got too many people to feed, but not enough to harvest?"

Angela shook her head. "No. That was my initial thought too. But the problem is the security. Transporting enough people into the fields, along with their protective details? We don't have enough for that either."

Angela looked bitter, and for a moment Lee felt his own stomach sinking because he heard the hopelessness in her voice, and he counted on her to have hope. He could make it through the slog of every day misery, but not if those around him didn't have hope.

"Jeff says that we'd only be able to harvest a small percentage of it before the rest rotted in the fields." Angela shifted her position in the bed, wincing in pain. "He says it'd probably get us to the end of the year. But no further. And that's maintaining reduced rations as they are now."

They were silent for a moment, lost in considerations. That endless, web-like series of analysis where every choice leads to a consequence, and all the choices sucked and all the consequences were bad.

Well, as long as we're on the topic of shitty news...

"I think we have a problem with the primals."

Angela looked at him again. "When do we not?"

Lee thought about whether he should even tell Angela at this point. But she deserved to know what might be coming down the pipeline at them. "We recovered one of them today, at Field Twenty-Nine. One of the primals. It was still alive when we got there. We put it down."

Angela waited, sensing there was more.

"It was small. Looked young. I think it might prove Jacob's concept."

"The breeding concept?" Angela frowned. "I thought we'd already proven that."

"No, we know they're breeding but...this is more to do with how *quickly* they're breeding. I think what we recovered today was one of the juveniles that we've reported seeing."

Angela lowered her eyes. "Oh."

"Doctor Trent is taking a look at it. Trying to determine the age of it. He doesn't agree with my theory. He says that he objects to it in—" Lee put up air quotes "—the strongest terms possible."

"Okay," Angela said. "What is it that you think?"

Lee sighed. "I don't know what to think. I hope Doc Trent is right. I hope it's just a small primal. Maybe it's the opposite of bad news. Maybe it's a good sign. Maybe the small primals are a sign of...I dunno...malnutrition or something."

"That's what killed off the regular infected."

Lee gave her a fractional nod. "That. And the last two winters. And the primals hunting them. Now the primals don't have them as a food source, and they're turning to the next easiest prey. Which is us."

"This thing you recovered...you think it was born in the last couple of years?"

Lee shrugged. He had no other answers for her.

Angela had grown very still. Over the last three years of hell on earth, she'd become accustomed to the rising tides of fear that would come upon them. And she had learned how to press it all down. How to calm the seas within herself. How to compartmentalize.

That was good, Lee thought, as he watched her grow steady again. A valuable trait in a leader. It had its own consequences: eventually you didn't feel much at all—even the stuff you *wanted* to feel. But that was a butcher's bill that had to be paid later.

Much of what they did was on credit, building up debts against themselves that they hoped they would eventually pay off in some far-flung future when things were going to be "normal" again.

A future that Lee often thought was more fantasy than anything else.

Angela smoothed the wrinkles out of her blanket. "We need fuel. That is priority number one. Without the fuel to harvest the crops, we starve. If we starve, then the primals are a moot point. As of right now, we have the power back on, and that is keeping the currents running on the fences, and that is keeping the primals out."

"For now," Lee said. "They've been testing those boundaries, though."

"Yes, they have."

Eventually they were going to figure out how to get past the electric fences. Just as they'd figured out how to defeat previous fortifications. It was only a matter of time.

Angela was right. They needed fuel.

Fuel to not only keep the populace from starving, but fuel to reinstate the hunt and destroy missions, which they'd put on hold because of their diminishing fuel reserves. In retrospect, perhaps they should have continued to seek out the dens where the primals gathered.

If they could've impacted the population of primals, maybe they wouldn't have had to waste so much fuel building the damn fences to keep them out.

"Fuel," Lee said, refocusing himself.

Angela nodded in agreement. "We have to turn the pumps back on."

"The Gulf, then."

"That is where the pipeline leads, yes?"

"Yes."

They'd gone over all this before. The mission was half-planned already, because they knew that this was going to happen. They just didn't think it was going to happen so soon.

They knew virtually nothing outside of the four members of the United Eastern States: North Carolina, South Carolina, Georgia, and Florida. They would need to cross a lot of unknown territory to turn the pipelines back on. They had no idea what was around the pipelines, if anyone was currently in control of those pipelines, and if the pumps and refineries were even still operable.

They would need more than a dozen people to get the oil flowing again. But they would need an advance team to figure out what was going on. To take the temperature of the locals. To make alliances. To build connections and allies.

"Well." Lee nodded, feeling a sinking feeling in his gut that he couldn't quite explain in that moment. "I'll tell the team."

EIGHT

CO-ORDIN-ATIN'

ELSIE FOSTER WAS A stone cold bitch.

That's what Mitch was thinking as he watched her.

They were in Carl's office on the bottom floor of the Support Center. They'd scrubbed the room of anything relating to their ongoing investigation of the Lincolnists.

Mitch had suggested they leave it up, including the cork board with pictures and notes attached to it, linking certain dubious individuals to Ms. Foster. Mitch thought it might rattle her.

But Carl liked to keep his cards close to his chest. And it was his office. And ultimately, his investigation.

Carl was seated at his desk. Elsie was directly across from him. Mitch was cattycorner, sitting on the side of the desk.

"So," Carl said, in his flat, calm voice. "You had no direct dealings with John Burke."

"That's not what I said," Elsie corrected, mirroring his level tones.

She was a middle-aged woman with mouse-brown hair that she kept in a tight braid and was beginning to show streaks of gray. She had a kind face, on the surface. A nice, polite smile. But her eyes were like little nuggets of dirt, and they gave nothing away.

Elsie knew better than to volunteer information. She let Carl probe, and answered only what she had to answer.

Carl rested his elbows on the table and sighed. "Okay. What was it that you said?"

"I'm sure you recall, Mr. Gilliard. I said it less than a minute ago."

Carl watched her in silence. A classic interrogator's move. Give the suspect silence, and sometimes they feel compelled to fill it.

Elsie was not that type of person. She simply sat there, smiling back at Carl, like this was all just a civil discussion taking place at some social gathering. She was waiting it out. Completely comfortable with the silence.

What Elsie *had* said, was that she'd met John Burke a handful of times, during meetings where the Lincolnists discussed peaceful solutions to their issues with the UES. The way she told it, John Burke had seemed edgy, and had a lot of disagreements with the rest of the peace-loving Lincolnists, and that they all got a bad vibe from him, but he'd never explicitly told them he was going to do anything violent.

It was a load of shit, and everyone at that table knew it. Carl and Mitch knew it was shit. And Elsie knew that they knew. She just didn't care. Because she also knew that their hands were tied by none other than Angela herself. Angela wanted *proof*, and until she got it, she wasn't going to authorize any sort of action towards the Lincolnists. It was their right to peaceably assemble, after all. It was their right to discuss things, as long as those discussions didn't turn into a safety hazard. And so far, not a single Lincolnist interviewed had said anything other than what Elsie was saying now.

They all claimed they wanted a *peaceful* solution. Without bloodshed.

Carl could rattle the sabers, so to speak. Make threats. But Mitch knew he wasn't going to do that. Carl never made threats that he couldn't back up. And even if he could back up those threats, why give forewarning?

And so, Elsie Foster's bullshit statement, and her current silence, brought their efforts to a stalemate.

Elsie blinked a few times. "Mr. Gilliard," she said, still with that simpering smile. "As much as I enjoy staring into your handsome visage, I have things that I need to do today. So are we done?"

Carl shrugged. "Is there anything else you'd like to tell us?"

"No. Are there any other questions that I can answer for you? That is, questions that I haven't *already* answered?"

"Did you arrange to have Angela assassinated?"

Elsie didn't even blink. "Of course not. What a ridiculous accusation. We want a peaceful solution."

Carl gave her a smile as stale as a three-week old saltine. "That's very reassuring to hear." He raised his hand from his desk and gave a small *shoo* gesture, as though Elsie Foster were a gnat on his desk. "You may go now."

Her eyes flashed, but that was it.

But any reaction was a victory.

Elsie rose from her chair and departed without another word. She knew better than to fire back at them. She knew better than to do any of the stupid shit they hoped that she would do.

Mitch had to give her credit. She knew exactly how to play this game.

When she had left, Mitch rose, went to the door, and closed it. He turned on Carl and crossed his arms over his chest. "Fuck it. I say we put her and her Lincolnists on work detail in one of the new fields, then cut the power to the fences. Let this problem work itself out."

Carl leaned back in his chair. "Mitch, if there was a way to bury these people and not raise suspicions, they'd already be dead." He put a finger to his lips, thoughtfully. "We need to get someone inside. Gain their trust. Get them to talk about the shit we know they're talking about."

Mitch nodded in agreement. "You got anybody in mind?"

"No, not yet," Carl admitted. "I guess I'm still holding out hope that Angela is pissed enough after getting shot that she just authorizes us to take them out."

"If I had to take a bet," Mitch said. "I'd say you might want to start looking for that undercover."

There was a knock at the door.

Carl glanced at Mitch, then nodded at the door.

Mitch opened it.

Tomlin leaned in. "What's up, Mitch?" he said, then looked at Carl. "Team meeting in The Cave. Lee's got something for us."

—

The Cave was a windowless room on the second floor of the Support Center.

Only six people were allowed entry to this place, and that was Lee and his team. It was their briefing room, their armory, and often their hangout.

The lack of natural light didn't mean that The Cave was dark. It was well-lit by a collection of several gaudy lamps that they had acquired over the course of their two years doing missions together.

The lamp-thing had started with the finding of a tacky, stained-glass table lamp, which featured, of all things, dolphins. Tomlin had unearthed it in the manager's office of a tire shop that they'd raided to outfit their pickup trucks. Tomlin, who was often the instigator of shenanigans, had insisted that it go on Lee's desk in The Cave.

Since then, the lamp collection had grown.

A crystal lamp.

A lamp with a pink, fuzzy shade.

A lamp with a giraffe as its base, and a cheetah-print shade.

The gaudier the better.

The lamps provided plenty of light, because the room was fairly small. Maybe twenty-by-thirty, with a single door on the narrow side. It was just big enough for all six team members to claim a space, which then turned the room into—as Abe had once observed—an Epcot Center of personalities.

Lee's desk—the only desk, in fact—stood in the far left corner. He actually shared that space with Carl. The two of them generally kept the desk orderly, Carl's side moreso than Lee's, partly because Carl was more orderly, and partly because he had his own office. If you were facing the desk, Lee's locker and gear box were on the left, and Carl's were on the right.

Clockwise from the desk, the next corner belonged to Abe. His area was neat, and mostly free of mischief, although he was the owner of the Africa-motif lamp. Other than that, just a folding chair and a dartboard on the wall. Disputes were known to be settled by a game of cricket.

Julia's station was up against the flat of the right wall. She had an additional locker, which held all her medical supplies. Charts of human anatomy and books about battlefield trauma marked her area. She had been studious in her role as team medic. Almost obsessive.

The next corner was Nate's area. Being the only one of the team besides Julia that had no prior military experience, his area was festooned with things that the others had brought him to "help" him.

A diagram of the nomenclature for an M4 rifle had been erected on the wall because Nate had once failed to identify the gas key. Except that all the names for the rifle's parts had been crossed out and replaced with "NATEnclature": The muzzle was labeled, "BOOMY END"; the magazine was labeled, "INFINITY BOOLITS"; the buttstock was labeled, "SHOULDER KICKY THINGY"; etc., etc.

On the wall over Nate's gear trunk was tacked a plastic baggie filled with little paper squares that Tomlin and Abe had lovingly cut out. It was labeled, "grid squares." He had fallen for the old "Get the keys to the Humvee" trick, but had realized he was being fucked with when they'd asked for him to find them some chemlight batteries.

Nate took it in stride, with a laugh and a roll of his eyes. Despite all the picking on him, he'd become a good operator. The rest of the team liked and trusted him. His operational experience in the world after the collapse of society was all the resumé that he needed.

Tomlin's place was directly across from Nate's, and was by far the messiest area of the room. Tomlin insisted that it was "organized chaos," and that he knew where everything was.

Lee had put a perimeter of duct tape on the floor around Tomlin's section to mark his "boundaries," and if ever an item attempted to cross Lee's perimeter, he gave it a swift kick back across the border. It didn't help that Abe, Nate, and Julia routinely tossed random items into Tomlin's area—

a street sign, an old baby doll, bits of trash, and, most famously, a large, purple, two-sided dildo.

The dildo now sat in a biohazard bag atop Tomlin's locker, a permanent part of the décor.

The wall adjacent to Tomlin's gear locker held a large paper sign, on which was inscribed in bold block letters, one of Lee's favorite exclamations upon walking into The Cave and seeing Tomlin's area: JESUS CHRIST, BRIAN! POLICE YOUR SHIT! Abe and Nate had erected the sign so that, if Lee was ever *not* present, Tomlin would still be reminded to police his shit.

The team was now gathered at the only empty space left in the room, which was the section of the left wall between Tomlin's area and Lee's desk. On this wall was a large cork board, and on the cork board was tacked several maps of the southeast.

Lee stood to the side of the corkboard and indicated a red circle on the map of Georgia, in the center of the state, and a little bit to the west. This was the Butler Safe Zone. One of only five Safe Zones that existed in the United Eastern States.

"We're going to stay a night in Butler," Lee said. "Catch up on sleep and refuel. Reload, if necessary, but we're hoping to make a clean run, starting early tomorrow morning." Lee glanced at them quickly. "*Hoping* being the operative word there. Our last intel on the route to Butler is nearly a month old. It was clear at that time, but who knows what the fuck popped up in the last few weeks. So, we're going to proceed down the route with due caution. *Hopefully*, the malcontents and primals will stay out of the way."

Not everyone in the four member states considered the UES to be legitimate. Many of them held similar views to the Lincolnists. And some of those pockets of survivors had become problematic for their convoys in the past.

"If we do encounter any trouble," Lee continued. "We will not have QRF, so we will respond appropriately, and make a game-time decision on how to proceed."

Abe tilted his head. "Why no QRF?"

"Partly because we're going to be a long way from Fort Bragg."

"We could arrange QRF with nearby Safe Zones as we come into their territory," Abe pointed out.

Lee nodded. "Yeah, well, that's the other part of it. We're going to be keeping this operation quiet. We're not alerting any of the other Safe Zones about it. We're not even calling up Butler until we're right on their doorstep." Sensing additional incoming questions, Lee held up a hand. "In light of what the Lincolnists have been up to, we don't want them trying to sabotage our efforts."

Julia frowned and shook her head. "Getting fuel benefits everyone. Including them."

"Yeah, you're right, but it also benefits the UES," Lee said.

Carl nodded along with Lee, then turned to Julia. "These fucks just want to see the UES fail. I wouldn't put it past them to try to throw a wrench in our gears, even if it negatively impacts them as much as us. I think secrecy is called for."

Julia shrugged and said nothing more about it.

Lee turned back to the map, looked again at the Butler Safe Zone. "Once we leave Butler, we're going to be crossing the border into Alabama, and from there, we're in The Wilds."

They'd been so busy trying to get the power back on and secure themselves against the constant probing by primals, that they'd had no chance to mount expeditions beyond their borders to see what the rest of the southern states looked like. With the exception of the northern interior states, which they knew aligned with Acting President Briggs, the rest of the country was a mystery.

AKA, The Wilds.

"Once we cross into The Wilds, our mission is to make friends and try to figure out how to get fuel back to Fort Bragg. Ideally, we want the pipeline that runs straight to Bragg up and running again, but that requires a helluva lot of infrastructure that I'm not sure we'll be able to take advantage of. So, we're just going to have to play it by ear." Lee held up two fingers and ticked them off: "Make friends, and figure out how to get fuel."

Tomlin crossed his arms over his chest and smiled. "Sounds like we're going to be doing some *subvener-atin'* and *refectus-in'*."

Lee finished Tomlin's litany: "Co-ordin-atin', for sure." He hooked his thumbs into the pockets of his pants. "Of course, we don't know how friendly everyone down south is going to be. So we're just going to be very careful and take it one step at a time."

The team nodded their assent to that. But no one moved away. And Lee didn't conclude the meeting.

He stood, looking pensively at the ground in front of his feet.

The others, sensing that there was something else, waited.

Lee drew his eyes up and met their gazes, his eyes circulating the room. The people he knew best in the world. The people who had his back through thick and thin. And now it was time for him to have their backs. It was time for him to get them out of this shit-cycle.

"I know we've talked about it in the past," he said. "So it won't be a complete shock. But I wanted to tell you guys first, before I made it official with anyone else: This is going to be our last mission together."

No one spoke to that. They all just kept watching Lee.

"We've all been doing nearly continuous operations for close to three years straight. I think it's about time we pass the baton. So, once we get back from this mission to the Gulf, I'll be removing myself as your operational leader, and I'll begin training replacements for each of us. The hope being that soon after we will all be replaced and there will be an entirely new team here in The Cave."

There were a few small nods along with this.

None of them could really decide whether this felt like an immense relief, or whether it scared the shit out of them and left them feeling empty and purposeless. For the last three years, the team had been their entire world. The work stretched them thin, and chipped away at them. But it was difficult to imagine doing anything else.

"And besides giving ourselves a break," Lee continued, with a note of caution in his voice. "If things continue the way they've been with Acting President Briggs and Colorado…well, we're going to need more than just the six of us. We need new teams trained up. We have willing recruits. But we've been so busy keeping the UES afloat, we haven't been able to give them the training they need. And I don't think that's something we can continue to ignore. Not if we expect to be able to stand up to Briggs."

"So," Tomlin spoke up. "We all gonna be training cadre after this?"

Lee shrugged. "I trust each and every one of you. I'd love for that to be the case. But it's also up to you. And it's also up to the needs of the UES. I can't guarantee we'll all be working together. The other Safe Zones need experienced training cadres, too."

Julia inclined her head and flicked a finger into the air. "Did you bring this up to Angela yet?"

Lee shook his head. "No, she's got enough to think about. I'll tell her when we get back." He looked at them all pointedly. "Actually, we've *all* got enough to think about. So let's not put the cart before the horse. We've got a mission. Let's focus on getting that done first."

NINE

PROMISES

LEE LEFT THE SOLDIER SUPPORT CENTER as the sun touched the horizon, splashing the Fort Bragg Safe Zone in orange light.

The broken windows at the entrance of the Support Center were now boarded up. The glass swept away. A lone shell casing that had escaped the cleanup glittered on the pavement.

Lee stopped. Looked down at it. Grabbed it and pocketed it.

"Fuckin' day," he mumbled.

He walked toward home.

Home.

The word had lost much of its meaning to him.

At the moment, home was a single-family dwelling that used to house soldiers and their dependents, and now housed Lee, Abe, and Tomlin.

A few years ago, it had been an old trucking facility called Camp Ryder. Sometimes, it was The Cave, or the back seat of a pickup truck. Other times, a musty, abandoned house, out beyond the borders of the Safe Zone.

Home was…wherever it had to be.

He felt sometimes like a rootless drifter. He went where his business took him. And mostly his business was violence.

The streets of the Fort Bragg Safe Zone were starting to empty out. People were going home from their day's work. Most folks led an agrarian lifestyle—they were up at dawn, and in bed shortly after dark, and they put in a lot of work in between.

Lee still wore his combat pants, but he'd doffed his combat shirt in favor of a light gray hoodie, which concealed the Glock 17 on his hip. It was his secondary weapon when he was in full gear, and his primary when he was in "semi-civilian" clothes.

It was his companion at night. Sometimes he kept it on the nightstand by his bed. Sometimes, when the night seemed to stretch blackly over him and his heart wouldn't stop telling his brain he was in danger, he would leave it on an empty chamber and grip it under his pillow.

He walked on. Hands in his hoodie pockets. Heading west, away from the Support Center, and into the glow of the setting sun. A cool breeze blew at his back. Smelled like spring, and dusk.

The topic of stepping down as operational leader—of breaking the team up, essentially—terrified him. On the one hand, there was a part of him that wanted desperately to be done with…all of this. It was the part of him that recognized the inherent toxicity of living that life without ever having any relief from it.

There was only so long that you could live in the black headspace of constant conflict. There was only so long you could be switched on and ready to roll at a moment's notice, before it began to reshape the very structure of who you were.

And, unfortunately, Lee suspected that that point had already come and gone for him.

He knew he needed to get out. Or at least take a break.

But there was still a part of him that was scared shitless that he was wholly incapable of doing anything else, of *being* anything else. This was such a monumental part of who he was, of everything that he had become over the last few years, he wasn't even sure if he would know himself without it.

And wouldn't it be giving up? Wouldn't it be abandoning the mission?

The only thing that gave him solace was his hatred of Briggs. And hatred was not too strong a word. Briggs had sent people to kill Lee on multiple occasions, so Lee felt that he was justified in wanting to rip the man apart.

But if they ever wanted to beat Briggs, they would need more fighters.

More teams.

More operators.

And who better to train them than Lee?

So, the objective of training the next generation had been the only point in which he could make the two discordant halves of himself reconcile their differences. At the end of this mission to the Gulf, he would step down and begin to train the next generation of operators. It would give him and his team the break they so badly needed, while ultimately still pushing the mission forward.

On the sidewalk ahead of him, a man and his young son were walking in the opposite direction. The boy seemed oblivious at first, prattling on about something to his father, but as they drew closer to Lee, the boy looked up, stared at Lee like he was spotting a mythical—and perhaps dangerous—beast.

The boy grasped his father's hand.

Lee nodded to the two of them, then looked away, his chest tightening with the fervent desire not to speak with anyone.

The boy whispered: "Is that Captain Harden?"

The father gave the boy's hand a small tug. "Shh."

They kept walking.

Lee wasn't looking at the boy. But he felt the gaze on him. Hot and pressing.

The father drew his son to the edge of the sidewalk, allowing an exaggerated amount of space for Lee to pass by. Lee gritted his teeth, forced a smile and another nod, and kept going.

Two paces past them, the boy's voice lilted up again: "Thank you."

Lee felt his mouth twitch in an unpleasant grimace. He stopped. Forced neutrality into his face. Turned and looked at the boy.

The father seemed flustered. "Sorry. He's just…we hear a lot about you."

Lee thought about asking what the hell the kid was thanking him for, but instead decided on a more tactful approach. "Sure," he said, figuring that covered a gamut of things.

The boy looked pleased, simply to have garnered a personal reaction from Captain Lee Harden. The father gave Lee a look that said, *Hey, we're adults, I know what's up.*

"Thanks for what you and your people do," the father said.

It was useful for Lee to remind himself in these situations, that this "civilian" wasn't the same as the civilians that had populated the country a few years ago. Most of those civilians were dead now. This civilian was a survivor. He'd made it this far, and kept his son alive, to boot. So maybe he *did* know what was up.

Lee bowed his head. "No problem," he said.

The father and son turned, and continued on their way.

Lee turned and continued on his.

No problem.

Dead friends? *No problem.*

Dead enemies? *No problem.*

A life spent fighting, with no end in sight?

No fucking problem.

He encountered no one else, which was a relief.

He walked across Reilly Road, through a path in a thin stand of trees, and out onto the street where his home now was. Down the sandy, tan sidewalk. Identical, single-family dwellings on either side. Down towards the last house on the corner. The one he shared with Abe and Tomlin.

Less than a block from the place he currently called home, he spied a bit of paper, stuck to a light pole.

He knew what it was before he approached it.

There was a part of him that wanted to pass it by.

But there was a larger part of him that couldn't help himself.

He stood, looking at the paper. Wondering how it made him feel. Realizing that he didn't feel much of anything at all. The anger was there, simmering low inside of him. But it didn't jump up to him like it had in the past. These stupid flyers didn't get to him like they used to.

This one was very similar to the others. It was a cartoon, drawn by someone with less than stellar artistic skills. It featured a caricature of a soldier, with helmet, body armor, and a rifle with the bayonet attached. The face of the soldier was wild and insane. Teeth bared. Eyes wide. No pupils drawn into them, so the soldier looked like a mindless drone. Blood dripped off the bayonet. A cluster of skulls lay beneath the soldier's feet.

An over-large nametape on the cartoon-soldier's chest read HARDEN.

Down below the picture were the hand-printed words: FUHRER ANGELA'S DEATH SQUAD.

Lee grunted. Sat there for another moment, waiting to feel angrier about it. But he didn't. He thought about ripping the thing off and tearing it up, but that felt like a childish and silly reaction to someone else's childish and silly reaction.

Whoever had stapled it to the light pole had probably considered themselves very brave for posting it there, such a short distance from the place where the monster in question slept.

Lee took it down off the light pole, but was careful not to tear it. He folded it in fourths, then pocketed it, and continued on his way.

Inside his house, he found Abe and Tomlin at the kitchen table, playing dominoes. Deuce was laying on his side on the floor. He scrambled up when he saw Lee, wagged twice, as though relieved, then adhered himself to Lee's left leg, as usual.

"Hey-oh," Tomlin greeted him, not looking up from his tiles.

Abe turned to see who had come through the front door. "What's up?" he said, then turned back to the game.

"Gentlemen," Lee said. He stopped at the table and drew the piece of paper from his pocket, which he then unfolded and placed on the table. He forced a chuckle. "We got a new one."

Abe leaned forward. Eyeballed the drawing. Rolled his eyes and sat back. "Fuckin' people."

Tomlin craned his neck to see the picture right-side. "I dunno, man. They're getting better. I think it looks like you this time."

"Yeah?"

"Oh yeah. I've seen you make that face before. You psychotic bastard."

"Fridge," Abe intoned.

Lee took the paper and turned to the fridge, which was not even plugged in and held nothing in it. But, on its surface, held by old magnets, were four other, similar posters. Different artwork. Same sentiment. Captain Lee Harden was a psychotic killer. Angela's little attack dog. He lived only for death and destruction.

He posted this one with the others. "Good to be famous," he sighed.

"You want us to deal you in?" Tomlin offered.

"Nah. Gonna make it an early night."

"Suit yourself. Don't murder any neighborhood kids on your way up, you scary fuck."

Lee left the kitchen, and Deuce followed him. He trudged up the stairs to the second level. Lee's room was the one on the end. He went in and closed the door.

Deuce posted up on a mini-fridge in the corner of the room. This one *was* plugged in, and it contained Deuce's food.

Lee took the metal dog bowl from the top of the mini-fridge and set it on the floor. "Sit," he instructed, and Deuce obeyed. His big, pointed ears rotated as far forward as was caninely possible. Staring at the mini-fridge.

Lee opened the fridge. Drew out the white bucket, which was the only thing that it contained. The smell of animal's blood wafted up at him. Deuce's meals for this week were from last week's cow slaughter.

There really wasn't a part of the cow that the humans didn't eat. They were good about that. But most of the "mystery meat" that was left over was ground up into big, mushy bricks, and divvied out as a sort of gristly sausage. This included trachea, tripe, tails, intestines, and testicles. Perhaps some other stuff. Lee wasn't sure.

People ate it, but they didn't like it. Lee was usually able to score a brick or so of this stuff for Deuce, who was the only being in the Fort Bragg Safe Zone that looked forward to eating it. Still, despite everyone else's hatred of the stuff, and Deuce's obvious infatuation with it, Lee had to keep this quiet. He went discreetly to the guy that ran the slaughtering of the cows, and the guy would pass him a few pounds of the stuff on the sly.

It would be seen as unacceptable to be feeding an animal when the populace was so close to running out of food. But in Lee's mind, Deuce did more to keep him and his team safe than anyone else in this fucking place. Deuce earned his meals.

If anyone asked him how he fed Deuce, Lee planned to tell them that Deuce ate from Lee's own rations. Which wasn't *entirely* a lie. Lee also portioned off small amounts of his own rations, which he then let dry out in the sun and then stored them in a nylon bag.

He carried this with him to feed Deuce during longer missions. It was easier than carrying around raw animal parts. Also, a less attractive scent for the primals.

It'd been a while since they'd been on a multi-day mission, so Lee had a decent-sized bag of his home-dried, this-and-that dog food stored up.

Which was good. Because they were going to need it.

Lee scooped out a mound of the ground mystery meat with a cold metal spoon that stayed with the bucket in the mini-fridge. He plopped it down into

Deuce's bowl, and at the same time admonished the dog, "Sit. Wait."

He tapped the spoon off. Stuck it back in the bucket. Stuck the bucket back in the fridge.

Deuce hovered over the bowl, as still as a statue.

"Deuce," Lee said.

The dog's ears twitched. But he remained transfixed with the gunk in his bowl.

"Deuce."

Finally, the dog looked up at him. Held eye contact.

That's what Lee wanted. Deuce needed to learn to take his instructions always from Lee. The dog was continuing to learn, and Lee was continuing to teach him. But they had a good partnership.

"Eat," Lee said.

Deuce attacked his bowl with reckless abandon.

Lee sat himself on the edge of his bed, and smiled at Deuce. And for the first time that day, he didn't have to force it. The smile came out, genuine and unstrained.

It felt good that this animal didn't think Lee was a psychotic killer. It felt good that this animal appreciated what Lee had brought him.

Deuce knew what survival was about.

Deuce was a kindred spirit.

But more than that, it simply felt good to bring life to something.

As Deuce ate, which never took long, Lee pulled off his hoodie and slung it to the foot of his bed. Then took off the Glock and set it next to him.

He stared at it for a few moments, sitting there next to him. The black, polymer handle. The dim sheen of the dark metal slide.

The simple practicality of it…

Lately, an image had begun coursing its way through his brain, and when that image came to him, he felt the click of the trigger in his right index finger, and he visualized the striker pin hitting the primer, the primer lighting the propellant, the gases expanding, shooting that bullet out, and that bullet flattening as it met his own skull, pulverizing his brain matter, and then…

Lights out.

Release.

The image didn't frighten him.

Nor did he crave it.

It just sort of…came to him sometimes.

In fact it was looping through his head right at that moment.

He didn't think he would ever do it. But he had to admit, if only to himself, that what he felt most strongly when he imagined that bullet snuffing the life out of him, was *relief.*

Then again, when he thought about somebody *else* trying to put a bullet in him, he got angry. So he figured that meant he still had some fight left in him.

He pulled his eyes off the pistol. Reached over to the nightstand. Took a black composition notebook from it.

He opened it to the first page. His own handwriting filled the spaces.

The woods are lovely, dark and deep.
But I have promises to keep.
And miles to go before I sleep.
And miles to go before I sleep.

His handwriting, perhaps. But not his words. They were the last lines from a poem by Robert Frost called *Stopping By Woods On A Snowy Evening.* And, frankly, the only words from the poem that he could remember.

He had transcribed them into his notebook because they gave him a measure of comfort.

They served as a reminder to him. And he felt that he needed that reminder now.

He looked up, and found Deuce watching him, as though he knew his master's mind.

Lee smiled at his dog again.

But I have promises to keep.
And miles to go before I sleep.

He took a heavy breath and flipped the notebook to one of the middle pages. The last page that contained any writing.

Lee didn't write in a consistent hand, he'd found. Sometimes his writing tilted to the left. Sometimes to the right. Sometimes it was neat. Sometimes hasty and nearly illegible.

In a rare display of humanity, Carl had given Lee the notebook a few months ago.

"You should write stuff down," Carl had said, in his typical aloof manner.

Lee had frowned at the notebook. "What kind of stuff?"

"Your thoughts. Drawings. Whatever's on your mind." He'd sniffed, as though not wanting to get too personal, God forbid it. He concluded with, "It helps."

So Lee had started writing down…whatever was on his mind.

Most days he didn't write. But somedays he did.

He didn't bother dating any of the entries. That made it feel too much like a diary. He just separated the entries with a line in between them.

An entry from several weeks ago read, *Wonder what I would've done if I hadn't signed up for Proj. Hometown. If I'd just taken my fucking dd214 and gotten the fuck out. Would I be dead now? Would I have survived? I think I would have. Maybe would've ended up in Fort Bragg anyways. Maybe would've ended up doing the same shit. Who knows right? Maybe this is my fucking destiny. Maybe I couldn't have avoided it if I'd tried.*

The next entry after that was, *This is fuckin dumb. I got nothing to say.*

There were several entries like that. Except that he never did throw the book away.

Maybe Carl was right. Maybe it did help.

Today, he'd thought a lot about wires, and boundaries, and barriers, and the fact that they were all clustered here in this little military installation in the middle of a world that wanted to wipe them out. They were an enclave. An island. Everything beyond their electrified fences was hostile.

And now it seemed that even some of the things *inside* the fences were hostile, too.

He wrote a single sentence that day, as the world outside dipped into darkness.

We are born surrounded, and spend our life fighting to the death.

That was the last entry he wrote.

He slept that night with the Glock underneath his pillow.

BACK IN THE PRESENT

TEN

HURTSBORO

JULIA AND ABE WERE HOLED UP in the small house in the northeastern corner of Hurtsboro with Lee's unconscious body.

Nate was dead.

Tomlin and Carl were captured.

Over the course of the last three days of hiding out in the basement of that little house, Julia had managed to sneak out to where they'd abandoned their pickup trucks. The first day, she just watched for hostile movement. The second day, she recovered one of the trucks.

The other had four flats and a shot-up radiator.

She scavenged as much gear as she could, and packed it back to their little hideout.

She found it odd that whoever had ambushed them had not looted the pickups.

If not to rob them, then why the hell had they ambushed them in the first place?

In the basement of the split-level house, Lee lay on the lumpy mattress of a pullout couch, his chest rising and falling. But he still hadn't woken up.

Deuce lay alongside his right leg. They'd lost the dog during the ambush. But he'd found them on his own. Sniffed his master out in the basement of that little house. Since being reunited with Lee, he'd refused to leave his side.

Julia and Abe sat on the floor. Abe had his leg propped up on a cushion borrowed from the pullout couch. His leg was bandaged at the calf. His pants cut away at the knee. He kept his boot on. He'd been shot through the calf, but it was muscle only, and he could move if he needed to.

As Julia unpacked an MRE, her gaze went from Lee's body to the small basement windows. Through the overgrown natural area that the windows peered out from, she could see that the light was fading from the sky.

The basement was sinking into darkness.

"I'm going out again tonight," she said.

Abe tore open his own MRE. He gave her a sidelong glance. Then nodded. "You want me to come with?"

She shook her head, dumped the contents of her MRE out. Located the entrée box and peered at it in the gloom. Chicken and rice. She was okay with that. "No, I want you resting."

"I'm fucking rested. What I want is to hurt somebody."

"Yeah, me too. But I'm just trying to put eyes on. You know I won't make a move without you."

"Yeah, I know."

She located the side dish. Found it to be jalapeño cheese. She didn't care for that. She passed it to Abe. He passed her his Skittles. No negotiation necessary. This was standard operating procedure.

"You goin' back to the airfield?" Abe asked, then started shoveling his own cold entrée into his mouth.

"That's my best guess." She took a few bites of chicken and rice. Swallowed. "Somebody was out there."

At first, Julia had figured that Carl and Tomlin were dead. She'd gone back to the apartment complex when she'd felt it was safe, and gone into the apartment where Carl and Tomlin had held a base of fire to try and let the rest of them escape.

The evidence of the gunfight was there.

But…

No bodies.

And no blood either.

Which meant that Carl and Tomlin hadn't died.

The next, most logical possibility to Julia, was that they'd been captured.

Julia had spent the previous night searching the surrounding area outside of Hurtsboro for signs of habitation, figuring that whoever mounted the ambush might have a base nearby. She was looking for light and listening for sound, but what she got instead was the smell of cigarette smoke.

She'd been out near a small, local airfield. Maybe a mile outside of Hurtsboro proper. Airfields were popular for squatters. They had fences, which meant you were at least *slightly* insulated from the primals.

It was a good bet that the cigarette smoke was coming from someone at that airfield. And it was also a pretty good bet that it was the people that had ambushed them.

If she found them, she might find Tomlin and Carl.

Julia felt her throat thicken. Tighten.

She stared at the dim contents of the foil pack in her hands.

If they're still alive.

Abe watched her for a moment. Seemed to read her thoughts. "There's no reason for them to capture Tomlin and Carl and then kill them. They coulda killed them when they ran out of ammo, and they chose to take them alive."

Julia didn't respond. She was thinking, *Take them alive so that they could hang their heads from trees, or their bodies from power poles, like the fucking Followers did?*

But she didn't want to give voice to that.

The truth was, the act of the cold clinician that she put on was just a façade. It was her armor. Her protection against the terrible truth that…she had very little left.

The unconscious man on the bed, and the one sitting next to her sharing a shitty meal—they were all that was left in her world.

Over time, Julia's "interest" in combat medicine had become an obsession. It began with the fact that Lee wanted her to be the medic for his team. And it progressed further and further, as she began to view each member of the team as a member of her family.

She tried to distance herself from it, but it was too difficult. The demands of the constant operations had whittled her down to nearly nothing. It had carved her down to one ultimate goal: *keep them alive*.

Part of it was because she was actually good at medicine. But the darker part of it was that she did not think she stacked up to some of the other operators on Lee's team. She felt the desperate need to become irreplaceable in the one area where she excelled.

That's all you gotta do, she would tell herself, to focus through the fear that stalked her nearly every waking minute, and sometimes into her sleep as well. *You just gotta keep them alive. You just gotta keep their hearts beating.*

Up until four nights ago, she'd been able to do that.

Then she'd lost Nate.

And she might lose Lee.

And Tomlin and Carl were captured.

The very foundation of who Julia was as a person had been so utterly shaken that for the last few days she'd often felt like her legs might just give out on her. Simply crumble to dust underneath her, and her chest would cave in like a heavy stone arch that's lost its keystone.

The only thing that kept her moving, the only thing that kept her holding on, was Lee on that sofa bed, and finding Tomlin and Carl. Because as long as Lee was breathing, then she still had a purpose.

And as long as she didn't find Tomlin and Carl's bodies, then they were still alive in her mind—which meant she could still save them.

The blow of Nate's death felt like ruination in a part of her that she could never hope to rebuild. But as long as there were lives that were counting on her, then she had a reason to press on.

"You sure you don't want me to come along?" Abe asked.

Abe was the one that wanted to come along. He was going stir crazy in that basement all day.

"Yes, I'm sure. I'm just reconning, and you're gonna slow me down." She glanced at him, like she was gauging how deeply her words might've cut. "No offense."

Abe seemed hurt, but he said, "None taken."

What Julia was really thinking was *I can't lose you too, Abe. I can't do it again.*

What she said was, "Besides, if the primals show up again, you won't be able to run fast enough."

Abe gave a single nod as he chewed, recognizing the unpleasant truth.

"How is it feeling?" She asked around a mouthful, nodding towards his wounded leg.

"Fine," Abe replied.

Which was probably bullshit. He'd said it was fine ten minutes after being shot, too.

That was another thing that made her job difficult: none of the hardasses on her team would ever admit to being in pain. They ignored hurts, which sometimes turned them into injuries that could've been avoided.

Julia cradled the contents of her MRE in her lap and leaned carefully forward towards his leg and gave the bandage a sniff. Then she leaned back. "Well. It's not gangrenous. So that's good."

"Super," Abe mumbled.

They ate the rest of their meal in silence.

She washed it down with some water from her Camelbak. They kept 8-gallon water jugs in the beds of the pickup trucks. Four jugs per pickup. Only two of the jugs had managed to make it through the firefight unscathed. But it was enough to see them through.

Julia rose from the floor and pulled her armor back over her head again, tightening the straps down. The inside of the plate carrier was still moist from the day's sweat.

She checked her gear with a few pats of her hand. Then stooped and took up her rifle.

She nodded at Abe. "Needa shit?"

Abe shook his head. "Nah. You?"

They didn't stand over each other while they did their business or anything like that, but it was nice to have someone with a rifle close by when you were in a compromised position.

"I'll be fine for now." Julia pulled the strap of her rifle over her head. "Alright. I'll be back in a while. Three shots if I need you."

"I'll keep an ear out."

Yesterday, the batteries on their radios had died. They'd plugged them into the little solar recharger that they carried and stationed it on the south-facing side of the house, but, of course, it had been cloudy all day, so they were still without comms.

As she reached the door, she heard a groan behind her.

Her heart leapt up into her throat. She turned and looked at Lee.

On the pullout couch, Lee's head bobbed back and forth, and his eyes flickered open for a second, and Julia thought that maybe he was going to speak to them, but then they closed again. His leg kicked once, and he was still.

Chest rising and falling, evenly.

Deuce had perked up and was looking back at his master, expectantly. After a moment, he laid his head back down, disappointed.

Abe and Julia watched Lee for almost a full minute.

He didn't move again, or make another sound.

Abe looked back at her. "I can take care of him," he said. "Go find our guys."

—

It was fully dark by the time Julia made it to the other end of the town.

She could no longer distinguish between the sky and the trees. The temperature had dropped. Downright chilly when the wind blew. A few stars had shown up. But no moon yet.

She slipped between buildings and stopped often to watch and listen.

She did not like the darkness, but it would hide her. And she needed to be hidden.

They'd come to learn that the primals preferred to nest in pre-existing structures. And why shouldn't they? Why would they dig a den out of the dirt when they could easily live in the convenient shelter of one of these abandoned buildings?

Julia wondered if it was some passing instinct from their time as normal humans that made them seek out these manmade shelters. Something that whispered to them of home and civilization and things that they could no longer feel, like love, and comfort.

The thought always made Julia melancholy. But she brushed it away.

They hadn't seen any primals since the night of the ambush, but that didn't mean much.

The best bet was to be quiet, listen carefully, and trust your gut if it told you something was wrong.

Julia squatted on her haunches by a dumpster on the side of a Dollar General building. She peered down the road where the blackness of night had swallowed everything up.

Trees.

Forest.

She was going to have to go in there.

Primals might like to nest in the city, but they hunted the woods just as much as the city. They hunted wherever prey might be. And Julia held no illusions: she was the prey.

The American countryside had become something like how she imagined the African savannah might feel to a lonely traveler on foot—rife with the potential to be ripped to shreds.

Tomlin and Carl, she told herself. *You gotta do it for them.*

She stood up and leaned briefly on the side of the dumpster. The metal was cool and she felt it through the sleeve of her shirt. She held her breath for a four count and listened past the thrumming of her blood in her ears, and then she crossed the street at a soft jog.

That was the last building. The last of the town. Now it was just the woods.

She made it to the other side and slowed so that she could pick her way into the woods without making too much noise.

She stopped inside the treeline and gave her eyes a moment to adjust to the deeper darkness.

The shapes and the shadows shot up and around, all skewed and asymmetrical, and it was impossible to see what was there ahead of you until it moved. A primal could be hiding within plain sight of her and she wouldn't know until it started charging her.

She sniffed at the air.

Fallen leaves and dew and bark.

The rustle of some branches in the breeze.

Stillness.

She kept moving.

She felt how wide her eyes were stretched, trying to let in all the light they possibly could.

After about a half an hour, she came to the wide open area that she guessed was some sort of quarry. There were pits dug into the sandy soil, and mountains of it piled high and pale in the starlight. A manmade industrial pond sat to one side, glittering faintly with the rippling of the wind. Earthmoving equipment sat abandoned and forgotten.

She stayed for a moment, staring at this strange Martian scene.

She was about halfway to the airfield now.

Julia was about to step out again when she heard a cry.

It sent electric shivers straight up her spine, spiking out to her hands and fingers, and she froze where she was like she'd been turned to stone.

Be smart, she told herself, even as her body started to react to it with a slamming heart and burning lungs. *Think. Use your head.*

Sounds could be deceptive. She knew that. Sometimes they could seem like they were right on top of you, when in fact they were much farther away.

And she knew that the primals didn't make a habit of calling when they were actively pursuing prey. When they were hunting for something, then yes, they would call to communicate. But when they'd locked in—then they stayed silent.

Julia realized she'd sunk to her knees.

"Fuck, fuck, fuck," she heard the words on her lips, hardly louder than the rustling of the breeze.

It's not close. And they haven't found you. If they'd found you, they wouldn't be calling.

It was logical. But it didn't make her want to move her feet.

You gotta move, she told herself.

She worked her grip on the rifle. Felt the ache in her knuckles. Thought she heard something behind her. Whipped around to look, but it was only dark and still woods.

Acutely aware of how alone she was in this dark, dangerous world, Julia forced herself to her feet.

She began to circumvent the sandy quarry, moving to her right.

She stopped every ten paces or so in order to listen to the forest around her. A few times, her courage almost gave out and she felt like her feet had grown roots, but it never lasted for more than a second or two.

The quarry was about ten minutes behind her when she smelled smoke again.

Not cigarette smoke this time, but wood smoke.

Were they burning a fire?

Foolish, she thought, thinking of the primals.

Firelight could be visible from a long way off. And any unusual sights, sounds, or smells could draw unwanted attention.

After a few more minutes of slow, steady movement through the woods, Julia caught the faint flicker of firelight through the trees.

She felt a faint sense of victory amid the tension and the fear.

She craned her neck around, until she had a good fix on where that tiny little tongue of light was coming from, then oriented herself to it.

She moved in the direction of the light.

She kept her rifle up higher than she had before. Her steps had more tension in them. She tried not to stare at the light of the fire. Even that little bit of light could affect the acuity of her vision.

A highway materialized out of the gloom. She saw it ahead of her. If her mental image of the map was correct, that would be Highway 51. And directly across that road, stood the airfield.

The fire was clearer now. She saw the individual flames licking up from what looked like a trash can or barrel.

She also saw faces, seeming to hover, detached, over the fire.

She was too far away to identify them.

The closer she got, the slower she moved. She chose her footing carefully, and kept the trunks of trees between her and the faces she saw around the fire.

A small thrill went through her. A dangerous feeling.

She could see them, but they could not see her.

They did not know that she was there.

She could kill them right now...

Shots'll draw primals, she admonished herself. *And you're a long run from home base.*

She found an open spot in the brush, right at the edge of the tree line. She now had a clear line of sight across the highway to the airfield. She perceived the fence, but it was easy to see through. Beyond it, a building. It was off the side of this building that the fire burned.

Two figures standing near the fire.

And two other figures sitting. Their backs against the wall of the building.

She felt a little spark of hope, but was careful not to give it too much credence.

Hope could make you hurt.

Things rarely worked out the way you hoped.

She fished a pair of compact binoculars off of her chest rig and brought them to her face with one hand. Found the fire. Twisted the focus knobs.

The two men around the fire came into focus first. They both had dark hair and dark beards. One had an AK on his back. The other held an M4 lazily in his arms. She saw their mouths moving, but couldn't hear their voices. They were speaking quietly over the fire.

She panned down.

The two sitting against the wall.

Hands bound behind their backs.

Tomlin and Carl.

Julia felt elation, like oxygen breathed onto that spark of hope.

She almost cracked a smile, but before it could find a way to her face, it died enroute.

Tomlin and Carl.

Captured.

By unknown gunmen.

Were there more than just these two?

And how long did Julia have to figure out how to get Tomlin and Carl out of there?

She found herself cursing under her breath again as her mind suddenly sprang in seven different directions. She was still mumbling curses when a spear of light shot out from her right and she snapped her head in that direction.

Down the highway.

Headlights.

There was a vehicle coming.

ELEVEN

STRANGERS

TOMLIN SAT AGAINST THE COLD brick wall, and he waited.

He waited, and he observed.

Beside him, Carl was very still.

Across from them, the trash can, glowing with fire and spilling an acrid-smelling gray smoke. Their two captors stood around the fire, one facing the road, and one facing the prisoners.

So far, they'd gotten no answers. Tomlin had asked a question once, and he'd lost a tooth for it.

Still, Tomlin had managed to extrapolate some things on his own.

First, there had been more captors initially, which made sense, since Tomlin recalled no less than a dozen people shooting at them during the ambush. After they'd been captured, most of those people had departed, and they had been guarded at the airfield by five people.

Then three more of them had left, departing in an old, brown Suburban with a cylinder that ticked like a time-bomb. Which left them with their current two guards.

The second thing that Tomlin knew, was that these two guards were disciplined. They never had to talk amongst themselves to figure out what to do, when to give water, how to give it, or how to administer piss breaks. They did it like it all had been laid out beforehand.

They never laughed. Never joked between themselves. Their guarding of the two prisoners was almost manic, and often bordered on paranoia.

If Tomlin didn't know any better, he would say that these two guards were terrified of the men they held captive.

All this thinking had led him to the question that had gotten his tooth knocked out.

"Are you with Briggs?" he'd demanded, and then he'd watched his captors for any tell.

But, no tell had been forthcoming. Only the flash of a buttstock and then ringing in his ears and blood in his mouth.

Smooth move, Brian, Tomlin had chided himself as he spit his tooth out amid dirt and gravel.

So after that he'd stayed silent.

He knew two things.

Suspected a few others.

They hadn't given him much to work with.

Two guys, both mid-thirties. Both of them were dark-haired, with beards. The easiest differentiation between them was that one of them was dark-skinned, and the other light-skinned.

The light-skinned one smoked hand-rolled cigarettes, but not often. It seemed a nightly ritual. Tomlin hadn't seen him smoke one during the day.

He was smoking one now as he and his companion stood around the trash can fire. The warm smell of tobacco mingled with the harsh stink of the fire, which was built with scraps of office furniture.

Tomlin thought it was stupid to have a fire. And he especially didn't like having his hands tied behind his back while these two idiots burned a fucking signal to every primal within a mile of them.

He wanted badly to communicate to Carl, but knew that he couldn't.

The two captors talked amongst themselves, but they were still paying attention to their captives. Still checked them often. They spoke in low tones so that Tomlin knew he'd be heard if he tried to whisper to Carl.

They'll make a mistake, Tomlin told himself. *Eventually. Just keep your eyes peeled.*

It was through this fog of thoughts that two headlights twinkled between trees, and pierced the gloom of Tomlin's mind.

He blinked a few times, wondering if he was seeing things.

But no.

There.

Out beyond the runway, passed the fence and through the thin skein of trees.

A pair of headlights flashed and drew closer.

He felt his heartrate and respiration coming up from an idle.

Was this a good thing or a bad thing?

At the fire, the guard whose back was turned to Tomlin and Carl caught sight of the headlights and stirred. He mumbled something to the other man, who glanced quickly over his shoulder, and then back to the captives.

It was the light-skinned one. The guy with the cigarette burned down to a nub between his lips. "Both of you. On your knees. Now."

Tomlin and Carl twisted their bodies to get their knees underneath them. In the gloom, and in the movement, Tomlin managed to catch Carl's eye.

The other man's gaze was hard and intense and it seemed poised and ready to act.

Good.

The two of them got their knees under them and then waited.

Out on the highway, the headlights were drawing closer. Slowing down now.

The two guards shuffled behind Tomlin and Carl.

"Keep your eyes on the fire," the darker one said.

Tomlin and Carl did as they were told.

Tomlin watched the flames dance. Knew that they were destroying his night vision.

Then his vision winked out.

Cloth. Over his eyes.

Blackness.

He felt the blindfold being tied tightly at the back of his head.

He didn't like that. Not one bit. Reminded him too much of a firing squad.

"Both of you stay still," their captor said. "This is the wrong time to do anything stupid."

Tomlin heard the vehicle approaching now.

Big vehicle.

The roll of tires on concrete.

And…

The ticking of a faulty cylinder.

Our friends are back.

The engine was slowing.

The lightest squeak of brakes.

The rattle of chain link as a gate was drawn aside.

Then the engine rumbled up again, and this time Tomlin heard the tires on gravel, and it was growing very close now, close enough that for a grim moment he thought they were going to get run over.

But then the vehicle stopped. The engine went into an idle.

The faulty cylinder ticked the seconds and half-seconds.

Tomlin waited.

He couldn't observe. But he could listen.

A door opened. Then closed.

Feet on concrete.

The crunch of boot heels traversed the empty space in front of Tomlin, and then stopped. Tomlin could not see the person, but he could *feel* the shadow of them, as they blocked the radiant heat of the fire.

No one spoke for several beats.

Then: "Which one of you is Lee Harden?"

The voice.

Heavily accented.

If Tomlin were to take a guess, he'd say Spanish was the speaker's first language.

Between Tomlin and Carl, there was only a moment's hesitation, and then they both happened to come to the same idea at the same exact time.

"Who?"

Another moment of silence.

The slight chuff of a snicker.

"Fine," the stranger's voice said. "Take them both."

—

"Shit." Julia breathed the word. She watched the red eyes of the vehicle's taillights disappearing rapidly down the road, and then they winked out of existence as it turned into a curve.

She had the ridiculous urge to get up and chase after the vehicle.

Gone. They're gone.

The strangers had piled Tomlin and Carl both into that old Suburban and driven off, their tires chirping as they hit the asphalt, heading away from Hurtsboro.

They're gone, and I have no fucking clue where.

Suddenly she felt the loneliness of her position. With the vehicle gone, and the distant light of the trash can fire now extinguished, and all the human beings that had occupied her thoughts now fading in the distance, she felt abruptly like she was cut loose and adrift in the space between planets.

I've got to get back to Abe and Lee.

She started moving.

The distance between her and the basement of their hideout seemed to have grown. Stretched. Become continental.

She knew that it was still only a few miles.

But they were long, slow miles, and her fear continued to put the spurs to her. She had to willfully resist the urge to begin running all the way back to the hideout. Running would be noisy. The primals might hear her. And she knew they were in the area.

Her fear began to boil down into panic.

She'd heard the primals calling to each other.

And then not heard them again.

When you couldn't hear them calling—that was when they were right behind you.

She became religious as she moved, the words coming out in the huffs of her breath: "God, please get me back. God, please get me back."

The street that preceded their hideout was like crossing the finish line of a marathon.

When her feet hit pavement, she felt her whole body give up the tension of fear that had gripped her. She was close. So close, that it seemed nothing bad could happen.

But as she reached the basement door, she noticed four bullet holes in it.

Three in the body of the wooden door, and one through the glass.

All four appeared to have been fired from within the basement, directed at something outside.

Julia drew back from the door.

Shaking hands gripped her rifle. Staring at the door, trying to piece it all together, trying to make sense of it, to form some logical and linear course of events that would hopefully explain away what she was seeing.

What had Abe been shooting at?

People? Or primals?

And were they still here?

Shit, shit, shit...

She put her back to the wall of the house and looked behind her, checked the nearby overgrown yards, and the nearby houses, sitting in amongst chest-high weeds with their roofs charred black and their windows broken and their insides gutted from fire or looting.

Who was there?

And was Abe still alive?

Was Lee?

"Julia?" a voice hissed.

From inside the basement.

In any other circumstance Julia would have been confident that the whisper belonged to Abe Darabie. However, in that moment, she wondered if you really could correctly identify someone by their whisper?

She chose not to respond.

Her rifle was up, without her thinking about it.

The optic filled her vision, the small red dot hovering right where someone's chest would be if they came through.

"Julia!" Maybe-Abe's voice said, louder this time, and more stern. "Get the fuck in here. It's okay. We got company. Don't fuckin' shoot them."

It's a trick!

She thought she heard something behind her.

She twisted to look, but there was nothing there.

She snapped back to the door, her finger going to the trigger out of sheer jumpiness.

"No!" she called out. "Whoever's in there, come out here where I can see you! Come out of the basement with your hands up!"

She didn't actually expect them to comply. She was stalling for time. Trying to think how she was going to figure this out without putting her ass on the line...

Something tapped the back of her head.

She instantly knew that it was the muzzle of a rifle.

"Don't fuckin' move," a voice said.

Julia felt like her stomach was imploding. Gone supernova. Sucking reality into it.

Her vision went white and sparkly at the edges.

"Finger off the trigger," the voice said.

She pulled her finger off the trigger.

"Let that rifle hang, and put your hands up high, and don't make a move for it."

Julia did, and it was only when she stretched her hands up high that she remembered to take a breath, and some of the white sparkles disappeared from her vision.

"Now, walk into the basement so we can get outta the open."

Julia stepped forward.

Thought about spinning and trying to disarm whoever was behind her.

Thought about making a run for it.

Thought about refusing.

Somehow, each imagining ended in some sort of disaster, and then, before she could come up with any worthwhile plan, she was standing in the doorway of the basement and looking in.

Their solar lantern was sitting there, burning brightly on the pullout couch where Abe was seated, next to Lee's body.

Abe had his rifle in his arms, but it wasn't held ready.

Another armed man was standing behind him, at the side of the pullout couch.

Abe looked at Julia and shook his head. "Jules, chill out. We're all friends here."

TWELVE

MESSAGES

LEE WAS STANDING IN a place.

It seemed passingly familiar.

Bright sunshine poured over him. But it didn't heat him. He still felt cold. He was surrounded by green grass that billowed in a breeze. In the distance was a hill. On that hill, a tree.

That was it. There was nothing else.

He felt...distraught.

Out of place.

Like a trespasser.

"Do you recognize this place?" someone asked him.

He turned and looked.

Angela stood next to him. And he was not surprised to see her there. Like she was supposed to be there. Like she belonged in this place, although he was still not sure where this place was.

"I think I do," he said. "But I don't know."

Angela only shook her head at him. "You don't know it. You've never been here." She seemed disappointed in him. She gave a small shake of her head, then turned away from him.

Lee was not sure what to say.

Not sure where he was.

Angela took a few steps past him and looked over her shoulder. "Who are you, anyways?"

And Lee felt the hollowness of nothing. Felt it like a big empty space, how every movement echoes and the wind sighs through it because there is absolutely nothing there.

"I don't know," he said.

And then, abruptly, he was no longer in that green field. He was in the hollow place of his imaginings, a vast, empty cave, and the ceiling vaulted blackly over his head and down at his feet there was the sad leftovers of a fire, embers barely glowing in all this darkness.

Seated cross-legged at this depressed fire was Julia, and Lee had the sense that she had somehow sprouted from Angela, that Angela had *become* Julia.

Julia looked up at him and smirked. "This is where you belong, Lee. Down here with us. Down in the ground where the light doesn't reach."

—

Lee came back into his body like he had been dropped into it from a great height.

His eyes opened before he was fully conscious. The strange dream world of fields and hills and trees and dark caves had melted into something else. A dim room. There were people in it. He recognized Julia. He recognized Abe. The others were strangers.

There was a moment when he thought that he was still dreaming.

And then, in the next moment, for no particular reason, his brain snapped into place and he knew this was reality.

Julia, across the room. An armed man behind her.

Abe, sitting beside Lee on what looked like a bed.

Another armed man, standing at the side of that bed.

Lee had no idea what the fuck had happened, or where the hell he was. His only recollection was of a life-threatening sense of *oh shit*. A knock of adrenaline hit him like someone had injected it straight to his chest, and his heart started slamming.

Three things made it through the whiteout of panic that rushed over him.

He was aware that he was injured—he felt it in the deep and horrible ache in his body.

He was aware that he had no weapon and no armor—not even a shirt.

And he was aware that the armed stranger at the side of the bed was within reach of him.

He did the only thing that he could think of to do.

Lee's eyes latched onto that stranger's rifle—an SKS—and he lurched up, which caused a wave of apocalyptic pain in his chest, and he grabbed the man's rifle.

The room turned into bedlam.

Lee got his left hand on the foregrip and his right hand seized the buttstock, and he ripped backward. The man yelped, shouted, and started pulling back.

Lee hadn't even noticed Deuce laying at his side, but the dog bolted off the mattress and started barking savagely.

Everyone was yelling.

Abe launched his body over top of Lee's, smacking the rifle out of his grip. Abe's voice punched at his eardrums, but it took a second for Lee to register what he was actually saying.

"No, Lee! Stop! Stop!"

The stranger behind Julia crossed the room in a flash and pointed his rifle at Lee, yelling, "Put it down! Put it down!"

The SKS clattered to the floor, and the man who had held it two seconds earlier dove for it.

In a wash of paralyzing confusion, Lee allowed Abe to flatten him back into a laying position. Abe had one hand posted on Lee's sternum, which made his entire upper body feel like it was on fire, while Abe's other hand pumped the air.

"Stop!" Abe shouted. "Everyone chill the fuck out!"

Lee lay there, struggling to breathe, wondering why he was struggling to breathe, wondering why it hurt so damn much. Over Abe's shoulder, he watched the second armed man dip his muzzle a few inches.

It was enough of an acquiescence that Abe turned away from that man and faced Lee.

Lee's whole body was shaking. He realized he had Abe's shirt clutched in two handfuls. He released them and held up his hands, not sure if that was the right move. It felt wrong, but Abe was telling him to stop. His hands hovered in the air, and they trembled violently.

The other armed stranger had scooped up his rifle and backed off to the far side of the room, holding it at a low ready, his eyes darting as he swore vehemently.

Deuce had planted himself between the two strangers, his head low, his tail between his legs, growling fiercely.

Abe grabbed Lee's head, holding him steady, anchoring him to reality. Abe's dark eyes were locked on his, searching them for reason.

The image of Abe's bearded face suddenly blurred.

Tears of pain and abject confusion were springing out of Lee, like the bedrock of his being had been cracked open. He couldn't control himself. His mental defenses were shattered.

"Lee. Are you with me? You see me?"

"What the fuck is going on?" Lee coughed out, sending another rack of pain through his chest. He inhaled sharply, and it hurt and shivered his body. "What the fuck is happening?"

"These are friends," Abe said in the tone of someone speaking into an abyss of insanity. "We're all friends here, okay? Can you relax? Can you sit back?"

Lee realized he was still straining against Abe's grip, trying to sit up against it. He released the tension in his core, and some of the pain in his chest abated.

"There you go," Abe counseled. Then he turned to the armed strangers. "We're good. Everyone's good. Let's all stop fucking pointing guns, okay? Let's all be calm."

The two strangers exchanged a worried glance, and then lowered their rifles further.

Lee's pulse was hitting so hard that it was twitching his whole body. His breathing was too fast.

Slow it down. Think.

Compartmentalize.

Get your shit together.

He started pulling air through his nose and breathing it out slow through pursed lips.

What happened? Why are you here?

The pain his chest went from a widespread blaze to a small, localized flame. The left side of his chest. His ribs.

His hands fluttered to his side. He craned his neck to look.

"Ah-ah," Julia's voice, shooting through the darkness of his confusion like a searchlight in a storm. "Don't touch that."

Lee glanced up, his brows still furrowed, his eyes still wet. He distinctly recalled this feeling. This shattered feeling. He had felt it once before. On a forest floor. Lying there, left to die, after a bullet had skimmed along his skull and jangled his brain.

I've been injured...

Lee blinked. Focused.

Julia was on one knee at the side of the bed, next to Abe. Her eyes were on the side of his chest, but then they flicked up and met his. Julia gently pushed his fingers away from his ribs, away from whatever it was she didn't want him to touch.

Lee strained again to see his ribs.

A mound of bandaging, taped around a plastic tube that was protruding from him. Thin, watery-looking blood spotted the inside of the tube, like condensation.

"The fuck is that?" Lee croaked.

"It's a chest tube," Julia said, her voice calm and clinical.

Calm and clinical.

Julia.

Julia standing over him while bullets screamed through night air.

The memories hit him like a geyser.

He remembered looking up at her. Seeing the stars behind her. He remembered the pain in his side. Remembered her telling him to breathe, *try to breathe...*

We are born surrounded

The ambush. The shooting. The running through the woods. The flicker of muzzle flashes in the night. The cold, hard truth of tactics like a thin veil over the fear of imminent death. The feeling of something hitting him hard in the chest.

And spend our lives fighting to the death

"You were shot in the chest," Julia said, her words slow and enunciated. "Do you remember that?"

Lee did remember it. "How long?" he blurted. "How long have I been out?"

"Three days. Almost four. This is the fourth night since it happened."

The surrealism of lost time hit him like a right hook. It didn't seem possible. Almost four fucking days? How could all that time simply disappear?

A more urgent thought occurred to him.

"Where's everyone else?" he said, his eyes going wide, flicking between Abe and Julia. "Where's...? Where's Brian? And Carl and Nate?"

Julia averted her gaze. Blinked like something was caught in her eye.

Abe's throat bobbed. Constricted. "Nate was killed in the ambush," he said, his voice low. "Tomlin and Carl were captured."

Lee's mind seemed to spasm. His stomach felt like it was an elevator, and the cables had just snapped. His thoughts lurched to one thing, and then the other. *Nate's dead*, and then, *Tomlin and Carl are captured.*

Lee's first instinct was to ask about Nate, but then he realized the stupidity of the question. It didn't matter that the truth was too large to be absorbed. Abe was looking in his eyes and telling him that Nate was dead. Was there really a question to ask?

Nate's dead.

Lee reeled. Remembered to breathe. Sucked in air.

He couldn't accept it. But he deflected. He went to the other question. The one that *did* need to be asked.

"Carl and Tomlin," Lee said, coming up onto his elbows with significant effort. "Who captured them?"

Julia and Abe didn't answer. But Abe raised his head and looked at someone.

Lee followed his gaze to the man standing across the room. The stranger that he'd tried to disarm. Probably would have, and then shot dead, if Abe's reactions hadn't been so quick.

Lee took stock of both of the strangers.

The one with the SKS was a younger guy with sandy blond hair sticking out beneath a black watch cap. He had quick, cautious eyes. He carried a pack on his back and was dressed in jeans and a dark blue jacket. He had no other weapons or ammo on him, unless he carried it in his pack.

The other stranger was similarly dressed, but older, with short-cropped, balding hair, and he carried an AR variant with a hunter's scope on it.

The younger one took a step forward and appeared to relax some. "It's Lee, right? Lee Harden?"

Lee nodded once.

"I'm Braxton." He nodded towards his older counterpart. "That's Trey. We've heard a lot about you. And the UES."

Lee didn't care about that right now. "Who took my guys?"

Braxton blinked, shook his head. "Look, we don't know for sure…"

"It might be some guys we're familiar with," Trey spoke up.

Lee pivoted his attention to the older guy.

"We were in the area, scavenging, when we heard the ambush," Trey continued. "We saw what happened. Hightailed it out of town. Went back to our group. Our main guy, I guess our *leader*, so to speak, he told us to come back and try to make contact with anyone that survived. Thought we might have some mutual interest in the people that took your guys."

Lee felt a rush of frustration heat the back of his neck. Made him suddenly feel sick. He tried to speak, but the air that he gathered for the words turned to acid in his chest and he started coughing violently.

Julia put a gentle hand on his chest. "Try not to cough, Lee."

Lee did his best to stifle the racking pain in his lungs. Let out a wordless growl.

Trey held out a placating hand, and waited until Lee's coughing fit had ebbed before speaking quickly. "Listen. Our guy, Paolo, he told us not to give you all the deets here. He's got his reasons for being circumspect. I'm sure you understand. We're willing to build some trust here, but we don't know you people, and you don't know us. We're not just going to spill everything we got when we don't even know who you are."

Lee was struggling to reset his mind to reality, like putting your house back in order after a burglar has ransacked it.

You have to be in control.

You have to TAKE control…

"You know my name," Lee managed. "You know we're from the UES."

Trey nodded, coolly. "Sure. That's what you say. But things are…tricky out here."

"Well, where the fuck's this Paolo of yours?" Lee demanded.

"He's at our place. We'll take you, if you want. Paolo will meet you there. He's the one that wants to talk to you. He'll let you in on the details."

Julia snapped her eyes to Trey. "Why should we trust you people?"

Trey shrugged. "You don't have to. But Paolo knows who took your guys."

"So Paolo wants something from us," Julia realized.

Trey didn't respond to this, but his silence felt like answer enough.

Julia glared. "What's to stop us from taking the two of you and beating the information out?"

Trey and Braxton both tensed again, going back on high-alert.

Before the situation could muddy any worse, Lee held up a hand, stifling another cough. "Stop. Both of you stop." *Take control.* "No one's beating anyone."

Julia continued to stare menacingly at Trey, and Trey held her gaze, unflinching.

Lee had to slow his respiration again. Every time he started breathing hard, the pain in his chest mounted and made him want to cough. But even in the last few minutes of being awake, he was adapting to it. Learning to control the need to cough. It reminded him of drown-proofing.

This is who you are. This is what you do.

We've got a mission, Lee was thinking rapidly. *Make friends, and find fuel.*

"Trey," Lee said, controlling his voice, working some command back into it. The other man tore his defiant gaze from Julia, and met Lee's eyes again. "We'll talk to Paolo, okay?"

Trey pursed his lips. Then nodded, curtly.

Lee looked at Abe and Julia. "Has anyone managed to get on the line with Fort Bragg?"

"Our satphone got shot in the ambush," Julia said. "I tried to piece it back together, but it's done. Power source was shredded."

"Fuck." Lee tilted his head back and breathed steady to quell the sickening frustration. *Control. Command and control.* "Any idea how we can get comms with them?"

"Radios won't reach," Abe pointed out the obvious. "Nearest settlement with a satphone is back in Butler."

Lee closed his eyes. They felt hot and feverish behind his eyelids. He thought. *Forced* himself to think through his physical discomfort. Forced himself to compartmentalize all the bad shit into another place in his mind, and simply focus on the problem standing before him now.

They had to get comms with Fort Bragg. Fort Bragg needed to know what had happened in Hurtsboro, and from there, they might be able to dispatch a reaction force.

But a trip back to Butler would cost them time. And time, they did not have. They had already lost four fucking days.

Lee felt Carl and Tomlin's absence like a cable tied to his chest. The longer they waited, the further they stretched away, and the cable was taut to the point of breaking. They had a trail to pursue right now. But if they let that trail go cold…

We are born surrounded…

The thoughts were almost invasive. Hard to beat down.

Images from the ambush peppered his brain like stray bullets.

Muzzle flashes in the night.

The nightmare feeling of his lungs collapsing.

Fucking FOCUS!

Lee opened his eyes again and looked at Trey, then at Braxton. "Do you guys have a vehicle?"

Trey considered this for a moment, as though unsure whether or not to volunteer that information. Then he nodded. "Yes."

Inwardly, Lee was struggling to maintain a grip on his train of thought.

Outwardly, he didn't let it show. He *couldn't* let it show.

"Okay," he said. "I need one of you to take a message back to Butler, Georgia."

Trey chuffed. "What? No. Absolutely not."

Lee skewered him with a look. He knew he was not cutting the most imposing figure, laying wounded on a bed, but he also knew that rumors and legends grew tall in people's minds, and apparently these people had heard of him. He might use that to his advantage.

"Your man, Paolo," Lee said. "He wants something from us. And I'm the one that can get it for him. Vehicles, weapons, ammo, medical supplies, food…" *Well, we can't really do the last one.* "You name it. But if Paolo wants what we have, then this is the first step. I can't go meet Paolo without sending a message back to my people. So, if you wanna play, then there's gonna have to be some give and take. Got it?"

Trey's bottom lip peeled back, exposing his lower teeth. It was an ugly look. But…he didn't immediately dismiss Lee this time.

Lee gave it a moment, then pressed. "I'll give you the passcodes to get into Butler. I'll tell you who to meet up with. You tell them that I sent you, there won't be any problems. You do this for me, then I'll go meet your guy. Tomorrow."

Trey gestured at Abe and Julia. "Why not send one of them?"

In his current mental state, it took monumental effort for Lee to continue speaking civilly: "No. This is what's left of my team. They're staying with me. That's the deal. Take it or leave it."

Maybe they'd just go with Julia's idea. Pop Trey in the back of the head and take Braxton prisoner. The prospect of violence had a centering effect on Lee. It was familiar and comfortable, like the soothing touch of some dark mother.

This is who you are. This is what you do.

But no.

As often as violence truly *was* the answer, that was not the case here.

"They're both wounded," Julia spoke up. "Lee's the one that Paolo wants to speak to. He's gotta be there. Abe is shot in the leg. You can't send him—if something goes wrong with the car on the way, he'll be fucked. I'm the medic, and I have to stay with my two wounded guys."

"It has to be one of you," Lee said, trying to give it the feel of a final stamp.

Trey and Braxton still had options, but Lee didn't want them to *feel* like they had options. People with options never did what you wanted them to do. They were slippery. You had to corner them. Coerce them, sometimes.

"Alright," Trey said suddenly. "Here's how it's going to work." He leaned back, narrowed his gaze. "I'll send Braxton to deliver the message—"

"Gee, thanks," Braxton mumbled.

"—But that means you guys are staying with me as collateral until he gets safely back. Life for a life type of thing. I take you to meet Paolo, and then all three of you remain there, until Braxton gets safely back home."

Lee didn't hesitate. It was a relief to simply come to an agreement, some form of clarity in the chaos, even if that meant he became someone's collateral. "That's a deal," Lee said, and before anyone could object to any of the terms, or continue the God-awful argument any further, he turned to Braxton. "Butler, Georgia," he reiterated. "You're gonna ask to speak to Ed. He'll be able to get you in contact with Fort Bragg."

Braxton's lips had pressed down to a grim, displeased line, and for a moment, Lee thought that, despite his best efforts at hurrying this thing along, Braxton might continue to argue.

Instead, Braxton sighed through his nose. "Fine. What's the message?"

Lee did his best to not look thankful. Then he told him the message that needed to get to Fort Bragg.

THIRTEEN

LITTLE TALKS

THEY SPENT THE NIGHT in that basement.

Five people. Three strangers on one side, two strangers on the other.

Such was the necessity of their circumstances.

The only talking that occurred between the two groups was initiated by Braxton.

He was watching Lee from the other side of the room with a sort of half-doubtful, half-hopeful expression.

Lee was lying on the sofa bed, trying not to feel sick. Deuce had rejoined him on the mattress, and Lee's fingers absently worried at the fur on Deuce's neck.

Julia and Abe were settling into the spots that had become their beds over the last four nights. Julia, beside the pullout couch, and Abe on the other side of her, up against the wall.

On the other side of the room, Trey had already chosen a spot and was ostensibly trying to sleep now. His small, battered backpack was his pillow. His rifle next to him like a cold lover.

The only light was from the fading solar lantern, which didn't reach to the edges of the room, and would be reduced to dully-glowing LEDs in an hour.

Still, it was enough for Lee to become aware of Braxton's stare.

Lee tried to avoid meeting the young man's gaze, knowing it would be taken as an invitation to speak. And Lee did not want to speak. But it happened anyway.

"Is it true what they say about you?" Braxton asked, suddenly. Like he was afraid everyone might fall asleep before he had a chance to ask.

Lee felt his chest tighten. He finally allowed his eyes to hit Braxton's.

The younger man's face was barely visible. The whites of his eyes glittered like ghost lights in the distance.

"I don't know," Lee said. "What is it that they say about me?"

"They say you stopped a horde of millions of infected. That the horde would've wiped out the entire east coast if it wasn't for you."

"Well, I didn't do it single-handedly, if that's what they're saying. There were a lot of people that risked their lives to stop that horde." Lee paused. "A lot of people that died, too."

"So it's true," Braxton said. "There actually was a horde of millions. And you guys killed them all."

"We didn't kill them *all*," Lee said. "But we killed enough to stop them. And if you ever meet a Marine artilleryman, you can thank him. They were the ones that did the lion's share of the work."

The image of that night would never leave Lee's brain. It would always live there in perfect clarity, and when he recalled it, he always felt exactly as he had that night: Terrified, awestruck, and relieved, as he watched from the deck of a helicopter as fire rained out of the sky and leveled the town of Smithfield, and the millions of infected that had gathered there.

He didn't think that memory would ever stop making his heart stutter-step, as it did now.

"They also say," Braxton began again, his voice more shrewd this time. "That you will kill anyone who stands in your way."

"Braxton," Trey grumbled in a warning tone.

"Even if they're your friends," Braxton finished.

"Would you shut the fuck up?" Trey snapped, pulling his head up from his backpack and looking sideways at his partner.

Braxton kept staring at Lee. "It's a fair fucking question. Seeing as how we're *friends* now."

Trey reached out and backhanded Braxton's shoulder. "Let the man sleep." Trey harrumphed back down onto his pack, turned his body away from Braxton. "For that matter, let *me* fucking sleep. Sittin' around, yappin' your jaws like it's a goddamn slumber party…"

Trey trailed off.

Silence overtook the basement.

In the cold, fading light, Lee could still see Braxton's eyes.

They watched each other in the dark.

Maybe Braxton thought that Lee was staring him down, but behind his eyes, Lee was seeing his dead friends. The truth was, they haunted him because he had killed them all, hadn't he? Through his mistakes, through his bullheadedness, through his misplaced surety in himself, they had all died.

But the one that stared back at him most accusingly was Lucas.

Lucas, his fellow Coordinator.

Lucas on a forest floor, bleeding out.

Lucas, staring up at Lee with confusion on his face.

Lee hadn't known how to interpret that confusion at the time, but in the hundreds and hundreds of nights since, it had become horribly clear what that confusion had meant.

Lucas had come to North Carolina to help Lee.

And Lee had shot him dead.

He wondered what Lucas was thinking in that moment when he'd looked up at Lee. Had he felt betrayed? Had he felt misused? Or had he simply been confused, like a dog who's been beaten but can't remember what it did wrong?

A thousand times he'd replayed that day in his mind, thinking of how he might have changed the outcome. And a thousand times he ended up hating himself, not because he'd missed a sign that might've saved Lucas's life, but because he could never think of a single thing he would've done differently.

This is who you are. This is what you do.

For the first time since waking, he remembered the dream he'd had, and it came back to him in an unpleasant wave, and the dream-version of Julia stuck while the rest of it washed away, like storm tides leaving detritus on a beach.

This is where you belong, Lee. Down here with us. Down in the ground where the light doesn't reach.

He fell asleep, eventually, holding onto Deuce, with those words sitting inside of him like a festering wound.

—

There was one other occasion of wakefulness that night.

Lee wasn't sure of the hour, or how long it had been since he'd fallen back asleep, but he woke to the rumble of Deuce's growl, a vibration in his hand, and up against his leg. He twitched up out of sleep.

It was a Pavlovian reaction for Lee. Except that he was the dog, and Deuce's growl was the stimulus—every time Lee heard it, he felt like his heart was trying to make a fast exit out of his throat.

Feeling his own pulse rocking his head, Lee reached out and touched Deuce on the chest and said, "Ssh…"

Lee couldn't see the others in the darkness, but he had the impression of them, and he could hear them stirring.

Deuce had stopped growling—he was at least learning the command to be quiet—but he was still issuing soft, stressed breaths, nearly whining, but without using his voice.

No one spoke. No one moved.

Lee prayed that Trey and Braxton knew enough to keep their fucking mouths shut. All it would take would be one of them to start talking...

From somewhere upstairs came a sound.

Like a fingernail on glass.

Tap...

Tap-tap...

Lee became terribly aware that he'd allowed himself to fall asleep without any weapons at hand.

He knew why—because Julia had taken all his weapons away until he regained his senses. As they'd seen earlier, sometimes when you awaken from an injury, you react violently.

It was logical on Julia's part, but Lee found himself loathing the decision and cursing Julia in his head.

Tap.

Tap.

Were the windows intact? Were the doors secure?

Please tell me Julia thought of that. Please tell me that she didn't remember to disarm me, but forget to secure all the entrances...

A long time passed.

Lee heard nothing else.

Deuce eventually stopped his whisper-whine. Huffed, as though exhausted, and then relaxed.

A quiet voice from beside him: "Lee."

Lee felt Julia's fingers touch his left arm, slide down until they had his wrist. They pulled his hand out, and he felt the familiar grip of his Glock being pressed into his palm.

"Chamber's empty," Julia whispered.

Lee didn't respond. He held the pistol in his left hand, against his chest, like a child might hold a favored stuffed animal, and he stared at a black ceiling that was indistinguishable from the blackness behind his closed eyes.

—

Braxton left the next morning, before first light.

Trey insisted on going with him to where they had hidden their vehicle. Gave Lee a searching glance before he closed the basement door behind them, as if to say, *Don't go disappearing on me.* Then the two of them slipped out into the early-morning darkness.

Lee felt marginally better than he had the previous night. That was enough for him to seize on and keep telling himself, *you're healing, you're building back up, you'll be okay.*

While he'd been unconscious, Julia had staved off dehydration with IV's. But she'd run out the day before Lee woke up.

She'd given him some water last night, to test his stomach. When he held that down, she gave him some water mixed with grape drink-mix from one of their MREs. She'd been saving those up for him. Figured he'd need some quick calories, and his stomach might not be ready for solid food.

She was right about the need for quick calories. Wrong about the food.

As the grape drink hit Lee's stomach, he realized that a large part of his overwhelming feeling of nausea was actually extreme hunger. He hadn't eaten in three days. And his body was trying to heal itself, robbing him even further of his miniscule fat stores.

After he managed to keep the first grape drink down, he asked to eat, and Julia found the least harsh MRE that was left, which happened to be chicken and noodles. Lee ate it, while Julia hovered and occasionally told him to slow down.

"Chew. Swallow," she advised. "It's not going anywhere."

Lee did as the doc ordered. Chewed. Swallowed. Waited for a moment to see if he was going to toss it back up. When he didn't, he shoveled another gigantic spork-full in.

"Just like Mom used to make," he mumbled around the mouthful.

"Your mom must've been a shitty cook."

Getting calories into his body had done wonders for him. He slept hard and dreamlessly and he woke up feeling much less like he was about to die.

A far cry from full strength, but progress is progress.

"How long until I'm one-hundred-percent?" Lee asked as he struggled up into a sitting position on the pullout couch, the Glock still in his hand. He racked a round into the chamber. Press-checked it. Tapped the back of the slide. Set the pistol off to the side, still warm from being hugged to his body all night.

Julia had Lee's three-day-pack, which she hauled across the floor and propped up against the bed, next to Lee's bare feet. "Couldn't say," she said. "Depends on rest. Recovery. Nutrition."

"So…never."

Julia smirked at him. "Could be anywhere between two and six weeks. Knowing you, I'd bet on the outside numbers."

Lee lifted his left arm, regarded the tube coming out of his ribs, and couldn't suppress a shudder. Sometimes he thought he could feel the other end of the tube, inside of his chest. "When does this come out?"

"Soon. Not right now. I want to see how you do when you get mobile. If you do okay, I'll take it out tonight."

Lee nodded, looked down at his pack.

Three bullet holes marred the surface. Wide and gaping. Probably exit holes. He tilted the pack to see the backboard area, and saw the entry holes. They kept most of their packs and gear in the truck beds. It looked like his pack had gotten shot up, along with a lot of other stuff.

He opened it and dove inside, while Julia moved over to check on Abe's wounded calf.

At the top of the pack, luckily unmarred, was the bag of Deuce's home-dried, this-and-that food. Lee felt relieved upon seeing it. He'd been so out of it the previous night that he hadn't even thought about feeding Deuce. But he saw the bag was emptier than he recalled it being, so he knew that Julia had been feeding him.

On the floor at the foot of the bed, Deuce perked up at the sight and smell of his food bag being opened.

Lee scooped some out onto the floor, and only made Deuce wait for a moment before letting him attack his food. He watched the dog with a faint smile, then noted that there wasn't much food left in the bag.

Lee folded it up and put it off to the side. Went back to his pack with a frown.

The rest of the contents of Lee's pack were predictably perforated. But not necessarily unusable. He was currently dressed only in his skivvies. He had a fresh pair of underwear (no holes, he noted), and swapped those out with the skivvies. Found his spare combat shirt. A bullet had gone through it. The way the shirt had been tightly rolled, he now had a series of ragged holes that traced down the middle of the shirt, front and back. He pulled it on gingerly, careful not to disturb the chest tube.

His pants had been similarly rolled, and sported a similar collection of holes, this time starting at his right hip and going all the way down the right pant leg.

Socks were unmarred.

"Alright," Lee mumbled to himself, feeling better now that he was dressed. More in control. "I can work with this." He looked up at Abe, Julia still inspecting his calf. "How you doin'?"

"Better than you," Abe said. He saw that Lee was dressed, and smiled. "What a transformation. You look like you might even live."

Lee grimaced as he twisted to pull on his boots. In the middle of a groan of pain, he managed to scoff. "Ain't found a way to kill me yet."

But he felt the hollowness of that bravado.

If it hadn't been for Julia, he *would've* been dead.

Ten minutes later, Trey got back. When he opened the door, Lee saw the first glimmers of dawn turning the sky from black to navy blue. Trey closed the door behind him again, then stood there, looking at them.

They were packed and ready. Julia insisted on carrying Lee's rig and pack. Lee insisted on carrying his rifle, with his pistol back in its battered holster on his side. Abe carried his own things, but favored his right leg.

Trey sniffed. Eyed them critically. "Be honest, y'all don't look like much."

Abe frowned at him. "Sorry. Next time we'll try not to get shot so much."

Trey shrugged. "Let's go meet Paolo."

—

It wasn't a dream. More like one of those memories that assaults you the moment you awaken.

Angela opened her eyes and knew where she was, knew what had happened in the last two years, but for some reason her mind was on a rooftop under a beating summer sun. An empty jug of water in one hand, and the other holding onto her daughter, while her husband paced the yard below, gone mad, obsessed with trying to kill them.

She lay there in her bed, staring at the ceiling of her bedroom, knowing that she was in the Fort Bragg Safe Zone, but feeling the dread of that day as though she were living it again right then and there.

On the roof. Stranded.

That's how Lee had found her, almost three years ago.

She remembered seeing Lee emerge from the wood line close to their house.

She remembered seeing her husband—or at least what had *been* her husband—charging towards Lee.

The *pop-pop-pop* of Lee's rifle.

Her husband going down.

Abby screaming "Daddy! Daddy!" because she didn't understand that it wasn't him anymore.

A knock on her bedroom door startled her.

Back in the here and now.

"Angela, hon?" Marie's voice coming through the door.

Angela rolled upright, sensitive to the pain of her bullet wound healing in her side. "Yeah," she said, trying to sound more awake than she was. "I'm up."

"Breakfast is on."

Angela dressed with painful, wincing care, and made her way out to the kitchen.

Her home was one of the houses on the base where active duty troops and their families used to live. It was one of the single family homes in the middle of a circular street called Hoyle Plaza. Most of the homes in that neighborhood had been given over to the civilian refugees.

It almost felt normal sometimes.

Almost.

In the kitchen, Marie was tidying up the breakfast mess. Her short crop of curly brown hair wiggled and bobbed as she scrubbed a sticky patch on the counter with an intensity that it seemed only Marie could muster.

At the kitchen counter, perched on a stool, was Abby. Her frizzy blonde hair hung around her face as she poked at breakfast. Which, Angela noticed, was eggs and some homemade bread.

Fresh eggs, by the look of it. A nice change from the powdered eggs they'd been subsisting on for the past year. But Angela realized she felt guilty for having the eggs.

She ate from the same ration boxes that Marie handed out to the rest of the populace, but she remembered acutely how people didn't believe that to be the case. She would've preferred to eat *worse* than everyone else, just to prove a point.

And to get rid of the guilt.

Angela went to the pot on the stove that contained steaming instant coffee. She poured herself a mug and eyeballed her daughter, who had yet to acknowledge her mother's presence. "Good morning, Abby."

"Morning, Mom," Abby sighed back.

Angela exchanged a glance with Marie.

Marie gave a slight roll of her eyes.

Angela sipped her coffee and didn't notice that it was bad because it'd been years since she'd had real coffee and she couldn't remember what good was. In fact, there'd been several times that she'd gone with hot water steeped with burnt bread crusts.

So, compared to that, instant coffee was stellar.

She gestured towards Abby's plate. "Those are fresh eggs, you know."

"I knooow-uh."

Angela's mouth quirked, loading a rebuke. "Well there's no Pop Tarts and Cap'n Crunch. Eat your breakfast." She almost said "Eat your *damn* breakfast" but caught herself at the last second.

Abby proceeded to eat in the least enthusiastic way possible.

Angela watched her over the rim of her mug and wondered how the hell a kid got spoiled in a world like this. Was she doing something wrong? Was she coddling Abby too much? Or was this normal kid behavior?

Marie reached across Angela and pointedly slid an identical plate of eggs and a slice of the bread in front of Angela. "You too."

Marie had insisted on helping out while Angela fully recovered, and hadn't taken no for an answer, though Angela had tried valiantly. In the end, Angela was glad she was there. Recovery was harder than she thought.

Angela started into her breakfast.

Marie sipped her own cup of coffee, relaxing back onto the counter. "How you feeling today?"

"Better," Angela said around a mouthful. "The eggs are good. Thank you. When did we get fresh eggs?"

"They been laying for a bit now."

"Really? I didn't know."

Marie smiled. "That's why you delegate, hon."

"So the egg lottery is working, then?"

"Looks like it. Most families can get a half-dozen at least once a month. I'm told when the warmer weather gets here we might could bump that up. But that's Jeff's domain."

"I'll have to ask him about it." Thinking of Jeff made her think of the meeting she'd had with him right before being shot. Made her think about the dire warning that Jeff had given her.

Which made her think of the fuel situation.

Which made her think of Lee.

Marie's thoughts must have shadowed Angela's, though her concern was less for Lee, and more for her sister, Julia. "Any word?"

Angela shook her head. "As soon as I know, I'll tell you."

Marie found something on the counter to scrape with her fingernail. "What about the Lincolnists?"

Angela's neck stiffened. "What about them?"

Marie gave Angela a sidelong glance. "They're tearing us apart, Angela."

"They're just...people."

Marie twitched, started to say something loudly, then remembered Abby was sitting on the other side of the counter, and spoke just above a whisper. "Look what they tried to do to you! You think that was a one-off? You think they won't try it again?"

"We don't know that it was them."

"Oh, come on, Angela!"

"We can't prove it."

"I feel like you're being intentionally dense."

Angela shot her friend a look. "I'm *trying* to play by the rules, Marie. You don't think I want to send Carl and Mitch after them?"

Marie took a moment to scrape a fingernail along her eyebrows, exasperated. "Angela. I respect what you're trying to do. I respect that you're trying to hold yourself to the law." She leaned in closer to

Angela. "But just because we've reinstated a form of civilization, doesn't mean that we're civilized."

Angela looked at her friend for a long moment after that.

Was she right? Was Angela playing this too soft?

They tried to kill me, for chrissake!

But if Angela didn't follow the rules, then how could she expect everyone else to?

She couldn't be above the law.

That was one of the things everyone hated about the old government.

It was one of the things that they hated about President Briggs.

Abby, oblivious as ever to adult conversation, interrupted loudly. "Where's Sam?"

Angela turned to her daughter. "He had guard duty last night. You know this. How many times do I have to answer this question for you? You'll see him when you get home from school. Which reminds me, you need to get ready, it's almost eight."

What a normal mother-daughter conversation.

Sometimes you could almost forget that you were just a few short months from starvation, and that if you stepped outside the high-voltage wires that surrounded you, there were things in the woods that would rip you to shreds.

Almost.

—

Sam.

A few years ago, he'd had a family.

They'd all died.

He'd been on the run with his father.

He died too.

And right as Sam was about to die, a man snatched him up and carried him out of danger. That man had been Lee Harden. He'd hauled the kid into a hiding place in the woods, shoved him under the roots of a fallen tree, and given him a pistol. Then he'd gone back, to deal with the men that had killed Sam's father.

Sam remembered sitting under those roots, bits of dirt and bark going down the back of his collar, flinching at every gunshot, cringing as men cried out as they were killed.

The kid hiding in the roots had been named Sameer al-Balawi.

That was not him anymore.

He was just Sam now.

They'd done a census in the Fort Bragg Safe Zone. They'd asked Sam for his full name. Sam had told them his name was Sam Ryder, because that was the first damn thing that popped up into his brain, and that's what he'd decided to go with, knowing full well that they couldn't fact-check him on it.

Still, knowing he was clearly of Arabic descent, and that he was from Camp Ryder, the officer taking down the paperwork had frowned at him, as though perceiving the truth through Sam's lie. In the end he'd shrugged. Coming to the same conclusion that Sam had come to.

There was no way to prove him wrong.

So, Sam had become Sam Ryder, and that was that.

He'd been thirteen then, and though he was only just about to turn sixteen, the intervening years may as well have been a lifetime. Fifteen was the new age of consent, as far as the leadership in Fort Bragg went, and at the moment, on that chilly April morning, Sam—AKA Private Ryder—was wearing his second-hand ACU uniform that he still needed to grow into.

He'd already checked his M4 back in with the armorer.

He didn't like to be without a weapon, even though they called it the Safe Zone—or the *Relatively* Safe Zone, if you were feeling cheeky—but now the little .22 rifle that he'd toted back in Camp Ryder seemed a piddly thing compared to the full size rifle he'd grown accustomed to.

Plus, he would have to go back home to Angela's house to retrieve it. And he was headed other places at the moment.

Like any almost-sixteen-year-old, his thoughts were consumed with a girl.

He met her out back of the Ste Mere Eglise Community Center.

Charlie Tucker was fifteen, long, thin, and dark haired. To any adult she would have been a pretty-but-mousy girl that could turn either homely or beautiful, depending on how her later years treated her.

Of course, Sam was not objective, as no young man has ever been objective about a young woman he thinks he is in love with.

His heart stutter-stepped when he saw her. He hoped he looked good in his uniform. And he tried his best to be cool, because feigned apathy is a teenager's best defense.

She smiled when she saw him.

He kept his own reaction to a smirk.

"Hey, Soldier Boy," she teased. "You just get off work?"

"Yeah. You?"

She gestured to the muddy tan overalls she wore. "Well, I don't wear these for fashion."

Sam thought she looked cute in overalls.

"You got classes this morning?" He asked her, falling into step with her as they veered away from the Community Center and towards the cut through to the neighborhoods.

"I got deferment on first," she said. Meaning her early morning work allowed her to skip first period.

"What'd they have you doing today?"

"Tuggin' on cow tits."

He laughed and she grinned at him.

She lifted an eyebrow. "You?"

"Walking the fence line, as usual."

"We still safe?"

"*Relatively* safe."

"Of course."

They took a well-worn path that ran through the middle of a copse of trees. To their left, a neighborhood. To their right, a road.

"How's your mom?"

"She's not my mom. You know that."

"Right. Your *adopted* mom."

Sam eyed Charlie as they walked. He wished Charlie wouldn't have that tone in her voice when she talked about Angela. Like she was talking about the village idiot. But at the same time, Sam didn't care to be associated with Angela.

There was a lot going on there that Sam wasn't able to put his finger on. He just knew that he wished more people liked Angela, but at the same time, he knew that sticking up for her would knock him down a few points. And, at this age, life was very much a scoreboard, and the points could only ever be awarded by your peers, and they were awarded strictly on the basis of opinion.

In the end, Sam chose a very neutrally-toned "She's fine."

Another few steps in silence.

It didn't escape Sam that Charlie's sunny nature had clouded over.

"Did you know him?" Sam asked.

Charlie cast a glance in Sam's direction. She nodded. "Yeah, I knew him."

They reached Longstreet Road. No vehicles coming or going. Why would there be? There was barely any gas to run them. Fuel was for IMPERATIVES ONLY.

They crossed Longstreet Road, headed towards McFayden Pond.

Sam became aware that he was just following Charlie now.

"Where are we going?"

She didn't answer him immediately. And he didn't press her. Kept walking beside her. Felt good just to be with her.

Finally she stopped.

They weren't in any particular place.

Just another path through woods.

Up ahead, because the trees had not completely leafed out yet, Sam could just see the glint of sunlight on water. In another month, that wouldn't be visible from where they were standing now.

He looked at Charlie and found that she was facing him, watching him.

Like she was trying to figure out whether or not to trust him.

"Can you keep a secret, Sam?"

Sam frowned at the question, because it seemed odd. He considered himself a trustworthy individual. He thought of times people had told him things in confidence and he'd kept it to himself. So he nodded. "Yeah. Of course."

She looked away from him. "You say that so easy. Like it doesn't even mean anything."

Sam raised his hands in supplication. Felt indignant that his confidence was being questioned. "What do you want me to say? You asked and I said 'yes.' Is there a special way you want me to say it?"

She looked at him sharply, then started walking again. "Never mind."

Sam immediately felt bad.

Insert foot in mouth.

He stepped quickly after her. "M'sorry, m'sorry, m'sorry," he muttered.

She stopped walking away from him. Looked at him. But with her shoulders up. Arms crossed over her chest. Pure defense.

"I'm sorry," he said, more articulately. "Charlie, you can tell me anything. I promise. You can trust me."

"Even though you're wearing that uniform? Even though..." she cut herself off, rolled her eyes, then shook her head. "You know what? Never mind. I'm sorry. I shouldn't have asked you."

He let her get a few steps away from him this time.

"Charlie."

She turned back to him. About ten feet away.

She expected him to say something.

He supposed he expected himself to say something too.

He had a moment of sardonic clarity. One of the few gifts that came with watching the world burn was that it gave you a sense of perspective, even at a young age. And what he thought, with an inner smirk at himself was, *Well, this didn't go how you thought.*

Of course, what he thought was what every guy his age thinks: that every encounter with the opposite sex at least has a *good chance* of getting physical.

He finally went with, "I care about you. I want you to trust me."

She watched him for a long time, with that same gauging look in her eyes.

Long enough for the back of his neck to feel hot and for his feet to tingle like they needed to get moving.

"Be here tonight," she said, suddenly. "Seven o'clock." Held his eyes for another pointed moment. "And don't tell anyone."

And then she left him in the woods.

FOURTEEN

PAOLO

THEY STOPPED IN THE MIDDLE of some misbegotten farm road in Alabama.

Lee thought he knew what rural looked like.

He was wrong.

This rural was borderline wilderness. Whatever farmsteads there'd been, which seemed few and far between, had long since been abandoned, ransacked, or wiped out by infection.

"Let me get in the bed," Trey said, kicking his door open and exiting the vehicle. Before he closed the door, he looked back in at Abe and said, "Go slow."

Abe nodded.

Trey shut the door and clambered into the bed.

Lee watched him. He couldn't help but be suspicious.

They left the windows down, and the back glass open, so that they could communicate to him in the bed. Deuce took the opportunity to shove his snout out the window and huff deeply.

Trey stood up against the cab of the pickup and withdrew a yellow piece of cloth, which he then held high in the air like a banner and began to wave it back and forth.

"Go ahead," Trey called to Abe, and the pickup truck started rolling forward. "Somewhere in the next mile some guys with guns are going to come out of the woods. They're our friends. Please don't shoot at them."

They rolled forward at about twenty miles an hour for about two minutes before the welcoming party suddenly appeared from the wood line on either side.

Four individuals in homemade ghillie suits, bits of burlap and branches and leaves obscuring their faces. Two on either side of the road. They pointed guns at them.

Lee gripped his rifle a little tighter. Thumb touching the rifle's safety.

One of them stepped closer to the road and held up a hand.

"Stop," Trey called out.

They stopped.

Trey raised his voice. "It's Trey. I got friends with me. Everything's good."

The ghillied one that had held up a hand stepped up to Trey's window and peered in. Deuce let out a rumble, low in his throat, not fond of the stranger's intrusion, but Lee shushed him with a firm hand to his chest.

Closer now, Lee saw that it was a woman. She had a mean, hatchet face and she peered in at them with suspicion, but seemed friendly enough when she glanced to Trey in the truck bed.

"What's this?" she asked.

Trey leaned on the top of the cab, causing the sheet metal to thump and rumple. "These are the folks from Hurtsboro the other night. What's left of them anyway."

"Hrm."

"We need to get to Paolo."

The woman leaned back and gave the pickup truck a glare from stem to stern. "The fuck you gonna do with this?"

"Put 'er in the woods. The usual spot."

"Hrm." Her lips twisted from side to side. "Where's Braxton?"

"He's got our car. He went to a town called Butler, in Georgia."

"The fuck did he do that for?"

"Deliver a message."

"For who?"

"This guy."

The woman squinted a single eye at Lee and his team. She wagged a finger at them. "You three. Let me have some deets. Who are you, where you from, and where you going."

Lee leaned forward into the space between the two front seats. "I'm Lee Harden. This is Abe. This is Julia. We're a team from Fort Bragg, United Eastern States. Heading to the Gulf Coast."

She lifted an eyebrow. "No shit?"

"No shit."

"Hell, I didn't think you guys really existed. That's…" she leaned on her elbow. "Well, I don't exactly know how I feel about that. The Gulf Coast you say?"

"That's what I say."

"Hrm. Well. Yeah. You definitely want to talk to Paolo about that." She pushed off the truck, gave it another unsavory look, then addressed herself to Trey again. "Make sure you cover it good. You know the way."

Trey nodded. "I do indeed."

A slight pause. She nodded to him. "Glad you made it back okay."

The woman gave them a single wave.

Abe started forward again.

The four figures in ghillie melted back into the woods.

"That's Eileen," Trey said, kneeling down to speak through the back glass. "She's a bit much, but…good people."

"Where am I going?" Abe asked, both hands on the wheel.

Trey motioned vaguely ahead of them. "Up here a bit. I'll show you where to turn."

Trey guided them forward perhaps another quarter mile. There was a cut into the woods to the right of the road, and about a hundred yards down this overgrown path, the tall weeds tickling the undercarriage, there was a large area of trash.

Lee was familiar with places like this. In rural areas with no trash service, it often cost money to take things to the dump. Not many folks that lived in regions like this had money, but they often had land, or at least knew of a spot of land, where they could dump random shit.

Defunct washers and dryers. Baby strollers. Pallets of moldering roofing shingles. More than a few large, plastic containers that probably contained used motor oil. Etcetera, etcetera.

Trey directed them between two mounds of old appliances. Lee noted recent tire treads in the dirt. Perhaps this was their customary spot for hiding vehicles.

Abe nosed the truck into a thicket of brush, and that's where they parked it.

Abe left the keys in the truck, in the center console.

Trey took notice of this. "You guys aren't worried about someone stealing your truck?"

Lee, getting painfully out of the back of the truck, irritable at his own weakness, shook his head. "We don't know which one of us is gonna bite it next. If it's me, and the keys are in my pocket, then one of my teammates has to come back to my body, either under gunfire, or while primals are circling, to try to get the keys out of my pocket. Puts the whole team at risk." Lee stood on his feet and took a deep breath to steady himself. "No, the keys stay with the vehicle."

Trey nodded along with the thought process. "Interesting. Never looked at it like that. What the fuck are 'primals'?"

Lee glanced at the man, realizing that he'd used a term that was unique to the UES. "The primals are…the infected. But not the regular ones that died out. The new ones. The…mutated ones."

"Oh," Trey said. "We just call 'em 'Big'uns'."

Lee managed a smile. "Well. That's as good a name as any."

There were pre-cut pine boughs laying around. They used these to camouflage the truck.

"We got about a half-mile hike," Trey said when they were done. "You guys think you can make that? Abe, I know your leg's fucked up. And Lee, you look like shit."

"I can make it," Abe waved him off.

Lee just nodded.

"Alright. Y'all can keep your weapons, but do me a favor and let 'em hang, and keep your hands visible."

Trey led them out.

Lee kept his eyes on the woods. Not just scanning for primals, although that was the immediate concern. He also wanted to see if he could spot any more guards hidden in these woods. Whoever this crew was, they were cautious, and they were prepared, and they seemed well-organized.

Lee didn't know whether that made him feel better or worse.

They're cautious, Lee thought. *But it's a little more than that.*

These people seem like they're at war.

"I meant to ask," Trey said, his voice low. He gestured towards Deuce, who was currently making wide circles around the group as they moved, constantly sniffing the perimeter. "What's with the dog?"

"Team mascot," Abe answered.

Trey glanced at Abe. Then Lee. Then Julia. Then Lee again.

Lee nodded at him.

Trey shrugged and left it alone.

"You doin' alright?" Julia asked him, about five minutes into their hike.

At that point, Lee's breathing was starting to elevate, which made him irritable all over again. A slow stroll through the woods shouldn't have done that to him. It showed him the depleted state that his body was in.

With the elevated breathing, his chest felt like someone was tightening woodscrews into his lungs. And he was sweating, despite the mild temperature.

"I'm hurtin'," he said, honestly. "But I'll make it."

"Hurt-hurt or injury-hurt?"

"Just hurt-hurt," he replied.

She watched him for a few more paces. "Well, let me know if that changes."

"Oh, I'll let you know," Lee said on a heavy exhale.

The trees opened up suddenly in front of them, and Lee caught his first look at their destination.

It was a series of three, long, metal buildings.

Large vent fans that sat still and rusting in their cages on the sides of the structures.

Three years ago, Lee would have smelled this place before he saw it. And it would have been the ammonia-stink of chicken shit.

Trey angled for the central building. Lee surveyed the place with a strategic eye.

Decently defensible. A few exits for emergencies, but easily guarded. And relatively secure against primals. As long as you kept the doors locked and barred.

At the end of the building they were heading towards was a door, and above it, one of the enormous vent fans that kept the chickens inside cool and ventilated under the hot summer sun. Also kept them from choking to death on the fumes of their own excrement.

Twenty yards from the door, a voice called out, "Stop!"

Lee noted the metallic echo of it, and he stared into the shadows between the still blades of the vent fan. Thought maybe he saw the glimmer of a face in there.

"That Trey?" the voice said, the edge coming off. Deep, down-home accent.

Trey held up his right hand. "Yeah. It's me."

There was some muffled banging around.

The door below the vent fan opened up and three guys with guns came out, giving the newcomers a quick look over, and then directing their attention outwards.

"Come on, then," said one of them, and Lee recognized the voice of the speaker from the vent fan.

Most people don't match their voices. This guy did. Sway-backed. A rangy walk. T-shirt. A mesh cap that had once been John Deere green, and was now a smudgy gray.

He held a silver six-shooter, which he dropped into a leather holster, then grinned at them.

Christ. Who's this fuckin' guy?

The man strode forward, and jammed his hand out into the air. "Paolo."

Abe received the hand first and gave it a solid pump. "Abe Darabie." He motioned to the other two. "That's Julia. This is Lee. He's the leader."

Paolo gave Lee a dubious once-over. "Shit, son. You alright? You look a bit green in the gills."

Lee made sure that his handshake was firm. "Right as rain, Paolo."

Paolo shrugged. Turned his attention to Julia. "Well. Ma'am."

He didn't shake her hand so much as caress it.

Her mouth tightened. Eyes staying locked on Paolo's.

Paolo seemed to realize that his attentions were not wanted and he quickly withdrew himself and changed the subject. He smiled at the newcomers. "Now, I'll go ahead and address my name, because I know you all thinking it: Only blue-eyed Mex-ee-can you ever seen."

The intro had the flavor of something told and retold, but Lee also saw beyond the script. He saw someone that had spent a lifetime gleaning humor out of not fitting in. Barring anything else that Lee might learn about this man, he at least gave him credit for that.

"Momma was a southern belle, Daddy was a migrant worker—God rest their souls. Fell in love on a peach farm. Cutest damn story you ever heard. And now I'm Paolo Johnson."

"Well, Mr. Johnson—"

"Paolo, please."

Lee nodded. "Paolo, then. No offense, but let's not fuck around. My people were ambushed in Hurtsboro. You already know that. I'm told you might know who did it. So let's talk."

For the first time Paolo's gaze went down to something less than the flamboyant congeniality they'd dished out so far. There was circumspection there. Calculation.

"Right." He said. "Well. Let's get indoors."

Paolo and his entourage led them into the abandoned chicken farm, closed and bolted the doors behind them.

Lee didn't like the sound of those bars being placed over the door.

Walking away from them, Paolo gestured to their environs, which were dimly lit by skylights. A big open area with a lot of moldering feathers strewn about and the ghost of pine shavings and chicken litter tinging the air. "Our humble home for the last month. No more chickens, unfortunately. But we make do. This way."

He led them down the length of the structure, which must have been a hundred yards long. Went to a room on the side of the building that Lee saw was once used to store equipment for the upkeep of the chickens. The door was open and Paolo went inside. There were shelves, but they were mostly empty. A few cots. A few chairs that looked like they might've been liberated from the trash heap where they'd parked the truck.

Paolo gestured Lee and his team into the room, then gave a nod to Trey who had accompanied them this far. Trey returned the nod and retreated. Paolo closed the door to the room, so it was just him and Lee's people.

A show of trust, perhaps.

Paolo took a seat in one of the chairs, motioned for them to do the same. "Take a load off, gents. And lady." Then with a half-frown at Deuce. "And dog. Who is hopefully yours and not some stray that wandered in."

"He's mine," Lee said, then took a seat.

Lee, Abe, and Julia sat erect, none of them relaxing and leaning back in the chairs.

Paolo kicked one leg over the other and let his gaze scour over his guests. His eyes still held that cautious glint. "Tell me about yourselves and how you came to be in Hurtsboro."

Lee gave him the same rundown he'd given Eileen at the checkpoint. Finished with the ambush at Hurtsboro and the fact that two of their number had been captured, another killed.

Lee said these facts like they had nothing to do with him. Like he was speaking about someone else's friends. It was the only way he could remain even-keel. He had to pretend.

Paolo listened, and stayed focused on Lee the entire time.

Lee leaned forward and put his elbows on his knees, his rifle laid across his lap. "Trey says y'all know these people. He says you might be willing to point us in the right direction."

Paolo's propped up foot wiggled once. Then he was still. "Yeah. I might."

He didn't give anything else.

"Alright," Lee said, one corner of his mouth quirking up in a wry smile. "It's obvious you want something from us. So why don't you tell me what that is."

Paolo shrugged, trying to sell a measure of indifference that Lee wasn't buying. "We want the same thing, I think. Different reasons, but the same thing."

"To get rid of the guys who ambushed us," Lee said. "Who are, apparently, enemies of yours as well."

Paolo's eyes flashed serious for a moment. "We're fighting a war. I think you probably gathered as much on the way in. But we're the guerillas, and they're the big army. We need help. You guys can give us that help. And the end result is something that we both want."

"Okay," Lee said, allowing himself a few beats to gather his thoughts. "We're willing to help. Especially for a common goal. So consider us a tentative 'yes.' But we're going to need more information on what we're dealing with here. Otherwise, we don't know how much help you need."

Paolo pursed his lips, nodded slowly. But he didn't speak.

"You mentioned," Lee probed. "That you'd been here for about a month. Where were you before that?"

Paolo gave him a humorless smirk. "Astute. That's good." He took a big breath, and Lee saw the man thinking about what to say, and also *how much* to say. He smacked his lips, as though testing the flavor of his chosen words. "Well, we were at Bullock County Correctional."

Lee maintained a neutral expression. "So you guys were prisoners?"

Paolo let out a laugh. "No. Well…" he waffled a hand in the air. "Not *all* of us, anyways. But truth be told, there's several in our current crew who were inmates there. Don't worry. They're all good people. It was just a medium security, so, mostly drug shit. Some folks ran afoul of the slightly lighter side of the law, for sure. But no rapists or murderers or shit like that. I assure you."

Lee didn't feel entirely assured. He had a memory of a psychotic man named Milo who had given him a lot of trouble when the world had first gone to shit. That man and his crew had also been petty criminals. And yet they'd become very dangerous.

"Alright." Paolo slapped his boot down on the ground and folded his hands in his lap. "Lemme explain, then. You'll have to pardon my hesitancy to just drop trou and bare all to you folks, but I'm gonna go with my gut feeling here and say that we are indeed on the same team."

Lee gave him a nod of encouragement.

"Most of the original folks, including myself, were residents of Union Springs. Little town a couple miles west of Bullock County Correctional. We did our best to hang onto the town but…well, you know how the story goes." He rolled his hands over each other. "Skipping, skipping, skipping. Bullock was a safe place because it had fences and bars, and it didn't take us long to figure this out. When shit hit the fan a few years ago, there'd been a break out from that facility, but some of the inmates chose to stay behind because they saw the writing on the wall and knew that their prison had become the safest place for them to be. It was them that took us in out of Union Springs when we hightailed it out of there." A sniff. "Now, I'd be lyin' if I told you there wadn't drama when our two groups first came together, but we pushed past it. I was *kind of* in charge of the Union Springs folks, but the Bullock guys didn't really want to listen to me, they had their own guy, Little T. Of course, everyone from Union Springs didn't want to be led by a convict—which I think is understandable—but anyways, once we settled down and differences were put aside, me and Little T kind of ran shit as a partnership."

Lee tilted his head back, discerning. "Until about a month ago."

Paolo nodded. "Yeah. Until about a month ago."

"What happened?"

Paolo looked pained. "You ever hear the phrase *plato o plomo*?"

"That Spanish?"

Paolo nodded. "It means 'silver or lead.' Basically, 'take the bribe, or get shot.' That's what we got offered at Bullock. By some group I'd never heard of before. Never heard of 'em, but let's just say...they were *convincing*. Little T and a good portion of the folks—even a bunch from Union Springs—chose the *plato*. I guess I chose the *plomo*. Though they hadn't been able to *plomo* me yet."

Lee frowned. A cancerous feeling was beginning to metastasize in his stomach.

Abe leaned forward. "So the ambush was cartel? Our guys were captured by cartel?"

Paolo gave a small shrug. "No cartel I ever heard of. Nor had Little T. Nor had any of the other inmates at Bullock. But if it looks like a duck and quacks like a duck..." Another shrug. "They called themselves *Neuvas Fronteras*. It means 'new borders.'"

Lee shook his head, his jaw tight. "The fuck's a cartel want in this world, Paolo? Drugs are a fucking commodity. Everyone's just surviving. And what the hell do they have to gain?"

"Well, based on what they choose to call themselves, it seems they want to gain territory. The United States must seem like a goldmine to them. And now the defenses are down. Have *been* down for a long time. Seems like a land-grab to me."

"It doesn't make sense," Lee said. "There's no currency."

Paolo squinted an eye at Lee, like he thought Lee was missing something. "Currency is whatever gets you power, my friend. It's whatever you can use to manipulate others into doing what you want. I can tell you this: these fucks showed up at our door with military vehicles and a fucking helicopter." Paolo raised his eyebrows. "When's the last time you seen that many gas guzzlers in use?"

Lee felt like the wind had been taken out of him. He felt questions being answered, connections being made, but the picture that it was creating was not one that he liked.

He wasn't sure what he'd been expecting.

Maybe just some group of hell raisers like Milo's crew had been. Or, at worst, some religious fanatics, like The Followers of the Rapture. Both of those groups had been hard enough to deal with.

But this…?

"They're *huachicoleros*," Paolo said, the Spanish word pronounced effortlessly in the midst of his southern drawl. "Fuel thieves. They're not in it for drugs and money. They're in it for oil. And these days, oil means power. And control."

Power. Control.

He who has the gold, makes the rules.

But gold didn't matter anymore.

Oil did.

"Well," Julia cleared her throat. "At least we answered one question."

Lee nodded. His voice sounded hollow. "Yeah. We know who controls the pipelines."

FIFTEEN

CO-ORDIN-ATIN'

THEY'D DRIVEN FOR A long time.

Carl listened to the sound of the engine, and he kept track of time.

Time and speed.

That might give him a distance.

And distance might give him a radius.

An approximate location of wherever they stopped.

So far, he'd been able to mark the hours by the fingers on his hands that he could barely feel anymore. They were at about three and a half hours. Probably averaging about sixty miles an hour.

Still, keeping count of the seconds turning into minutes turning into hours, along with keeping track of the speed he thought they were going, required his complete focus. Focus he might've spent on trying to learn a bit more about his captors.

What he had been able to note, pretty much right off the bat, was that two of their captors were native English speakers, and two of them were native Spanish speakers. Carl didn't speak Spanish fluently. He knew what he called "survival Spanish" from a few counter-cartel operations he'd taken part in as a member of Delta. So he was able to identify the language at least, if not everything they said.

But there wasn't much to learn. His captors kept quiet.

After being taken from the airfield, Carl and Tomlin had been driven to a place that was less than twenty minutes away. They had spent several hours there, crammed into the Suburban, not allowed out. Not allowed to speak to each other.

Outside of the Suburban, while Carl and Tomlin waited for whatever was next, they heard muffled arguments.

Then their captors—or maybe a new set of them—had gotten back in the vehicle, and had been driving them non-stop ever since.

Back to counting seconds.

Minutes.

An upcoming hour.

Three hours and forty minutes.

At three hours and fifty minutes, they slowed, took a gentle turn, and began to coast.

Is this it? Are we at the final destination?

He waited, thinking *three hours and fifty minutes, three hours and fifty minutes*, to make sure this wasn't just a simple stopover. But then the vehicle came to a complete stop, and the engine was killed.

Doors were opened and closed.

A few shouts in Spanish.

Hands grabbed him.

"Out," was the accented command. "Out."

They hauled him out of the seat. Stiff legs and numb feet hit the ground. What felt like gravel under his boots. The air was thick and humid.

Two men on either side of him. They snaked their arms up behind his and forced his upper body down, propelling him forward while they did it so he stumbled to keep up, bent over double.

Three hours and fifty minutes at sixty miles an hour.

Where are you?

They jerked him to a halt. Kicked the back of his knees, sending him to the ground with a grunt. His knees hit the gravel, sharp pain sticking through them.

Focus.

He felt metal on the back of his neck. Knew what it was.

"You feel that?" an American said. "You move, you die."

It came down to a mile a minute, Carl figured. That was a good rough average, and it made for easy math.

230 miles.

That's clear across the state of Alabama, Carl thought. *Either southern Alabama, or we've gone into Louisiana.*

For a moment, he was bewildered by this.

They'd punched through "The Wilds" in three and a half hours. A trip through the backcountry of Alabama that Lee had figured would take them a week.

But Lee and the team would've gone through slow and methodical. Not knowing what lay around the next corner. Reconning towns, and circumventing cities.

These people had no such reservations. Which either meant they were reckless...or it was their turf.

Either way, Carl didn't like it.

You're a long-ass way from home now, Toto. Now, focus on killing these motherfuckers and getting out.

He heard footsteps in front of him. The grind of hard souls through gravel.

The footsteps stopped.

Carl smelled...

Soap.

And cigarette smoke.

"You American?" a voice asked him. The accent was obvious.

"Yes," Carl said, because he didn't think it would do him any good to deny it.

"Take off his blindfold," the voice said. "I want him to look at me."

The muzzle of the rifle that was against his neck pressed harder.

Someone tugged at the blindfold. Pulled it up off his face.

The air felt cold against his eyes after being forced shut so long.

Carl blinked rapidly and found himself in daylight. It was morning.

He was kneeling in the middle of a collection of pipes, conduits, and tanks. Cisterns. Power cables. He realized for the first time there was the thump and rumble of working machinery in the background, though it was faint.

The fuck is this?

He let his eyes take one circuit around his environs before he affixed them to the man standing in front of him.

The man had dark, shaggy hair that hung nearly to his shoulders. He had a soft, kind face, with a bit of stubble on his chin. He smiled down at Carl like they knew each other from way back when, though Carl didn't know the man from Adam.

The man wore gray slacks and a white linen shirt that looked rumpled, like he'd been sitting down for a long time.

Oddest of all, he wore black cowboy boots.

It was not the style of the boots that made them appear odd, but rather the spit-shined polish of the perfectly-maintained black leather, and the chrome nubs on the pointed toes.

"You like my boots?" the man asked.

Carl nodded. "I was just thinking…"

"Yes?"

"Those are the cleanest, most impractical shoes I've seen in a long damn time."

The man laughed. Set one of the boots up on its heel and played the toes back and forth. The sun glinted brightly off the chrome nub. "Perhaps. But they've not always been this clean, you know? Sometimes I get dirt on them. Sometimes blood."

Carl raised his eyes to the man. Grunted.

The man shrugged. "I just clean them. If you take care of nice things, they last a lot longer. You know?"

Carl waited because he felt like there was more to what the man was saying. But he was apparently done talking about his boots. He shoved his hands in his pockets and looked off. Carl took the opportunity to let his gaze roam over the man. Saw the bulge in the front of his waistband. The ghost of a gun visible through the light, linen fabric of his button-down.

"You know what this place is?"

Carl took another good look around him, and the man with the boots didn't seem to care that he did. Carl noted that there were six men with guns around them. Two more than had been in the Suburban with them. He also noted that Tomlin was still inside the vehicle.

"If I had to hazard a guess," Carl said. "I'd say this is a pumping station."

"Very good. You are a man who knows his oil." He flashed a smile and inclined his ear. "Listen! You can hear it. You can hear it moving through the pipes. Like blood in your veins." He pointed in the direction of some pipes. "That's pure power, flowing through those pipes." He looked under his eyebrows at Carl. "And you cannot have it."

Carl gave the surroundings another glance, then went back to the man with the boots. "What is it that you want from me? I'm thinking you probably didn't bother to capture and transport me all the way across the state of Alabama to show me a bunch of shit I can't have. So what's the point?"

The man with the boots gave a look of sheer innocence. "But…that *is* the point." He walked over to stand closer to Carl, his gait displaying lazy insolence. "I want you to answer me something."

"What's that?"

"Are you Captain Lee Harden?"

"I have no idea who that is," Carl replied.

The man with the boots stared down at him for a long time. Then he said, "Interesting," and raised his head to someone else that was behind Carl. "Bring me the other one."

Carl registered the sound of the Suburban's doors opening.

He felt his stomach twist. For the first time, he started to consider how this was going to end.

The sound of shuffling feet.

They kneed Tomlin down on the gravel, about five paces to Carl's left.

The man with the boots walked over to him, hands still in his pockets. He bent at the waist. Tomlin still had the blindfold on. Couldn't see. "Are you Lee Harden?"

"Who the fuck's that?" Tomlin spat, managing to sound genuinely confused.

The man in the boots straightened. "Well. How strange." Then he turned and looked at Carl over his shoulder and the good humor crumbled off his face. That softly-stubbled young-man's chin was now hard and severe. "*Bañar el crudo.*"

Two men jerked Tomlin off the ground and dragged him forward. They stopped at a red pipe that ran off the others and pointed to the ground. They slammed Tomlin down on his belly.

Carl watched. Not sure what was next. Feeling the uncertainty grow inside of him.

He felt off-kilter. Which was a rare feeling for him.

The man with the boots walked back to Carl. "Keep watching."

One of the men dragged up what looked like the body board from an ambulance and they laid it on top of Tomlin, then rolled him over and started to strap him into it.

Carl began to see what was going to happen. "Stop," he said.

The man in the boots shook his head. "No. First, you tell me who you are."

Carl didn't answer. Kept watching.

Tomlin was now fully strapped to the board. Lying face up now. Underneath the pipe.

Someone walked to a wheel valve and cranked it hard three times.

The pipe rattled. Gurgled.

Black-brown liquid gushed out, engulfing Tomlin's face.

He thrashed violently but had no room to move in the straps. His head and chest were instantly and completely smothered in viscous black. He tried to turn his head, tried to get air, but couldn't escape.

He's gonna drown. He's gonna drown in that shit...

"Alright!" Carl shouted.

"Are you Lee Harden?"

"No!"

"And is he Lee Harden?"

"No!"

The man with the boots held up a hand and the flow was cut off.

The pipe silenced its gurgling, a thin stream of it still trickling out.

Tomlin coughed. Gagged. Spluttered. Little eruptions of black droplets spewed from his mouth.

Carl searched for Tomlin's face, but couldn't find anything recognizable under the oil slick that covered him. Like he'd been dipped in tar.

Carl heard someone shift, just before something hit him hard in the side of the head.

Bells rang in his ears. Stars in his eyes.

Carl only just kept himself from hitting the ground. He struggled upright again, blinking to try to clear his vision.

The man with the boots stood there, a large, chrome 1911 pistol in his hand. A chunk of bloody scalp and hair still caught under the butt of the magazine.

Carl's skull ached. His face tingled.

The man with the boots didn't point the pistol at him. Let it hang in his hands. "Who are you then?"

Carl took a moment to breathe through the cloudiness. Grunted. "I'm Carl."

"You're Carl. Hm. And who is he?"

"That's Brian."

"So. Neither of you is Lee Harden?"

Carl was trying to think a step ahead here. The blow to the face wasn't insurmountable. Carl was a man who spent his life using his head to figure things out. And at the moment, he couldn't see a good endpoint if he continued lying. And he couldn't see the harm in telling some small truths at this point.

"Your men shot Lee during the ambush in Hurtsboro," Carl husked. "He's dead for all we know."

The man in the boots stood up. He gestured flippantly with the chrome 1911. "Here's what *I* know, Carl. I know that you and your team are from the so-called United Eastern States. And I know that you came down here, sniffing around for *my oil*." He shook his head. "I'm going to let you live, Carl, because you are going to take a message back to your people." He placed the muzzle of the pistol under Carl's chin and lifted his face to force eye contact. "I am *El Cactus*. We are *Nuevas Fronteras*. And everything you see belongs to us. You will tell your people not to send anybody else. There is nothing down here for you but death. Do you understand the message you are going to deliver?"

Carl's teeth were clenched down, grinding each other. "Yes," he hissed through his teeth. "I understand."

The man in the boots suddenly reached behind Carl's head, grabbed him hard by the scruff of his neck, and twisted him to face Tomlin's body. The muzzle of the 1911 jammed into the side of his face, like the man was trying to spear it through Carl's cheek and into his mouth.

His breath was hot and forceful in Carl's ear. "The only oil you'll ever get from me is whatever you can pump out of your friend's dead body."

The creak of the wheel valve cranking again.

Tomlin's oil-coated face searched blindly through darkness. He managed to get out a single, sad word: "Carl?"

The deluge of crude oil guttered out over him again.

Carl jerked against the grip on his head, but the man didn't relent, only seized down harder.

Tomlin's head and shoulders disappeared under the black waterfall.

His feet kicking, stirring up dust.

"You sonofabitch!" Carl screamed.

The man in the boots took Carl's head in both hands and brought it down hard on his own knee. Carl's mind left him briefly, but he came back to himself a moment later, sprawled back and on his side, still facing Tomlin.

People were kicking Carl. Boots slamming into his chest, his back, his sides, crunching, cracking, breaking, but all he could think about was the man that was ten yards away from him, but for whom he could do nothing.

Carl remained conscious long enough to see Tomlin's body go still.

Then someone kicked him in the face.

—

Carl Gilliard wasn't the only one that watched Brian Tomlin die.

And he wasn't the only one who knew exactly who Brian Tomlin was.

From the backseat of an SUV, Major John Bellamy watched his old friend drown under a spew of oil. He watched with one hand braced against his mouth, as though he didn't want anyone to see the disgusted set of his lips, though there was no one else in the vehicle.

His eyes flicked to the man called El Cactus—Mateo Ibarra Espinoza—and wondered for the tenth time that day why he wasn't there to put a bullet in the man's head.

Then he spared another look at the man who they were currently beating the snot out of, but he was curled on his side, facing away.

That was okay. John had already seen his face.

He looked down at the tablet in his lap and scrolled through a list of names and faces. Likely candidates, based on the intel that they had about who Lee Harden was with, and the fact that they had come from Fort Bragg.

When President Briggs had called upon the military to abandon the coastal regions, and consolidate in the center states, most of Fort Bragg heeded the call. Through reports from the soldiers that had evacuated to Colorado, along with simple process of elimination, they'd been able to compile a list of players that they thought were still alive and active in Fort Bragg.

About halfway down this list he found a face and stared at it.

Master Sergeant Carl Gilliard stared back at him.

A classic, hard-assed military personnel photo. Flag in the background. Master Sergeant Gilliard unsmiling, as though he were, in the moment of the camera's click, considering how best to kill the photographer.

Delta, John noted. Bad Mama Jama.

The door to John's left opened up. He glanced over, saw Espinoza climbing in behind the driver's seat. The man inspected his ridiculous boots. Found something offending. Reached down and scrubbed it with his thumb. Then leaned back in his seat and looked at John.

"Satisfied?" he asked.

John peered past Espinoza without answering. They were hauling Carl Gilliard's limp body up off the ground. Unstrapping Brian Tomlin's from the backboard that had held him in place. "Yeah," was all he decided to say.

Espinoza smiled. "You don't *seem* satisfied."

John went back to his tablet, simply because he didn't want to look at Espinoza.

"Were they friends of yours?"

John gave a brittle smile to the tablet. "Ask me no questions and I'll tell you no lies."

Espinoza shrugged. "The supplies then."

John reached down between his legs to the small pack that sat there. He pulled out a Project Hometown GPS device. Plugged a wire into it. Then plugged the other end into his tablet. Ran through a few security protocols in order to open the necessary program on his tablet.

Reassignment protocol.

Captain Perry Griffin, the Coordinator for Alabama, was currently safe in the Greeley Green Zone. He was no longer in need of his GPS device, as Alabama had essentially just been bartered off to *Nuevas Fronteras* for oil.

Not the choice that John would have made. But it wasn't his choice to make.

He turned the GPS device to Espinoza and indicated a small black square at the base of it. "You're going to put your thumb there and take it off a couple of times so the system gets a positive link to your thumbprint. That's what will allow you access to this GPS and the bunkers. Do you understand?"

"Yes." Espinoza frowned at the little device. "Is that all that's protecting these supply bunkers? Just a fingerprint?"

"There are other security measures. But we've deactivated them. For our purposes, it's simply easiest to allow you access with a fingerprint. Is that a problem?" John smirked. "Or would you rather an autocannon chew you to shreds if you forget a mnemonic?"

Espinoza smiled broadly. "No, I think a fingerprint will do just fine."

John nodded. "Then go ahead and put your thumb there."

Espinoza placed his thumb.

John walked him through placing it on and taking it off, while the system calibrated the device to its new owner. When it was fully calibrated, he handed it to Espinoza. "It won't fully activate until I'm in Greeley and can confirm that we have the first fuel shipment in hand." He gave Espinoza a stern look. "Aviation and diesel fuel. That's what we need. As soon as we have it, I will issue a remote command. Then you'll have access to the bunkers."

Espinoza pocketed the device. "Well. Let's get you back to your plane, then."

SIXTEEN

MPG

MITCH SAT IN CARL'S OFFICE staring at the corkboard.

On that board was a pattern of pictures and jumbled notes scrawled in a combination of hands from all the members of his team. The collage was familiar to him from his days working counter-terrorism in Delta. He usually wasn't the one to create such boards back then, but he'd seen his fair share in briefing rooms.

This one hit closer to home.

The faces in the pictures were his neighbors.

It was very hard to come by a solid connection amongst the Lincolnists. They knew that Elsie Foster was at the center of it, and she had her associates, but so far nothing had been proven, and Angela didn't want to make a move until things could be proven.

Her would-be assassin had only complicated the network on his whiteboard.

More associates.

More questions.

Zero answers.

He rubbed his beard with a tired sigh and thought for the umpteenth time how quick this could be resolved if Angela would just let them off the leash. Or if he simply decided to break free of that leash on his own…

A knock at the office door broke him out of this tempting train of thought.

He swiveled his seat back around to the desk. "Yeah. Come on."

The door opened and Rudy poked his hounddog face in. His normally placid eyes were crinkled up with concern. He was holding one of their satphones. "Mitch. We got a call from Butler, down in Georgia." He crossed the room and held out the phone to Mitch. "I think it's a message from Lee."

Mitch stood up from his desk, all thoughts of Lincolnists and diagrams and enhanced interrogation dissolving. This wasn't a scheduled contact. Which meant that something was either really great…or something was really bad.

And things were rarely great.

He grabbed the satphone and put it to his ear. "This is Mitch."

A man's voice. Older. Gravelly. Thick, southern accent. "Yeah, hi, this is Ed from Butler."

Mitch nodded in recognition. He'd only met the old man twice, but he made an impression. "Yes. Ed.

This is Sergeant Mitch at Fort Bragg. We met a few times."

"Yeah," Ed said, distracted. "Hey, look, I got this fella, showed up out of the blue, never seen him before, claims to know Lee."

"Does he check out?"

"Well, he had the passcodes and all. So, I guess 'yes.'" Hesitation. "He says he's got a message from Lee."

Which meant that Lee wasn't there himself.

Mitch's gut soured.

Why send a messenger?

"Is he there with you now?"

"Yes, he's—" the line broke apart in a wash of static.

Mitch winced at it, squinted to try to hear through it. *Goddamned satellites.* Their orbits had been decaying for some time now, making satellite communications iffy. "I'm sorry, Ed, you broke up. Did you say that the guy is there with you?"

Ed again, sounding flustered by the ratty connection. "Yeah. I have him here. You wanna speak to him?"

"Yes. Put him on."

A pause.

The line rattled and hissed in his ear.

A new voice: "Uh. Yes? Hello?"

Mitch frowned at his desk. Glanced up at Rudy, who was still standing there, watching Mitch carefully like he might glean the highlights of the conversation from the expressions of Mitch's face. "Who is this?"

"My name's Braxton. I have a message from Lee Harden?"

As though Mitch was supposed to know who the fuck *Braxton* was. He looked at Rudy again, motioned for him to close the office door. Rudy took a step back and gently swung it shut.

"Yeah, Braxton," Mitch said. "This is Fort Bragg. Go ahead with that message."

"Uh, yes, sir. You got a pen and paper?" Bashful. "He told me to tell you to write it down."

Shit.

No one ever made you write down good news.

Mitch scrambled about his desk for a pen and a scrap of paper. He found the paper. Made writing motions with his fingers. Rudy located a pen and shoved it at him. "Alright, Braxton. Go ahead with the message."

The stranger named Braxton spoke.

Mitch wrote it down, feeling worse with every word.

—

Angela was preparing to leave her own offices when Mitch entered, escorted by a stern-faced Kurt Barsch, and Claire Staley trailing behind.

Claire gave Mitch the evil eye as she edged quickly around him into the room. "Tried to call ahead," she said in a clipped tone. "But someone didn't want to wait."

Kurt also didn't seem terribly happy with Mitch, but then again, he'd been edgy since the assassination attempt.

Mitch didn't seem to care much about Claire or Kurt's disapproval. He strode right up to the desk behind which Angela was standing. "Sorry to barge in, ma'am. We just got a call from Butler. It's serious. And I need to speak to you in private."

Angela glanced in Kurt's direction.

She and Kurt both knew and trusted Mitch. But still, her guard looked hesitant to leave the room. She gave him a nod. "Thank you, Kurt. Claire. Give us the room, please."

Kurt and Claire silently exited.

Kurt closed the door behind him.

Mitch waited until he heard it latch, then produced a scrap of white paper, which he placed in front of Angela. "The message is from Lee, but it wasn't him I spoke to. He sent a guy named Braxton. Some guy he just met in Alabama. That's all we got right now."

Angela held to Mitch's eyes for a second, trying to divine from him how bad it was. Trying to temper herself for what she was about to read.

People are dead. That's what it's going to say. We lost more people.

Finally, she grabbed the note from her desk and read it carefully.

AMBUSHED IN HURTSBORO, AL.

LOST NATE. CARL AND BRIAN CAPTURED.

UNKNOWN AGGRESSORS.

LEE, JULIA, ABE PURSUING.

DISPATCH SMALL ELEMENT TO BUTLER. WAIT FOR COMMS FROM LEE. WILL COMM

IN FIVE DAYS OR LESS. NO COMMS = ASSUME DEAD.

Angela placed the note back down on the desk so carefully, you would think it was made of volatile explosives. The words ran laps in her head, and she was distantly surprised to see how still her hands were.

Assume dead.

"The guy said he received the message last night," Mitch said.

Angela felt her head buzzing. "How soon can we be in Butler?"

"We can be there by tomorrow morning."

Her teeth were set on edge. Lips tight. "You and your team."

Mitch nodded. "Rudy's prepping everyone now."

Angela pressed her fingertips down on the table, bending them until the knuckles were white and painful. "You take what you need. You do what you need to do. And you keep me in the loop. You understand? I want to know everything that's happening. And I wanna know who the fuck hit our people, and how we can hit them back."

Mitch had nothing else to say, and neither did Angela. She'd given him the green light, and that was all he'd come for. He gave her one curt nod, left the note on her desk, and then left her office with an urgent clip to his step.

Claire and Kurt, who had been waiting just outside the door, slipped in and closed the door behind them.

"Is everything okay?" Claire asked.

"I need Jeff in here." Angela met Claire's eyes. "And your father. ASAP."

—

Thirty minutes later, they met in Angela's office.

Colonel Staley, Claire's father, was the commander of the Marine forces that had been relocated from Camp Lejeune to Fort Bragg. A consolidation of forces, you might say. It hadn't been a completely seamless transition, but in the end, Fort Bragg had electricity from the local nuclear plant, and Camp Lejeune was dead, so most everyone appreciated the reasoning behind it.

Angela didn't rehash anything she didn't need to. She let the message from Lee speak for itself, passing it first to Staley, and then to Jeff.

They both read it in silence, and Jeff handed it back, obviously confused as to why he was present for this, since he was the Director of Agriculture and had nothing to do with military operations.

"Our conversation doesn't leave this room," Angela opened, looking at each of them in turn.

They nodded their assent.

"Mitch and his boys are putting together a small team. They're heading to Butler tonight. But Lee might need a bigger force than that, and if he requests it, I want the logistics already in motion." She sat down at her desk. Felt nervous energy making her want to stand again, but she held herself down. "What I need to know is, given the fuel situation, if we suspended all farming operations, how much diesel would we have available, and how many Marines can we send to Butler with what we have?"

Jeff's eyes widened. "I, uh…well…" he looked at Staley as though hoping for rescue.

Staley had remained calm the entire time. As though such things were a matter of course. He wore his desert digital BDUs with the silver eagles on his collar. His hands placed carefully in his lap. He essentially ignored Jeff, and spoke directly to Angela.

"Ma'am, I can commit whatever you feel is necessary." There was a caveat in his voice, and it followed quickly. "What you need to understand is that, while I can probably fuel up several trucks full of Marines and send them south, that's probably not going to be the answer that we want."

Angela's middle finger smarted. She looked at it. Realized that she'd been ruthlessly chewing at the nail. It had torn down to the quick and a bit of blood was welling up. She flicked the pain out of her finger, then interlaced them and placed them against her lips. From behind them, she said, "What do you mean?"

Staley leaned forward. "What I mean is that a combat effective detachment is more than just Marines with rifles. It's support, too. They need equipment, food, water. The more people you send, the more support has to go with them. And that support requires a lot of fuel. There's a point of diminishing returns." He held up his hand. "Ma'am, my Marines are the finest fighting force on this planet, there's no doubt in my mind about that. If push comes to shove, and you give me the orders, I'll send my boys down with what they got on their backs, and I know that they'll make a good showing. But what you need to understand before you issue that type of order is that it heavily reduces their effectiveness and puts them at a serious disadvantage."

Angela had one of those moments where her mind seemed to depart from her body and take up residence somewhere around the ceiling, looking down at her and wondering, *how the fuck did you get here? What are you doing, sitting behind this desk, playing with people's lives?*

She'd read once that mentally disassociating yourself from reality was unhealthy.

But it was about the only thing she could do in that moment to stay calm and collected.

So she disassociated.

This wasn't real. These weren't people's lives she was discussing. This was all just a game.

She took a long, bracing inhale. "Colonel, how many Marines can you send, with full support?"

Finally, Staley turned and seemed to acknowledge the presence of Jeff, the Agricultural Director. "That depends on how much fuel we have left."

Jeff looked like a kid that hasn't done their homework and then gets called on by the teacher. His shoulders scrunched up. He leaned forward, elbows on the arms of his chair. A slight panic in his eyes. "Uh. Well. Last I checked was last week. When we talked about the situation. And that was when we got to the halfway point on our last seven thousand gallon tank. Since then, we've continued our farming operations. If I was to take a guess, I'd say we were down in the neighborhood of two thousand gallons right now."

"Two thousand gallons then," Angela said, turning back to Staley. "What does that buy us?"

For the first time, Colonel Staley's face betrayed uncertainty. "Well, ma'am. I'll have to run the numbers on that. But…off the top of my head…not much."

"Not much," Angela echoed.

"Unfortunately, fuel efficiency was not high on the list of Uncle Sam's requirements when he commissioned fighting vehicles for the Marine Corps."

Angela knew he was right. Half the damn vehicles they had topped out at five miles to the gallon. It was the reason that most of them were parked, and Lee and his team had been running their operations out of civilian pickup trucks.

Pickup trucks that got a whole whopping *fifteen* miles a gallon.

Unfortunately for their fuel conservancy efforts, hybrid sedans weren't great for off-road capabilities, and with the derelict state of the roads, off-road capabilities were necessary. No one wanted to get bogged down in a washed-out road while primals were hot on their tail.

Angela bit down on her sense of surrealism and laid her hands flat on the top of the desk. *Take control. That's what you were elected to do. So do it.* "Here's what we're going to do, gentlemen. Jeff, you're going to immediately suspend all farming operations. I don't want a single tractor running by the end of the day, you understand?"

Jeff nodded, eager to be of some use, but his face clouded. He was a farmer at heart and she saw that her order to *stop* farming made him uneasy.

Angela looked at Staley. "Colonel, I need you to coordinate with Jeff to take control of whatever fuel we have left, if the need arises. And I want you to run the numbers for two possibilities. Number one, how many Marines can you send with full support. And number two, how many Marines can you send with just their rifles and whatever supplies they can carry."

Angela pushed herself up from her chair. "And in the meantime we'll hope that Lee can make it back to Butler and tell us what the hell is happening down there."

—

When Claire looked up from her desk outside of Angela's office, she saw that Doctor Trent was standing there in front of it.

She jumped at the sight. She hadn't heard anyone approach.

Claire put her hand to her chest. "I'm sorry. You surprised me."

Doctor Trent stood there, hands limp at his sides, looking down at her like she hadn't even spoken. Behind his glasses, his eyes were somewhere else.

Then they blinked a few times, came back to the real world, and he straightened. Seemed to realize that he'd just been spoken to.

"Right. Sorry about that. I need to speak with Miss Houston, please."

"I'm sorry," Claire said. "She's in a meeting."

Doctor Trent gave her an inscrutable look. "It's…important."

"Well. You can wait if you'd like."

Doctor Trent stared at her for a few beats longer, then simply chuffed through his nose. "No. I'll come back. Just…tell her that I was trying to meet with her." He turned as though to walk away, then stopped and turned back. "You can tell her it's about the thing that Lee brought me. That might get her interested."

"Ooh-kay," Claire said, then picked up a pen and wrote a big bold note so that Doctor Trent could see. Claire dictated to herself as she wrote it out: "Doc…Trent…About…the thing…from Lee."

Doctor Trent nodded.

He turned and walked away, leaving Claire wondering what the hell Lee had brought him, and why the hell it would matter to Angela.

SEVENTEEN

TIDES

JULIA PULLED BACK THE BANDAGE that covered Lee's chest tube.

Lee refused to watch. He stared at the wall and grit his teeth. The fact that there was a foreign object protruding from his chest still made his stomach flutter.

Paolo had been kind enough to give them the privacy of the room.

Lee and Julia were seated on one of the cots in the room. Abe sat in a chair across from Lee, alternately watching Julia work, and watching Lee's face for a reaction.

"Does it hurt?" Julia asked.

She was prodding around the tube. Lee felt it moving inside him, and while it didn't exactly *hurt*, it was uncomfortable and he despised the sensation.

"It's fine," he mumbled. "Do what you need to do."

"I'm gonna remove it," Julia said. "Then I gotta tie off the sutures on the wound."

Lee tapped his foot. Nodded disconsolately.

"You trust this guy?" Abe asked, perhaps just to get Lee's mind off of the tube removal.

Lee raised an eyebrow at Abe. Realized he was talking about Paolo. "Absolutely not. I trust you. And I trust Julia. There's not many other people I trust. But..." he considered his words for a moment. "Beggars can't be choosers. And right now we're begging for allies. Not friends, mind you. But allies. And I think Paolo is an ally. I believe his story."

"Take a deep breath and hold it," Julia instructed.

Lee inhaled. Felt a dim pain as he held the air in his lungs.

He felt a pull inside of him. "Don't tense up," Julia said, and then it was out.

Lee coughed, stifled it because it hurt. "Fuck. That's unpleasant."

Julia set the chest tube off to the side. "It's out now." She had a finger pressed tightly to the hole of his wound. "I'm gonna pull the sutures closed. It'll hurt."

Lee clenched his teeth and waited.

He felt her hands moving. The pinch of the purse-string sutures being pulled, the two flaps of skin coming together tightly. Then the flicking of Julia's fingers as they expertly tied off the knot, closing his wound.

"Alright," she said, leaning back and inspecting her work. "Gonna bandage it again. Then you're done."

"So, is my lung healed?"

"No."

"It still has a hole in it?"

"It'll close," she said. "Unless you over-stress it."

"Which I probably will."

She leaned over to make eye contact with him. "Well. Maybe you shouldn't."

"Don't have a whole lot of choice here, Jules."

"Hold still." She swabbed the area clean. Applied an occlusive dressing to the site.

Abe leaned back. Stretched. The bags under his eyes had become luggage. "So what's the plan?"

"The plan," Julia answered over Lee. "Is for Lee to sleep so he can think clearly."

"I slept last night."

"You just woke up from a three day coma, and you're still injured."

Lee had to admit, he felt exhausted.

He looked at Abe and nodded. "We need to coordinate with Paolo and his people. See what our options are before we come up with a plan."

Abe frowned deeply. Puzzling something out.

"What?" Lee prompted.

Abe looked at him. "So these cartel fucks. Apparently they have at least *some* control of the oil, although how much remains to be seen. Okay. That's all well and good, and maybe that's true, or maybe Paolo just wants us to ice these guys because he's got a bone to pick with them." Abe's jaw worked for a second. "What still doesn't make sense to me is why they hit us the way they did."

"Like they knew we were coming," Lee said, picking up on Abe's train of thought now.

"Yes. And why the hell they took prisoners."

Lee shook his head. "You're right. That doesn't make sense."

"None of it makes sense."

Julia settled back and gave the two of them a look. "Maybe it would make more sense once you've had some sleep."

Lee glanced at her. "What? You got a better idea?"

"Not right now," she answered, then got up and moved to where she'd set up her gear. "Abe, you need to rest up too. I'll stay awake."

Abe rubbed his face, seemed to melt into his chair. His eyes looked red when he pulled his hands away. They looked far-off. After a moment, he smiled. Chuckled to himself.

"What?" Lee asked.

Abe shook his head. "Just thinkin' about my life."

"Well, don't do that."

Abe looked at him. "Yeah. This is it, right? This is life. Sleepin' in fuckin' chicken coops. Working with crazy people so we can make it another day."

Lee smiled a rickety smile. "*Subvenir-atin'* and *Refectus-in'*."

"Co-ordin-atin'," Abe sighed.

"Co-ordin-atin'," Lee agreed.

—

What was nice about the room was that it had no windows, so when they extinguished their little lamp, it was dark, except for the line of daylight under the door.

What was bad about the room was that Lee's brain ran amok in the darkness.

In the darkness anything was possible. And his mind pursued every if, but, and shoulda-woulda-coulda. Lee's worries and fears were an animal trapped in a cage, running around and around and around, and all Lee could do was visualize closing the door on that sad animal and hoping it would tire itself out in the dark.

Exhaustion didn't exactly win out. But it took the parts of Lee that it could corner and carried them off to a twitchy, anxious sleep.

He was in the field again. The bright, green, rolling hills.

Beautiful sunshine.

Angela there with him.

Even as he stood there, he was aware that he was dreaming, and he thought, *More of this? Why can't I just sleep in blackness for once in my goddamned life?*

Green grass. Rolling hills.

The dream version of Angela indistinct. A mere impressionist painting of the woman who had taken up residence in his brain. She didn't speak this time around. She had nothing to say. She seemed to be basking in the warm sunshine.

In the distance, Lee saw the tree again. The only feature of the landscape. Distant. On the top of the hill.

The leaves shimmered in the sunlight as a light breeze stirred them, though he himself could not feel the breeze. For that matter, he could not feel the sunshine. He could not feel anything.

After a moment, he saw something else.

Underneath the branches of that tree.

A figure, in the shadows.

Small.

He squinted, tried to make it out, but couldn't.

He started to walk towards it.

He fell through the ground.

Plunged into darkness.

The pit. The cavern.

Blackness.

He scrambled for something. His hands flying about.

There was a horrendous banging noise.

A door opened in the darkness and light came rushing through, silhouetting three figures...

Lee's hand found what it was looking for. It found the warm metal of the rifle that lay with him. He swung it up. He heard shouting, peripherally, but it didn't make any sense to him. It sounded like animals howling.

Infected. Infected. They got inside...

He put the rifle to his shoulder and hit the light.

The beam from his weaponlight smashed the darkness.

One of the figures was walking towards him. Stoop-shouldered, hitching gait. The beam of light hit the thing's face and lit it up, pale and almost white in the glow of the halogen beam. It was swollen and cut-up and demented.

"Lee," it said in a broken, croaking voice.

Kill it! Kill it before it eats you!

"Lee, I'm sorry."

Lee's finger descended to the trigger as his heart tried to smash through his sternum.

More shouting.

Something hit him hard, pushing his rifle out of the way.

"Lee! Look at me!"

Reality swirled. Half in and half out of a nightmare.

A slap across his face. Hard. Stinging.

Fingers grabbing him, pulling his face to look in another direction.

Found Julia staring at him.

"Lee! Wake up!"

Lee blinked panic-widened eyes, sickly and disconnected, hallucinating. "Infected," he mumbled, and it was only when he heard the rasp of his own voice that his mind found a connection to reality and swung back into place, like the pins and cylinders of a lock lining up.

"There's no infected," Julia said, her voice sinking into a forced calm. "It's just us. No infected. There's no danger. Chill the fuck out."

Lee's eyes shot over to the figure in the room.

Not infected.

The face was malformed because it was swollen and bruised.

"Carl?" Lee came lurching upright on feet that felt like sacks of needles.

The two figures that were supporting Carl were Paolo and—surprisingly—Braxton, as though he'd shown up out of thin air. Both of them were staring at Lee with concern.

Carl Gilliard had one good eye. The other was swollen shut. He had to angle his face to make eye contact with Lee. His swollen, split lips moved. "Sorry, Lee."

Lee thought he was apologizing for scaring him. "Not your fault." He came up off the cot where he'd been sleeping. "Sit him down. Shit. What the fuck happened to you?"

Paolo and Braxton navigated Carl to the cot and eased him into a wincing sitting position. Carl was holding one arm across his belly.

"I'm sorry," Carl said again.

"It's fine, it's fine," Lee insisted. "It was just a nightmare. You know…"

Carl shook his head with obvious pain, then reached out and grabbed Lee by the wrist. "I'm not talking about that." The battered operator looked up at him with his one good eye. "They killed Brian, Lee. They fucking killed him and I'm sorry."

—

Lee stood on the side of the pickup. Elbows up on the bed. Looking down into it.

Abe stood next to Lee.

Paolo was at the rear of the bed, near the tailgate.

Their truck was now parked outside of the chicken house. Lee supposed he'd slept for several hours, because the sun was down below the trees, slanting through them in hazy yellow bands.

"Sorry for taking liberties with your truck," Paolo mumbled.

When no acceptance or rejection of his apology came forth, he cleared his throat and kept going. "Braxton spotted them on the side of the road when he was coming back, but he was too scared to stop by himself. Thought it might be a trap. He got back while y'all were sleepin', so we took your truck to go investigate. Figured…" Paolo puffed through his lips. "Figured we might need the pickup bed." A long pause. "Your man Carl was lyin' in the middle of the road. Bound up like a trussed hog. And…" A nod towards the bed. "He was lyin' there too."

"Brian Tomlin," Lee murmured.

"What's that?"

"That's his name." A pause. "*Was* his name."

Except it didn't look like Brian Tomlin. To anybody that didn't know the man's face by heart, he would've just looked like a black blob.

Lee smelled the sulfurous, petroleum stink of crude oil.

Paolo nodded once. "So this was your guy."

Lee didn't answer. The answer was self-evident, and he didn't feel much like talking.

What am I supposed to feel right now?

Was it rage? Was it grief?

That's what he thought he *should* be feeling. But the truth was that he felt hollow. He felt as empty as the cave from his dream, and just as dark.

Are you done?
Are you dead inside?

He wanted to feel something. Anything. And knew that Tomlin's death would eventually settle on him. But every death came differently. Some came like hurricane winds and blew you down. Others crept in slow like a soaking fog.

It was just that, right now, it was too big.

He couldn't metabolize it. He couldn't absorb it.

Perhaps worse than any tangible emotion, what Lee felt like doing in that moment was hiding. The urge of it was compelling, and comforting, and childlike in the way that he was completely overwhelmed.

He wanted to crawl into the backseat of the truck and lay down on the floorboards. He wanted to lay there and be left alone.

The place in his brain where Tomlin lived was suddenly cut off. Closed down. Like a boarded up business. That part of his brain that catalogued the life and actions of those he held dear would never be added to again.

They were now just memories of yet another person that was gone.

And it took the energy out of him.

It sapped his strength like a chronic sickness.

"Do you want help burying him?" Paolo asked.

Lee blinked a few times, found that he'd been staring at the black image of Tomlin's body so long that it left a ghostly afterimage behind. "Not gonna bury him out here." Lee shoved himself off the bed of the truck, feeling like lead weights had been attached to his limbs. "Not gonna bury him where the goddamn primals can dig him up. We'll take him back to Butler where his body can be left alone."

Like you want to be left alone.

Is that what you want, Lee? You want to crawl into your grave?

...the woods are lovely, dark and deep...

...but I have promises to keep...

But Lee didn't much feel like keeping promises.

He turned around and faced the chicken house.

"Uh," Abe started.

Lee looked over his shoulder at him.

Abe's eyes were red-rimmed, but dry. His face held his emotions back like an unstable levee. "It'll be dark soon enough. If we leave him out here..."

"We're not gonna leave him out here." Lee's voice lacked inflection. "I'm going to go in there and I'm going to get Julia and Carl, and then we're going to leave for Butler."

Lee walked back into the chicken house, and Abe walked with him. And for every bit of rage that Lee thought he should be feeling, it radiated off of Abe like a blast furnace with the doors open. And it was contagious.

By the time they made it back to the maintenance room, Lee felt something kindling in his chest, and he sheltered it jealously, glad to be feeling something, even if that something was destructive.

It was an endless circle, he knew.

But what else was he supposed to do?

The tides pulled him. Like it was all a current, and he couldn't fight against it. His destiny would always carry him to a place of wrath and tears.

In the room, Carl was leaning back on the cot, his mouth open because his broken nose was too swollen to breathe through, his arm cradled across his midsection.

Julia was hunched over him, probing for broken bones. Lee could immediately tell, just by seeing her face in quarter-profile, that she was crying. He saw it in her jaw, and in her cheeks, and in her shoulders.

Lee knelt beside Carl, conscious of his own injuries, even as he felt sympathy for Carl's. He put his hand on Carl's leg—gently, because he didn't know if it was bruised or broken. Lee had something to say, and Carl's one eye watched him carefully while he struggled to grasp what exactly it was.

He finally blurted, "Don't you dare fucking apologize."

Carl's eye blinked, and his lips twitched. He didn't shed a tear though. Lee had never seen Carl shed a tear. But Lee could see that it was only barely held in check.

"Not your burden to shoulder," Lee said.

"Whose is it then?" Carl asked.

"Can you tell me who did it?"

Carl's nostrils flared. He nodded.

"Then that's whose burden it is," Lee said. "And they're gonna shoulder every bit of it." He stood up with a wince. "Can you walk?"

Julia took that opportunity to speak. "He's got broken ribs, I think. But I can't be sure without an X-ray. No *obvious* signs of internal bleeding, but that doesn't mean it's not happening."

Carl leaned forward with what looked like a good deal of effort. "I can walk."

"You only gotta walk to the truck," Lee said. "Get your shit. We're heading back to Butler."

—

Paolo had stayed with the truck.

He wasn't a huge fan of having the thing parked in front of his hideout, but with the two guys with guns all torn up about the death of their friend, Paolo had figured it wasn't the time to bring it up.

Paolo figured that someone should stay with the body. So he turned around and leaned back against the tailgate, not wanting to look at the poor dead fuck inside the bed.

He began to think about things. Began to think about Bullock County Correctional, how nice and safe it had been, and how it sucked to be shacked in a chicken house. Also thought about Little T, that backstabbing, sellout sonofabitch, and whether or not he had been involved in whatever had happened to these people.

He eyed the hideout, and wondered how much longer he was going to hole up in this fucking place? Aside from being relatively secure, it didn't have much else going for it. It was a place of stagnation, and stagnation was anathema to Paolo, who had lived his life always moving forward to the next thing.

He was like a shark. He had to keep moving, or he would die.

Maybe it was time to do something. Maybe it was time to take some risks.

Breaking inertia was always risky. That's what made stagnation so easy.

Because stagnation was usually safer. At least short-term.

A whistle reached his ears, coming from the woods.

Two notes. Up-down. Almost like a bird call.

He twitched. Came upright off the bed of the pickup.

Two notes.

And then an echo, deeper into the woods.

And then another echo.

Not echoes, he knew.

It was a danger signal, passing from one of his spotters to the next.

"Shit," he murmured to himself, just as the first of his spotters burst through the woods at a dead sprint.

"Big'uns!" the spotter shouted as he ran.

Paolo shoved himself off the truck and ran to the door to his safe house, repeating the call: "Big'uns comin'! Infected! Infected!"

EIGHTEEN

―

PRIMALS

LEE AND HIS TEAM were halfway out the door of the equipment room when the alarm was raised.

"Infected! They're comin'!"

"Motherfuck," Lee spat, and slung into his rifle. His armor pressed against his new stitches and they smarted. He started moving forward quicker, but Abe caught his arm and turned him back.

"What're you doing?" Abe had the other hand on Carl's elbow, offering nominal support because Carl insisted he could walk by himself.

Julia exited the door, swinging her big medical bag onto her back. "I think they're tryna batten down the hatches, Lee."

Lee jabbed a finger towards the main door, through which heavily breathing figures in makeshift ghillie were already stumbling through. "Yeah, and we got a window to get the fuck out. We're gonna use it,"

"You have no idea how close they are," Abe argued.

"At the very least, I'm not leaving Tomlin's body out there for them."

Paolo and two of his spotters met them halfway down the long chicken house. "You hear me? Big'uns comin'. You don't wanna be outside."

"How close were they?"

One of the spotters spoke up. "'Bout a half mile back. Moving fast. No calls. They got our scent."

"It was the fuckin' truck," Paolo mumbled to himself. "Knew I shouldn't have driven that shit up here."

Lee was moving, and he realized in that instant that there wasn't shit that anybody could say to turn him back. "We're taking the truck and heading to Butler. Maybe we'll draw them off."

"Lee…" Julia had a warning tone in her voice.

Lee ignored it. The decision was made.

He glanced at Paolo. "I want you to come with us."

"What?" Paolo's face screwed up. "I can't fuckin' leave…"

"Your people know how to take care of themselves, Paolo. Isn't that right?"

Paolo didn't answer.

"I know it's short notice, but we're going to meet some people that can help us. And I need someone who knows the lay of the land down here. That's you." They reached the door, which had yet to be closed and barred. Lee put his shoulder to the doorframe and peered out. There was one spotter still coming in, straggling.

Eileen.

"Pack of 'em!" she called between gasping breaths. "They're close! Get inside!"

It was now or never.

Lee turned and seized Paolo by the shoulder. Looked the man in the eyes. "Paolo, if you want our help, if you want the help of the UES, then you need to come with me. This is bigger than you realize."

"You're tellin' me!" Paolo snapped back. "You have any idea what you're up against?"

"Yeah. I got a dead friend and a cartel that killed him. I know what I'm up against. Do they?"

Paolo touched his forehead, his eyes wide and sick-looking. "Shit. Fuck."

Eileen burst through the door. Two big bellows of air. She put her hands on her knees. "About two hundred yards back!" Gasp. "Close the fuckin' doors!"

Deuce had slipped outside the door while they were talking, and he halted about two yards outside. He started to growl, and it immediately built up to a bark. He was staring out into the woods, like he was seeing something the rest of them couldn't.

Lee couldn't wait any longer. He simply nodded to Paolo, said "Let's go," and then exited the hideout.

Lee's team followed without hesitation—if one was going, they were all going.

The second they hit daylight, their rifles came up.

Carl—unarmed—simply made a beeline for the truck.

Paolo's feet danced in indecision. "Wait!" he shouted at Lee's back, but Lee wasn't into talking anymore, and it was the fact that Lee had said "Let's go," like everything had already been decided, that Paolo finally caved.

"Shitfuckdammit!" He spun on Eileen, who was now standing up straight. "Eileen, I'm goin' with 'em."

"WHAT?" Eileen barked like she'd been bit.

"You're in charge while I'm gone." Paolo ripped the silver six-shooter out of his holster. "Now bar the goddamn doors and keep everyone alive."

At the truck, Lee hit the bed and vaulted up, swinging his leg up into it. He'd fixated on the concept that whatever was coming through those woods was going to try to feed on the body of his dead friend, and Lee was fully prepared to die to keep that from happening.

Maybe that didn't make sense to someone on the outside.

But to Lee, in that moment, it made all the sense in the world.

Carl hauled himself into the backseat, Deuce squeezing in between his legs. Abe went to the driver's seat, and Julia crossed to the front passenger's side.

Lee planted his feet over Tomlin's body, and hunched over the roof of the cab, bringing his optic up to his eyes.

Are you really doing this?

He scanned the woods around them.

Yeah, I'm fucking doing this.

He heard Paolo's voice behind him. "What are you doing in the bed? You can't—"

"Get in the fucking truck!" Carl shouted at him from the backseat.

"Alright! Alright!"

Out of the corner of Lee's eye, he saw Paolo jump into the back of the truck, and the engine roared to life.

Behind him, the doors to the chicken house were shut. The heavy metal sound of bars being drawn across them.

And that was it.

They weren't getting back in there.

The only way out was by going forward.

Do or die time.

"Hold on!" Abe shouted, and that was all the warning Lee got.

The tires spun in the dirt, then found purchase. The truck lurched forward.

Lee flattened himself down on the roof of the cab to keep himself steady.

An unpleasant moment of clarity struck him and he realized what a godawful idea it was to be exposed in the truck bed like this. Especially when he wasn't at full strength.

Too late now.

The dirt road cut through the trees, heading to the main farm road, and the mouth of that opening gaped ahead of them, the truck already hauling at thirty-five.

But Lee had seen the primals latch onto some pretty fast moving cars.

He scanned.

When they hit, they hit fast.

The first one came out of the woods, right in the bend of a blind curve, and it hit the side of the pickup before Lee even realized it was there.

He had time to yell "Contact!" and then the thing was in the truck bed with him.

It was a massive male, with not a strip of clothing left on its body. Not a bit of fat to cover the coils and bunches of unnaturally-evolved muscles. Wild, dreadlocked hair spun around its head, eyes locked onto Lee, wide and inhuman, and the mouth gaping unnaturally wide. Disproportionately long arms reaching towards Lee.

Lee recoiled from it, trying to get a reactionary gap. He yanked his rifle so the buttstock was over his shoulder—the only way to keep himself from feeding the muzzle of his rifle right into the primal's grasp.

It made a swipe at the rifle.

Lee kicked hard, separating them momentarily. It tottered on the edge of the bed—so did Lee. He felt his balance going and did the only thing he could. Let his legs go out from under him, slammed his butt right down into the truck bed.

Fired reflexively—*pop-pop-pop.*

The primal's face ripped away, head snapped back, tilted over the edge.

Lee felt iron claws grab his shoulder, his neck. He tried to twist out of it.

A burp of automatic rifle fire, not from his weapon.

The grip loosened.

Lee ripped his arm up, swam out of the grip, pivoted like a turtle on its back.

Saw the long, corded arms go tumbling off the side of the truck.

Julia, leaning half out of her window on the passenger's side, rifle stuck out in an almost blind-firing position. Her eyes locked to the rear of the vehicle. "Behind you! Behind you!"

From the position that Julia was in, she couldn't sight through her rifle. She couldn't risk firing over Lee's head.

Lee rolled from his back to his stomach.

Was halted by the speed bump of Tomlin's body.

But he could see enough.

A third primal, swinging itself over the tailgate.

Two more on the road behind it, chasing after the truck with inhuman speed, but Abe had the truck hauling now, must've been going close to fifty.

Lee fired from his awkward prone position, watched his rounds lance through the tailgate. The primal danced to the left, clutched the side of the bed, sprung itself off the tailgate. Lee had time to get his rifle up between his face and the primal's.

The thing tried to bite him over the rifle.

Lee struck out hard and close with the buttstock, cracked the thing across the face. He was twisted onto his back again, everything topsy-turvy, pinned between the sidewall of the bed and Tomlin's body. The buttstroke bought him a bare second, the primal stunned, its grip on the rifle loose.

Lee ripped again, jerked the rifle back into his full possession. Thrust the body of it straight up under the primal's chin while he still had the chance and managed to create enough of a gap between the bodies that he got his leg up, and then he kicked out as hard as he could manage.

The thing growled with the sound of animal effort, getting its feet on the sidewall and pushing back. Stronger than Lee.

Shit

Lee took a gamble.

He released one hand from his grip on the rifle. His fingers crabbed across his chest. Found the handle of the fixed blade knife that sat behind his magazines. He yanked it out, knowing that the primal was getting ahold of itself, reasserting its physical dominance.

There was nothing fancy about working someone's body with a knife. When it was close in like this, it was more like a shanking in a prison yard. He held the thing in his right hand and plunged the blade into the chest of the primal, then tattooed it as fast as his arm could work, pistoning back and forth.

As many holes as possible.

He got five or six good holes before the primal yipped and pulled back, and that was all Lee needed.

He dropped the knife. Grabbed the grip of his rifle. Pulled it in close to his body and fired from his hip. He pulled that trigger, and he tracked the rounds in by watching their impacts, guiding them in until they found flesh, found bone, punched the life out of the creature in front of him.

The thing reeled. Tottered on the sidewall, close to the cab. Looked like it might rally.

Lee brought his rifle up to his shoulder to get himself a finishing shot.

A silver revolver protruded out of nowhere and fired a single shot that clove the primal's head from temple to temple.

It went limp. Fell like a bag of bones.

Nothing moved but the mouth. Like a dog in a seizure. Jaw snapping.

Lee considered putting an additional round into the thing's head but its head was right in front of the hump of the tire-well, and Lee didn't want to give them a flat.

Lee's chest ached for more oxygen, then burned violently when he gave it. What was that that Julia had told him? Try not to work too hard?

He brought his rifle up to his shoulder, which took surprising effort. He scanned. Watched the little red dot of his optic dance with his breathing, with his heartbeat, with the exhausted shaking of his limbs.

"Clear!" he shouted, his voice cracking.

Only then did he pull his face away from his sights and look at Paolo, whose torso was out of his window, the silver six-shooter still held straight out in his grip. Only when Lee nodded to him did the pistol begin to lower.

"Thanks," Lee shouted to him over the buffeting of the wind.

"Lee!" he heard Julia's voice. "You good?"

"I'm good!" he shouted back. "Keep going!"

Lee slid down onto his ass, his back against the cab, his dead friend's body to his right.

His heart and lungs still going wild. He took a few big gulps of air, the stretch of them painful like they might pop his chest, and then he forced himself into combat breathing.

In through the nose. Out through the mouth.

In for a two count. Out for a four count.

He felt the electricity in his fingers and toes.

The shockwave after a nuclear blast of adrenaline.

It wasn't the nearness of death that set him off so much as the thoughts after the danger had passed. The thoughts about what *could* have happened. The thoughts of how you *might've* died. How close you had come. Those were like little secondary disasters in his brain, causing his adrenaline to surge again with each thought. Like how fallout can claim more lives than the actual blast itself.

As imminent death began to fade like a signpost in the distance, Lee felt it all coming out of him. He felt like a scarecrow, like a straw man who's suddenly been emptied of everything that kept him upright.

The shakes came on. Bad.

Not just the after-effects of fear this time: he'd taken what little reserves his body had and thrown them to the wind. Every muscle in his body felt like over-stretched elastic. Threadbare and loose.

If he had to fight again, he didn't know if he could.

You would have to, he told himself. *Because...*

Because what?

Because you fucking have to!

A wash of sickness came over him. Made him feel for a moment that he was going to vomit, but then it travelled up his body, through his chest, and landed in his head as a dull, throbbing ache.

He closed his eyes. Felt vertigo, and opened them again.

"Fuck me," he mumbled to himself. Then spat a gob of saliva between his feet.

He sat there, legs splayed out in front of him, body in a near state of collapse. Mouth open. Trying to regulate himself again.

They made it to the main road and went another two miles before Abe finally let up on the accelerator. He heard Abe's voice, floating back to him from the cab: "We're gonna stop so you can get in here with us!"

Lee lifted a thumbs-up. Feared his voice would be too shaky to respond.

You're good, he told himself. *You're good now.*

Abe found a spot in the road that wasn't surrounded by trees. Fallow fields on either side. They had a good, 360-degree line of sight here. The truck slowed, and then stopped. A wash of churned dust from the shoulder billowed over Lee. He smelled dirt and exhaust.

His heartrate felt like it was back down into a normal zone. But his lungs still hurt.

He pulled himself upright, feeling sludgy. He was weak. He hated it, but it also frightened him. This was not a world that showed mercy to the weak.

He climbed stiffly out of the pickup bed and hit the ground on shaky legs. He tried to move with urgency, but his body wasn't cooperating. He pulled the rear driver's side door open and Carl made room for him in the backseat.

Lee clambered in, trying not to put his weakness on display. And when he was seated, he tried not to gasp for air for the effort it had taken him. He kept his hands locked in his lap, where the others wouldn't see them shaking.

Funny how they all felt the need to hide that from each other.

Everyone got the shakes. But no one wanted to admit it.

They could guard each other's backs while they took shits, but couldn't let each other see their hands shaking. No, that was much too personal.

Abe looked into the back at Lee. "You good, man?"

"Yeah. I'm good." He glanced around the cab. "Everyone else good? Carl, how you feeling?"

"Useless," Carl growled. "I need a fuckin' gun."

"We're moving," Abe said, and started accelerating again.

They drove in a strange pall of silence for several minutes.

Lee let his head fall back onto the headrest. Closed his eyes.

Green fields. Rolling hills. A tree in the distance.

Why could he not picture anything else?

He opened his eyes and stared at the gray fabric of the ceiling, preferring that over thinking about that dream. The dream that made him feel like he would never be free…

"So," Paolo shattered the silence. "Y'all just gonna relax and take naps now? You not gonna talk about that shit?"

There was a long pause.

Lee turned his head to the man sitting in the back seat.

Paolo's eyes were jagging back and forth between the other occupants of the truck.

Abe was largely ignoring him. Carl issued a facial shrug and continued looking straight forward.

"What's there to talk about?" Julia responded from the front, not bothering to turn. "We made a decision and we rolled with it. All's well that ends well. Right?"

Lee felt that this was directed at him. In Julia's mind, he'd made a poor decision by getting in that truck bed. And maybe he had. But he was still alive, wasn't he?

"Well," Paolo shifted in his seat and finally slid his pistol back into his holster. "I guess…thank you. For drawing those fuckers off. Guess that's all I gotta say."

No one replied to his thanks.

NINETEEN

OUTSIDERS

SHE WAS WAITING FOR SAM in the same spot that she'd left him.

It was nearly dark and Sam didn't see her until she stepped out from behind a tree.

"You come alone?" Charlie asked.

"Of course."

A slat of moonlight caught her face as she stepped toward him. He could just make out her eyes taking him in, up and down, and then looking behind him, as though she couldn't take his word for it.

That stung.

"Alright then," she said. "Come on."

She started away from him, but he caught her wrist.

"Wait." He looked around. "Where are we going?"

She took his hand. The insistence of his thoughtless grab turning to something tender. She moved in close to him. Electrically close. He could smell her. "Do you trust me?"

"Yes?"

"Because I trust you."

He shuffled his feet. "Yes, Charlie. I trust you."

Then she leaned forward, and up, and their lips touched.

Firecrackers in his mind.

It was a brief kiss, not much more than a peck, but her lips were soft and warm and they filled his mind with pink. He felt a stir all through his body. A rush of wanting.

Then she was pulling him along with her. "Then come on."

He allowed himself to be led for a time, and when she became sure that he would follow without her towing him, she released his hand.

Even though Sam knew the borders were secure, that the fences were high, built up higher, and topped with powerful electrical lines, he still never felt safe in the woods. Especially in the dark. During the day he could shrug it off, but when everything was shadows, every shadow felt like a threat.

He never communicated this to anyone. It was his own personal problem to deal with.

He was too old to be afraid of the dark. He was a soldier now, for chrissake.

A soldier like Lee. And Lee wasn't afraid of the dark.

She led him into the clearing of McFayden Pond, and they skirted the edge of it, all the way around to the opposite bank, and then she began to descend the bank towards the water.

"We goin' swimming or something?" Sam said in a hushed tone. He stared at the shimmering dark waters and thought *no fuckin' way*. Then thought that if Charlie started disrobing and getting in the water, he probably would too.

"I hope not," was Charlie's only answer.

They came to a small cement dam. A washway. Something to drain off the pond during heavy rain. Charlie negotiated herself over the slick concrete, and Sam followed. The dam was now between them and the pond. She kept descending. Into darkness.

It wasn't until he saw the big, black opening of the culvert that he came to a stop.

Charlie halted at the mouth of it. It was huge. Her shadowy figure barely came to the halfway mark of its height. She looked back at him expectantly.

"You want me to go in there?" Sam hissed.

Charlie pulled something out of her pocket. It clicked. Light speared the darkness in the culvert. By the glow, Sam saw she was smiling. "It's fine," she said. "I've been through it before."

She shown the light down the length of the culvert. The darkness swallowed it. The beam never reached the end of the tunnel. She headed in, like the deep black tunnel was nothing more than a manicured path through a park.

Sam looked over his shoulder. Compared to the tunnel, the rest of the night seemed well-lit by the moon and he realized that he would have preferred to skinny-dip in the pond. But he headed into the culvert, knowing it was too late to turn back now.

And secretly, he didn't want to lose the glow of Charlie's flashlight.

The culvert was long. It smelled of wet concrete and a sort of forgottenness that went with things that never saw sunlight.

It had been a while since they'd had heavy rains, but still the bottom of it was wet. There was a layer of silt there, and he could see tracks in the silt. Charlie walked with a sort of bowlegged gait, straddling the little stream of murky water at the bottom of the tunnel, and Sam mimicked her to keep his shoes from getting wet.

A few minutes into the culvert and he was wondering how much farther they would have to go. He looked behind him and couldn't see the entrance of the culvert. He looked ahead of them and couldn't see the exit.

He wondered what would happen if her flashlight ran out of batteries.

Another few minutes of walking. His hips were getting tired from the strange gait they were using. Up ahead, her flashlight finally flickered off of something.

Twenty-five more yards and they reached it.

It was a heavy drain gate. It covered the entire opening, but there was a section of it that was hinged, just big enough for a man to get through at a crouch. It was closed.

Charlie shown her light on the opposite end of the hinges. The gate was held closed by nothing more than a little red carabiner. It looked like a new addition, and when he looked around at the bottom of the culvert, he saw the glimmer of a heavy padlock lying in the silty water. Its shackle had been cut through.

"Why are you showing me this?"

Charlie laughed like Sam was a child trying and utterly failing at understanding how the world works. She grabbed the carabiner, undid it, and pushed open the gate. "I'm not showing you the gate. We're going through it."

"Are we on the outside?"

She stepped out of the culvert, held the gate for him. Watched him expectantly. "Yes. We're on the outside."

Sam didn't move. "We don't have guns."

Charlie reached down and grabbed the hem of the hoodie she was wearing, lifted it up to show her waistband. The handle of a revolver showed. "Speak for yourself."

He stepped one foot out of the gate and looked at her darkly. "Charlie, if you think one fucking revolver is gonna solve your problems if it comes down to it—"

"I've been out before, you know. Not just out here. We *came* from out there. Remember? You're not the only one that has a shitty past, Sam. I can fend for myself." She raised her eyebrows. "Now are you coming or not?"

Sam realized his heart had begun to throttle up. He felt that threadiness in his lungs that told him they wanted to breathe harder, but he controlled it. He wanted badly to go back, but he was looking at Charlie, back in the moonlight, and he was remembering the kiss that she'd given him.

He swung his other leg through, cleared the gate so that she could close it. It squeaked as she did, and she re-clasped the carabiner to keep it closed.

"I wish you'd told me we were going outside the wire," Sam whispered. "I would've brought a weapon."

"If I told you that, I don't think you would have come."

"I would have come," he insisted, though he knew it was a lie.

She just shrugged. "Well, maybe next time."

The culvert emptied into a creek with steep banks. It took some working, but they got topside to the bank and found themselves in woods. Charlie began walking with purpose now. This wasn't just a stroll in the woods. She knew where she was going.

"So if the primals show up," Sam kept his voice low. "I'm just supposed to hide behind you?"

"What?" she said with a note of playfulness. "You have a problem with a girl protecting you?"

He looked sidelong at her. "You wouldn't have a problem with a boy hiding behind you?"

"It doesn't matter anyways. No one's standing behind anyone if the primals show up. If the primals show up, we run."

She said it so casually. As though it were just that simple.

He frowned at her. "You *have* seen a primal, right?"

She looked uncomfortable. "I've dealt with the infected before."

Sam touched her arm, pulled them to a stop. "Charlie, I'm not talking about the regular fucking infected."

"Infected. Primals. Same thing."

"It's not the same thing!" he snapped. "I've seen them. I've dealt with them. They attacked Camp Ryder when I was there." He realized he was shaking his head and his eyes were growing wide with the memory of that terror. "They're faster. They're stronger. They're smarter. These aren't just crazy people like the other infected were. They...changed somehow. Adapted. Or...evolved."

Charlie was not pleased to have been stopped. She huffed and looked skyward.

"I'm serious, Charlie. I've seen them climb fucking walls like spiders. I've seen them hurtle a six foot fence. Hey, look at me."

She looked at him with an expression of pure passive-aggression.

Sam didn't care. She needed to understand. "If the primals come, you're not gonna outrun them."

"Well, then I guess we'll just have to hope they don't come." Then she pulled away and kept walking. "Go back if you're scared, Sam. I'll give you my flashlight."

Sam wasn't going to go back unless she was with him. And she knew that. She was just trying to get him to shut up.

Sam was now angry, and the anger was helping to diffuse some of that fear. "No, I'm going with you. I just want you to understand."

"I understand fine."

You don't understand shit.

But they kept going.

Luckily, not for long.

Very suddenly, the woods ended, and Sam realized that they were standing in a backyard. To his right and left, there were more backyards. Houses. Neatly arranged on little quarter-acre lots. Defunct and abandoned. A few of them fire-gutted. It was hard to see the details of their demise in the moonlight, but Sam could infer based upon every other abandoned and looted neighborhood he'd seen.

"See?" Charlie said, as though she had been vindicated. "We're less than a hundred yards from the culvert. We can make it back quickly if anything bad happens. Or we can just stay here."

You can't make it back, he thought, but didn't say. Instead, he went with, "Where's 'here'?"

She pointed between the two houses in front of them. Across the street was another house, this one facing them. And in the darkness, Sam thought he saw a slight glow coming from the windows. Not the heavy yellow glow from a house that had power and ceiling lights. But the pale glow from flashlights or lanterns, barely distinguishable from the moonlight itself.

"There," she said. "That's where we're going."

She began walking towards the house. Sam followed, but his eyes tracked to the other dark and abandoned places around them and he thought about dens.

"Has anyone cleared these houses?"

"If there were infected here, we would've heard from them already."

Sam frowned. "How many times have you been out here? And who's in the house?"

"We've been out here a few times. And they're friends."

They walked up the front steps of the house. To either side, the lawn was a sprawl of brown, waist-high weeds that had died and fallen over in the winter. New growth writhing up between the old stalks. At the front stoop, two massively overgrown boxwoods crowded the front door.

Charlie slipped between their grasping branches and knocked.

No special knock. Just a few quick raps with her knuckles. Quiet.

The door opened almost instantly.

Claire Staley stood there in the doorway, smiling at Charlie. "Hey…" Then she trailed off as her eyes caught Sam, and the smile fell off her face.

Charlie swooped through the door, gave Claire's stiff body an embrace, and said, "It's okay, Claire. He's with me."

Claire extricated herself brusquely and stuck her head out of the front door, looking around, then thrust herself into Sam's face. "The fuck are you doing here?"

Sam was taken aback. He didn't really know Claire that well. He saw her around. Knew that she was Angela's assistant. They traded small talk every once in a while. "What the hell are *you* doing here?" was the only thing he could come up with.

Charlie inserted herself between them with a hand on Claire's shoulders. "Claire. I said it's cool. He's with me. Everything's cool."

Claire looked at her. "He's a soldier."

Charlie nodded. "And you're the colonel's daughter. What's your point?"

Claire held her ground for another moment, then stepped back into the door, leaving the space open for them to enter the house. "Wish you would've run this by me."

"Didn't know I had to," Charlie replied. "He's just here to hang out."

Claire made a small, dissatisfied noise, then waved them in. "Come on then."

Charlie stepped inside, then looked back at Sam and gestured him in with her head. "Come on, Sam. Don't hang out in the fucking doorway."

Not seeing another option at that moment, he stepped into the house, and Claire closed the door behind them.

They were in an old living room that looked like it had been preserved from the time before everything went to shit. It was dimly lit by the light of a few battery-operated lanterns posted on a few end tables, and by their pale LED glow, Sam saw furniture that stood, as normal as could be, centered around a dead TV.

The house smelled musty, but that was it.

There were perhaps a dozen people inside. All of them young, but they ranged from teenagers to people in their early twenties, like Claire.

Charlie sauntered in, comfortably. Sam trailed her, self-consciously. Feeling everyone's gaze on him as they paused their quiet conversations to greet Charlie, and then look at him like the outsider that he was.

Charlie found a boy that was probably twenty years old, sitting on the end of one of the sofas, beside a girl that stared off like she wasn't sure any of it was real. Sam recognized the guy from around Fort Bragg, but didn't know his name. Just one of the many survivors that had come to stay inside the Safe Zone.

He smiled when Charlie approached, and gave Sam nothing but a sideways glance before refocusing on Charlie. Sam watched the guy. Didn't like the way he looked at Charlie.

"Hey Ben," Charlie said in a lighthearted tone. She reach out and gave him a playful nudge on the arm.

Ben caught her in a light grip, held the tips of her fingers. "Hey, Charlie-girl. What you up to tonight?"

Sam stared at their fingers, touching, and his mind lit on fire. Felt his face flush up. Wanted very abruptly to murder him. But he was the stranger in a strange land here, so he just stood there stiffly and did nothing.

The girl with the far-off eyes turned languidly to behold Charlie and Ben's exchange, but gave no indication that she cared. Sam thought she was sitting awfully snug with Ben. Thought that maybe they were an item or something. But Ben seemed to have forgotten the girl in Charlie's presence, and neither Charlie nor the girl seemed to give a shit about the other.

"You bring anything for us today?" Charlie asked.

Ben leaned back in his seat, looking mock-offended. "Is that all I am to you, Charlie? Just the guy who brings the good stuff?"

Charlie grinned. "You know what they say. Don't bring it if you didn't bring enough for everybody."

Ben shrugged, sat forward, and took hold of a mason jar filled with clear liquid. A stack of paper cups next to it. "Alright. You got me." He pulled two cups off the stack, started to fill one from the mason jar. He glanced up at Sam. "What about this guy?" he said, as though Sam wasn't there and couldn't answer for himself. "Does he drink?"

Charlie gave Sam a pointed look. "Yeah. He does."

Ben nodded and poured a second cup. Then handed them both to Charlie. Once again ignoring Sam. Charlie handed one of the cups to Sam. Took a sip from her own.

Sam took the cup with stiff fingers. Out of place. Awkward. Angry. And, to be honest, a little frightened. He brought the cup to his face, looked in it, smelled it. Harsh alcohol vapors tingled his sinuses.

"This moonshine?" Sam asked.

It wasn't exactly *illegal* in Fort Bragg, but it was an unwritten rule that, in their current state of supplies, they couldn't waste anything to make alcohol. The corn to make moonshine, the fruit to make wine—they could all be used in better ways, either directly as food for humans, or as food for the animals that would become food for humans later on.

But there were still plenty of people that felt that alcohol made the strict rationing more bearable.

Ben planted his elbows on his knees and finally deigned to look at Sam with a frown. "Why? You gonna report me?"

Sam looked back at him over the top of the paper cup, the moonshine stink enveloping his face. There was a part of him that was still a scared teenager, out of place in a new crowd, and wanting to please, wanting to be friends, wanting to get that terrible scrutiny off of him.

There was also another part of him, the part that had killed and fought and aged far beyond anything his years could show, and that part of him thought about throwing the alcohol in Ben's eyes to momentarily blind him, and then strangling the man to death. Or beating his head against the sharp corner of the coffee table until the skull cracked like a split pumpkin and the twitching stopped…

"Of course not, Ben," Sam replied. He forced a smile, but the words came out wooden, and he knew that the smile didn't reach his eyes. "I'm just here to hang out."

Ben watched him for a moment, calculating.

"Cheers, then," he finally said, and he drew his eyes away from Sam, and they went back to Charlie, and Ben smiled again, back to being smarmy and semi-flirtatious.

Then all three of them drank.

They made quiet small talk for a few minutes—or at least Charlie and Ben did. Sam just stood there, the silence seeming to compel him to drink from his cup faster than he had intended to. He kept looking at the girl sitting next to Ben, who had apparently had too much already. She looked on the verge of nodding off.

After a painful time of Sam wishing he was someplace else, Charlie finally disengaged from Ben and dragged Sam towards another end of the dim house. But as he was being dragged away, Sam saw Ben reach his arm around the girl that was falling asleep next to him.

Saw his hand fondle her small breast.

Ben turned. Saw Sam watching him.

Sam's heart did a double-step, thinking Ben was going to get mad and defensive.

But instead, Ben simply smiled with all his teeth, and winked one eye.

Then he turned back to the half-conscious girl in his arms.

—

Angela arrived home just before eight o'clock at night. It'd been a long day, and her body was feeling it. She was supposed to be taking it easy, but that apparently wasn't in the cards for her today.

Besides, she was dealing with the issues surrounding Lee, his team, and his single message to them. And she couldn't help but push herself when she thought about them, out in unknown territory, with no support, and dead friends.

Nate's gone, she reminded herself.

She didn't know him well. Only through Lee. But still. She *knew* him. And that never stopped hurting her. No matter how many times she experienced it, it seemed like she would never build up a callous to it. Like a rock in your shoe that you can never get out.

She wished she could be more like Julia.

Then she proceeded to scoff at herself. She was a grown woman. In charge of the UES. She was who she was. And she had her own strengths, even if they sometimes escaped her own recollection. Strengths that others saw. Which is why they'd foisted this ridiculous, massive responsibility on her.

She didn't *feel* up to the task. But she *was*. She *had been* up to the task for the last two years. Despite the naysayers. Despite the Lincolnists and all their bullshit.

Still, she managed to feel the inescapable mom-guilt as she entered her home and saw that it was just Marie there at the kitchen counter, Abby having been escorted off to bed already. Another day with mom too busy to be with her.

It didn't matter that she was fighting for their survival.

Her maternal side would never cut her any slack.

Marie turned and stood up from the kitchen counter, already gearing up to fuss over Angela. "Eight o'clock!" she exclaimed, though it was only fifteen 'til. "You're runnin' yourself too hard. Come on. Sit down. Have some dinner. Have you eaten anything yet? Of course not. Sit. I'll get you a plate."

Angela sat, self-recrimination keeping her silent, forcing her to smile, because she knew that Marie was implacable. She was going to make sure that Angela ate her food, got her rest, etcetera, etcetera.

"Abby already in bed?" Angela asked.

"Uh-huh." Marie went into the kitchen and started fixing a plate from what was on the stove. "I told her you'd go up and kiss her goodnight when you got in. She made me promise." Marie gave Angela a wink over her shoulder. "Kid sleeps like a rock, though. You could always just say you did it in the morning."

Angela smiled back, guilty that the deception was tempting. "No, I'll go up."

"After you eat."

"After I eat."

Marie put the plate in front of her. Got her a glass of water.

"Thank you," Angela said. "I'm so sorry it took so long today."

Marie waved her off. "Don't even mention it. It's the least I could do."

Angela began to eat. A bit of crumbled mystery meat on grits.

Grits had become a staple in everyone's ration boxes. They were easy to make out of the field corn they grew, and it kept well in storage.

"Where's Sam?" Angela asked.

"He's out with that girl."

"Charlie?"

"M-hm." Marie looked knowingly at Angela. "Got quite the crush on her."

Angela smiled at the wondrous inference of normal teenage life. Managed to feel proud of it for a brief moment. She had helped to create that. She had helped everyone in the Safe Zone experience as much of a normal life as could be had.

That was something to be proud of, wasn't it?

Marie shrugged. "What the hell the two of them are going out to do beats me."

"Stuff they're not supposed to," Angela said, thinking of her own younger years. Thinking of them with the blissful filter of adulthood that willfully chooses to forget all the angst and heartache that came with a lack of experience, a lack of wisdom, and a lack of coping mechanisms.

But things were different when Angela had been a kid. Obviously.

Kids nowadays…they were tougher. They'd learned plenty. Maybe not quite *wise*, but street-smart, at least.

"I told him to be back at a reasonable hour," Marie said. "Which I defined for him as no later than ten o'clock. Besides, he's got guard duty tomorrow. He'll get some sleep if he has half a brain."

Angela nodded along as she ate, part listening, part worrying, part thinking about every other thing that had happened that day.

Shit. You forgot to get back with Doc Trent.

She'd meant to swing by his place after work, but it had gotten so late…

Was it about the dead primal that Lee had brought back? That was the only thing that Angela thought it could be. Why else would Doctor Trent want to speak with her?

God, I hope it's good news.

It wasn't until that moment that Angela remembered her promise to Marie.

She rested her fork on the side of her plate. "Marie, we got a message from Lee's team today."

Marie stopped working. Looked at Angela with full attention. "Well? Don't hold me in suspense, hon. You make me worried when you do that."

Angela held up an apologetic hand. "It's not Julia. I think she's fine."

Relief, and then hard curiosity on Marie's face. "Who, then?"

"Nate," Angela said, and found her voice tight. She cleared her throat. "They got ambushed in a town in Alabama. They don't know who ambushed them. Nate was killed." Angela swallowed. "And Tomlin and Carl were both captured. They're still missing as far as we know."

Marie leaned back on the counter, braced her hands there like the wind had been taken out of her. "Shit," she breathed.

"No one else was mentioned," Angela said. "I guess that means they're okay."

"Shit," Marie repeated. "Jesus, Angela. That's half the fucking team."

Angela's appetite had fled her quickly. There wasn't much left on her plate anyway. Enough of it gone to satisfy Marie. "I know that. And, I know I don't need to say this to you, but this conversation stays here."

Marie looked troubled. "Of course. Is there anything I can be doing right now?"

Angela shook her head. "Honestly, Marie, we don't even know what *we're* doing right now. We're waiting to hear from them. Waiting to get further information from Lee. When there's something actionable and we have a grasp on the situation, I'll make it public, but not now. Not when everything's still so cloudy. The last thing I need is a bunch of people asking questions."

"I know, hon." Marie hoisted herself off the countertop. Straightened her shirt. Drew herself up. "They're gonna be okay," she said with confidence that may or may not have been feigned. "Lee will know what to do. And they'll be okay."

Any further discussion on the topic was cut off by a knock at the door.

Angela and Marie exchanged a quick glance, first at each other, then at the clock on the stove. It wasn't exactly *late*, but Angela's gut twisted anyway. It was still later than good news typically came.

"I'll get it," Marie said, with a slight off-note of apprehension, then hustled over to the door. She opened it a few inches, peeked out, then swung it wide.

Kurt stood at the door. An SUV idled at the curb behind him, the red taillights glowing.

"Just got contact from Butler," he said, holding up the satphone. "Lee's there. He wants to speak with you."

TWENTY

BUTLER

THE SMALL TOWN OF BUTLER, Georgia had started as an outpost, and over the course of the last year, had become one of the two Safe Zones in Georgia.

As the infected had rapidly mutated and evolved, human habitation had to evolve with it. Small outposts that had been defensible in the past were now laid waste by the primals. Barriers that kept the regular infected out, were no barrier at all to the primals. So small outposts began to die out.

Now Safe Zones were the only practical way to keep people protected, and in order to be a Safe Zone, you had to have high voltage fencing, which meant you had to have electricity. If you had those things, then you could grow. If you didn't, then you would die like the rest.

Butler had massive solar farms nearby, and so it had access to electricity. Their fences had expanded, little by little. Now they encircled a good portion of the actual town of Butler, and the population of Butler had rapidly grown from just a hundred or so, to nearly a thousand.

It was now the Butler Safe Zone, and Lee was glad to be inside of it.

The headquarters was in the Taylor County Sheriff's Office, and the Sheriff was a guy named Ed, and he was the one in charge. Ed no longer went by his title of "sheriff," but instead preferred to just be called "Ed."

He no longer wore the badge, but he still wore the gun. He was an older guy, and it was a large revolver, which befitted a sixty year old man who grumbled under his wiry white mustache about how semi-automatics were unreliable, as though it were still 1917 and they were newfangled and unproven things.

He referred to his revolver as a "wheel gun." He always wore his old khaki shirt tucked into his jeans. He walked like a man that had ridden a horse all day. He talked like he had a mouth full of chaw.

Lee liked him a lot.

"How long we gotta wait?" Ed commented from behind an industrial metal desk.

"Not long," Lee replied. It had only been a few minutes so far.

There'd been no fanfare upon their arrival. No debrief.

Lee and his team, battered and much worse off than they'd been when they'd left Butler nearly a week ago, had shown up at the gate in their one remaining pickup truck. They'd given the clearances, and once inside, demanded to speak to Ed. Once they were all in his office, they'd placed the call to Fort Bragg, and now they were waiting for a call-back.

The sheriff's station hadn't always been inside the Safe Zone. Before they'd managed to get the fencing around it, it had predictably been looted and vandalized by those who do not care for law enforcement. When Ed had eventually reclaimed his office, it had been a disaster. The ghost of the letters FUCK YOU COCKSUCKER could still be seen on the walls.

In his cleanup, Ed had only seen fit to rescue one item of memorabilia from his bygone days. A wooden plaque with a star on it and the words Medal of Valor with Ed's name below it. "For Valor In The Line Of Duty, May 18, 2001." It sat in a frame on the wall right between the YOU and the COCKSUCKER.

Lee had never asked him what it was for and Ed had never cared to tell.

Lee appreciated his chosen placement, though.

Ed put his elbows on his desk and jammed his stubby fingers together. "Well, while we're waiting, perhaps you'd care to fill us in on what the fuck is going on."

Lee gave him a quick rundown as he pulled his armor off and dropped the plate carrier at his feet with a dull *thud*. It was warm in the office from the gathered body heat. He was sweating already, and his tan shirt was wet and dark in the shape of his plate carrier. Still, it was a nice change from the night outside that had turned chilly and windy.

When Lee finished, Ed ran a hand over his mustache. "Well, shit," he said finally. "You still have his body?"

Lee felt distant from the question. As though they were talking about someone else's friend. Some nameless corpse. Not Brian Tomlin.

"Yes. He's in the back of the pickup."

A long pause under Ed's watchful gaze. Lee had to build up to the next words. Every time he was about to say them, he felt his throat thicken, and he didn't want the others to hear that. Finally, he managed to mentally distance himself from the concept of what he needed to ask, and he was able to get the words out.

"We were hoping we could bury him here. Inside the wire."

Ed nodded. "We'd be honored to have him. I'll rustle up a flag. We'll give him the twenty-one and everything."

Lee's jaw worked. "If it's all the same to you, Ed, I'd prefer to just do it quietly."

"I understand."

"If you just point me in the right direction," Lee gestured to his teammates around him. "We'll handle it in the morning."

Carl cleared his throat, shifted in his seat. "There is one other thing we're going to have to address with you. Maybe after we get done with the call."

Ed's gray eyebrows raised in question.

Carl glanced at Lee, and Lee gave him a nod to proceed. "I believe we're dealing with a leak, somewhere in the UES."

"Why do you think there's a leak?" Ed asked.

Carl was preparing to answer when the satphone on the desk rang.

Ed picked it up. Looked at the calling number. Passed it to Lee. "It's Fort Bragg."

Lee pressed the answer button and put it to his ear. "Hello?"

Angela's voice: "Lee? Is that you?"

At the sound of her voice, Lee felt something ebb inside of him. He had almost expected her voice to cause more tension in him, but instead he almost felt a release. He stayed stock still, though. Didn't let his shoulders relax.

"Yeah, it's me. Did you get my message?"

"Yes." An audible exhale. "We dispatched—"

"Hold that thought," Lee interrupted. "Where are you and who are you with?"

A pause on the line. "I'm in my house. Marie is here. And Kurt. Colonel Staley is on the way."

"Okay. First off, tell Marie that Julia is fine. She's with me right now, hale and hearty."

Angela's voice dimmed as she pulled the phone away from her mouth. "Lee says Julia is fine. She's with them right now."

"Alright," Lee continued, pulling the phone away from his ear and putting it on speaker. "You're on speaker right now. I've got the team here, plus Ed from Butler. Angela, I need you to find a private place to speak."

There was a long pause on the line. Rustling.

As they waited, Lee turned and nodded to Julia, who was closest to the door to Ed's office, which hung open. He motioned with his head, and she reached over and swung the door closed.

"Okay," Angela's voice said. "I'm in my bedroom. Alone. Kurt's outside the door."

"Alright. Don't put your satphone on speaker."

"I won't. Lee, what's this about?"

"We were just discussing with Ed about the possibility of a leak. I want to bring you into this conversation, because we don't know where this leak is coming from right now, so we need to play our cards close to our chest until we figure it out. I'm going to let Carl speak, because he's the one with the first-hand intel."

"Wait! You found Carl? Carl's there with—"

Angela's voice was suddenly washed out in static.

Lee twitched, grimaced at the unpleasant noise, and mumbled, "Goddamn satellites…"

They waited for the static to subside.

"Angela? You there?"

"Yeah, I'm here."

"We lost you for a second. What did you say?"

"I was just asking how you found Carl? And were you able to find Tomlin?"

Lee stared at the phone. Felt like it had bit him. He was surprised how much the question still stung him. Quick. Like a jab straight to his throat.

He held the phone out so it was relatively close to the middle of his gathered team. He nodded to Carl.

"Ma'am, this is Carl Gilliard. Can you hear me okay?"

"Yes."

"You're aware that Brian Tomlin and myself were captured after our team was ambushed in Hurtsboro."

"Yes."

Carl's eyes stayed fixed to the black satphone in Lee's hands. His gaze looked deliberately blank. A stone wall. "Tomlin didn't make it," he reported with zero inflection. "He was killed by the people that captured us."

On the other end of the connection, there was a sound that might've been a burst of static, or might've been a harsh breath from Angela's mouth. She didn't say anything.

"We were held at a local airfield for a few days," Carl went on woodenly. "Then we were picked up by an SUV and transported to another nearby location where we waited for several hours. This occurred at night. Then we were transported again, this time for over three hours. By my best calculations this put us either in Louisiana, or down into the coast of Alabama. We were taken to what appeared to be a pump station for the oil pipeline. The man in charge at that location is what I believe to be a Mexican national. He identified himself as *El Cactus*, and his group as *Nuevas Fronteras*. I'm informed that this translates to 'New Borders.'"

Carl brought his hands together, slowly. Clasped them to one another. "Local intel that we've managed to gather leads us to believe that *Nuevas*

Fronteras is a cartel of sorts, focused on controlling the flow of oil."

"Jesus," was all that Angela whispered.

Carl's fingers began to tighten on each other, the skin turning white. But his expression never changed. "He left me alive so that I could deliver a message, which I will do, not because he wanted it, but because I believe it is germane to our intelligence. He said to tell you not to send anyone else, that we would only find death. Then he said the only oil we would ever get from him is whatever we pumped out of Brian's body. He then…" Carl seemed to have run out of air. Took a deep breath, and finished: "He drowned Brian in crude oil."

Lee's eyes went sharply up to Carl's. He felt the back of his neck flood with heat, like someone was holding burning coals inches from his skin.

Carl met his gaze. Gave nothing. Just stared at him, full of empty hatred.

There is a certain tipping point that occurs in your head when wrong has been done to you. There is the desire for justice. Sometimes, the desire to extinguish the life of the person that has wronged you.

But sometimes what they've done puts them over the edge. And that is when killing them is not enough.

That is when you want to wipe their existence off the face of the earth. Not only them, but everyone they've ever loved, everyone who has ever given them safe harbor. That is when you want to plunder their entire world, burn it to ashes, and leave no stone standing on another so that a blood encrusted wasteland is all that remains as a monument to the fact that they once dared to draw a breath against you.

That is what Lee felt.

It smacked to the walls of his heart and stuck there, black and ugly.

He wanted—needed—the absolute destruction of the man that had killed Tomlin.

Ed's chair creaked as he leaned back. Shook his head. Looked at a wall.

Carl blinked a few times, as though waking from a brief fugue. He sucked in a breath. "This man, this so-called *El Cactus*, he knew certain details about us that I feel strongly he could not have learned of on his own. He knew that we were coming south to search for oil. And he knew that we were coming from the United Eastern States."

There were only a handful of times in Lee's history with Angela that he could recall her going cold. She was a compassionate and emotive person, so it did not happen often. But this was one of those moments. Her voice sounded flat. "And that is why you believe we have a leak."

"Yes, ma'am."

"Do you have any suspicions as to who it might be?"

"No, ma'am. But there is something else that you need to be aware of." Carl appeared to relax more, now that they were off the topic of Tomlin's death. "We've talked about it amongst ourselves. We don't believe that *El Cactus* had direct contact with anyone from the UES. The chance is simply too slim. There were limited number of people that knew the details of our mission, and I can't see a motive for them communicating with an oil cartel from the Gulf States."

Lee heard the frown of confusion in Angela's voice. "How'd he get the intel on us then?"

"Well," Carl sighed through his nose. "We think a more likely explanation is that someone is leaking information to Greeley, Colorado. And the *Nuevas Fronteras* are in league with President Briggs."

TWENTY-ONE

CO-ORDIN-ATIN'

"IN LEAGUE WITH PRESIDENT BRIGGS," Angela echoed, her finger questing up to rub her eyebrows, then her whole forehead. The question came to her head about why President Briggs would get in bed with a cartel, but then she answered her own question. "For the oil."

It was Lee who spoke up. "There are pipelines that go up that way, just like there's pipelines that head to us."

"I would think he would try to access the northern pipelines," Angela said, trying to find a hole in this unpleasant concept. "Out of Alaska."

"That's a possibility," Lee said. "It's also possible that he's more interested in *denying us* the oil. He knows as well as we do that that's the next step to independence. He knows if we can't provide energy for ourselves we're dead in the water."

Dead in the water.

Dead in the oil.

Like Brian Tomlin.

Maybe the bad news. Maybe the exhaustion of overworking her recovering body. But she felt like puking. Her mouth started to sweat. She sat down on the edge of her bed.

There was a knock at her bedroom door. "Yes," she said.

Kurt opened the door and Colonel Staley squeezed through. He was wearing a tan shirt tucked into green athletic shorts. He looked sweaty. Angela tried to remember seeing him out of uniform and couldn't.

"I was taking an evening run," Staley explained. "What's this about?"

Kurt closed the door, so it was just Staley and Angela in her bedroom. She thought peripherally that she should feel awkward—the bed wasn't made, the covers still tossed—but she couldn't feel anything but the situation bearing down on her like a truck.

"I'm on the line with Lee and his team. They're in Butler now." She frowned. "Lee, can I put this thing on speaker?"

"How comfortable are you with Kurt?" was Lee's answer.

"Comfortable."

"Then go ahead."

Angela pulled the phone from her ear and put it on speaker.

The colonel furrowed his brow and spoke. "Lee, it's Colonel Staley. How is your team?"

"We're safe in Butler, sir. What's left of us."

Staley glanced up at Angela.

"They lost Tomlin," she said quietly. Then she quickly brought him up to speed.

Staley listened, his frown deepening.

"Angela," Lee spoke up again. "You mentioned that you'd dispatched someone to Butler, reference my message."

"Mitch is on his way with four others," Angela answered. "He left this morning. Right after we got your message. He said he should be there tonight. I also asked Colonel Staley to run up some plans and prepare to dispatch a force of Marines to Butler if the situation calls for it. I just wanted options."

"I think that was a good idea," Lee said. "I'd like to hear what the colonel has."

Staley swiped a trickle of sweat from his eyebrow and patted his thumb dry on his shorts. "Well, the situation's not ideal. Angela asked me to run some numbers based on our available fuel. Which, unfortunately, is less than we thought. And what's left is only there if we suspend all farming operations. Which we have done, until we figure out what we're doing."

"You can't suspend the farming operations," Lee said, sounding surprised that they'd suggested it. "The whole reason we came down here was to keep them going. If we don't plant, we're not gonna have anything to eat."

Angela felt her grip on the satphone tighten. "If we don't get those fuel lines open, we starve by next year anyways."

Staley nodded, making eye contact with Angela. "She's right. But let me run through my numbers. I think we might have a solution in here somewhere."

"Alright," Lee said. "Give it to us."

"If I send them with full support, I can send one platoon. If I send only the Marines and their loadouts, I can send three platoons. That's almost a hundred and fifty Marines."

"As much as I want to burn their shit to the ground," Lee said. "That might be...unweildy."

"You are talking about possibly invading the land mass of what amounts to a small country. If these bastards are as bad as they sound like, you do not want them sneaking around your rear. You'll want protected flanks. And when you think of it like that, then you see that three platoons doesn't even scratch the surface."

"Exactly," Lee said. "We obviously don't have the resources to do a full invasion. I'm not even going to entertain that as a strategic possibility unless you, sir, see some reason why we should."

Staley shook his head at the phone. "No, I don't think that is our best option."

"I think small and well-equipped is what we want. We've got a limited amount of time to get this done, so there's no reason to have a Marine detachment that's outfitted for a long deployment. If we don't have this shit solved within the month...well, then I don't think things are going to go our way."

Staley cracked a grim smirk. "I believe we're on the same page here, captain. Which is why I decided to run an additional calculation." He looked up at Angela, as though to ask her permission to proceed.

Angela stood there holding the phone with one hand, the other hand latched to her face, and as Staley's look interrupted her tumult of thoughts, she realized she was gripping her face hard. She pulled her hand away and gestured for Staley to continue.

"If we keep enough fuel here at Fort Bragg to continue farming operations through the end of the month, then we'll have enough fuel left over for me to send one squad of Marines, with enough food, water, and ammo to last them two weeks."

Angela held up her hand in a *pump the brakes* motion. "Sorry. Civilian here. How many men are in a squad?"

"Thirteen men in a squad," Staley answered. "But I'm also leaving room for four additional, depending on Captain Harden's requests. Mortar teams. Assault weapons team. That sort of thing."

Angela's eyebrows went up. "Is that enough? It doesn't sound like enough."

"No," Lee interrupted. "It's enough. I know a squad of Marines can do plenty of damage. And we want quiet, too. We want quiet, and fast, and mobile."

"And," Staley said, with an obvious note of displeasure. "If we really are dealing with a leak here at Fort Bragg, we don't just need them quiet in the field. We need to be able to dispatch them quietly too."

Angela caught herself about to chew her sore fingers again. She forced them down, feeling childish for it. "If we do it too quiet, it'll be like whispering when you don't wanna get noticed—it's guaranteed to get you noticed."

Staley pursed his lips. "We can send them for another reason. To another location. On paper anyways."

"Pick an outpost away from our operation," Lee advised. "Something small. Say they're having an issue with the primals while they get their fencing set up. Some place believable, but that folks in Fort Bragg won't necessarily concern themselves with."

"We can do that," Angela nodded. "That's believable. Not a fan of lying to the public, though."

"Don't think of it as lying to the public," Lee countered. "Think of it as misinformation to whoever is leaking intel to Greeley."

Angela blew a faint, tired raspberry noise, but said, "Alright."

Staley shifted his weight. "Lee, what's your primary objective here?"

"Primary objective hasn't changed, sir. We're here to try to get fuel for Fort Bragg. But…" A pause. "That brings up some additional issues we need to work around."

"Such as?"

"If the Gulf States are enemy territory—and it seems like they are—then we're not going to be able to get the pipeline flowing all the way up to Fort Bragg. That would require physical occupation of all the pumping stations along the way, and the ability to route power to them. Now, from what Carl explains to me, wherever they took him, they obviously had power enough to get those local pumps working. Which means that they've managed to get some sort of power plant working. It's possible that power from that plant can be routed to the pipelines that lead to Fort Bragg. But, as I already pointed out, that requires us to own the geography. And that's a lot of geography. Too much for us to own right now."

Staley's normally mellow demeanor showed its first signs of stress. He ran a brisk hand over his face. "So we're back to a full scale invasion of the Gulf. Which we don't have the fuel to accomplish."

"You're right," Lee answered. "We don't have the fuel for that. Not yet. But we might be able to do it incrementally."

Angela thought that she was tracking with Lee, but wasn't positive. She closed her eyes. "Okay. Keep going. What are you thinking?"

"*Huachicaleros*," Lee said. "Fuel thieves. That's what this cartel is, and that's what we're going to do. We're going to take a page from their own playbook and use it against them."

—

Sam walked.

The shadows of the woods surrounded him, and even though he was back in the wire, he still found himself looking over his shoulder.

The gathering at the abandoned house had dispersed.

Charlie had walked back with him, but she'd already split off towards her house, and now Sam was walking alone in the dark woods, without a light, and he hated it. The buzz of the moonshine took the edge off his fear, but a little voice in his head kept telling him *watch your back!*

This wasn't his first experience with alcohol, but close enough. He'd had a few run-ins with homemade beer that some of the other troops cobbled together from anything that had sugar in it (candies from MREs had been his last unfortunate encounter) and Sam had dutifully taken a drink of it to try and fit in.

This was, however, his first experience with liquor.

It still burned in his gut, and it made the world watery and unstable.

Something else burned in his gut, and those were Charlie's parting words to him.

"How do you feel about the direction that we're going?" she'd asked him just before splitting off for her house.

He'd frowned, thinking she meant their bearings in the woods. "What do you mean?"

"I mean the United Eastern States. How do you feel about where Angela is leading us?"

He had stopped walking and turned to stare at Charlie. The question seemed out-of-the-blue, and he realized that he had no answer for her. He'd never really considered it. He'd just...gone along.

"I...I don't know."

He recalled the way that Charlie's eyes had scoured over his face. No longer pleasant and flirtatious. Seeking. Probing. "You're not worried about how much they *don't* tell us?"

He blinked a few times. The liquor in his stomach making it hard for him to focus on her face. And he really didn't have anything to say but that he didn't know, and he'd already said that, so he stayed silent.

Charlie looked troubled. "You haven't seen anything weird going on?"

"Like what?"

"I don't know, Sam," she said, irritated with his density. "Just weird stuff. Like stuff it seems they don't want us to know about."

Sam didn't really have an answer to that one either.

Shit. *Was* he being dense?

He wanted to have something poignant and clever for her. Something that he'd seen that made her think he was sharp and observant. But he hadn't really paid attention.

He'd done his guard duty. He'd slept and ate. Went through the motions of his daily life. Glad to be surviving. Glad to be living in a Safe Zone.

He felt suddenly discontent with it all.

Charlie had simply shrugged and motioned with her head. "Well, anyways. I'm going this way." Her eyes caught him again, and she offered him a smile, but it had a shadow of disappointment in it. "I'll see you later."

Sam wondered if another kiss was coming.

It wasn't.

She just headed off towards her house, leaving him to make his way home on his own.

He came out of the woods now. His feet hit concrete. The houses around him glowed yellow through their windows. He felt marginally better.

But, somehow, the patina of everything suddenly seemed different. Aged. Defunct. Like noticing a stain on your favorite shirt.

He was heading home.

Home for him was a house full of strangers.

Were they really strangers?

It had never occurred to him before, but that's how it felt now.

He was just some Arab guy, living in a house with a white woman who kind of acted like his mother, and a little white girl that kind of acted like his sister.

As the strangeness of his situation dawned on him for the first time, he wondered if they felt the same way. Did they look at him and wonder who this stranger was that they allowed to live with them? They didn't fit together, did they?

One of these things is not like the other.

Very quickly, everything had become questionable.

You need to sleep. You need to go right to your room and not talk to anybody, and just sleep until that moonshine gets out of your belly. You're just thinking weird. That's all. Everything will be normal again in the morning.

But now that the curtain had been pulled back, he wasn't sure he wanted to close it again.

Now it felt like a lie.

He arrived back at the house with time to spare. It was only a quarter to ten.

He realized quickly that his chances of getting to his bedroom unseen were very low.

The lights were still on in the house.

A gray Tahoe, which replaced the black one that had been shot to shit, was sitting at the curb. A soldier was in the driver's seat, watching him approach.

Shit.

The man stepped out of the SUV as Sam approached. He nodded his recognition. Technically the man outranked Sam, and technically that meant something. But the rules were much laxer than they used to be.

"Ryder," the man greeted him. Not using his rank. Which was something of a common courtesy they all extended to each other: If you weren't in uniform, then you were treated as a civilian.

Still, he said, "Sergeant Hauer," more out of habit than anything else. "Is something going on?"

Hauer shrugged. "I just drive the car."

In other words: *mind your own business.*

Sam nodded, then headed for the door.

"Hey," Hauer called.

Sam stopped and looked back at him.

The man was giving him that eyeball that the old troops gave the new ones. Sam had become familiar with it by now. It said, *No, I'm not going to break the unspoken protocols of our common courtesy to each other, but you need to remember that I'm a real soldier, and you're just a pretend one.*

"Sir?" Sam said, feeling stiff and ungainly under that gaze.

"Where you comin' from tonight?"

Sam swallowed. Realized that his mouth was very dry. Like the liquor had sucked the moisture out of it. "The community center."

A thin smirk. "They got hooch at the community center now?"

Fuck.

Was it that obvious?

Sam blinked. Looked away.

Sergeant Hauer put one leg back in the SUV. "Better walk straight when you go in there, Ryder. And don't open your mouth." Then he sat back in the SUV and closed the door.

Sam turned clumsily on wooden limbs and went for the door.

Before he could reach it, it came open.

Colonel Staley stepped out, and Angela stood there in the door.

Sam froze where he was, eyes wide, like a burglar caught in the act.

Colonel Staley and Angela seemed to stare at him for long, interminable moments.

Are my eyes glassy? Am I swaying on my feet? Do I stink like alcohol?

He didn't think he'd had that much to drink. But under the scrutiny of their eyes, he suddenly felt like a staggering drunk.

The concept of saluting Colonel Staley flitted across his mind. Perhaps if he did it crisply enough, that would fool them…

Stupid. Just stay still.

Staley nodded to him. "Sam," he said, with a certain formality. Then he turned back to Angela. "Night, ma'am."

"Goodnight, colonel. Are you sure you don't want to use the car to get home?"

Staley headed down the front walk and called over his shoulder, "No, I think a walk will do me good. Thank you."

Sam wanted to edge towards the doorway, but Angela was still standing there, and then as soon as she moved out of the way, her body guard, Kurt, appeared in the doorway. He gave Sam a quick evaluation and then ignored him.

"Anything else you need, ma'am?"

"No, Kurt. Thank you. Sorry to keep you so late."

He shook his head. "Not a problem."

Then he too stepped out and walked for the SUV. Sergeant Hauer saw him coming and started the vehicle.

"You gonna come inside or sleep on the porch?" Angela was holding the door for Sam, watching him with a curious half smile.

Sam remembered Hauer's advice to keep his mouth shut, so he just smiled and nodded and slipped through the door like a plague hovered in the air there and he needed to get through it as quickly as possible—and without taking a breath. He headed for his room.

"You have a good time?" Angela asked.

A simple enough question, but Sam sensed an underlying curiosity. He stopped and turned when he felt he was a safe enough distance away that she couldn't smell his liquor-breath.

"Yeah. Just tired. Gotta work tomorrow. Gonna get some sleep."

"Marie made some dinner, if you're hungry," she called after him.

"I'm good, thanks."

Actually, he realized he was very hungry, but felt the need to be hidden in his room.

He made it to his room and closed the door behind him with a sense of relief.

It wasn't until he was lying in his bed five minutes later, staring at the dark ceiling, that Charlie's words came back to haunt him again.

Just weird stuff. Like stuff it seems they don't want us to know about.

What the hell had Colonel Staley been doing here this late at night?

TWENTY-TWO

BEST LAID PLANS

THEY BURIED TOMLIN in a quiet corner of the cemetery on Cedar Street.

The old cemetery was across the road. Its stone and concrete monuments visible.

In the new section of the cemetery, there was very little to mark the graves accept for the sunken ground of the old ones, and the raised ground of the new ones, and occasionally a crude wooden cross.

There had been a lot of death in the last two years.

Lee thought there would continue to be.

How long? Lee wondered. *How long is it going to be like this? Are things ever going to be normal again? Or will it be like this forever?*

Mitch and his team arrived close to midnight the night before. They woke up early enough to do the heavy digging. Julia insisted on helping them dig, and further insisted that her three wounded teammates not worsen their situation with heavy labor.

Lee, Abe, Carl, and Julia took the honor of lowering the body into the grave.

Lee stood, sweating in the mid-morning sun, looking down at Tomlin's form in the grave. Ed had provided them with a white bedsheet in which to wrap the body. Spots of it had turned brown as the oil still on Tomlin's body soaked through.

Lee swallowed gummy spit and cleared his throat. "Brian knew he was going to die. Just like all of us know we're going to die. Eventually." He kept his eyes on the form in the grave. Didn't want to look up into anyone else's gaze. "He told me that when he finally went, not to do the thing where everyone says a bunch of sappy bullshit. His words, not mine." Lee wanted to smile at the memory of Tomlin's blunt manner, but couldn't. "He told me that all he wanted was to know that whenever we were together around a campfire, and especially if we had something to drink, that we just pour a bit out and remember him, and that would be enough."

Lee took a deep breath that stretched his heavy chest. He nodded to the departed. "And we will."

Then Lee bent down, tossed a handful of dirt in. And then everyone else did as well.

We are born surrounded, Lee thought. *And spend our lives fighting to the death.*

Mitch and his guys shoveled the dirt back in.

Lee walked away from his friend's grave, speaking to a ghost.

What am I going to do now, Brian? What's the team going to do? Without you to pick us up, all they got is my gloomy ass. We needed you, Brian. I have no fucking idea what we're going to do now.

But he knew what they were going to do. It was the only thing that they could do. It was the only answer to the question. It was the only solution to the problem. It was the punchline to every god-awful joke. It was inescapable for them.

For him.

For who he was.

It was the tidal pull of violence, like it was all the oceans of the world, and every river led to it eventually.

—

They met in the roll call room of Ed's sheriff's station-turned-headquarters.

Mitch's team included the old Huckleberry Hound, Rudy, as well as Morrow, he of the wild mountain-man beard and hair—topped by his ancient Multicam ballcap—and their two younger operators from the 82nd Airborne, Logan and Blake.

Ed and Paolo were also in attendance. Ed, because he wanted to know what was going on, and Paolo, because he was their only source of local intelligence for Alabama.

The roll call room was small, because the department had been small, but they all fit in. There was a single long table at which all of them were able to sit, shoulder-to-shoulder. Lee stood at the head of the table and looked at Paolo.

"How much do you know about *Nuevas Fronteras*?"

"We had some ties with other local groups," Paolo said, thinking as he spoke. "The ones further south were the first to go under. Which I think supports your theory that they're coming out of the south."

Carl put his elbows on the table. Steepled his fingers. "What do you mean 'go under'?"

Paolo shrugged. "They were taken over by this cartel. Or what I now assume to be this cartel. It makes sense that it would be the same people, but I can't tell you for certain."

"I think it's a safe assumption," Lee said. "What do you know about how they took over?"

"Same way they took over my place at Bullock County Correctional. They swooped in. Made threats to the folks that lived there. And the folks that lived there either went with it, or they went packing. Or they were killed." He raised his eyes to Lee. "Honestly, I think most of the people just went with it. I only heard about one instance where they might've just wiped the whole settlement off the map."

Lee planted his hands on the table and considered. "Here's what we need. Ultimately, we need to confirm the location of a place from which we can steal their fuel. That might be the location where they took Carl. Or there might be a better place to hit. But that's what we need to find out."

Mitch leaned forward, putting his elbows on the table. "How confident are we that they even have the pumps running? That they even have refined oil?" He arched his eyebrows. "I mean, it's not like the oil rigs are just taps you can turn on and out comes JP-eight, you know?"

Carl nodded. "You're right about that. All I can say is that it was definitely a pumping station, and it was definitely pumping. Now, all I saw was crude oil." A pause here. A flash of grimness across Carl's features. "But they had that much running. And it's obvious that they themselves have access to fuel. It's possible that they're getting it out of old fuel reserves, but…"

Lee picked up where Carl trailed off. "Look. Here's where I stand on it: If the UES had the wherewithal to get a nuclear power station up and running again, then I suspect that a powerful cartel could get people working for them to get the oil rigs running again, and the refineries pumping out fuel. It's not that big of a stretch for the imagination."

Mitch scratched at his beard. "I suppose that's true."

Lee turned back to Paolo. "What we need to figure out is where the fuel is coming from. Is it all stored in one location? Or do they have the infrastructure in place to be pumping it through the pipelines? We need to know how they're keeping their people fueled up."

Paolo shook his head. "I'm sorry, Lee, I can't really speak to that."

"I know you can't. I'm not asking you to. What we're going to need is someone who *does* know, and in my mind, that means it has to be one of these cartel motherfuckers."

Mitch raised his head. "So you wanna snatch one of them."

"Yes. But the problem is, the most likely place to find one of them is going to be from one of these settlements that they've taken over. And when word gets back that one of their guys got snatched, that's going to come back on the settlement. And I don't want to burn these people. We're going to need them working with us. And if they know that they're going to get massacred for helping us, then we're going to get a lot of doors slammed in our faces."

Carl frowned. "Back when we were Delta, we did a few operations in Central America." He looked at Lee. "The cartels rule these places through fear. And it is not easy to get a local populace to work with you. They're fucking terrified. And understandably so. The things that these animals do to people that betray them…"

"I know," Lee said. "And that's why we need to do this fast. We need to get in, get what we need, and secure the people that helped us before word can get back to whoever this *El Cactus* guy is. We have an advantage here, and that's that people can't just pick up a cell phone and dime us out."

"They might have satphones like we do," Carl pointed out. "In my experience, they're typically very well equipped. And, if they are in league with Briggs, who knows what kind of hardware they're getting from Greeley."

"They might have satphones," Lee acknowledged. "But if we select the right settlement, then we limit our chances of one of the locals using it against us."

Paolo blew a breath through his lips. "What constitutes the 'right settlement'?"

"Someplace that doesn't want them there," Lee answered.

Paolo shook his head. "Hell, Lee. I don't think anybody wants them there."

"Someplace where the people are pissed. That's what we need. If there's a settlement that got made an example of, then, yes, they'll be living in fear, but there's also going to be some folks whose family and friends were murdered. They're going to be the people that won't turn around and give us up."

Mitch flicked his fingers into the air and then gestured at Paolo. "What about his old place? The correctional place?"

Paolo made a negative noise in the back of his throat. "Shit. As much as I'd love to kick their asses out of my place, I just don't think it'll work. There's too many of the guys there that were a little too quick to accept their terms."

Lee looked at Mitch. "It's too hard of a target anyways."

Mitch smiled. "Too hard?"

"Too *risky*. I'll put it that way. I'm sure all you hellraisers could take the place. Eventually. But how many are we going to lose in the process?" Lee shook his head. "No. Truth is, there are no acceptable losses for us right now. We're already behind the eight ball. We can't afford to take that kind of risk."

"Well," Paolo said. "I think I might have a good target for you."

Collectively, the group turned their eyes to him.

"You remember Eileen, right?" He asked Lee.

"The ornery old lady from your group?"

Paolo smirked. "Yeah. That's her. She came from a different group. Group that got hit by the cartel. That settlement's still there. But…they're no friends of the cartel, I can tell you that. And neither is Eileen."

"Where's the settlement?"

"Not real far," Paolo said. "Little closer to the Mississippi line, I think."

Julia leaned forward to see Paolo around the bulk of Mitch. "Will she go with us? And will her people still trust her?"

Paolo looked at Julia. "Yeah, I think they'll trust her. And yes. She'll go with you. I think she'll do just about anything to get back at those people."

Lee pushed himself up off the table. "Sounds like we need to go get Eileen." He looked at Mitch and inclined his chin. "You said you brought some hardware from Bragg?"

Mitch smiled and nodded. "Oh yeah. We brought you some goodies."

Lee jerked his head to indicate the outside. "Well, I'd like to go see those goodies."

—

Lee pulled a long, tan Pelican case from the back of Mitch's truck, and set it on the tailgate. On the side of it was scrawled in magic marker, HARDEN.

"Honestly," Lee said over his shoulder to Mitch. "This is all I was hoping for."

"Yeah, I figured," Mitch drawled. "But we also brought plenty of extra ammo and mags. And a bit of ordnance." Mitch leaned over the truck bed and patted another, large Pelican case. "Brought my baby. You know. Just in case."

Lee managed a smirk. "It can't hurt."

Well, it *could* hurt. But mostly other people. Mitch's "baby" was an M32A1 multi-shot grenade launcher, with a revolving cylinder for six 40mm grenades. He'd used it to devastating effect in the past. And you just never knew when you might need to blow something up.

Back to his own cased weapon, Lee unsnapped it and lifted the cover. Packed into the foam interior was his M14, outfitted with a scope and a high, adjustable cheek rest. The rattle-can paint job he'd put on it still held the marks of its long usage. The handguard, grip, and cheekrest were all worn down to the original black. The polymer magwell chewed up from numerous reloads.

Lee typically stuck to his M4 and his trusted Aimpoint optic. But every once in a while, you needed to reach a little further, or hit a little harder. And for that, the .308 rifle, and the magnified optic mounted on it, were called for.

Lee snapped the case closed again. "Don't need it right now," Lee said, sliding the case back in amongst the rest of the goodies. "But, I got a feeling that as banged up as I am, I might be more useful on overwatch than on assault."

—

Major John Bellamy sat in his office in the Greeley Green Zone.

He stared at his computer. Stared at the prompt asking him ARE YOU SURE?

Am I sure? What a stupid fucking question.

The first shipment of fuel had arrived that morning, driven all the way from Louisiana. A convoy of ten HEMTT trucks with the fuel tanker attachment, dispatched from Greeley the week prior. Thirty-five thousand gallons of diesel, and thirty-five thousand gallons of jet fuel.

They were pumping their payload into fuel cisterns at that very moment. And then they'd be off again, to make the same round trip.

By the end of the month, Greeley would have enough fuel to run their tanks and helicopters again. Depending on how their relationship with Mateo Espinoza blossomed over the coming months, they might be fueled up for the foreseeable future.

And all John had to do was sign his soul over to the devil.

ARE YOU SURE?

No, I'm not fucking sure.

But it wouldn't be the first time in John's military career that they gave massive stockpiles of weapons to a contingent of people that might not be so friendly to them in the long run. For a military that was supposedly so good at strategy, it didn't seem like they thought about the consequences of their actions very often.

John's gaze rose from the insipid question on his computer to the large map of the United States that hung on his wall. On each state was the picture of a face. Each face belonged to a Coordinator from Project Hometown. Beneath each face was a single sticky note, and on those notes were written one of three things: GREELEY; NONVIABLE; or just a question mark.

His own face looked back at him there, posted in the center of the state of Wyoming.

The sticky note under his face read GREELEY.

Over in North Carolina, Lee Harden looked back at him, and under his face it read NONVIABLE.

Below that, in South Carolina, Brian Tomlin hung, and his sticky note also said NONVIABLE, except that now there was a big black X written in marker over Brian's face.

Dead.

The most NONVIABLE that you could ever be.

Most of the interior states—the Dakotas, Nebraska, Missouri, etcetera—said GREELEY. All of those Coordinators had heeded the call of President Briggs. They abandoned their original mission and signed their numerous bunkers full of resources over to the powers that be.

The northeastern states were all dead. Died when everything had gone to shit. The populations too dense. Too many people got infected and went mad all at once.

A few of the southeastern states, such as Florida and Georgia were labeled NONVIABLE, but their pictures had also been X'd out. They were dead because President Briggs had ordered them so.

Most of the West Coast was a question mark. No one knew about them. Had they made it? Were they NONVIABLE? Were they trying to get to Greeley? Or were they dead too?

His eyes then drifted down to Texas.

Oklahoma. New Mexico. Arizona.

All question marks.

He looked back to his computer.

To the prompt there on the screen.

ARE YOU SURE?

In the end, it wasn't about whether he was "sure" or not.

It was about whether he would follow his orders.

He clicked the button that said YES, and transferred control of eight bunkers full of weapons, ammunition, ordnance, food, and medicine, straight into the hands of Mateo Ibarra Espinoza. All eight bunkers in Alabama.

On the map, the face posted to the state of Alabama was Captain Perry Griffin, and his sticky note said GREELEY.

In fact, Perry's office was three doors down from John's.

He closed the laptop computer with an irritable snap.

He rose from his seat and walked to his office door, which hung open a few inches. He closed it, then went to his desk and unlocked the bottom drawer. He pulled a box of files out of the way and picked up the satphone that lay underneath. He extended the antenna. Dialed a number.

It buzzed twice on the other end before a voice answered: "Hello."

Not "Hello?" like a question.

The person on the other end already knew who was calling.

"Tex," John said, keeping his voice quiet. The walls around here could be thin.

"Whatcha got?"

John stared at the map on his wall as he spoke, low and clear and careful. "Lee is in Alabama. I think he's going to try to move on the *Nuevas Fronteras*."

There was a pause on the other end, as the information was absorbed.

Then: "Roger that. We'll find him."

And that was it.

John shut off the satphone. Collapsed the antenna. Put it back where he got it. Put the file box over it again. Closed and locked the drawer.

ARE YOU SURE? His mind seemed to ask him.

Yes. I'm sure.

TWENTY-THREE

―――

CAPTIVES

"WELCOME TO THE WILDS, GENTS," Mitch said as they passed the sign on the road that told them they were entering Alabama.

At the wheel, Rudy *harrumphed.*

Mitch looked at him with a half-smile. "What? You not skeered?"

"Ain't skeered," Rudy drawled.

Mitch turned in his seat and looked to Morrow, who was right behind Rudy. The man's dark eyes were looking out his window at the passing countryside. Everything around them was a dense and heavy green, darkened and thickened by the overcast day.

A strong wind was blowing out of the south, buffeting the truck, like it was trying to repel them. It shivered through the leaves in the trees, making them spin and flash, first green, then silver. It whipped up little walls of detritus from the roads which then clattered over the windshield.

Beneath the granite sky, darker smudges of clouds caught the strong winds and sailed towards them rapidly, like an invading armada.

"What about you, Morrow?" Mitch asked the man in the back seat. "You skeered by The Wilds?"

Morrow glanced at his team lead, then went back to his window. "I'm appropriately cautious."

"Appropriately cautious," Mitch nodded. "Mm. Wise words." He turned even further to look at Logan and Blake. "How about our two young padawans?"

Logan smirked. "Can't be any worse than Afghanistan."

Mitch chuckled and faced forward.

Rudy made another grumble noise. "It can always be worse."

Mitch nodded. "Huckleberry's right. It can always be worse. We could all be on fire."

"You know what I mean."

Mitch gave him a nudge with his elbow. "Yeah, I know what you mean."

Their pickup truck was in the lead. In the sideview mirror, Mitch saw Lee's truck behind them, keeping a sensible fifty-yard distance.

Logan spoke up again: "At least we haven't hit any roadblocks. You know?"

Rudy glanced up sharply in his rearview mirror. "Boy, you better knock on some fucking wood."

Logan gently knuckled his crotch. "Shit, Rudy. You're so salty today."

"Rudy's always salty," Blake agreed.

"We buried one of our own today," Rudy grunted.

Silence.

Mitch eyed his friend in the driver's seat, but Rudy kept his frowning face on the road.

"Now, that might not mean much to you hard chargers," Rudy continued. "But it means somethin' to me. Maybe y'all didn't know Brian Tomlin like I knew him, but I tell you one thing, the man was no slouch. No easy pickings." Rudy jacked a thumb behind him. "You see that pickup back there? Lee, Carl, Abe, Julia. They're no slouches either. And look at them. Shot through the fucking chest. Shot through the leg. Carl's beaten to a fucking pulp. Nate and Brian are just…fucking dead." Rudy gripped the wheel in both hands. "These ain't no goatherds we're dealing with. And y'all should remember that."

"M-hm," Morrow intoned.

Well, that took a dark turn, Mitch thought. But then he couldn't exactly deny what Rudy was saying. There was a survivor's wisdom in it. Being smart about your opponent wasn't cowardice. Some things should rightfully be feared. Young bucks had to convince themselves they were the baddest motherfuckers in the valley, but the wisened warriors walked on the edge of a harder reality: You are the man, until you meet the man.

"Rudy's right, gents," Mitch said with a sigh. "So's Morrow. Appropriate caution is the name of the game."

They drove on quietly for a bit. A splash of sun managed to pierce the cloud cover, and was immediately covered again.

"So," Logan began again, more circumspectly. "Y'all don't think we can take that prison?"

"I didn't say that," Mitch replied. "Fact is, I think we should. It'd be a nice defensible location for us to stage out of. Yes, I think it would be dangerous. But everything we do out here is dangerous. And I don't think they can match us. I think we could take that place over."

"Why didn't you say that to Lee?"

Mitch turned in his seat and looked Logan in the eye. "Because I've learned to—"

"Shit!" Rudy grunted and slammed on the brakes.

Mitch hit the dashboard hard.

Tires screeched.

Rudy yelled, "Contact! Contact!"

Mitch twisted, looked out the windshield.

Saw three figures in the road.

Three figures...on their knees.

Twenty yards behind them, a brown Suburban.

—

The second that their truck stopped, Paolo was out and running. He'd blurted, "That's Braxton!" and then threw his door open before Lee could reach in the back and restrain him.

Lee had no time to assess.

He'd seen the three figures, and he'd seen that they were on their knees.

But he'd also seen the brown Suburban further past them.

First instinct: *Get the fuck out!*

Second: *Cover Paolo!*

"Fuck!" Lee shouted at Abe, slapping the dash. "Go forward! Go forward! Get between the Suburban and them!"

Abe cranked the wheel hard to get around Mitch's truck, then rammed the accelerator, throwing them all back in their seats. The door that Paolo had left open slammed closed as the truck hurtled forward.

Lee shouldered his rifle and got his hand on his door latch. "As soon as we stop put fire on that fucking Suburban!"

The yardage between them and the string of three people evaporated.

Abe swung them wide around the left side of the three figures in the road, then brought them to a skidding halt.

Lee was focused on the Suburban, but he glimpsed the big coil of rope sitting in the middle of the road, a short distance ahead of them, and as he threw his door open and unassed the vehicle, his mind seized on it, not quite able to connect the dots.

He swung around the door and hit the front of the truck, using the engine block as cover, and bringing his rifle up over the top of it.

The rope

The brake lights on the Suburban winked out. A gout of gray exhaust plumed out of the tailpipe. The chirp of tires on concrete.

The rope

The rope.

One big coil.

A strand that went to the tow hitch on the Suburban.

Three more strands coming out of that big coil.

"Oh fuck," Lee murmured.

Someone started shooting.

Lee watched the back glass of the Suburban disintegrate as it sped away from them, rope unspooling rapidly out of the coil in the middle of the road.

Lee looked to his right, to the three figures in the road.

The three strands of rope.

Each ending in a knot tied around a neck.

In that microsecond, Lee made the connection, and acted all at once.

He dropped his rifle. Let his sling catch it. Snatched out his knife. Dove for the first strand of rope that was closest to him.

He got his hand on it. Gripped it hard. Put the knife to it.

It was Braxton. The younger guy turned on his knees, his eyes wide and terrified. The rope was tied around his neck. He blurted, "I'm sorry!"

"Don't—"

The slack in the rope ran out.

Lee's whole body jolted like he'd touched a live power line. The rope ripped out of his hands, went taut against his left leg, sent him flying. His whole body lifted up, his legs pulled out from under him.

But his eyes somehow stayed locked with Braxton's.

In midair, Lee watched the man's head separate from his shoulder.

Then Lee hit the concrete.

Braxton's head went spinning past him.

The three bodies in the road fell backwards.

Lee found himself on his stomach, staring up at the stump of a neck that spewed hot blood at him. Speckled his face. His whole body hummed from the shock of the rope hitting him. He tried to breathe and couldn't, his lungs and diaphragm locked up.

The three bodies didn't move.

Not a twitch. Not a stir.

Paolo hit the concrete on his knees, right in front of the middle body, too late to do anything. His hands flew up to his head, clawed the dirty hat from his scalp. His eyes wild and unmoored.

"Jesus Christ!" he screamed. "Oh Christ! Oh fuck!"

Lee pushed himself up off the ground as the rapidly-spreading pool of blood reached his fingertips. It touched. Wet and warm. He pulled them away.

He felt hands on him, pulling him upright, all the way up to his feet.

"You okay?" Julia asked him. "You with me?"

"'D'you get 'em?" Lee slurred. Coughed. Finally managed an intake of breath.

It was Abe who answered, limping around the front of the truck. "We got the Suburban. I don't know if we got the fuckers inside."

Paolo was still screaming.

Mitch and his team were running up.

Lee swayed on his feet, then roughly separated himself from Julia. He pawed his way around the front of his truck, the hood hot on his hands. He swung around the driver's door. Clambered into the driver's seat.

His lungs felt raw. Wet. He coughed. Wheezed. Didn't bother shutting his door. Pulled the truck into drive.

At the last second before he hit the gas pedal, Abe and Julia vaulted back into the car. Carl had never even exited the back seat.

The truck went forward. All the doors swung closed on their own.

The truck roared down the road and no one asked where they were going. They faced forward, one hand on the grip of their rifles, one hand on their door latches. Faces drawn. Eyes dark.

Lee's vision seemed overbright.

Did I hit my head?

It didn't hurt like he'd taken a blow, but he felt a hot-cold prickle on his scalp...

They blasted through a bend in the road.

Up ahead, about a quarter mile, the Suburban had gone off the road and crumpled itself against a tree.

Lee didn't let up on the accelerator.

The driver's door on the Suburban came open.

A man tumbled out. Saw them coming. Saw them chewing up the distance between them. Tried to run a few steps, then stopped, raised something in one hand.

It bloomed fire.

A bullet crashed through the windshield.

Lee went low behind the engine block.

He heard bullets hitting the front of the truck.

Glass trickled down on him.

He peeked up over the dash.

Saw the man's face, dead ahead.

Lee slammed on the brakes.

A hard *THUMP* reverberated through the truck.

They lurched to a stop.

Lee rammed the shifter into park.

The doors were opening.

Lee spilled out, his vision struggling to catch up with his movements. He couldn't seem to catch his breath.

The man from the Suburban had been punched in the chest with a two-ton fist. It had launched him ten yards down the road. He lay on his back, legs twisted underneath him, hands wavering insensibly in the air.

Lee staggered towards the form in the road. His breath rattled wetly. He tasted pennies.

Beyond the veil of physical pain, Lee felt a dark burning seething up inside of him. It seemed to pull him along, like a force that possessed his body, and Lee didn't fight it, he didn't *want* to fight it. All he wanted was to destroy.

The man on the ground watched Lee approach. His empty hands trembling.

"No!" the man struggled to say, kept showing his palms to Lee.

Surrendering.

Lee stood over him.

The man stared up.

Pathetic eyes, gone from killer to prey.

How quickly they go from merciless, to begging for mercy.

It only made Lee hate him more.

"Please, don't—" the man stammered.

Lee put three rounds into the man's head, shattering it against the concrete.

One of the hands fell. The other remained up, by some sparking of nerves, the fingers convulsing in the air, like they might find something to hold onto.

Then that hand fell, too.

Lee looked at what he'd done and felt nothing inside of him but a bitter and bracing satisfaction.

All rivers lead to it eventually.

Behind him, he heard Abe call out: "Got a live one!"

Darkness danced at the edges of his vision.

Something's wrong.

He tried to take a breath. Coughed more.

He turned. Looked back.

A short distance from him, their pickup truck. Beside it, the Suburban, with the passenger's side rammed against a wall of trees. Abe bodily hauling someone out through the driver's door, then slinging them onto the ground.

"Don't fucking move!" Abe screamed, punching the man in the face with the muzzle of his rifle, then kicking him over onto his belly and planting a knee in his back.

Lee started walking.

His feet felt like rubber blocks.

Julia stood there, covering the man that Abe had, but she looked up at Lee. Made eye contact with him. Her gaze was blank.

Irradiated. Uninhabitable.

Lee didn't realize his feet were scuffing the ground until he stumbled.

Julia's eyes narrowed. "Lee?"

Lee nodded at her, willed his feet to move properly. If he could just get a goddamned breath…

More coughing. He spat into his hand.

Bright, almost neon-red, across his palm.

Well, shit, he thought, and then collapsed.

—

Reality and unconsciousness swirled. Mixed. Intertwined.

Lee wasn't sure what was real and what was imagined.

He was looking at concrete. Black top. A layer of two years' worth of dirt accumulated there. It hurt to breathe. Julia was running towards him.

And then Julia was a tree.

The concrete and dirt turned to lush, green fields.

He was walking towards the tree again, the tree on the hilltop.

He was closer this time. He could definitely see someone there.

There was a swing hanging from one of the big branches.

The figure was on the swing…

And then he was in the truck again. Julia's face in front of his, slapping him.

"Wake up, Lee!"

I'm awake, don't slap me.

He thought he'd said it, but then realized he must not have, because she slapped him again.

"Fuck," he murmured.

"There you go," she said.

Lee became conscious of the engine. They were moving. Abe was driving. Lee and Julia were sprawled across the backseat. Deuce was on the floorboard, whining.

"Where's Carl?" Lee managed.

"He's in the bed with the guy," Julia said. "Can you lift your arms?"

She was trying to get his rig off of him.

Lee tried to sit up. Pain lanced through his chest. He lifted his arms and she ripped the Velcro straps keeping his plate carrier to his body, then pulled them quickly up and over his head. The rough canvas scraped against his ears.

Lee managed to catch a glimpse out the back glass and saw Carl sitting in the back, rifle trained on something that Lee couldn't see, something laying in the bed of the truck.

The guy.

The live one.

Lee felt the truck decelerate. Come to a stop.

The back passenger door behind Julia came open and Mitch thrust his head in. "What the fuck happened?"

"I don't know," Julia said. Her fingers went under Lee's shirt and lifted it up on his left side, looking at his stitched up wound.

"Was he shot?"

"I don't think so."

"I wasn't shot," Lee said. He grabbed the headrest on the front seat and used it to pull himself upright. "Help me sit up. I'm fine."

Julia helped him, but then put a hand on his shoulder and looked him in the eye. "Lee, you're not fucking *fine*. You were coughing blood and you passed out. That's not *fine*. Quit saying that you're *fine*."

"It just jarred me," Lee said. "The rope."

The image came back to him.

The rope going taut.

The heads coming off.

God...

Lee saw past Julia and Mitch. Saw the roadway beyond. The headless shoulders of one of the bodies, but he saw the spray of blood from each, darkening on the pavement.

"Where's Paolo?" Lee asked.

Mitch jerked a thumb over his shoulder. "He's in our truck. He was losing his goddamn mind."

Shouting from outside.

Mitch craned his neck and swore. "Well, he *was* in the truck." He shoved off the side of the truck and held up a hand. "Paolo, chill out, brother!"

Paolo's voice: "Is that the motherfucker that did this? Is that him? Is that him in the truck bed?"

Lee tried to move for the open door, but Julia held onto his shoulder.

He met her gaze. "Julia, let me talk to him."

"You can't do everything yourself, Lee."

But she took her hand off his shoulder.

Lee pushed himself out of the door. His feet hit concrete and he suddenly realized that Julia was right, he should have kept himself in the car. Coming upright took all the blood out of his head again, and his legs were watery like Jell-O left out in the sun.

He grabbed the side of the truck bed and barely kept himself from falling.

The south wind tugged at his pants legs, like it wanted to trip him.

Outside was calamity.

Bodies in the roadway. Blood spewed. Mitch raising his hands to try to get Paolo to back away from the truck bed, while Mitch's team quietly started to surround Paolo, sensing that things might go bad.

Paolo stood at the tailgate, looking up at Carl. His face was flushed red, his eyes wild. "You give me that motherfucker! You give him to me right now!"

Carl remained calm. "Not yet, Paolo."

Mitch, still pumping his palms at the man. "Easy, Paolo! Same team here, Buddy!"

Paolo drew his pistol from its holster, held it down at his side.

As one, the circle of Mitch's team tightened up.

Mitch slapped the side of the bed to get Paolo's attention. "Whoa! What the fuck is that? Put that shit away, Paolo!"

"Imunna fuckin' killim!"

Carl was trading his gaze between the man he was covering with his rifle, and Paolo. He didn't speak. Just shook his head.

Lee pulled himself along the truck bed and shouldered Mitch out of the way. He had to fight to take a big breath, but managed to belt out, "PAOLO!"

The man's blue eyes jagged to Lee, and they were about to go back to the target of his hatred, but something in Lee's face stopped him. For a second, Lee thought that maybe he just looked that pissed. But as Paolo stared at Lee and his expression of rage was edged out by something like shock, Lee realized that it was because of how bad he himself looked.

Based on the cold sheen of sweat he felt across his entire face, Lee guessed that his skin was dead pale. Hanging off the side of the truck like he couldn't support his own weight, lips probably still tainted red from coughing blood.

"Christ," Paolo mumbled. "What happened to you?"

Lee shook his head. "Don't worry about me. Worry about yourself, and don't do anything stupid."

Paolo twitched. He looked over his shoulder and realized for the first time that Mitch's team had edged very close to him. Close enough that all they had to do was reach out and touch him.

Lee hitched himself down to the tailgate so he was standing next to Paolo. "Look at me."

Paolo looked at him.

Lee raised his hand and motioned with his fingers, a gesture that said, *come closer so we can confide in each other.*

Paolo leaned close.

Lee spoke quietly. "You'll have your chance. But not before I bleed that motherfucker for everything he knows."

"I heard that!" the man in the truck bed suddenly wailed. "I heard that, and I'm not giving you *shit*!"

Carl raised his boot, put it to the side of the man's face, and mushed it into the truck bed until the man mewled in pain. Carl ground his heel to make his point. Then he leaned down, and a rare flash of intensity came over his features, causing his lips to curl in a savage sneer. "Quiet now, meatsack."

Meatsack obeyed, save for a whimper.

Paolo dragged his gaze back to Lee. Held eye contact for a moment longer, his jaw working like a dog that wants to bite. Then a fresh round of panic hit his features. "What about my people? What about—"

Lee cut him off with a sharp wave of his hand. "We're gonna find out about the rest of your people. And a whole lot more. But we can't go back to your hideout right now."

"But—"

"It's too dangerous. Could be a trap, and you know it." Lee took a hold of Paolo's arm, because he felt the need to make physical contact with the man, like he might serve as a lightning rod to ground him. "Give me tonight, Paolo. Just give me tonight."

A spattering of fat raindrops tumbled out of the sky, and started audibly smacking the concrete, the truck, and the people around it.

Paolo's face seemed to tremble. "But where are we gonna go?"

Lee had already considered that. "Back to Hurtsboro."

TWENTY-FOUR

TIMES CHANGE

THEY STRUNG THE MAN UP from the exposed rafters in the basement where Julia, Abe, and Lee had hidden for three days. The detritus of MRE wrappers were still piled in the corner. The pullout couch still tousled.

No one had spoken to the man yet.

He had tried to cry out several times, but every time he did Carl slammed him in the face with the buttstock of his rifle. After four iterations of that—split lips, a few lost teeth, and a broken nose—the man had finally gotten the picture and remained silent.

Lee was upstairs, sitting shirtless at a small kitchen table.

Julia sat beside him, correcting a few busted stitches in his chest wound.

The entire house was dim. The day outside had darkened even further into a violent twilight. Wind rushed at the house, and the walls creaked threateningly. Rain washed heavily over the windows in pale waves. Sometimes they heard the sharp *tick-tack-tick* of hail.

Lee looked down at Julia's hands. "Nothing serious then?"

Julia pulled away from his side, inspected her work, then propped one elbow on the table and looked at him. "It's all serious, Lee. You've been pushing too hard. You need rest, or this shit's not going to heal."

Lee felt the truth of that deep in his bones, as if his marrow was somehow aching. He thought that if he was back in his house in the Fort Bragg Safe Zone, he might collapse into his bed and sleep for days on end.

Deuce seemed to share his exhaustion. The high-strung dog apparently had burned himself out over the last few days. He was ten feet from Lee, just inside the living room, where the floor was carpeted. He'd walked away from Lee, found the soft carpet, and then simply laid down on his side and was now asleep.

Lee reached out and put his hand on Julia's. Looked at the dark ghost of blood that sat in the grooves and wrinkles of his hand. Saw the same thing under her nails.

"Thank you," he said. "I know it's not easy to do what you do. But I appreciate you..." he cracked a smile. "Managing me."

She lifted her thumb, brought it down so that it grasped his palm. "Well. Someone has to *manage* your ass. Obviously, you won't do it."

"You know I can't stop," he said. Thought of how he could clarify that, and decided to leave it as it was. A simple statement of fact.

Julia searched his face. Didn't find whatever she was looking for. She looked off into the kitchen. Not at anything in particular. Just staring.

Lee watched her. She was, at once, haggard and beautiful. She was an attractive woman, but no one looks their best after being in the field for a week. Still, there was something about how hard she pushed herself that made her beautiful to him.

Was that strange of him to think so?

No.

She was a kindred spirit.

"We were carrying you when we lost Nate," she said, her voice distant. "Me and Abe. We each had an arm. We were dragging you across a road. It was dark. You were practically dead. We'd been giving you CPR while we waited for the blood and air to drain out of your chest so your lung could re-inflate. I was only thinking about you. You and your chest. You and your wound. I couldn't imagine anything else. I thought you were going to die, and I thought that I had to apply every bit of myself to saving you, or…or…I dunno. Or I'd just evaporate. Like if you died there wouldn't be enough of me left over to be a real person."

Her eyes drifted. Crashed into Lee's. Veered away again. "Then, Nate was holding cover on the road, and we were carrying you, trying to get to cover, and the next thing I know, a round just catches him. Just…right in the head. Like that." She snapped her fingers. "That was it. That's all it took. A microsecond. And then he was gone. I was trying to keep you alive, and I lost someone else. And then I had to leave him there. Because…because fucking *triage*, Lee. Do you understand?"

Lee nodded, stiffly.

"Because you were still alive, just barely, but still alive, and the rules of triage say I leave him there and get you to safety. So I did. And I'd do it again. I loved Nate like a brother, but I'd do it again, because those are the rules. Because you have to triage."

"If you'd have gone back, they would have shot you, too," Lee said.

Julia waved him off. "It's not about that, Lee. That's not the point. The point is, I was trying to keep you alive, and I lost Nate. And then, you wake up, and I can't tell you how relieved I am that you're awake. And I take the chest tube out, and I think, *everything is gonna be okay, Lee's in the clear now*, and then I lose Tomlin."

Julia held out her hands, palms up, and her eyes spilled over as she stared at their emptiness. Then she clenched them and rapped them on the table top. "It's like fucking Whack-A-Mole, goddammit. The second I keep one of you alive, someone else goes down, and I don't know what the fuck to do, I don't know who to watch, I feel like everyone's on the ragged edge of dying and if I so much as fucking blink, or look away for an instant, I'm going to lose someone else!"

Lee wished that he had something to say. Something wise. Something poignant. Something that would salve the way that Julia felt. But it all sounded so broken and worthless in his own head that he didn't dare say it.

It seemed that anything that had ever been worth saying about loss had already been said at some other time, when someone else had been lost. And now it was all stale platitudes. There was no wisdom in death. There were no words that could make someone feel better.

Sometimes it was simply best to keep your mouth shut.

Lee looked at her hands on the tabletop, and he nodded, feeling his own emotions clench down hard around that little stone of grief inside of him.

That was all he could give her. He could only commiserate.

Julia sniffed. Made a noise as though disgusted with herself, and then swiped the tears out of her eyes like they'd rebelled against her, and then wiped her nose with the back of her wrist. She leaned forward, across the table, put her hand on the back of Lee's neck. Kissed his temple. Her breath and lips were warm against his skin. "We need you, Lee. We need you alive."

Lee said nothing in response.

Julia sat back in her chair again. Turned to look down the stairs that led to the basement.

She was silent. Thinking about something.

Her lips parted. Jaw worked. Her teeth shown for just a flash.

"Let me do it," she said, her voice as still and as dangerous as the surface of quicksand.

He wanted to ask her what she meant, but he knew.

It made him think of the road. Of killing that man, with his empty hands upheld for mercy. It made him think of the Julia he'd known at the beginning. The Julia who had trouble reconciling the slaughter of the infected, because she still viewed them as people. Crazy people, but people nonetheless.

Times change.

People have to change with it.

"Two years ago," Lee spoke like you might walk across broken glass. "You would've tried to stop me from killing that man today."

She eyed him. "Two years ago, I would've thought that I *could* stop you."

This is who you are. This is what you do.

"He deserved what he got." She jerked her head towards the basement. "So does this guy."

Lee didn't want her to go downstairs. And he questioned himself. He questioned why that was, and he knew that it wasn't because he thought Julia was not capable. It was because...

Because he wanted to protect her.

Her change made him sad, he realized.

On the one hand, there was something familiar and good about being of one mind about things. On the other hand, Lee wanted her to be better than him.

Has that ship sailed? He wondered.

Are any of us "better"?

Are any of us "good" anymore?

He didn't have an answer for himself.

"Fine," he said. He reached forward, took his shirt, slid it painfully back over his body. Then stood up. "Let's go."

—

Rudy, Morrow, Logan, and Blake had braved the squalling storm to kick out a few blocks and create a perimeter.

Abe and Mitch were upstairs in the bedrooms, providing overwatch on the streets, though the gales of rain severely lessened their visibility. But they were also keeping Paolo upstairs, and keeping an eye on him.

It was just Carl and Julia and Lee down in the basement.

And the man tied to the rafters.

Carl posted up on the door to the outside.

Lee sat in one of the wooden dining room chairs they'd brought down. About five paces from their prisoner.

Julia poked around in the corner of the basement, as though she'd previously seen something over there and was trying to find it. She came up with an aluminum softball bat.

The man watched her with a cocked eyebrow. "Sent a woman to do a man's work," he grunted.

Julia smiled. Tested her swing in the air. The bat made a humming noise as she warmed up like a batter who was next at the plate.

Lee sat erect with his hands on his knees. Slouching hurt his side. "What can I call you? I mean, besides 'Meatsack.'"

The man pulled his eyes off of Julia and looked at Lee. He hocked and spit, but the globule didn't reach Lee's feet. "You can call me Fuck You. That's what you can call me."

Lee remained placid. "Is that first name Fuck, last name You? Or Fuck You is your first name? Like Fuck You Johnson?"

"You think this shit scares me?" the man snapped. But there was a tremor in his voice. "You can't scare me. Y'all are fuckin' amateurs compared to what I've seen. You have any fuckin' idea who I work for?"

Lee shrugged. Looked at the ceiling, thoughtfully. "You remember those Tootsie-Pop commercials? How many licks to the center of a Tootsie-Pop?"

The man stared, not sure what to say, and choosing to say nothing.

"How many hits to the center of your spleen?" Lee asked. He looked quizzically at Julia. "You're the resident medical professional. How many hits until his spleen ruptures?"

"Four?" Julia suggested. "Maybe five?"

The man chuffed. "In your dreams, Sweetheart."

The sound of the bat hitting his midsection was at once a slap, a thump, and a bone-deep crunch.

The man's eyes went wide, his mouth open, his shocked diaphragm only able to issue a ghostly *gruuu-ungh!* out of the hole of his mouth.

A long, angry, red mark quickly appeared on his left side.

Julia's aim was impeccable.

"That's one," Lee noted. "Jules, what's the spleen used for?"

Julia adjusted her grip on the bat. "Fights infection. Filters your blood."

"Filters your blood," Lee repeated. "That sounds important. Will you die without treatment?"

"It's considered life-threatening," she said. "Internal bleeding."

"How long?" Lee asked. "Until he dies, that is."

Julia gave a facial shrug. "I dunno. Everybody's different. Days. Maybe a week."

"Fuck You," Lee addressed him formally. "You killed three friends of ours on the road with your little rope trick. What did you guys do to the rest of them?"

The man finally started breathing again, but it was obvious that it caused him pain. Having his arms up above his head didn't help. The body's natural instinct is to curl around an injury, to try to protect it. He couldn't do that. His injury was exposed for more abuse.

"We fuckin' killed 'em," the man gasped, but he put some venom into his words, and managed to raise defiant eyes to Lee. "Slaughtered them all. Stacked their bodies inside the chicken house for the infected. It'll be a nice little buffet for them—"

FWUMP

"Gaah!" A cough. A breathy swear.

Lee let him get his air back again.

"I gave you an answer," the man slavered. "Don't fucking hit me!"

Julia lifted the bat and used the tip to poke the red welts on the man's side. "I thought you were too tough for me, *Sweetheart*."

"Next time less editorializing," Lee advised the man.

In his own thoughts, his mind turned over what he'd been told. *That's bad news for Paolo. That's bad news for all of us. But he already knew it, didn't he? Of course he did. We all fucking knew it.*

"Hit him again," Lee said.

The man's eyes widened. "Wait—"

Julia swung for the fences.

FWUMP

No sound from Fuck You this time. After a few moments, a gagging noise.

Lee leaned forward in his chair. He held up three fingers. "That's three, Fuck You. You got one, maybe two more."

In all honesty, Lee thought Julia had probably already ruptured the spleen.

"You didn't even…ask me anything!" the man groaned.

"I want a pumping station," Lee said. "I want a place with a lot of diesel fuel where I can fill up several big-ass tankers. Tell me about a place like that."

A stream of drool was coming out of the man's mouth. He was looking up at Lee from under his brow. "You're gonna kill me anyways," he mumbled.

Lee chose not to address that concern just yet. He nodded to Julia.

She made another home run swing.

The man's side was beginning to look like hamburger. The raw, purple skin had broken and was issuing thin trickles of dark blood. The ribs were definitely broken. The spleen probably pulverized.

The man was crying now.

Lee couldn't blame him. He'd actually held out for longer than Lee had expected.

"Fuel dump," Lee said, reminding him, refocusing him. "I want specifics. Location. Guards. That sort of thing."

"You already ruptured it," he moaned. "I can feel it. You busted my insides."

"Yeah, maybe she did. But hey. Listen." Lee held his palms up like two sides of a scale being balanced. "You got two options here. And you're right, they both result in you being dead. But one is clearly better, and I think you'll agree. Option Number One: You tell me about the fuel dump, and then the crazy guy that wants to kill you can come down here and put a bullet in your head. It'll be quick. I'll make sure he doesn't fuck with you."

The man spat. His saliva was bloody. His voice was barely a whisper. "And what's Number Two?"

"Number Two is, we leave you where you are, tied to the ceiling rafters like a side of beef. We open all the doors. Your sweet stench wafts out there into the world. The primals come sniffing around. And they eat you. Whenever it is that they find you. Which, in my experience, will probably be pretty quick, but who knows, right? So, the mystery with Option Number Two is this: Are you going to die of internal bleeding after hanging there in agony for three or four days? Or will the primals find you quick enough to eat you while you're still alive?"

—

Lee and Julia were back in the kitchen.

Lee watched Julia carefully. She had her arms crossed over her chest. Contemplating her feet with a frown.

She realized she was being watched and looked up. "What?"

Lee's mouth made a grim line. He shook his head. "I shouldn't have made you do that,"

"You didn't *make* me do anything."

Abe, Mitch and Paolo trundled down the stairs, looking expectantly at Lee.

Lee found Paolo and motioned with his head towards the basement. "Make it quick. That was the deal."

Paolo snarled. "He doesn't deserve quick."

Lee didn't budge. "Make it quick."

Paolo stared at him for a long moment, rage flushing his face, tears shimmering at the bottom of his eyes. Then he nodded once, and went down the basement steps. His footfalls were slow and heavy.

Lee gestured Abe towards the table. "You got the maps?"

"Yeah." Abe stepped to the table and opened the map pouch on his vest, behind his magazines. He brought out a tumble of folded papers, limp from his sweat. "What do we need?"

"Alabama," Lee answered. "The southern portion, if you got it."

Abe fished around through the pile of maps, came up with one. Swept the others to the side of the table and laid that one flat. "Okay. Southern Alabama. What am I looking for?"

"City's called Andalusia," Lee answered, peering over Abe's shoulder. "Should be east of it. Looking for a regional airport."

"Hm," Abe nodded, his finger tracing over the map. "Everyone loves airports these days."

"Good fences," Lee said.

"Here's Andalusia," Abe tapped his finger. Traced eastward. Found the tiny airplane icon. "Must be this right here."

Lee nodded. Felt a measure of relief. "Well, he wasn't lying about it. So that's good."

A gunshot rocked the house.

Everyone twitched at the sound of it, but otherwise didn't react.

Abe glanced at Lee, then back at the map. "Good thing we confirmed that before he died."

Lee shrugged. "There's no confirming anything until we're there. Could still be a trap."

Mitch hunched himself over the map with them. "What's the significance of the airport?"

"Airport is where the fuel is. Some diesel, some regular automotive." Lee straightened up. "Pumping station is out, for now. Guy said there's no working pumping stations until you get down into Louisiana. I don't want to push us that far. However, this airport right here is where they cache tanker trucks. The trucks get filled up, then they get stationed here, then they get dispatched to whatever settlement needs them. According to the guy."

"How heavily guarded?" Abe asked.

"Pretty heavy."

Julia spoke up from beside Lee. "He estimated between ten and twenty guards. Said he'd only been there once. Hadn't really paid attention."

Abe looked at Julia. "You believe him?"

She shrugged. "If he was trying to lead us into a trap, I'd assume he'd try to make it sound like an *easy* target. I think he was telling the truth."

Abe crossed his arms. Rested them on top of his magazines. "Next question: Do we wait for the Marines or try to roll on our own?"

Lee made a pained face. "The ten of us to assault a possible twenty, in a fortified location?"

Abe let out a heavy breath through his nose. "We wait for the Marines, that still only evens the odds. Nowhere near what we need. According to the book."

"There are other intangibles that can make up the difference. Good intel. Surprise. Speed. Better weapons. Better training."

"Better weapons—maybe," Abe pointed out. "Better training—we hope. A lot of these fuckers in these cartels are ex-military. Depends on who they decided to staff their fuel cache with. A bunch of locals pressed into service? Or a bunch of hard-charging true believers?"

Mitch cleared his throat. "Lee, there's something else we need to think about."

Lee looked at him.

Mitch went into the side pocket of his pants. Came out with a folded piece of paper. He unfolded it, then passed it to Lee. "This was pinned to one of the bodies out on the road."

Lee took the paper.

Handwritten. Big block letters in black magic marker.

BUTLER GEORGIA

Lee stared at the letters for a while. Until they started to burn a pattern into his eyes. When he blinked, he saw their negative image hovering there in the momentary blackness. He laid the paper down on the table, to the right of their map.

Julia grabbed it by one of the corners, as though she were about to read it, but she already had, and she whipped it away from her. "The fuck's that supposed to mean? Is that a threat? Like 'turn back or else'? And how the fuck do they know about Butler?"

The paper had drifted to Mitch's side of the table after Julia's toss. He picked it up. Folded it again. "You read what I read."

Abe swore. "If we move on that fuel dump, we leave Butler exposed."

Lee held up a hand. "Let's not jump to conclusions. All we got is a scrap of paper with the name of a place on it. That doesn't mean shit."

Abe frowned. "It means they know about it. And why the hell would they tell us that if it wasn't a threat?"

Lee shook his head. "Abe, it won't be the first time we've had to make a gamble."

Abe didn't like it. "Shit, I understand where you're coming from Lee. I do. I just don't…I don't feel good about it."

Lee faced him, irritated. "You don't feel *good*? Well, fuck, Abe, I don't feel good either. I don't feel good about any of this shit. But we do what we have to do."

"This is how Lucas died."

Lee's hands clenched reflexively. He felt a wash of heat descend on his head. "How long have you been wanting to get that off your chest?"

Abe's lips pulled back like he had a biting remark, but then he seemed to snap it off with his teeth. "Lee, I've been with you every step of the way. I never fucking brought it up. Shit happens. But you can't make these gambles with peoples' lives."

"It's always a fucking gamble," Lee said through his teeth. "Every time we leave the fucking Safe Zone, it's a goddamned gamble."

Mitch had edged his way around the table and now interjected himself between them. "Alright. Both of you shut the fuck up. This isn't helping."

Before either Abe or Lee could retort, Julia spoke quickly. "We hit the fuel dump."

Three sets of eyes looked at her.

She nodded. "We wait for the Marines, then we hit the fuel dump. If we do it quick—like in the next day—then they'll react to that, and they won't go after Butler."

The basement stairs creaked.

Lee looked back, saw Carl standing at the top step, looking in at them.

"Everything okay up here?" he asked.

There was the slightest pause from the four of them.

Lee waved Carl off. "Yeah. It's good. Just...passionately exchanging viewpoints."

Another gunshot rocked the house, coming from the basement.

Carl spun around in the stairwell, jerking his rifle up. "The fuck...Paolo! You okay?"

There came no answer from the basement, and then all five of them were tumbling down the stairs in a rush of feet...

At the bottom, they stopped.

But they didn't move closer.

They just sort of huddled together at the base of the stairs.

The man that they'd interrogated still hung from the rafters, his body slowly twisting on its axis, a hole in his forehead, the back of his head still dripping.

On the pull-out couch, Paolo lay, in an almost peaceful repose. His silver pistol was still in his right hand. Gunsmoke seeped out of his mouth and nostrils. The wall behind him was speckled with blood and bone and brain.

It was like they were all waiting for someone to come up with something intelligent to do, but for the life of them, they couldn't figure out what that was.

"Motherfucker," Carl finally muttered. "I left him for two goddamned seconds."

"Why the fuck did he kill himself?" Julia wondered aloud, her tone only mildly curious. Almost academic.

"He found out about his people," Lee answered her.

After another long moment of silence, Carl reiterated, "I left him for two goddamned seconds."

The moment felt strange. Removed from reality.

Maybe they were all waiting for it to punch them as hard as they thought that it should.

But it just didn't.

After the violent deaths of people that they loved, the suicide of this relative stranger seemed like a distant tragedy. Something you hear about through the rumor mill.

Yesterday there had been an entire group of people. And Paolo had been their leader. And now they were just…gone.

But it didn't rise up in any of them.

They had already paid out their own grief, and gone bankrupt.

They could not afford to grieve for the loss of strangers.

They didn't have anything to say.

They didn't have anything to feel.

At the most, perhaps they felt bad for not feeling much.

Slowly, gradually, their eyes fell away from Paolo, and wandered over into the corners of the room, and then to each other.

Abe met Lee's eyes, and he dipped his head. "Sorry."

Lee wasn't sure if he was sorry for Paolo, or sorry for bringing up Lucas. He supposed it didn't matter which. He gave Abe a single nod. Water under the bridge.

Grudges were hard to hold onto when you lived in the shadow of death.

Julia shuffled her feet. Cleared her throat. "The little airfield where they held Carl and Brian. It's only a few miles from us now. I think we should try to secure it. Meet the Marines there."

Lee nodded slowly. Turned away from the scene in the basement. "Let's get our shit together. Get out of here."

TWENTY-FIVE

BREACH

I<small>T FOLLOWED THE SCENT TRAILS.</small>

It followed the beaten leaves.

The way was clear and required no thought. The Alpha could follow the path easily at a strong trot, and its sharp ears heard the movements of its pack mates following it.

The scent was the smell of the Easy Prey.

The Alpha knew that there were many trails through these woods, through all the land that it hunted, and all of those trails were from prey, because everything was prey.

But The Alpha also knew that some prey were hard and some prey were easy.

Some prey had teeth and claws. Some prey had horns on their heads that could gouge and gore. Some prey ran very fast.

This prey was none of those things.

This prey was slow, soft, clawless, fangless.

Easy Prey.

The Alpha gained speed as it followed the trail, faster and faster until it was loping through soft pine forest.

The trail ended in water. Water that trickled from a cave that was not a cave. A big, perfectly round cave. Something that the Easy Prey had made. The Alpha knew this, vestigially.

The Easy Prey's only defense was that they were clever.

But The Alpha and its pack mates were also clever.

It bent down to the murky water. Smelled it. Determined it was good enough to drink, and then refreshed itself. Then it sat on its haunches and looked at the cave, while the pack gathered around, chuffing softly to themselves, scenting the air.

The cave was where the scent of the Easy Prey was coming from. Strong.

The Alpha sidled up to the cave. Tilted its head to look at it from different angles. Deciphering it.

The mouth of the cave was covered. With sticks that were not sticks. Sticks that could not be broken. These sticks were cold to the touch. Not like sticks in the woods. It was familiar with these sticks. These sticks were also something that the Easy Prey had made with their cleverness. Like the long, thin strands that hummed menacingly and would kill you if you touched them.

The sticks that covered the mouth of the cave didn't hum. But still, experience told The Alpha to be cautious, so it reached out and batted at them to test them.

The sticks weren't dangerous.

It wrapped its long fingers around the sticks and tugged at them.

The sticks rattled. It didn't know what made them rattle, but it knew that if they rattled like that, then they could be defeated somehow. It chuffed to itself, then louder, to its pack mates. Turned in a short circle of frustration, and then came back to the mouth of the cave. Grabbed the sticks. Shook them again, but this time much harder.

And this time something else rattled.

The Alpha looked at the thing that had rattled. It was a small thing. Kind of a circle, but not quite a circle.

Intrigued, The Alpha pulled on the sticks again. The small, circle-thing caught. Kept the sticks from pulling away. Just that one, small, circle-thing. That was all that held the sticks in place.

One of its pack mates squeezed in, shoulder-to-shoulder, reached out and hooked a finger around the circle-thing. It tugged violently at it, but the circle-thing wouldn't budge. The pack mate retreated, mumbling disconsolately to itself.

The Alpha was more patient than its pack mate. Experience had taught it that it could go most places where the Easy Prey went. It just took time to figure out their clever tricks.

It played with the circle-thing for a time. Tugged it. Rattled it. Pushed it.

Finally, it *squeezed* the circle-thing.

The circle-thing broke.

Except it didn't really break. Not like a stick would break. Because when The Alpha released its grip, the circle-thing made itself whole again.

It grunted loudly at this discovery. Its half-human brain logged it in with the rest of its experiences. Learning. Adapting.

It squeezed the circle-thing again and again, repeatedly breaking it and making it whole.

If it could break the circle-thing, then it could *remove* the circle-thing.

The Alpha eyed the thing for a few beats of its rapid heart. Leaned forward and smelled it. Then leaned back again. Grasped it one last time. Squeeze. Break. And then *lift*.

The circle-thing came away.

The Alpha tossed it to the side, then pulled at the sticks again.

This time, the sticks came away from the mouth of the cave. They creaked with a familiar sound. A sound that meant *the way is open, the path is clear*.

The cave stood open before it.

The Alpha chuffed softly at its pack mates who had gathered excitedly behind it, and then they went in.

—

Sam met Charlie at the same spot in the woods as they'd met before.

It was earlier this time because Sam had overnight guard shift. The sun was just setting below the tree line and casting the woods in a dull blue, but he appreciated the light. The woods weren't as worrisome when it wasn't full dark.

Part of him was disappointed that he wasn't going to make it to…well, whatever it was that they called it when they met in the house beyond the Safe Zone.

A party? Not quite.

A hangout?

But he was also relieved that he wouldn't have to be outside at night.

Why did they even meet out there? Charlie had said that they did it so they could hangout without rules, but Sam had gotten the distinct sense when he was there that there was more to it. The sense that those who regularly hung out there were holding back because he was present.

Charlie was waiting for him out in the open this time.

She smiled when he got there, but it was constrained.

"Hey, Charlie," he said, and reached for a hug.

She accepted the hug and gave him a quick pat on the back.

He was hoping for a bit more than that and pulled back with a small frown that he quickly hid from her.

"You mentioned that you had something?" she said.

Cutting right to the chase then.

Sam felt off kilter. Couldn't help feeling dejected. "Right. Yeah."

She watched him, like a teacher waiting for their stuttering student to finally spit out the right answer.

After planning all day to tell her, Sam hesitated. "Charlie…" he shuffled his feet. "Why do you need this information anyways?"

Exasperation flashed across her features. "Because I want to know what the hell's going on around here. Don't you?"

"I guess. Yeah."

"Well?"

He nodded slowly, trying to see it from her perspective and not really getting there. But the big motivator was those eyes looking up at him, waiting for him to prove himself to her. And he felt keenly, though he couldn't articulate it to himself in that moment, that he needed to show how useful he was to her. Maybe *that* would impress her.

"Colonel Staley was at my house last night," Sam said, taking a glance around as though to make sure they were alone. He instinctively lowered his voice. "He was leaving just as I got home. He and Angela were having some sort of meeting. They didn't seem happy."

"Did you hear anything they were talking about?"

"No," Sam shook his head. Watched disappointment come over her face, and immediately jumped in to mitigate it. "But I heard some talk amongst the other guards."

Her eyebrows went up. Re-engaged.

Sam felt a bubble of satisfaction. "Some of the guys were saying that some Marines were gearing up today. Rumor was that they were going to head south tomorrow morning. But they didn't say what for."

"How many Marines?" Charlie asked him.

Sam felt surprised by the question. Why would she want specifics like that? "I'm not sure. The guys made it sound like it wasn't that many. Maybe a squad or two."

Charlie's eyebrows knit. She looked off into the middle distance. Processing.

Then she glanced at him. "Anything else?"

Shit. That's not enough?

He shook his head.

She nodded. Reached out and took his hand, and he thought, *Ah, now she'll relax...*

But she just gave his hand a squeeze, and then released him. "Okay. I gotta go."

He felt a wash of disappointment. He wanted to spend more time with her. He thought quickly, trying to prolong their togetherness. "Do you have anybody to walk with you?"

She looked up at him like he was stupid. "What?"

He felt his cheeks redden. Luckily, she wouldn't see that in the dim woods. "To the house. Or at least out the drain gate."

She shook her head dismissively. "I'm not going out there tonight. No one is."

"What? Why?"

"Spotters caught a pack of primals in the area. Too dangerous for now. You hadn't heard?"

"Oh. That. Yeah." Sam nodded, like he knew, but he didn't. It was news to him, and he felt silly for his ignorance. He guessed they'd mention something to him when he got to roll call.

Charlie offered him a bright smile that seemed to wipe away all the unsureness. It seemed to tell him that they were still...what? Together? Boyfriend and girlfriend?

"Thanks, Sam. I appreciate you meeting me. Just keep your eyes and ears open. You know?"

"Yeah." He smiled dopily back at her.

"I gotta go," she repeated. "See you soon?"

"Sure," he replied, in what he thought was a pretty suave manner.

Then she turned and left him, disappearing into the woods.

He stood there in the little clearing for a minute, feeling anti-climactic.

"Well, shit," he mumbled to himself. He checked his watch. He had thirty minutes to get to roll call. Which was ten minutes more than he needed. He supposed he'd just walk slowly.

—

Charlie walked about twenty-five yards through the woods. Soft feet quiet across the pine needle carpet. She stopped at the stump of an old pine that had rotted and fallen. She looked behind her. She couldn't see Sam anymore, but she could hear him walking away.

She waited for a minute or so. Until she could no longer hear him.

Then she whispered, "It's clear."

Claire Staley stepped out from behind a tree. She gave Charlie a smirk. "Have a good talk with your lover?"

Charlie rolled her eyes. "He's not my lover, Claire."

Claire shrugged. "Why not let him think it?"

"I'm not gonna have sex with him, if that's what you're asking."

Claire shook her head. "No, I'm not asking you to do that. Sorry, I didn't mean to piss you off. Just teasing."

"Well don't," Charlie said. "I'm just doing what you asked. And I feel bad about it."

"You shouldn't. It's not your fault he's just another horny boy."

Charlie crossed her arms and jutted her chin. A study in teenage petulance. "You want the information or not?"

Claire reached out and gently squeezed Charlie's shoulder. "Yes, of course. I'm only trying to make you feel better about it."

Charlie nodded. "Right. Well. He said your dad was at his house last night with Angela. They were having some sort of talk. Your dad was leaving just as Sam got there. He said they didn't seem very happy."

"I'm aware they had some sort of meeting last night," Claire answered. "Did he tell you what it was about?"

"Sam said he'd heard there were some Marines that were gearing up today. Supposed to head south in the morning. He wasn't sure how many Marines. Said he heard it was something like a squad or two."

Claire drew her head back. Considering. "Okay."

"Does this help?" Charlie asked.

Claire nodded. Smiled. "Yes. It helps a lot. Thank you."

Charlie's lips quirked, just slightly, like she wanted to smile, but then decided she was too irritable for such a display. She nodded once, as though to conclude the conversation and started to turn away.

"Wait," Claire said.

Charlie stopped. Looked back at Claire. "What?"

Claire shoved her hands in the pockets of her jacket and fixed Charlie with her halting green eyes. Her mouth, stern. "I didn't mention it the other night. It wasn't the right time. But...don't ever let me catch you taking a drink from Ben Sullivan again. Do you understand?"

Charlie frowned, and pulled her head back, both irritated at being ordered around so blatantly, and confused as to the nature of the order. "Why would you even say that? I didn't get drunk. I had, like, two drinks."

"I'm not worried about you drinking too much," Claire said. Then she paused for a moment, looked around the woods and found it predictably empty. Back to Charlie. "You remember the girl he was with? The one that was sitting next to him on the couch?"

Some of the irritation melted off of Charlie. Replaced with mingled curiosity and reticence. "Yeah. I remember her."

"Yeah? Well, she only had a couple drinks too. But Ben put something in hers." Claire rolled the final words around on her tongue, then spit them out. "And he raped her."

Charlie's mouth dropped. "What?"

Claire just nodded in confirmation.

"How do you know that?"

"Because I fucking saw it. And took pictures."

"You...you *saw* it? And *took pictures*?" She took a step towards Claire. "But you didn't do anything to *stop* it?"

Claire didn't move an inch. Didn't even bother to take her hands out of her pockets. She simply looked Charlie in the eye, then down, then up, as though taking her measure, and finding her wanting. It doused the indignation burning across Charlie's face, and made her feel like a silly little girl.

"No, I didn't do anything to stop it," Claire said, as though such a thing was foolish even to consider. "Listen. I'm only going to tell you this because I think you need to know it to get your head on straight: Ben Sullivan's mother is a nurse. She works in the Medical Center. I'm assuming that's how he's managed to get his hands on drugs. But in any case, there's no point in outing him right now, Charlie. The dumb bitch he fucked probably doesn't even remember it, and she put herself in that situation to begin with. But since I have the photographs, I have the evidence that it happened. And maybe that'll be useful in the future." Claire narrowed her gaze at Charlie, like you might if you were trying to ascertain whether a foreigner understood what you're saying. "Are you getting what I'm trying to explain to you, Charlie? There are bigger things at stake here than some little girl's first fuck gone awry."

Charlie didn't realize that she was still capable of being shocked. But she had to come back to her senses after a moment, and remember to close her mouth. She had a dozen things to hurl back at the young woman standing across from her, but all she said in the end was, "What the hell did they do to you?"

Claire's nostrils flared, but that momentary fire was snuffed out quick, and she was back to being cold. She gave a soft chuff through her nose. "Let's just say I would've been thrilled if they'd drugged me before they did the things they did." Claire leaned slightly closer, and lowered her voice. "You need to start thinking like an adult, Charlie. I like you a lot, but you need to grow up."

Charlie didn't say anything. She was just a cauldron bubbling over with hurt feelings and resentment. Claire cast a glance of pity at her, like she wasn't sure she could save this one, and then she just turned and started away.

She called over her shoulder, "Thanks for meeting with me."

—

Sam took his time walking through the woods.

This was an unusual move for him, because he didn't like the woods, and it was getting dark now. But it was almost a mental game.

He walked slowly not because he wanted to, but because he hated it. He wanted to inoculate himself to it. He wanted to be *cool* about it.

He saw the beginning of the neighborhoods, peeking through the trees, and he disliked how relieved he felt when he saw them.

You're in the Safe Zone, he told himself. *The Safe Zone is safe.*

He continued walking at this controlled pace.

Something rustled in the woods to his left.

He glanced in that direction, but couldn't see in the dimness.

His heart beat faster now. He forced his steps to remain even.

It's nothing. Just an animal. You're in the Safe Zone.

But it had sounded big.

He reached the edge of the woods and came out of them onto the street.

He'd never been so glad to hear his heels on concrete.

The neighborhoods stood before him. The houses lit invitingly.

A woman pushed a stroller along the sidewalk on the other side of the street, lighting her way with a flashlight. Heading home, or maybe taking a short walk around the block. Getting some fresh air for her and her baby.

It seemed so normal. He felt his heartrate slowing.

"You really need to get over this," he said aloud to himself.

He crossed the street to the sidewalk. Turned left. Heading for work now.

He passed the lady with the stroller.

By the glow of her flashlight he saw her face. She smiled at him. He smiled back.

"Evening," she said as she passed him.

"Evening," he replied.

Kept walking.

A whippoorwill urgently called out its name from the trees to Sam's left. Three times, as though announcing itself, and then it fell silent.

The night was getting cool. His fingers were starting to feel the chill. He shoved them in his pockets where they felt marginally better. The friction of his movement warmed them.

Some of the other soldiers had told him that back in the day—which meant back when they worked for the actual United States Army—you couldn't be caught with your hands in your pockets while in uniform. Nowadays, it was one of those things that had gone by the wayside. Sam was glad for that. Not that there was anyone around to catch him and berate him anyway—

A scream.

Sam's stomach jumped at the sound of it.

In the time it took his head to turn, he thought that it was probably just the kid, the kid in the stroller, got upset by something stupid…

Thirty yards behind him, the stroller hit the ground on its side.

The flashlight was turning circles, spinning alone on the concrete, creating a strobe effect.

The woman was screaming.

Sam could make out her light-colored sweatshirt in the darkness. She was halfway across the road. Someone had her by the foot. Someone was dragging her across the road. Someone who was just a hunched, shadowy figure.

"Hey!" Sam yelled, but his feet didn't move. He was too stunned to move.

What the fuck was he even looking at? Was she being robbed? Raped?

The flashlight spun and strobed.

The child in the stroller wailed.

Sam realized that his feet were moving, his mind caught in a loop: *Do something! Do Something! DO SOMETHING!*

His limbs felt like rubber. His legs ran awkwardly like they were stilts.

He became aware of more shapes. He couldn't count them, it was just *more*, and they were coming out of the woods, more attackers, a whole gang of them. The woman was screaming without words, clawing at the concrete as she was pulled violently towards the woods.

One of the dark shapes leapt onto her. Like it was trying to kiss her. Trying to kiss her throat...

Her screams were cut off.

The flashlight spun.

Strobed.

Lit the attackers for a fraction of a second.

Naked. They were all naked.

Thickly-muscled necks and shoulders.

Wild eyes that sparkled in the night.

Open jaws, too wide, far too wide...

Sam tried to yell, but the air wasn't in his lungs.

He almost stopped running, but the child screamed again. That momentary pause, like a building storm, and then the child's scream became hysterical—ragged and terror-born.

Sam's eyes fixed on the overturned stroller.

The kid. Don't let them get the kid.

He skidded to a stop on one knee, the concrete ripping the cloth of his pants, and then the flesh underneath like a cheese grater. Sam felt nothing. Nothing but panic like a lightning strike, overloading his entire system.

He grabbed the stroller and jerked it upright.

It flew out of his grip. No weight in it.

The toddler was on the curb. Hadn't been strapped in. It was clambering up onto its hands and knees, its entire small body shaking with its shrieks, its hands reaching out for nothing and finding nothing.

Across the road, the woman disappeared into the woods.

Two more dark shapes emerged.

Low on their haunches.

Sidling forward.

Sam couldn't tell whether they were moving to attack him, or to cover their retreat with their prize. He reached out, grabbed the child in his hands, hugged its struggling form to his chest and then he turned and ran, finding enough air in his lungs now to scream.

"Primals! Primals in the wire!"

TWENTY-SIX

RUN

Sᴀᴍ's ꜰᴇᴇᴛ ᴘᴏᴜɴᴅᴇᴅ ᴛʜʀᴏᴜɢʜ the sandy soil of Fort Bragg.

Shadows whipped past him.

He didn't dare look back—it would only slow him, and he had twenty pounds of screaming child already weighing him down. He didn't call out the warning anymore either—he couldn't waste the breath. His chest was heaving, and his legs were already burning from the dead sprint.

You can't outrun them!

He knew it was true, but panic was his engine right now.

He didn't think about cover until he saw the lights of someone's dining room straight ahead of him, and he saw them at their dinner table and he thought *safety*.

He didn't slow down. He angled his body and tried to shield the child from the impact as much as possible, then hit the door at near full speed. He crashed through. The impact rattled his teeth and shut down the kid's siren screech.

He stumbled into their dining room, barely keeping his feet.

"What the fuck?" the man yelled at him, standing still in shock, not able to compute what he was seeing.

"Primals!" Sam gasped, then thrust the child into the man's arms, turned on his heel, grabbed the door and slammed it shut on its splintered jam. "There's primals inside the Safe Zone!"

"What?"

Sam's face was pressed against the small glass window of the door, peering out into darkness, but the light from inside was making it hard to see. He caught a view of the street beyond the houses. Saw dark shapes moving along it.

He gulped a breath.

They weren't pursuing him. Not immediately, anyhow. But he'd seen them be cunning about this before. He'd seen them circle around before trying to get in.

"Guns," Sam panted. "Do you have guns?"

"What the fuck?" the man demanded again, a broken record of shock.

Sam turned his head and yelled at the man, just as the child started bawling again. "Guns! Fucking *guns*! There's primals outside right now! Do you fucking have guns?"

The man's wife, obviously more clear-headed than her partner, grabbed the child out of his arms and pushed him by the shoulders. "Get the rifle, Ben!"

Simple commands were best to people who were in mental vapor-lock, and it worked.

Still looking confused, the man turned quickly and ran deeper into the house.

Sam glanced back through the window. Couldn't see any movement. He planted his foot against the door, knowing it wouldn't hold for very long. He gulped air, his thoughts moving at a thousand miles an hour, bouncing off of each other like pinballs in a machine.

How'd they get in?

Shit, you gotta tell somebody!

Oh, God, that poor lady...

The door. Secure the door.

Sam looked down at his foot. A meager stopgap. Then he looked to the dining room chairs. He waved his arms. "Gimme a chair."

The woman was bouncing the screaming child on her hip, holding its head and shushing it. She grabbed one of the dining room chairs and shoved it towards Sam. He caught it, then used it to brace the door under the knob.

"That's not gonna hold very long," he said. He backed away from the door. "Get the kids. Kids, get away from the window."

The family had a boy and a girl, both around Abby's age. They stared at Sam like he had two heads, then looked at their mother. She hurried over to them, pulling them out of their seats. "Come on. Get away from the window. Do what he says."

The kids started to whimper in fear.

The toddler in the woman's arms was starting to quiet now, the piercing screams fading to a sobbing whine.

As a group, they backed their way out of the dining room and towards the center of the house, as far from any entrances as they could get. Sam was the last out of the dining room, uselessly using his body as a shield, as though that would do any of them any good.

"Do you have a phone?" he stammered. "Or, like, a radio or something?"

The woman's wide eyes crinkled at the edges, like he'd asked for manna from heaven. She shook her head. "No."

Of course they didn't. It was a stupid question born out of panic. Nobody had fucking phones. They had power, but they didn't have active phone lines. And why would a random family have radios that reached anybody of importance?

Sam let out a string of curses, and then somehow felt bad because there were children present.

They were in the living room area now.

The man appeared, holding a pump-action shotgun.

What the hell did that thing even hold? Four shots? Maybe five?

Like bailing out the Titanic with a teaspoon.

Sam kept that to himself.

How many primals had there been?

At least five. That he *saw*, anyway. There could be more.

Where'd they come from?

He felt like he knew, but couldn't grasp it at that point.

The more important question was how in the hell he was going to raise the alarm.

He raked his fingers through his short, black hair. "Shit. Sorry." Looked at the man, then the woman. "Is there any way that you can think of that we can use to notify Angela? Or Colonel Staley? Or anybody?"

The man stared with wide eyes and mouth agape, a fish on the deck of a boat, trying to figure out what the fuck's happening. "Uh...uh...there's a phone. An emergency phone. In the box. Out on the street. It's like, two blocks from here."

The emergency phones. Yes.

Sam nodded vehemently. They'd installed some hardline trench phones around the neighborhoods. A sort of rudimentary 9-1-1 system for emergencies. They didn't run off of a typical telephone network. It was a closed network and no matter what phone you picked up, the other end was always the Watch Commander, out at the Soldier Support Center.

"Okay," Sam said. "Good. Yes. I need to get there. Okay. Do you have any other guns?"

Both the man and the woman shook their heads.

"Shit. Sorry."

"Excuse me," the man said, his brow furrowing. "But who are you? And whose kid is this?"

Sam considered what felt like a million different possible responses to those questions, all of which required a lot of time and explanation. He simply shook his head. "I don't have time for that right now. Just listen to me. You need to stay in your house until you're told otherwise. Shut off the lights. Stay in a safe place. Keep that shotgun on you. Do you have extra shells?"

The man managed to nod.

"Keep them on you." Sam oriented himself briefly, found the front door. "I'm gonna go. Lock this door behind me."

—

The last thing in the world that Sam wanted was to be out on the street again.

But he couldn't hide in the house and wait for others to be killed.

He had to get to the emergency phone.

He stood in the shadowy front porch for a moment, trying to let his eyes adjust to the dark. He felt like he had to pee, and that made him feel like a coward. He couldn't stand just sitting in one spot, but he had to be able to see.

He decided that his best bet was to limit the amount of time he was on the street. That meant he needed to sprint to the phone. He needed to call the Watch Commander. Then he needed to get indoors again. Indoors wasn't a perfect situation, but it was better than being outside.

Shit. What about Angela and Abby?

He needed to get back home.

He looked down the street, his eyes slightly better now. He saw no movement, but that didn't mean anything. The primals were stealthy. They knew how to use concealment to their advantage.

"Just run," he whispered to himself, but his feet didn't move.

He looked to his right, two blocks down, as the man inside the house had said.

He saw an old light pole that no longer shed any light. He thought he saw the dull outline of the box in which they'd put the trench phone, posted to the side of it.

Maybe a hundred yards.

"Just run," he whispered again.

This time his feet moved, and once they started, once he left the fake safety of that front stoop, his legs started churning all out. He crossed the street and angled for the light pole.

Panic chased his heels.

Oh Jesus, you should have stayed inside!

When he was about halfway there, a howl went up, almost stopped him in his tracks, but he willed himself to keep moving. If they were howling, then they weren't directly on his tail.

He knew this, but the animal part of his brain, the scared little prey-animal inside of him, didn't believe it.

Just go

Just go

He reached the old light pole.

His worst fear as he reached it was that it was a mistake and this was not the right light pole.

But it was. The box was there. He ripped it open. Grabbed the receiver of the trench phone and wound the thing up. He heard it buzz on the other end. His breath huffed in the microphone. He looked over his shoulder. All around him. The shadows were deep and threatening, hiding anything and everything.

"Answer!" he whispered harshly into the telephone. "Fucking answer!"

"Watch Commander," the voice said on the other end.

Bored. Perhaps expecting some sort of stupid domestic dispute.

"L-T!" Sam shouted through the receiver. He didn't know which lieutenant it was. It didn't matter. "It's Private Ryder. There are primals inside the wire. You need to get a reaction force moving *now*!"

"What?" the voice slapped at his eardrum. More of an exclamation, than an actual question. "Shit! Private, where the fuck are you right now?"

Sam wanted badly to hang up the phone and keep running. His legs were tired, but his feet were dancing, needing to propel him onwards again. He was turning rapidly, looking in all directions.

"I think I'm just north of the Rec Center," Sam belted out. "They already killed someone. They killed this lady…"

"Alright shut the fuck up. How many did you see?"

"Sir, I don't have time for this shit!" Sam yelled. Was this guy really going to grill him right now? "I'm exposed in the middle of the street! Fucking get a reaction force moving! I gotta go!"

Another howl. Close by.

"Shit," Sam whispered into the receiver, and then hung up and started running again.

—

Angela had risen from her desk and was preparing to leave her office at the Soldier Support Center when Kurt burst through the door.

Angela jumped at his sudden entrance. "Christ. What…"

The look on Kurt's face silenced her. Made her stomach bottom out.

"What's wrong?"

"Ma'am," Kurt crossed the room to her, but then stationed himself on the other side of her desk. "Lieutenant Derrick just called from downstairs and said someone just reported primals in the wire."

"Primals in the wire?" Angela put a hand on the top of her desk to support herself. "You mean *inside the Safe Zone?*"

"Yes, Ma'am, that's the report. We're going into lockdown."

Angela was already shaking her head before Kurt had finished talking. "Kurt, I need to get home."

"I can't let you leave right now."

Anger surmounted the fear. She came around the table, her hands shaking. "Kurt! My fucking *daughter!* Abby's at my house!"

"We're sending someone to your house right now to pick her up."

"No! I need to go!"

Kurt held out a hand and placed it on her shoulder. "And what if this is a trap?"

Angela stared at him, his words sinking in.

He shook his head. "The call's not confirmed. It could be a trap. Could be the Lincolnists pulling some shit. We're going into lockdown. That's the procedure that we have. That's what we're going to do."

Angela shrugged his hand from her shoulder, bristling. She drew herself up, put command into her voice. "Kurt. I am *ordering* you to get me to my fucking house. We will come right back here if that's what you want, but we are going to get my daughter."

Kurt's eyes hit hers, then ricocheted off. "Angela," he said, with stiff resolution. "I'm sorry. This is a military matter right now, and I'm going to follow those orders."

"Are you going to forcibly stop me?"

"I'd really prefer not to."

"Kurt, it's my *daughter*."

Kurt's face flashed with something like anger. "Ma'am, I understand that. But this is reasonable and you know it. By the time we get down to your car, Abby will be on the way. You'll just be putting yourself at risk for nothing."

Every instinct in Angela's body told her to run, dart past Kurt before he could restrain her. But the logical part of her knew he was right.

She wilted backwards, sitting on her desk. "Please, tell me when they have her in hand."

—

Sam burst through the door, this time taking the half-second to work the latch so he wouldn't destroy it. He spun, slammed it closed, locked it, dead bolted it. Gasped for breath. Looked out the window.

Nothing out there.

"Sam?" Marie said from behind him. "Are you okay?"

He turned quickly. "Where's Abby?"

Marie's face went from confusion to apprehension. "She's in the kitchen. Sam, what's going on?"

From the kitchen he heard Abby's rapid footsteps. "Sam? Is something wrong?" Abby skidded around the corner, blonde curls flying.

Sam grabbed Abby and Marie and propelled them towards the staircase to the second floor. "Upstairs. We need to get upstairs," he blurted. "Primals inside the Safe Zone. They already killed someone."

The image of the screaming woman being dragged across the street shot through his brain again.

The three of them tumbled up the stairs, Abby and Marie both talking over each other with a slew of questions that Sam barely heard.

At the top of the stairs, he pushed them into his room, then closed and locked that door too. Jumped to his closet. Reached up top and pulled down his little .22 rifle. The rifle that Mr. Keith had given him what seemed like ages ago. Why he hadn't replaced it with something higher-caliber was beyond him. Perhaps he'd stupidly felt that they were *safe* in the so-called Safe Zone.

How'd they get inside? His mind demanded.

And he had the terrible thought that he knew exactly how.

He checked the chamber on the little rifle, saw the tiny cartridge inside.

It was all he had. It was the best he could do.

Where are the primals now?

When he'd been running, they'd stopped howling. Which meant that they'd found something else to hunt…or they were hunting him.

"Sam!" Marie shouted at him.

He looked at her, dazed. "What?"

"I'm asking you a goddamned question!"

"What?"

"How'd they get in?" Marie demanded.

The culvert. The drainage culvert. The gate with the carabiner clip to hold it closed.

He shook his head. "I don't know."

"Who'd they kill?" Marie's voice shook.

Sam felt exasperation hit him. "I don't know that either! Christ, Marie! I just ran, okay? I couldn't do anything about it! I didn't have a weapon! I couldn't…I couldn't fucking *do anything*, okay?"

Marie grabbed him by both shoulders. "Hey! Hey. No one's blaming you, Sam. Okay?"

Something rattled the front door. Sam heard it from all the way upstairs, and he jolted at the sound, feeling panic like static sparks in his fingers and toes.

"Ssh!" he hissed.

The door rattled again.

Then pounded.

A voice: "Abby! Marie! Open up!"

Sam stared at his bedroom door like he could see through it, all the way down to the foyer and the front door. He looked at Marie. "Just…stay here until I clear it, okay?"

Marie frowned at him. "What's there to clear, Sam? Primals don't talk. Let's go."

Not sure why he was so reluctant, Sam opened the door and the three of them went back down the steps they'd just come up. Abby hesitated at the bottom of them, and Marie stood with her.

Sam opened the door just as someone started to pound on it again.

Sergeant Hauer stood there, looking urgent and pissed. When the door opened a crack, he pushed it all the way. "Private Ryder. Abby and Marie in there with you?" He answered his own question by seeing them, then motioned quickly. "Come on. We're taking you to the Soldier Support Center. Now. Let's move."

Marie pulled Abby by her hand, leading them out of the house.

Sam came out, looking in every direction, seeing threats in every shadow.

Sergeant Hauer jogged to the SUV. Opened the back door. Sam realized that Hauer was by himself. There was no one else in the vehicle.

They should've sent more—

The shadows suddenly converged on them.

It was a flash of naked flesh. It hit Marie hard, sent her sprawling into the dirt.

Abby screamed, short and sharp.

Something had her by the leg. Yanked hard. Abby went down.

"No!" was all Sam had time to shout.

Sergeant Hauer was spinning around, raising his rifle.

Nothing was clearly defined. It was just a tangle of limbs, and Abby's blonde curls and frightened eyes staring up at Sam as she ran out of breath.

He saw the jaws, the head, thrust his little rifle out and jammed the muzzle into the space at the base of its neck, and he pulled the trigger rapidly. The thing went limp on top of Abby, spilling brains and blood across her torso.

Sam wasn't thinking. Just doing. He dropped his rifle because he needed both hands to grab Abby up. That was all he could do. That was his only concern. He snatched her by both of her arms and pulled her upright, already churning his legs for the SUV.

Marie was scrambling to her feet.

Sergeant Hauer shouted something at them.

Pale arms shot out from underneath the SUV. Latched onto Hauer's legs and pulled him under like he weighed nothing. All Sam saw was Hauer's hand, gripping the curb, trying to pull himself out as his shouts turned to screams.

Sam shoved Abby into the open door, and propelled himself in right after her.

Marie came in hot on his back, a tumble of limbs, everyone cramming themselves into the back as quickly as possible because the SUV was the only source of protection they had. Marie was making noises of desperation and fear; short, sharp bleats, as she turned in her seat and more shapes came out of the darkness.

She slammed the door. Smacked down the locks.

Something hit the door. Teeth flashed across the glass. The SUV shook on its chassis.

"Sam! Get us out of here!" Marie screamed.

The primal on the other side of the door started hammering the glass with its fist. If it were a normal human, the bones would have broken before the glass did, but Sam watched in horrified wonder as the glass held, then splintered, then cracked.

Drive!

Sam leapt headfirst over the center console and into the front seat. Knees and elbows scraping and banging into everything. The wipers came on full blast. The horn honked. He managed to get his ass in the seat and his hands on the wheel and his feet on the pedals.

The window shattered.

Abby and Marie both screamed, launched themselves towards the opposite side of the car.

"Drive, Sam!"

Sam yanked the shifter and hit the gas.

It seemed like an entire minute passed in the time it took for the transmission to catch up with the revving engine and actually shift into gear. In that terrifying eternity, Sam was certain that something was wrong with the car, it wasn't going to go, it had broken somehow, the primal that was feeding on Sergeant Huaer underneath their feet must have pulled something loose—

The engine banged hard.

The tires screeched.

The SUV lurched forward, then jolted as its rear tires tore over the body of Hauer and the primal that had him.

The wheel jerked in Sam's hands, hit the curb, and Sam almost lost control. He tightened his grip, somehow remembered not to overcorrect, and pulled them back onto the road.

They were up to sixty miles an hour, tearing down the neighborhood street before Abby's screams finally coalesced into words, and those words made it into Sam's brain.

"It bit me!" she was shrieking. "It bit my leg!"

TWENTY-SEVEN

LOCKDOWN

LEE'S TEAM TOOK THE AIRFIELD in darkness.

Lee, Carl and Abe provided overwatch. Carl had been re-armed through Mitch's delivery of weapons, one of which had been his Remington MSR, a .338 Lapua Magnum bolt-action that beat the piss out of Lee's M14 in nearly every category imaginable.

They figured that whoever had run the operation on Paolo's people had done so either out of the Correctional Facility, or the airfield. When Lee and Carl and Abe got into position—spaced out along the woods southeast of the single runway—they found the place had only two occupants.

Julia, Mitch, and his team, were stacked up in the woods off the front gate.

Lee lay in the wet leaves, his clothing already soaked through. The rain had stopped, but big drops of cold water were still dripping out of the trees. The water ran down into his eyes and he blinked it away. It touched his lips and tasted sharply of salt.

Lee watched through the scope on his M14. He spoke into the squad comms, his voice barely above a whisper. "I've got two. One in red plaid. One in gray hoodie. Both armed. Rifles. Carl and Abe, let me know when you got 'em."

There was a pause of about twenty seconds.

Carl transmitted first. "I got both. They're stationary at the front of the building."

"Good," Lee said. "Standby for Abe."

Another ten seconds passed.

"Yeah, I got an angle on one, but not the other," Abe said. "I got the guy in red plaid."

"Copy," Carl's voice mumbled. "I got gray hoodie. It's on you, Lee."

"Assault team," Lee said. "You in position?"

Mitch came back: "We're in position."

Lee took a deep breath, blew it out. He focused his reticle on the empty space between the two guards. He could provide a backup shot on either of them if Carl or Abe missed. He settled into the ground, melted his body into it, his face resting on his buttstock. Finger hovering over the trigger. He touched off his comms. "All teams go on my mark."

The two men three hundred yards away from them looked at each other and laughed about something.

"Three. Two. One. Mark."

Lee watched the two bodies jolt from impacts about a half-second before the rifle reports washed over him. Gray hoodie crumpled where he stood. Red plaid staggered forward, tried to bring up his rifle, then lost his legs and collapsed, dead.

Across from the gate, Lee watched the assault team coalesce out of the woods, Logan up front with bolt cutters. They breached the gate. Filed through at a purposeful but unrushed pace.

"Assault team is in," Lee said. "Overwatch, hold on doors and windows, Building One."

Two buildings. The main and largest one designated as Building One. The smaller one, not much more than a shed, designated as Building Two. With Carl and Abe covering Building One, Lee shifted to observe Building Two.

Mitch's voice: "Assault team's at Building One. Breaching now."

Lee opened both eyes. Through the unmagnified sight of his left eye, he saw Rudy put his foot through the door of Building One. The explosive sound of the slam reached Lee a second later. The assault team filed in, Julia and Mitch holding cover on the exterior of the building.

Lee refocused on Building Two. No movement.

After about a minute, Rudy, Morrow, Logan and Blake exited Building One, and started moving for Building Two.

Mitch and Julia still held their positions.

"No movement from Building Two," Lee advised.

They stacked up again and Rudy breached again.

Only Logan and Blake went into the smaller Building Two. They exited about twenty seconds after they'd entered.

"It's clear," Mitch said, louder and more confidently. "Grounds are clear."

"Roger," Lee responded. "Moving to you."

The entire operation had lasted less than five minutes, from first shot to all-clear.

In the time it took Lee and Carl and Abe to make it out of the woods, Rudy and Morrow had retrieved their two pickup trucks and parked them around back of Building One where they couldn't be seen from the road.

They secured the gates, posted Logan and Blake as sentries, and met inside the main building.

It was dark inside and they lit their way around using their weaponlights. They went to the office, which had a desk and some chairs. That was all they needed. Julia posted their trusty solar lamp, illuminating the room.

Mitch sprawled their map of southern Alabama across the desk while Lee pulled out the satphone that he'd borrowed from Ed. He quick-dialed Fort Bragg, put it to his ear and waited.

It rang.

He waited.

Ringing.

Waited some more.

He disconnected the call, wondering if the damned satellites had degraded so much that the satphone was rendered useless. But then, it wouldn't be ringing, would it?

He tried the call again.

And again, no one answered.

The occupants of the office had become very still, watching Lee. And watching the phone.

He tried to connect a third time.

He let it ring for longer this time. Almost a full minute.

A full minute, in which time his mind went to a lot of different places.

He put the phone down. "Something's wrong."

"Is it ringing?" Julia asked.

Lee stared at the phone like it was actively trying to stymie him. "Yeah, it's ringing. It's just no one is answering."

"That's not a good sign," Carl observed.

Julia nodded to Lee. "Keep trying."

—

Angela's office was thrown into chaos.

Thirty seconds prior to that, Angela had been on the verge of just duking it out with Kurt and seeing if she could make a break for the door. He'd lost contact with Sergeant Hauer, who was sent to retrieve Abby and Marie, and kept repeating "He'll answer up, he's just busy," but Angela wasn't having it.

Right about the point in time when Angela was considering how effective a surprise right hook would be on Kurt, they heard a commotion in the hall. Kurt raised his rifle to the door as it burst open, and luckily had the trigger discipline not to shoot Marie in the face.

She tumbled in with Sam on her heels, looking harried and scared, but Angela's gaze skimmed off her like a flat pebble over water and went straight to her daughter who was limping into the room, bawling hysterically with both arms over Sam's shoulders.

There was a lot of yelling. A lot of screaming. A lot of questions being shot out and not getting any answers. The truth began to coalesce out of the storm of words.

The primals had attacked them.

Sergeant Hauer was dead.

Abby had been bitten.

Had Angela been the same woman she'd been two years ago, she would've stood in shock, clutching her daughter to her and trying ineffectively to think of what to do next.

But times change. And people change with them.

Angela ran to her desk and with a single sweep of her arm sent everything on it clattering and fluttering to the floor. "Put her on the desk!" she shouted over everyone else.

Sam had already anticipated what she wanted and was there with Abby, sitting her down, then swinging her legs up so she was laying on the desktop, propped up on her elbows.

"Where'd she get bit?" Angela demanded.

Sam pointed to Abby's right thigh.

On the short ride over, Marie had done the only thing she could think of to help Abby. She'd used her own belt to tourniquet the leg. Despite the fact that everyone knew tourniquets were not an effective barrier against infection.

Angela grabbed Abby's hand and squeezed it. She brushed hair from her daughter's face and mumbled, "It's going to be okay now, Sweetie, it's going to be okay. We have you now."

"I'm gonna die!" Abby shrilled. "I'm gonna turn infected!"

Angela couldn't help her own tears, didn't even think about them as they blurred her vision. "You're not going to die!" she told her daughter. "You're going to be okay." Then she bent over the leg and looked at it.

She knew that she'd seen worse, and as hard as it was to be objective, that's what she chose to fixate on: *I've seen worse.*

The bite had broken through the fabric of Abby's jeans, and there was blood coming out, but it didn't look like the monster that had done it had ripped a chunk out. The bleeding was manageable, and she knew that bleeding was the first priority.

God, I wish Julia was here...

She turned to Kurt and snapped her fingers. "Knife. I need a knife."

Kurt ripped his folding knife from his vest and handed it to her. "You can't amputate with that," he told her as the knife left his fingers.

Angela flipped the knife open. "I'm not amputating my daughter's leg!"

"You're gonna amputate my leg?" Abby gasped.

"No, Sweetie, no one's going to amputate your leg."

In the back of Angela's mind, the memory of her first night in Camp Ryder scuttled through her brain on insect legs. There'd been a girl that had been bitten. They'd amputated to try to prevent infection. She'd died of blood loss.

But how are you going to stop the infection?

Angela grabbed the cuff of Abby's jeans and used the knife to cut upwards, creating a long slit all the way up to the tourniquet, exposing the wound.

The teeth marks were evident. A full bite. Top and bottom teeth. Blood oozed, but didn't gush.

That's good, she told herself, even as the sight of it made her feel faint. Not the blood by itself, but the fact that it was *her daughter's* blood.

Kurt had negotiated himself to the opposite side of the desk, the side where Angela usually sat. He had already taken a small pouch from his vest and ripped it open. What the guys called a "blowout kit." He pulled a little green pack from inside of it and handed this to Angela.

"It's gauze. Put it on the wound and hold pressure." Then he grabbed a Combat Application Tourniquet, pulled it loose, and applied it expertly, directly below Marie's makeshift tourniquet. He started cranking the windlass and Abby cried out in pain.

"That hurts!"

Angela had to reign herself back from her immediate instinct to smack Kurt's hands away.

Kurt looked at her daughter with a shade of tenderness that Angela had never seen in him before. "I know, honey. But it's gonna help you, okay?"

Abby squeezed her eyes shut and buried her face into Sam's arms. He cradled her head, staring down at the wound, and then up at Angela, his eyes a question about how they were going to proceed. Angela noticed that his hand snuck around and gently covered Abby's exposed ear.

She looked up at Kurt. He had finished with the windlass and was now securing it in place. He looked up at her and the warmth was gone from him. There was only clinical urgency now. "You have to," he said, his voice low.

"I'm not," Angela shook her head fiercely.

Kurt held out his hand. "I'll do it then."

Angela pulled his knife away. "*No one* is going to do it!"

"Angela, it's the only fucking way, and you know it."

Angela jabbed a finger at him, getting furious and scared all over again. "No, I don't know that! No one knows that! This is the first time someone's been bitten by a primal and survived!"

"You think it's gonna be any fucking different?" Kurt hissed, getting angry right back at her.

Angela grabbed hair that was getting in her eyes and yanked it back from her face. She spoke very deliberately, like the words were an incantation: "There is anecdotal evidence that the primals' bites are not infectious anymore."

Kurt's eyes crinkled up at the edges and he tossed his hands up. "Oh, *anecdotal evidence*! Bullshit. You talking about some guy who says he knows a guy that knows a guy that got drunk and claimed to survive a bite? Bullshit, Angela. It's fucking bullshit and your daughter's life is on the line!"

"Hey!" Marie butted in, then lowered her voice below the ascending level of the argument. "You guys mind taking this over to the corner of the room?" Her insistent eyes jagged pointedly to Abby.

The three of them shuffled over into the corner of the office. By the time they got there, Kurt's expression had melted into a hard-swallowing regret.

"Ma'am, I spoke out of turn," he said, stiffly. "I apologize. It's just…"

Angela was still pissed. "We're not cutting my daughter's leg off with a pocket knife!"

Kurt squeezed the rest out: "I had a daughter. I couldn't do it either. And she died."

Angela stared at him, shocked by that revelation. Kurt seemed so young, she'd never thought he could have been a father.

Marie touched Kurt's shoulder. "No one's taking away from that horrible situation you went through," she said. "But this is not that. Three years ago, anecdotal evidence was the reason we started amputating after a bite, and it saved some lives. Now we have anecdotal evidence that says something different, and I'm inclined to believe it. But besides that fact, Angela is right. We don't have the equipment to keep Abby alive through an amputation. If we start trying to do it with what we've got lying around she *will* die. If we wait, there's a chance that she won't."

Kurt looked pained, but didn't respond.

Angela's anger had gone. She was back to fear. Back to thinking through dozens of different possibilities, none of them good. "Can we get her to the hospital?"

Marie made an unsure face. "Even if we could, it's eight o'clock at night. Doc Trent's not going to be there."

"We could go find him," Angela spurted out. "We could find him and bring him to the hospital."

"It's not safe out there yet," Kurt said. "You gotta give the response crews time to clear the streets. Look what happened to Sergeant Hauer, just trying to retrieve Abby!"

"How long until they clear the streets?" Angela demanded.

"I don't know," Kurt responded, then indicated his radio earpiece. "They're out there now. But we gotta give them time. If we run out there, we're just going to create a worse situation. You try to get Abby to the hospital, there's no telling what might happen between here and there. Is that something you really want to risk?"

"I don't know!" Angela suddenly shouted, then grabbed her face with one hand like she was trying to stifle any more outbursts.

Marie spoke calmly. "Listen. Angela. I know you don't want to hear the bad stuff right now, but I'm going to shoot straight with you, okay?"

Angela nodded, feeling her eyes burn, her vision swimming again.

"The tourniquets aren't affective against infection. They never have been."

Angela squeezed her eyes shut. Felt tears drip over her cheeks. "Jesus, Marie…"

"Listen," Marie repeated. "If the primals' bites are infectious, then even if we go and get Doc Trent and we somehow get Abby to the hospital, it's going to be thirty minutes, maybe even an hour before he operates. Do you understand what I'm telling you?"

Angela opened her eyes. Took unsteady breathes.

She's saying if the primals' bites are infectious, then Abby is already infected, or will be by the time we can do anything about it.

She nodded, suddenly feeling odd and out of place, stuck in a nightmare. Everything surreal and obtuse.

Marie took Angela's hands and squeezed them in her own. "I don't think they are, Angela. I believe what people have told us. I think Abby's going to be okay."

"But you don't *know*."

"No one knows. But we're gonna hope and pray, because that's our best option right now." Marie untangled her hands from Angela's, and used those same hands to cup Angela's face, forcing eye contact. "I love you like my own family. I love Abby too. I wouldn't say it if I didn't think it was true."

"Jesus, I don't think I can do this," Angela whispered.

"You can. And you will. Because you have to."

There was a sharp knock at the office door, and then it opened.

Lieutenant Derrick stepped in, looking around the carnage of the room with surprise. He held a satphone in his hand. His eyes finally found Angela, and he held the phone up. "Ma'am, it's Captain Harden."

Angela stared at Lieutenant Derrick, thinking, *I can't do this. I'm not cut out for this shit. I can't strategize with Lee while my daughter's life is on the line. I'm in over my head…*

Marie cut off her thoughts. "Angela, let me coordinate with Lee, okay? You focus on Abby."

—

"What the hell is going on out there?" Claire sidled up next to the window and pulled the shades apart, looking out onto the street where a Humvee roared by, a soldier in the turret blaring his voice through a loudspeaker: *Stay in your houses. There are primals inside the wire. Lock your doors. Stay in your houses…*

"Come away from the window," a woman's voice said behind her.

Claire turned away from the window, letting the curtains fall closed again.

Elsie Foster stood across the kitchen from her, one arm hugged across her chest, the other propped up with the fingers thoughtfully at the side of her mouth. "You're pretty sure about the information? About the Marine detachment?"

Claire shrugged. "Charlie says she's sure. I suppose I trust her."

"Okay," Elsie nodded. "You should send that information as soon as possible."

"I'll figure out a way to get it out. Tonight."

"That might be tough." Elsie frowned at Claire, her eyes knowing. "Do you know how the primals got inside?"

Claire inhaled sharply. Exhaled. "The drain gate."

Elsie nodded, concurring. "You can't use that again."

"The meetings weren't good for recruitment anyways. Everyone was just showing up to have a good time. Just a bunch of drunk kids. Their eyes glazed over at the slightest mention of dissidence."

"Well." A grim smile crossed Elsie's lips. "It did get us Ben Sullivan."

"If that ever even becomes useful."

Elsie was very still. Considering something. Watching Claire carefully.

Claire fidgeted under the gaze. "What?"

Elsie took a step toward Claire. They were close together now. Elsie put her hand on Claire's shoulder. "It's very dangerous, Claire. I don't expect you to go."

"I'm going."

Elsie's lips pressed together in concentration. "Primals in the wire. A tragedy for others. An opportunity for us." She looked earnestly at Claire. "I need you to find out what's happening in Angela's office. But only go if you think you can make it there safely."

Claire looked towards the window again, a little sliver of nighttime beyond visible between the two curtains.

Out in the darkness, a string of gunfire rattled.

"Yeah, I can make it there. I've been through worse."

Elsie squeezed her shoulder. "You're so incredibly brave, Claire. I hope that someday people know about what you've done for this country."

TWENTY-EIGHT

SLIM TO NONE

IN THE SMALL, DARK OFFICE of Building One, Lee and his team sat in the muted refraction of a few flashlights, all of them staring at the satphone, which was placed in the center of the desk, on top of the map.

They heard Lieutenant Derrick knock on a door and then they heard some commotion in the background.

Julia shook her head, eyes still affixed on the satphone. "That doesn't sound good."

The phone rustled and Marie's voice came over the line. "Lee? Are you there?"

"Yeah, we're here, Marie," Lee answered. "What the fuck's going on? We've been trying to make contact for the last twenty minutes."

"Primals got in the wire somehow," Marie said. "We don't know how yet. The whole place is in lockdown. And Lee…" Marie hesitated and lowered her voice. "Abby got bit."

Lee drew a hand over his mouth. "Okay. I copy that. Is Angela with her?"

"Angela's right here. We're in her office with Abby. I'm gonna handle this phone call for her. Is that okay with you?"

"Fine. Are you aware of the situation?"

"Halfway aware. Fill me in."

Lee did so quickly, hitting the main points. He finished with, "What are the chances of that Marine detachment actually leaving on time in the morning?"

Marie blew out a breath that rattled in the microphone. "Shit, Lee. I'd say slim to none at this point."

Lee's hand crept back up to his face, found his eyes, rubbed them. *This is not what I wanted to hear.* "Okay. Marie, you're on speaker phone right now. Stay on the line with me, but we're gonna discuss amongst ourselves for a minute."

"Is Julia there?" Marie asked.

"I'm here, Sis," Julia said, a note of genuine affection coming out in her voice.

"Are you doing okay?"

"We're doing fine. It's been rough, but we're fine."

"Good," Marie said, sounding like she was choking back tears. "Y'all go ahead. I'll be right here."

Lee looked up at his gathered team. "We can't wait."

Abe folded his hands and rested them on his magazines. "So you're talking about hitting the fuel cache by ourselves."

"If we wait, there's a chance they go after Butler. If we hit these fuckers hard, and soon, then they won't have time to go after Butler—just like Julia said. The clock is ticking. We gotta take this fight to them. The opening is now. I say we exploit it."

"Why not wait?" Mitch weighed in. "I mean, I'm not saying we shouldn't go after them now. I'm playing devil's advocate here. But if we wait for the Marines, how much longer could it possibly take them? A day? Maybe two?"

"Because right now they don't know that we're on to them," Lee said. "In two days, or even one, they're gonna realize that we hit those motherfuckers in the brown Suburban. And they're gonna realize that they've lost contact with the two boys we just took out. Which means they'll know where we are, and they'll know that we're on the warpath. Right now, they're thinking they made they're point with Paolo's people, and for all they know, we've tucked tail and run back across the border to Georgia."

Carl cleared his throat and spoke quietly. "I'm with Lee on this. And not just because I'm pissed and ready. But once they find out what we've done, it's not too much of an intuitive leap for them to assume that we got some information from one of their guys. They already know we're here for fuel. It won't be hard for them to figure out our next step."

Lee nodded along with Carl's rationale. "Right now we've got the biggest force multiplier, and that's the element of surprise. If we hit them hard before they expect it, then we even our odds on that assault."

Abe didn't look entirely convinced, but he remained silent, weighing the arguments in his mind.

Lee looked at him, felt a surge of anger. What Abe had said about Lucas still stuck in his craw. But he pushed past it. That's what they had to do right now. "Abe, I'm not gonna do anything stupid. You have my word on that. If we go and scope this place out, and it's too hard to hit, then we'll figure something else out."

Abe nodded once. "Okay, Lee. I trust you."

Lee looked down at the phone. "Marie, can you take down a location to send the Marines to as soon as they can be ready to roll?"

—

Sam seemed to be the only one that noticed Claire slip into the office.

He jettisoned himself from the desk and approached her as she quietly closed the door behind her.

"What are you doing here?" he said, keeping his voice down.

Claire looked over his shoulder at everyone gathered around Abby. "I came when I heard we were in lockdown. I thought Angela might need me."

"How'd you get here?"

She shot him a glare. "I ran, Sam."

Sam noticed that she did seem out of breath. He sidled closer to her and spoke in a whisper. "You know how those fuckers got in, don't you?"

Claire's mouth tightened. "You don't know that."

"How else could they have gotten in?"

"I don't know," she snapped.

"One of your people left the gate open."

Claire gave him a dangerous look. "No one left the gate open."

"Then they figured out how to get it open."

"No way."

"It was a fucking *carabiner*, Claire!" Sam hissed. "They can open *doors*. What makes you think they couldn't figure that out?"

"If you were so worried about it, why didn't you say something before now?"

"I did say something. To Charlie."

Claire brushed him off. "Just stop talking about it."

She broke away from him and walked further into the room.

Angela was clearly preoccupied with Abby. Holding her hand. Soothing her. Kurt was hovering, looking like he wished he could figure out a way to be useful. Marie was on the satphone. She glanced at Claire, but didn't seem to take too much notice of her sudden appearance.

"Yeah," Marie said into the phone. "Hold on."

She crossed to the desk. Or rather, the pile of papers and objects that Angela had swept off of it into a pile on the floor. She bent down, rifled through, found a pen, then grabbed a sheet of paper.

She crossed back to the wall of the office. Put the satphone against her shoulder and put the paper against the wall. "Okay. Go ahead with it."

Claire crossed to Marie, just as she scrawled something on the paper.

"Is there anything I can do?" Claire offered.

Marie held up a finger to Claire, silently asking her to wait. She listened to something else that was being said over the satphone. Then she seemed to recover a sense of discretion, took the paper, and folded it in half, so that what was written on it was covered.

"Yeah," Marie said into the phone. "I'll pass it along. Okay. Yes. You guys stay safe." She hung up, and then handed the satphone to Claire. "Can you take this back down to Lieutenant Derrick?"

Claire nodded, looking earnestly glad to be of some use.

—

It was a late night for Major Bellamy.

He was tired of being in the office. Tired of doing bullshit.

Hell, he'd take a trip down to Louisiana to meet with that psychopath Espinoza over the cat-herding he was currently doing.

He longed to leave his office and get back to his quarters, because in his mini-fridge was a gift from one of his operators. They'd happened across an un-looted convenience store during a clearing operation in the Colorado foothills last week, and managed to liberate several cases of beer.

Two cans of Coors Original were chilling in Bellamy's fridge at that moment, and they'd been calling to him all day.

He got as far as shutting down his laptop and standing up from his desk before Captain Perry Griffin knocked on the jam of his open door.

Bellamy looked up, hoping for a simple "see you tomorrow" but bracing for more work.

Griffin held a sheet of paper in his hand. His eyes did not look like the eyes of someone about to bid him goodnight. They had an excitable glimmer to them.

Bellamy's heart sank.

"What?" Bellamy griped.

Griffin waggled the paper in the air, making it snap. "Just got a call from our girl."

Bellamy straightened up. "Bragg?"

Griffin nodded. A ghost of a smile. "She's got a solid location where Harden is going to be."

Bellamy held out his hand, waggled his fingers—*gimme.* "When?"

Griffin stepped fully into the office and handed him the paper. "Sometime in the next day or so. Timeline is unconfirmed."

Bellamy held the paper up. "Andalusia, Alabama," he read the big scrawl of hasty handwriting. "Airport." He lowered the paper. "What's there?"

Griffin shook his head. "Fuck if I know. But she said Fort Bragg is dispatching a small group of Marines to that location. Something about an assault. Something about fuel."

Bellamy slapped the paper down on his desk. "This is good work, Captain."

Griffin nodded. "Anything I can do right now?"

"You can close the door," Bellamy said. "I'll handle this."

Griffin backed out of the door, and obediently closed it behind him.

Bellamy remained standing behind his desk, staring at the door, while he listened to the sound of Griffin's retreating footsteps. Then he sat down and unlocked the drawer with the satphone in it.

—

"We gonna rack out tonight?" Mitch asked after Lee put the borrowed satphone away.

"Not here," Lee replied, then grabbed his rifle. "We don't know when more people are gonna show up to check on their boys we just took out. Get Logan and Blake. We're leaving right now. Me and Carl will catch some Z's on the way there. Find us a good place to hide out. Me and Carl will insert and have eyes on the airport by morning. You guys sleep during the day, and when me and Carl get back, we'll put together a plan."

Lee looked around at his team, waited for objections, but none were forthcoming. "If we can pull it off, we're hitting it tomorrow night. Hopefully the Marines will get there in time for us to fortify the airport against a counterattack. If not, we'll take what we can and get the hell out."

Nods all around.

Rudy spoke up. "What do you wanna do with this place?"

"Pack any Claymores?"

Rudy smirked. "But of course."

TWENTY-NINE

ROOTS

GUNFIRE RATTLED ON AND OFF into the night.

Every so often a truck would drive by outside and they heard the voice of one of the soldiers over a loudspeaker, telling everyone that the lockdown was still in effect and to remain indoors.

Kurt monitored the squad comms and gave Angela updates that usually consisted of a tally of confirmed kills. They were up to eight now. Eight primals confirmed dead. Which meant that the pack that had gotten into their Safe Zone had been a large one.

They'd moved Abby to a chair and she'd recovered her calm. She was now comforting Angela more than the other way around.

"I think I'm gonna be okay," Abby said, and squeezed her mother's hand, who was sitting next to her. "I feel fine."

Angela smiled and nodded, though she only felt worse. "I'm sure you'll be fine, Sweetie."

You don't know that.

They'd taken the tourniquets off an hour ago. There was logic to it, and that's all that Angela could cling to at that moment. The tourniquets were not effective against infection, and Kurt told her that "limb morbidity" could set in after a few hours with them on. Which meant nerve damage if they left them on. Which meant that if they left them on, and Abby remained uninfected, she could lose the use of her leg.

Angela knew that there was no purpose in leaving the tourniquets on. But taking them off had felt like signing a death sentence for her daughter, no matter how illogical that was.

Claire got some water from the Watch Commander's office, where he kept an emergency supply. She offered to get them something to eat, but it didn't seem like anybody was hungry.

They'd been in the office for almost four hours when Kurt perked up and walked over to Angela. "No contact for the last thirty minutes," he told her. "They're conducting a final sweep now. Last they saw of the primals they were heading towards the border near McFayden Pond. They're gonna sweep that area for a breach."

Angela sat up. "Does that mean we can move to the hospital?"

Kurt looked unsure. "They haven't lifted the lockdown yet."

"But they haven't had any contact for thirty minutes," Angela argued. "And the primals were running. Retreating. Is that right?"

"I don't know how they would characterize it," Kurt replied.

"Well can you ask them if it's safe to move to the hospital?"

Kurt considered this for a moment. He reached for the PTT button on his chest rig, then stopped. He looked at Angela. "Ma'am, this might be one of those situations where it's better to ask for forgiveness than to ask for permission."

She stared at him. Unsure of what he was saying.

"If I ask, and they say no, then I'll have disobeyed orders. If you tell me to take you right now, after they've said that the grounds are *mostly* clear...then I can articulate I made a reasonable judgement call. And I might not be in too much trouble."

Angela swallowed. Nodded. "Kurt, I want you to take us to the hospital. Right now."

They left Claire at the office, in case anyone came looking for Angela.

Kurt led the way out, followed by Sam, Angela, Abby, and Marie.

They moved quickly to where Sam had left the SUV parked haphazardly on the curb. The hospital wasn't very far away, but in the steeped darkness of midnight, the SUV was at least some protection.

They piled into the SUV, with Sam driving again, because Kurt wanted to keep his rifle up and ready. For his inexperience, Sam drove quickly and carefully, without too many jolts to the brakes. It hadn't been an issue before because he'd simply been standing on the accelerator.

When they rounded the corner of the medical center, Kurt pointed to the front doors of the Emergency Room. "Pull us up right there. Leave the engine running and stay behind the wheel in case we need to beat a retreat."

Sam nodded gravely and did as he was told.

Kurt exited first, scanning up and down and all around. He went briskly to the door and peered inside. He rattled the doors, but they wouldn't budge. He glanced around, and then pounded on the glass with his fist.

In the SUV, everyone wanted to watch the doors but smartly kept their eyes peeled for moving shadows.

"Hey!"

Everyone looked around.

Kurt was motioning them out. There was a woman in scrubs on the other side, unlocking the door and pulling it open. It was Nurse Sullivan.

Sam waited behind the wheel of the running SUV until they were all through the doors, then he cut the engine, pocketed the keys and ran inside with the rest of them.

Sullivan closed and locked the doors.

"Have you been stuck here the whole time?" Angela asked her.

Sullivan shook her head and turned to them. "No. They went and picked up me and Doctor Trent just in case we were needed."

"Who picked you up?" Angela demanded.

The nurse shook her head. "I dunno. Soldiers?"

Angela looked at Kurt, but spoke to Sullivan. "How long have you been here?"

"A few hours."

Kurt looked stricken. "I'm sorry," he mumbled to Angela. "They didn't say anything over my channel. I didn't know."

Angela didn't trust herself to respond in a civil manner. She turned to Sullivan. "Is Doctor Trent available right now?" She indicated Abby, who was standing on her own. "She's been bitten."

The nurse looked at Abby and then at Angela, and the expression on her face was like the tolling of a death bell. She started leading them into the Emergency Room. "He's treating one of the soldiers right now. And there are two others. Two other civilians that got here within the past hour."

Angela's stomach was in upheavals. "Was anyone else bitten?"

"Just the soldier he's working on now. They had to amputate his arm."

"What about the civilians?"

"They were caught in the crossfire. Minor gunshot wounds. I got them stabilized."

Nurse Sullivan hustled them into one of the ER rooms. Angela saw the two other civilian patients as she entered the small room. They were laying on hospital beds. One was a man who appeared to be asleep or passed out. The other was a woman who watched them keenly.

Sullivan directed Abby to sit on the bed and lay back. She smiled reassuringly at the girl. "You must be Abby. Angela's daughter?"

Abby nodded, looking unsure of everything now. Her conviction that she was okay was starting to melt away. She'd noticed the look on the nurse's face before.

"Well," Sullivan said, pulling a white hospital blanket over her. "You just stay warm. I know it's a little chilly in here. Do you need anything?"

"No," Abby said, her voice small. "I'm okay."

Sullivan nodded, then looked at Angela. "Can I speak to you outside?"

Angela looked over to Marie, who was standing beside Abby's bed. Marie put her hand on Abby's and nodded back, letting Angela know that she would stay with Abby.

Angela and Sullivan slipped out of the room and walked a few paces down. The other woman pulled her into an empty adjacent room. Her smiley demeanor was gone. She looked serious now.

"How long ago was she bit?"

Angela felt her heart in her throat. "It's been...five hours, I think."

Sullivan tried and failed to conceal her dismay at that news. "Look. Angela. I have to be frank with you."

Angela's hand went up to her forehead. She didn't like the sound of those words. They made her tongue gum up and her throat constrict.

"If it's been that long, there's not much we can do," Sullivan said. "The final say-so is up to Doctor

Trent, but I don't think there's going to be any point in amputating the leg after five hours."

Angela's voice didn't come when she tried to talk. It was caught somewhere deep inside of her. Her words were a threadbare whisper. "There must be something you can do."

Pity flashed across Sullivan's features. She touched Angela's arm with all the reassurance she seemed to be able to muster. "Angela, we're going to do everything we can. I'm going to treat that bite mark. We don't have much antibiotics, but what we have, we'll give to Abby. But those drugs aren't useful against the FURY bacterium. You know that."

Angela didn't respond. She was looking at the ceiling.

"Listen to me," Sullivan said. "I've heard that the bites aren't as infectious as they were at the outset."

Angela managed a shaky nod.

Sullivan seemed to want to have something else to say, but couldn't come up with anything. Finally she gave Angela's arm a gentle squeeze. "Go and sit with her. I'm going to do everything I can."

—

Lee's sleep was not restful.

His chest ached, and fits of wet coughing would startle him awake. He was sitting in the back seat of the truck, smooshed against the passenger door. It was not comfortable, but he was exhausted, and that exhaustion would take him down under again.

When he slept, he dreamed of the fields and the tree, but his mind wouldn't let go of his body completely, and the pains that he felt made it into the dreamscape, so that when he walked through the fields he would look down and see that he was dragging a long, bloody tube that was coming out of his chest, and that tube was pumping out his blood and leaving a trail of it behind him.

When he looked at the path he'd made, he saw the ragged, inhuman shapes of primals, slipping like wraiths through the long grass, tracking along his blood trail.

He hurried faster, but his heavy breathing burned in his lungs. Made him feel hot and feverish all over. The sky was turning from a clear, polarized blue, to a messy, congealed-looking orange.

He reached the hill on which the tree stood. The primals were close behind. He thought that maybe if he could climb that tree, he might get away. He had no weapons. And, as he reached the tree, he realized that he had no clothes either. He was naked. Exposed. Cold, and then hot. He felt like vomiting.

He staggered up to the tree, trying not to trip on the long tube coming out of his chest.

The tree.

The massive branches.

The swing that hung from one of them.

He heard it creaking, merrily.

A little girl was seated on the swing, and she flew high, back and forth, like a pendulum, smiling at him as he coughed and tried to tell her that she was in danger, that she needed to climb the tree with him to get away from the primals.

She just laughed. "Everything will be okay."

But it wasn't going to be okay. Couldn't she see that?

She laughed and kept swinging.

Lee was sinking into the dirt. He couldn't climb the tree. He was going underground.

Then he was beneath the tree.

He was in the cavern, and the roots of the tree were deep and dark and gnarled like witch's fingers. He stood there, coughing and bleeding and feverish, and Julia was there, with a shovel, and she was working hard, sweating and dirt-streaked, shoveling soil into a pit.

Lee staggered to the edge of the pit and looked in.

There were bodies. Stacks of them. A mass grave.

On top was Tomlin, covered in oil.

Julia tossed another shovel-full of dirt in. It pattered over Tomlin's dead body. She rested. Planted the shovel's tip in the dirt, and leaned on the handle of it. "It's what we do. We bury them down deep. It's good for the roots." She nodded into the pit of bodies. "Look."

Lee looked.

The roots of the tree were moving like snakes. They slithered out of the walls of the pit, and joined with the bodies. Piercing them. Draining them. Consuming them. They crawled over Tomlin's body, questing, searching like blind worms. They found his nostrils. His mouth. His ears. His eyes. Went inside of him.

Lee wanted to cry out for him, but he couldn't stop coughing.

"Good for the roots," Julia said, and then continued to shovel in more dirt. "Makes strong branches."

Lee hacked and coughed. Collapsed onto his knees. Spit blood.

"Jesus," Julia said. "You alright? Lee? Lee?"

—

"Lee?"

His eyes blinked open. Bleary. Hot.

Back in the truck. His chest felt raw on the inside.

Julia hung over him, the dirt and grime from the cavern beneath the tree was gone from her face. Her cool hand was placed on his forehead, concern scribbled on her features. "Shit. You're runnin' a little hot."

"He okay back there?" Abe questioned from the driver's seat. He had the cab light on so that Julia could see.

"I'm not gonna lie," Lee said. "I feel like shit."

"Here," Julia said, tugging at his chest rig. "Get this off."

"I'm sure my stitches are fine."

Julia was opening her medical pack and pulling out her battered stethoscope. "I'm not worried about the stitches. Take the rig off."

Lee grumbled like an ornery dog but did as he was told.

When he sloughed the thing off like a dead skin, she lifted his shirt and put the paddle of the stethoscope to his chest. "Breathe in deep."

He did so, and she listened.

"Again."

He felt his lungs rattling as he did.

She took the stethoscope away and leaned back. She gave him an evaluating look and bit her lip.

"What?"

She bent to her bag again, started to rifle through it. "I'm putting you on antibiotics."

"You think it's pneumonia?" he asked.

She nodded, pulling out a bottle of pills and checking the label. "Normally, we'd run a test to confirm that before putting you on the pills, but…I don't have that capability. So we're going to take a bet that the antibiotics will do more good than harm."

Lee put his hand on her wrist. "We don't have many antibiotics left. Don't waste them."

Julia looked at the bottle in her hand, seriously considering the ramifications here. Lee was right, and she knew it. Antibiotics were in short supply, and no one was making new ones. They couldn't afford to simply shell them out every time someone had an infection. They had to let people's bodies do their best.

"If I don't give you these," Julia said, reasoning it out at the same time that she spoke. "Then there's a strong likelihood your condition is going to worsen. Which will make you inoperable. Which puts the whole team in jeopardy." She turned her gaze on him. Her eyes were calm and emotionless. "This isn't a heart decision I'm making here, Lee. I'm giving you these antibiotics because the alternative will turn out to be more costly."

Lee's mouth twitched. Then he nodded. "Whatever you say, Doc."

She gave him the first round, which was several pills. She counted them out in her hand. Lee didn't. He shoveled them in his mouth and washed them down with water from his camelback that was body-heat warm and tasted like plastic.

Carl was twisted in the passenger seat, watching Lee. "You gonna be operational?"

Lee leaned back. He felt the ache of sickness in his limbs. He nodded. "Gonna have to be."

Carl pursed his lips and exchanged a glance with Julia, then turned back forward. "We're almost there."

Maybe it was the sickness. Maybe it was the exhaustion. Maybe it was the cobwebs of the dream that still hung about in his mind, or the fact that Paolo had just blown his brains out hours ago, but the image came to him again.

The trigger clicking against his finger. Striker hitting primer. Igniting propellant. A bullet blasting through his own head. That sequence playing on loop.

The woods are lovely, dark and deep, Lee thought.

But I have promises to keep.

And miles to go before I sleep.

And miles of rivers that lead to violence, eventually.

Lee blinked at the ceiling and felt something give inside of him.

Like giving up on stridently paddling upriver. Simply letting the current take you.

Because you can't fight it. Destiny is a river, and all the rivers lead to the same place eventually.

And that was Lee's destiny. To forever bypass the dark and lovely woods. To forever continue on, because there are promises to keep. Lee was not made for peace, was he? He was not put on this earth to be the kid that was able to swing from the branches of the tree and enjoy the sunshine and the cool breeze, like all the other normal people.

Lee had been put on this earth to fight. To go down into the dark where the normal people never went, and to bury the bodies that kept that tree strong. He would never swing from that tree. It simply wasn't his destiny. That was not where his rivers led.

He couldn't fight the river anymore.

He could make himself miserable looking at the normal people and wondering why he could not be like them. Or he could look at the tree as more than just branches and sunshine, but also as darkness and roots, which supported the entire structure of it all, and take his quiet measure of pride in knowing that none of those normal people could do what he did.

Perhaps the violence in his nature was not an affliction.

A wild fire destroys, but it is also a part of the natural cycle.

That is who I am, he realized. *That is what I do.*

He was the reset.

He was the tare that balanced the scales.

Lee didn't find peace on those dark Alabama highways. That was not for him. And he thought that it never would be. And that…that was okay. What he found was acceptance.

—

They would've preferred some industrial site. Something with concrete walls and big metal doors. Those had proven to be the best places to hide out while on the road.

But as the miles dwindled between them and their objective, all they could find was a farmhouse, set back off of Covington County Highway 67. It was abandoned, and didn't look like it had been utterly destroyed, although most of the glass was broken, shards of it sticking up from the window frames like busted teeth.

Time was short. It would have to do.

Mitch and his team approached the house with caution and cleared it of anything that might be hiding inside. Humans. Primals. Packs of dogs. All legitimate concerns.

When Mitch gave the all-clear over the squad comms, they parked the trucks tight around the back of the house, and went inside.

"It ain't the Ritz-Carlton," Mitch said as they walked in the back door. "But it'll do."

The back door opened them into a cramped kitchen with a sink piled full of dirty dishes that had been there so long they weren't even moldy anymore. Rain and leaves from nearby trees had come in through the shattered kitchen window. Created a tiny ecosystem right under the window, which spilled into the sink with all the dishes. There was a tiny sprig of a tree growing up out of the sink, reaching for the window with its grand total of three leaves.

The house smelled of dampness. But, for all of that, it didn't look like it'd seen much traffic. A lot of these abandoned houses had been used and used again by God-knew who. Lee wasn't sure who those people were, or what sect of society they came from, but they inevitably scrawled stupid things on the walls and took shits in the corners.

Luckily, graffiti and old piles of human excrement were not in attendance.

Someone had lived here. And then abandoned it when it could no longer keep them safe. And that appeared to be the end of this house's story. At least until about five minutes ago.

Lee stood in the kitchen and looked around. The turbulence inside him was calmer this morning. He felt like he was no longer fighting himself, and that was good.

But there were still concerns. Fears. For his team. For their lives.

This was still a long-odds mission, no matter how they cut it.

He worried about how Julia would take it if he died that day.

She was strong. She would be okay. He knew that. But he wondered, with a wispy sort of reticence, if he'd ever come right out and told her how much she'd meant to him. And he didn't think that he had. And he wondered if she knew.

But you can't expect people to know things if you don't say them.

He thought about it now, but it seemed strange.

He didn't want to have a deathbed conversation right now.

He wanted to do his work. He wanted his team to have confidence. Not to be worried that he was gonna kick the bucket. They needed to be focused on the objective right now, not on mortality.

Lee looked away from her. Turned to Carl. "You ready?"

Carl dipped his head. "Yeah. You?"

Lee stifled a cough. "Let's roll."

It was an hour before dawn when Lee and Carl dipped into the woods, heading south towards the airport. Lee, armed with his M14, and Carl with his much fancier MSR.

Deuce tread quietly along, sticking close to Lee's legs. He looked up at Lee as they went, and Lee put his finger to his lips, and shushed him. Hoped the dog would obey.

The woods were quiet and serene. Just the susurration of Lee and Carl and Deuce moving through the leaves. In the darkness, Lee saw Deuce perk up a few times at something, but he never issued a growl.

The sky was turning gray when they came to the top of a hillock. Through the half-leafed trees, Lee saw a sprawl of tarmac ahead of them. Buildings were light gray and white shapes.

Carl and Lee came together, shoulder to shoulder and listened.

Birds were starting to rustle and wake. Calling out to each other through the woods.

"I'm hedging my bets here," Lee whispered.

Carl nodded. Looked around at the lay of the land. "Alright. Find yourself a hide." He raised a hand, pointing to another rise in the landscape off to their right. "I'm going to make my way over there and see if I can cover another angle."

Carl started moving in that direction.

Lee picked his way across the hillock, going slow, often kneeling and inspecting the skein of trees for a window. On the southern side of the hill, he found what he was looking for. It was a slight clearing right before a steep downslope. The trees opened up here, creating a window for Lee to view through.

He knelt down again and looked around. He couldn't see Carl anymore.

He touched off his comms. "Mic test. Mic test. How copy?"

Carl came back with a whisper: "Carl copies."

A moment later: "Abe copies at the Crash Pad."

Lee got himself situated at the side of a downed pine tree. He sat cross-legged and propped his rifle up onto the crumbling bark of the dead tree. Glanced to his left and saw Deuce standing there, looking out into the woods. He clucked his tongue to get the dog's attention and then motioned for him to come over.

Deuce seemed to consider this for a moment. Then he sauntered over.

Lee held up a hand. "Sit. Stay."

Deuce chose to sit with his body up against Lee's, either for warmth or comfort. He leaned heavily into Lee. Lee gave him a scratch behind the ears. "Good boy."

Then he settled down over his rifle. The cheek rest was cold against his face. He focused on being comfortable. Didn't want to be fidgeting. He spread his legs out, and managed to squirrel them underneath the pine tree so that the trunk of it created a comfortable bench for him to lean on. He relaxed into it.

I can sit here all day.

Which was good. That was the point.

A rattle and bang echoed its way through the woods. A distant noise, carried through the cool, clear air. Then the sound of a voice.

Lee sighted through his scope. Panned it around the airport.

From his vantage, he could make out what appeared to be two large hangars. Off the side of one, he spotted two figures. One was moving about, doing the Early-Morning-Shuffle. The other was raising a large rolling door. The rumble of the rolling door reached Lee's ears a second or two later.

Lee used the mildots on his reticle to size up the two men. Took a quick mental average of their heights. Judged the distance to be approximately six hundred yards. But he didn't plan on taking shots yet. Just gathering data.

Lee spoke into his comms, just above a whisper, slowly and deliberately so that his words were clear. "I have two hostiles. Located at the east side of that easternmost building. Both armed with rifles. AK variants."

Carl's response took a little longer this time. "Copy. I'm just now getting into position. Standby and I'll let you know what I can see."

Lee watched the two men for a moment more, taking a mental note of their clothing so that he could differentiate them in the future. One was wearing a gray top. What looked like a hooded sweatshirt. The other was wearing a green, 1960's-style military jacket.

Lee pulled away from his rifle and with slow, purposeful movements, pulled out a sheet of paper and a pen, which he used to start taking notes.

"Alright," Carl's low voice came through. "I'm situated. I *do not* have a good view of the eastern side of the hangar from my position. I can see the tops of them, but not the doors. But I got a good line on the other set of buildings. I got a tall one with a white roof, and a short one with a gray roof. You see those?"

Lee settled back into his rifle. Panned to his left. "Okay," he responded. "I can see the two buildings that you're talking about. I have a good line on the short building with the gray roof. I *do not* have a visual on the front of the tall one with the white roof."

"I copy. I have coverage on the front of the tall one."

"Alright, Crash Pad," Lee said. "Prepare to copy."

Abe answered up. "Go with it."

"Airport is inhabited by hostiles. At this time, we are focused on four buildings. These buildings are located on the north side of the airport, with the tarmac running east and west behind them. Short building with gray roof will be Building One. Tall building with white roof will be Building Two. These both face approximately northwest. The next two buildings are both the same size. Going from left to right, they will be Building Three and Building Four. Buildings Three and Four face approximately north-northeast. On Building Four, I have a visual on hostiles using entrances located on the delta-side."

Lee used the agreed upon terminology: The front face of a building was referred to as "A," and then, moving clockwise, the sides of the building were B, C, and D.

Abe came back after a moment. "Crash Pad copies. Any visual on tankers?"

Lee scanned the compound in the distance and felt the first note of misgivings. "Crash Pad, I have no visual on tankers."

Lee moved his rifle a fraction and brought Building Four back into his sights. Despite the feeling of his gut souring with not-so-great news, he said, "Now let's hold off judgement. Buildings Two through Four are all hangar-sized. Plenty big enough to hold fuel tankers."

Carl responded. "I agree. And that's where I'd put them."

"Crash Pad copies. Is there any way that you guys can see inside one of those buildings and confirm whether there are tankers present?"

"From my current vantage point," Lee said. "I can see there's a sizeable rolling door that they just pulled up. I think it's big enough for a truck to get through, but I can't see inside. Carl, can you advise any better?"

"Negative," Carl said. "I can't even see the doors you're talking about from this perspective. Are you able to move closer, Lee?"

Lee glanced sideways at Deuce, laying at his side. "I can, but I got Deuce with me. If he smells something and starts barking, the jigs up."

"Roger that," Carl said. "I'm going to move now before it gets any lighter out. See if I can't get a look through that big door."

Up to this point it had been long-distance recon. The closer Carl got, the more their chances of being seen rose. And Carl would be looking into the rising sun. Which meant, in order for him to see inside that dark doorway, he'd practically have to be in the shadow of the building.

The thought made Lee's heart start knocking inside of his chest.

They had one chance to do this, and it was entirely predicated on them having the element of surprise. If they blew that, they might get out alive, but they couldn't just come back later and try again. The hostiles inside the airport would be on high alert.

Lee couldn't, in good conscience, tell his team to assault a compound when they weren't even sure that what they were risking their lives for was there.

They *had* to confirm the presence of fuel tankers.

Lee didn't like it. He felt like the circumstances were forcing his hand.

There's another option, he thought. *You just have to think about it...*

"Carl, standby," Lee ordered. "Everyone hold on for a minute. Let me think about this."

Silence on the comms.

Lee's mind pursued several possibilities, like a chess player thinking through the cause and effect of his next move.

But this was more like speed chess. A decision was needed quickly.

"Alright," he transmitted. "Carl, maintain your current position. Crash Pad, I think there's another option here. I think it's a better option. It'll involve less risk. But…" he trailed off, pursuing trains of thought again. Released the PTT button while he considered them.

After a moment, Abe prompted him. "But…?"

Decision.

Do or die time.

"But it's going to move our timeline up," Lee answered. "Sorry, I don't think anybody's gonna get any sleep. Abe, grab a paper and a pen and get ready to start drawing."

THIRTY

TANKERS

MILES TUGGER—BETTER KNOWN as Little T—pulled up to the tiny airfield outside of Hurtsboro at about nine in the morning.

Little T wasn't exactly little. He was short, yes, but he was very broad across his shoulders, and his chest was the approximate size and shape of a whiskey barrel. His hands looked more like thick-cut steaks with five muscly protrusions apiece. They looked more suited to crushing bone than pulling triggers, but he still had his shotgun in his lap.

Little T was unhappy and worried, although he could not express worry, so it came out as anger. His broad face was scrunched down into a Neanderthalic expression of distaste.

His driver pulled them to a stop, facing the gates.

The wheel-man was *actually* little. Small in height, and small in frame. Wiry. A redhead with a mouth full of teeth that ran off in separate directions from his gums, like his tongue had called out a bomb threat and the teeth were fleeing in panic. Little T legitimately couldn't remember the guy's actual name. Everyone just called him Ginger.

"I don't see the Suburban," Ginger said, then cast a worried glance at Little T.

Little T glowered and didn't say anything. Inside, though, his stomach was in knots.

The *Nuevas Fronteras* boys had come out to the airfield to do their dirty deeds against Paolo's little group of dissidents. They were supposed to send word back to Browers County Correctional when everything was clear.

They wouldn't be sending the word back to Little T, mind you. They didn't give a fuck about Little T. He was just a means to an end. They played nice with him so that they didn't have to waste the ammo to exterminate him and his people.

No, the message was supposed to be sent back to one of *El Cactus's* lieutenants, a slim, sallow-faced Mexican who's entire demeanor exuded insanity. *His* name was *La Pala*, which Little T understood to mean "The Shovel." Presumably because he buried people.

La Pala was not happy that his boys hadn't brought the good word of Paolo's destruction back to them. So he sent Little T to figure out what the fuck was keeping them.

Little T didn't care to be ordered around, but he was terrified of *La Pala*. He was terrified that the news he might bring back would be bad news. *La Pala* didn't subscribe to the old "don't kill the messenger" way of thinking.

"You want me to honk the horn?" Ginger asked.

"No," Little T answered quickly. "Don't do that."

Little T shuffled his thick self around in his seat so he could access the pocket of his jeans. He pulled out a silver key. The key to the lock on the chain that kept the gate closed. He passed this over to Ginger. "Open the gate."

Ginger nodded and hopped-to. Exited the vehicle. Walked over to the chain with his weird, scarecrow gait. Fiddled with the lock. Stopped.

Little T watched him in annoyance. Was the lock too much for this cretin to handle?

Ginger turned around and held up the lock for Little T to see.

The hasp was cut through cleanly. Bolt cutters.

Well, that's not a good sign.

He rolled down his window and poked his head out.

"What do you want me to do?" Ginger asked.

"Open the fucking gate so we can figure out what happened," Little T answered.

This is gonna be bad news.

Maybe I can send Ginger to deliver the bad news.

Ginger shrugged, tossed the broken padlock off to the side. Undid the chains.

Little T settled back into his seat with a huff.

Ginger pushed the gates open.

The world exploded.

Ginger's body seemed to come apart at the seams.

The windshield of their truck shattered in a dozen places.

Little T felt something hit him high in the shoulder.

Out of pure reaction, Little T ducked in his seat, his angry eyes gone wide with fear. Behind the glove box, he turned his head to look at his shoulder and saw the ragged wound there, dribbling blood. His ears rang, committing the rest of the world to silence.

Little T waited for gunshots. Waited for more explosions.

They didn't come.

After a few ragged breaths, he straightened in his seat. Peeked over the top of the dashboard. But he couldn't see anything out of the pebbled windshield.

He pushed his door open. Slid out of his seat and stood on unsteady legs.

The gates were mangled by the blasts. Smoke that stank of high-explosive wafted through the air.

What was left of Ginger was piled in the spot where he'd pushed open the gate. It wasn't recognizable as human.

Booby-trapped, Little T thought. *Someone booby-trapped the gate.*

And it sure as shit hadn't been the *Nuevas Fronteras* fucks.

Little T evaluated himself after a moment of standing in shock. The wound to his shoulder was bad, but survivable, he thought.

Still, he found his stomach doing loops.

Bad news.

And now Ginger was dead.

Which meant that the only person left to deliver the bad news to *La Pala* was him.

For a moment he considered running away. But just as quickly he dismissed it. Where the fuck would he go?

His unsteady legs began moving again, and they carried him around the front of the truck. The hood looked like someone had gone to town on it with a pick axe. A lot of big holes in it. Shrapnel. But…it was still running. For now. The radiator would be fucked at the very least.

Little T realized that his biggest fear at that moment was the truck dying. Which would delay him getting back to the Correctional Facility. Which would delay him getting to *La Pala*. And while he didn't even want to report to *La Pala*, he thought that maybe if he did it quickly, *La Pala* would appreciate his diligence. But if it took him half the day to hike back…

Little T shuddered.

He shuffled to the driver's seat and got in.

It was still warm from Ginger's skinny ass.

He slammed his door closed. The engine was making funny noises, which only increased Little T's sense of urgency. He backed out onto the road, turned, and headed quickly back to Browers County Correctional to deliver the bad news.

If he delivered it fast enough, perhaps *Nuevas Fronteras* could stop whoever it was that had blown Ginger to pieces. And maybe that would save Little T's own hide.

—

Carl slipped through the trees, a few hundred yards from the fence line of the airport.

It was getting on towards eleven hundred hours now. The sun was still ahead of him, but it wasn't glaring into his eyes as it had been that morning. It would have been better if the sun had been at his back. Would have been better for his visuals, and also to conceal his movements.

But you had to work with what you had.

Carl had set out from his hide on top of the hill over an hour ago. Moving down the face of the hill, he'd kept low to the ground, duck walking when the trees created a wall that would conceal him, and low crawling with his face in the dirt when he was exposed. Inch by inch.

His clothes were soaked. Sweat was pouring down his face and into his eyes. A stalk was no easy task when you were healthy. With an injured ribcage it was slow and agonizing.

But he kept picturing Tomlin's body under that flow of crude oil, and that made his injured ribs seem like a small thing.

He kept picturing the heads of the men inside of that compound snapping back as he put .338 Lapua Magnums through their brains, and that gave him the energy to keep moving.

Lee had kept a running tally of hostiles over their squad comms.

So far, there were thirteen men accounted for. What sounded like a roving patrol of six that skirted the perimeter in pairs. Three more in a truck with an

M60 machine gun on the back—one to drive, and two to serve the weapon. Four more that Lee had identified, just milling about the compound, going in and out of the buildings.

Carl couldn't see any of this from where he was.

When he'd been slithering down the face of the hill, he'd spotted one of the roving patrols, but that was it. And the truck with the machine gun was sitting stationary between the two sets of buildings, covering the gated road into the airport.

Now he was at the very bottom of a draw in the land, and coming back up. He couldn't see anything, but the nice part about it was that because the earth around him was over his head, he could walk upright.

He started to make his way up to the top of the draw, getting lower as he did.

Through the trees, he saw the top of the roofline of Building Four. It glinted brightly in the sunshine. The closer he got to the top of the draw, the more of the building came into view, and the lower Carl had to crawl.

At the top, he was on his hands and knees, breathing heavily. Everything around him was the scent of his own sweat, mixed with the earthiness of the forest floor. When he held his breath for a moment, he clearly heard voices. They seemed very close.

He estimated his distance to the building. Maybe a hundred yards?

He chose a thick oak tree and used this as concealment, keeping it between him and the building as he crawled toward it.

One of the more unnerving parts of a stalk was hearing all the leaves rustle beneath you. It sounded like you were raising a racket, but Carl knew from experience that no one more than twenty yards from you could actually hear it. It was difficult sometimes to put your faith in the tricks of the trade, when you knew your life was on the line.

He got to the base of the oak tree and stopped. Took a moment to catch his breath and give his ribs a chance to stop aching so damn bad. Then he leaned out, very carefully.

He saw the fence ahead of him, at about the fifty yard mark. Beyond that, open space for another fifty yards. Then the face of Building Four. Huge. Tall. Broad.

From this perspective, he could see the shape of the open rolling door that Lee had identified earlier. But there was still too much visual interference. There were a lot of trees between him and that door, and there was a particularly dense bit of evergreen that was sitting right in the middle of his view.

"Shit," he whispered to himself.

He tried anyway. Lowered himself to the ground, painstakingly slow. Brought his rifle up.

He was hoping to get a keyhole through that screen of evergreens.

But the image was just a green blur.

He cursed again, adjusted the focus on the scope, trying to see *through* the copse of green, but still, no joy.

Carl was not a man to be easily daunted, but an hour of stalking while injured had sapped him hard.

He laid his head on the rifle stock and whispered another litany of curses at the dirt.

Alright. You gotta shift.

Lee's voice in his ear: "How you doin', Carl?"

Carl leaned back behind the concealment of the oak's trunk and keyed his comms, keeping his voice at a whisper. "I'm within a hundred yards. But I came up on a bad angle. I'm going to need to adjust. Give me another fifteen minutes."

"You got it, Bud. Take your time."

—

Seven of them, crouched in tense silence in the woods.

They were close enough that Julia felt like she couldn't breathe without being heard.

It had taken them most of the morning to get into position. Everyone was tired and ragged. But they held their positions despite aching muscles and cramps. They *had* to. They were fifty yards from the gate, and the woods were thin. If they started rustling around, they'd be seen.

Julia was prone in the leaves. She didn't have cover. She was acutely aware of that. Cover stopped bullets. Concealment didn't. All she had was the underbrush to hide her.

She leaned her head to the right. A little window through the brush that provided her with a view straight ahead into the airport. She saw the tall fencing. Beyond that, the truck with the machine gun on top.

She heard the men in the bed of the truck talking. Laughing.

They were speaking Spanish, she was pretty sure. She was close enough to hear the individual words, but she didn't understand them. She was close enough to see the expressions on the men's faces. Close enough to see that one of them was very young and had the wispy beginnings of a macho mustache. The other was older. Clean shaven. A military bearing to him, even as he laughed and made conversation.

She kept thinking how that M60 would chew through her pathetic concealment.

And her body.

A daytime raid was no one's idea of a good time. But Lee had a point: if Carl was spotted, their only chance was to assault the objective while they still had a few seconds of surprise on their side.

If all went well, they'd exfil quietly after dark, get a few hours of sleep, and hit it in the early morning hours.

At least I'm prone, she kept telling herself, trying to look on the bright side. *At least I'm comfortable.*

But if she was being honest, she couldn't wait for darkness to fall so she could get the hell out and stop staring down the barrel of that machine gun.

—

Lee was coughing and trying not to.

A cough could be heard from a long ways off. Maybe even six hundred yards.

He bent down below the cover of the fallen pine tree and wheezed, as quietly as he was able. Then held his chest still, trying to overcome the urge to hack through sheer willpower.

When the coughing fit past, he spat what was in his mouth onto the ground. It was dark and unpleasant looking, but at least it wasn't bloody. That was a step in the right direction, he thought.

You're good to go, he told himself.

He raised his head back up and settled back into his rifle.

Behind the scope, he moved the rifle by small increments, scanning along the fence line closest to where he estimated Carl to be, and then branching out from there.

Two of the roving patrols were on the far side of the airport. The third patrol was coming around and would be directly in front of Carl. But it would take them a while. They were lazy and didn't think that anyone was after them. They sauntered, and they spent more time looking at their feet and laughing at each other's jokes than watching the woods.

"Carl," Lee transmitted. "Just as a heads up, you're gonna have a roving patrol adjacent to your poz in about five minutes."

Carl clicked his mike twice to indicate silently that he understood.

Lee shifted his scope to the left, all the way to the truck with the M60 on the back.

That was going to be a problem.

But if Mitch did his job, then hopefully they could mitigate the damage. That was the best they could hope for at this point.

He scanned the grounds again, looking for any additional hostiles. He kept track of them by their clothing, or any other distinctive features. Sweatshirt Guy. Bloused Boots Guy. Cowboy Hat Guy. Etcetera, etcetera.

He spotted no one that he hadn't already made note of.

Carl's voice, very quiet on the radio: "Standby. I have a keyhole on the big door…"

If it hadn't been for that transmission, Lee wouldn't have scanned to his right, back to the big door, back to the side of Building Four.

If he hadn't scanned over to Building Four, he wouldn't have seen something there that he hadn't seen before.

A slim line, just barely protruding from a high window on the side of Building Four.

Angled down into the woods.

That's a rifle barrel…

Lee didn't have time to consider the consequences.

The second he realized what it was, he slapped his PTT: "Carl! Cover!"

At the same instant, he put his reticle on the side of the building, superimposed to where he thought a body might be holding that rifle, and—he had no choice—he took the shot.

The rifle boomed, and a second later, the sound of the bullet striking the metal siding of the building was clearly audible. He fired twice more in quick succession to the first shot, squeezing the rounds off as soon as his reticle settled back into place.

The rifle barrel disappeared into the building.

"Shots fired!" Lee transmitted.

He swung his rifle towards the truck with the M60.

The gunner was already swiveling the machine gun to bear in Lee's direction.

Lee fired. The gunner jolted, crumpled over the M60.

Lee was reaching for his PTT to call an abort when Carl transmitted: "Tankers confirmed! Tankers confirmed! Hit it! Move!"

The second man in the truck bed grabbed his buddy's corpse and shoved it off of the machine gun. Through the rifle scope, Lee saw the man's wide eyes, and they seemed to be looking right back at Lee.

Then the truck exploded.

THIRTY-ONE

THE AIRPORT

THE FIRST GRENADE FROM Mitch's launcher took the truck right below the hood and launched the whole vehicle about a foot in the air in a plume of white smoke and concrete dust.

His second grenade hit the cab, and shattered the structure of the vehicle. Fire flashed out of the windows and windshield, the doors came off like they were held there by nothing more than tape, and body parts scattered.

Mitch took two bounding steps to his left. Exposed in the middle of the road. The gated entrance to the airport dead ahead.

He hit the pavement on his belly and sighted through the optic on the grenade launcher, unleashing another grenade with a shoulder-pounding thump.

The round hit the concrete at the base of the gate and went off with an ear-punching BOOM.

The gate blasted open.

Mitch put his face over his shoulder and shouted: "MOVE!"

Abe was already on the road, rifle up, moving swiftly towards the breached gate. Rudy, Morrow, Blake, Logan, and Julia stacked up behind him.

Mitch scrambled to his feet and took up the rear, behind Julia.

Mitch felt his mouth going dry and his blood singing in his ears, but it never touched his mind—the body fears, but the mind is cold.

The gate was a natural bottleneck, with woods on either side. Beyond it, there was about thirty yards of open space between them and the smoking ruins of the truck.

Which was their first point of cover inside the compound.

Abe went to his knees inside the gate and held his position, rifle oriented to the right to cover Buildings Three and Four. Rudy posted over top of Abe, covering Buildings One and Two.

Morrow paused behind Abe and Rudy.

"Moving!" he called, then hesitated.

Two shapes appeared around the corner of Building Two. They were both armed, but they weren't ready.

Rudy and Morrow fired at the same time, a burst of three shots from each.

One man wilted to the ground, dead.

The other's legs went out from under him and he rolled back into cover.

"Move!" Rudy commanded, and Morrow broke for the ruins of the truck like a racehorse coming out of its gate. He sprinted across the pavement and slid into cover at the front of the crumpled hood of the truck.

Mitch shuffled up behind Julia, smacked her shoulder to let her know he was there, then decided that now might be his only chance to reload the launcher in his arms. He broke it open, swiped his fingers across his tongue, and yanked the still-scalding 40mm shells from their ports, the spit on his fingers sizzling.

He shucked three replacements out, filled the empty ports, and snapped the launcher closed just as Blake hauled ass across to the truck, lugging the M249 Squad Automatic Weapon. Morrow saw him coming, shuffled to make room. Blake hit the ground, the bipod on the SAW already extended, and plopped the machine gun onto the ground, creating a base of fire for the rest of them.

With Morrow and Blake's base of fire now covering the left and right, Abe jolted to his feet and pointed a firm knife-hand at the side of Building Three, dead ahead of them. "Everyone on my ass!"

Mitch squeezed Julia's shoulder. "You good, Doc?"

"I'm good."

"'Cause shit's aboutta get spicy."

"Moving!" Abe bellowed over to Morrow and Blake.

Blake shouted back: "Move!"

Then the assault team sprinted for Building Three.

—

The worst thing about hiding was the shakes.

When Carl was in the mix, moving and running and gunning, the adrenaline had a place to go. When you were posted up behind a thinner-than-desirable tree, that adrenaline had no outlet.

Carl sucked in air through his nose and blew it out as slow as his thrashing heart would allow him.

He heard shouting to his right.

The roving patrol.

He heard their feet pounding pavement.

Carl held his next breath. Leaned out from his dismal excuse for cover.

Two men, jogging up along the side of Building Four. Their eyes were focused on the corner, where the gunfire was coming from. They stuttered to a stop just before the corner, jabbering to each other. One inched closer to the corner while the other hung over his shoulder.

Their backs were to Carl.

It was too easy to pass up. Even if it cost him his secrecy.

He lifted his rifle, put a bullet through the head of the one peering around the corner.

The other reacted faster than Carl would have liked. He spun, firing his AK from the hip, the bullets splashing through the brush all around Carl.

Carl cringed and held his aim as best he could while he racked the bolt, hoping to God that one of those bullets didn't seek him out, then put a single .338 projectile through the man's heart.

The man curled up like a pillbug and pitched forward onto the concrete.

Carl spun around and pointed himself towards the draw that was his only escape now. He racked a fresh round into his rifle.

Shit, he really shouldn't be this close in with just a fucking bolt-action.

You're done! Get the fuck out!

He sprinted for the draw.

Shouts behind him.

The rattle of automatic gunfire chased him.

A bullet split a branch about six inches from Carl's head.

He hunched his shoulders and piled his body forward, hit the draw, went down on his ass and slid through about ten feet of leaves. When he came up, the forest floor he'd just been running on was over his head.

He gasped, out a breath.

Pain from his ribs torqued his body for a moment. The slide down the draw had crunched them good. He waited for it to pass, then hobbled up onto his feet, pointed them north along the draw, towards the road and the gate that the assault team had just breached, and he started running.

—

Lee's whole world was barely-maintained control.

The fundamentals of marksmanship at 600 yards required complete control of the body, control of the head, the eyes, the trigger finger, the breathing.

But it all teetered on a razor's edge, and it required Lee to go to a different place in his mind, a place where nothing mattered, lives didn't matter, he was just doing a job.

He was just hammering nails.

Complete control.

Put the reticle on the target.

Steady rearward pressure on the trigger.

The gun bucks. The target goes down. Find the next one.

He couldn't think about Julia. He couldn't think about *any* of his team. He was like a surgeon, who, in order to maintain a steady hand, couldn't think about what would happen if he fucked it up.

He was letting the river take him. He wasn't fighting that tide anymore. He knew where it would lead. He was an agent of destruction, because sometimes that's what's needed in order to give life a chance.

Lee focused on the roving patrols. Two pairs of them were on the far side of the airport, and they were running across the tarmac towards the action.

They were running straight at Lee. That made his shots easier.

Windless day.

He only had to account for bullet drop.

Hammering nails.

He took the first of the four men in the pelvis.

Eighteen inches low.

The other three went prone. A smart choice, but they had no cover. They could only make themselves smaller targets.

The math ran through Lee's head. No time to second-guess it.

He cranked the elevation knob on his optic. Ten clicks. He put the reticle on the first of the three. Fired.

The round splashed in front of the man, spewing dirt in his face.

Shit.

Lee didn't adjust the optic again. He held the reticle higher, just over the top of the man's frightened face. Squeezed off another shot.

The man's face caved in. Disappeared.

Lee shifted to the next man.

Same point of aim.

Took off his jaw.

Maybe not dead, but out of commission…

Another clatter of gunfire to his right.

He opened both eyes and glanced at the side of Building Four.

Two dead bodies, slumped against the wall, and two live hostiles hosing the woods where Carl had just been.

Lee didn't have time to adjust his optic. He held low, right at the first man's feet—Bloused Boots Guy—fired. Caught him in the chest. Killed him instantly.

The other man jumped back into Building Four.

Lee opened both eyes again. Saw the assault stack moving along the front of Building Four, towards the corner. He touched off his comms. "Abe! Hold on that corner, you got a hostile on the other side."

The assault stack came to a stop, about ten feet from the corner.

Lee closed his left eye. Focused again.

Don't think about them dying.

Don't think about them screaming.

Don't think about failure.

Lee kept his finger on the trigger. Reached up with his left hand and cranked the elevation knob back to its original 600 yard point of aim. Held on the opening of the rolling door.

The hostile peeked out, just the side of his face.

Lee fired through the thin, sheet metal wall.

The face recoiled.

A second later, a hand flopped out onto the concrete, still and dead, and Lee felt a deep and frightening satisfaction.

That's what 175-grain, .30 caliber projectiles were for.

Because fuck you, and whatever you're hiding behind.

"Hostile's down," Lee said over the comms. "I don't have an angle in that door, though. I'm blind once you're inside."

"Roger that," Mitch's voice answered for Abe, because Abe was focused on the corner.

Lee did a rapid mental count, and then hauled himself up out of the leaves.

Three dead in the truck. All six roving patrol dead. Two more at the entrance of the rolling door.

Lee transmitted as he ran, Deuce jolting up to follow him. "You got *at least* two more inside that building," Lee huffed. "I'm moving to the compound now!"

—

Abe held on the corner.

Julia looked behind her. Mitch was slinging the grenade launcher off to the side and pulling his carbine up—they'd all agreed that grenade launchers and fuel tankers don't mix.

Her heart was pounding in her throat. She hated going through the door. But she would never vocalize it. She didn't want the others to know that it scared her as bad as it did. Maybe it scared them as well. Maybe they all just kept that shit to themselves.

The reason that Julia did all the things that she was afraid to do was because she knew that she had to be there with them, in the thick of it, or risk not being fast enough to save one of them if they got injured. It was her job. It was her *purpose*.

Don't let them die, she kept telling herself. *Don't let anyone else die.*

Mitch settled himself and rested his hand on her shoulder. "Set."

"Ready," Julia said, nudging Logan in front of her.

The nudge was passed from Logan to Rudy to Abe. Abe moved forward at a steady pace. Then hit the corner hard, followed immediately by Rudy.

No gunfire.

The stack was moving.

Julia held her breath and forced her feet into action.

Logan's back, right in front of her.

They cleared the corner.

Abe was at the opening of the rolling door. He had a tiny slice of vision on the inside and he scanned it with a fast, expert eye, inching forward while the stack scrunched together again, right at the entrance. The next corner they turned would be into Building Four...

Gunshots.

The sheet metal between Abe and Rudy sprouted holes. The holes started lancing back towards Julia.

Abe moved.

Rudy grunted, stumbled. But then kept moving, right behind Abe.

Logan hunched, lurched forward, and then his left leg let out a puff of red and he went down with a yelp.

Julia's first instinct was to grab him, and at the same moment that she bent down for Logan, she knew it was the wrong call. Mitch seized her shoulder, propelled her forward, staggering over top of Logan's body.

"Keep moving!" Mitch barked.

Her head buzzed horribly.

God, please don't let Logan die before I can get back to him!

The opening of the rolling door loomed. She had time to bring her rifle back up, back into her sights, grit her teeth, and then she hit the corner. One step out. A hard turn. She was facing darkness. Her sun-dazzled eyes wouldn't let her see anything for a half second, and all she could do was keep moving her feet.

Muzzle flashes split the dimness.

The ghost of Rudy's shape, dead ahead of her, and Abe's shape cutting crosswise to her right.

Go where the man in front of you hasn't gone!

She twisted, pivoted on her heel, swinging left inside the door.

An obstruction nearly smacked her in the face. A vehicle of some sort. She saw its small, boxy shape, the heavy tires. A forklift that had been parked up against the side wall.

Movement directly behind it.

Julia juked to her right to avoid running face-first into the lift.

A man in the corner, sighting down a rifle at Rudy's back.

Julia didn't even think that she aimed. She just pulled the trigger. She watched the bullets slam through the man's chest. Track up. Obliterate his face. He spilled backwards against the wall, and she didn't stop firing until she registered that he was on the ground.

She reached him, her ears ringing, her veins burning, every square inch of her body horrifyingly electric.

She kicked the rifle out of his dead hands and sent it skittering across the floor. For some reason, she couldn't bear to turn her back on him. So she put another round into his already-chewed-up face. Then she pivoted again, her back to the corner of the building, rifle scanning the darkness.

You did that.

You did that.

But louder than that voice was the thought, *I saved Rudy. I saved one of my guys.*

Tanker trucks. That's the first thing she registered. A lot of them.

—and the stink of spilled gas—

—and then the shapes of her comrades—

Abe, out to the right. Rudy in the middle. Mitch, peeling to her left, taking the left wall directly in front of her.

More muzzle flashes, sparkling like fireflies in the night.

The sound of bullets striking metal. Ricocheting with terrifying whines. Fragmentation from the projectiles ticking and tinkling all around her.

Julia didn't want to move from the corner. She wanted to sink down on her ass and sit next to the man that she'd killed. But she couldn't let everyone down. She had to keep them alive.

She propelled herself forward to catch up with Mitch.

Mitch moved quickly along the left wall of the hangar, then came to a sudden stop and jumped to the right. A smattering of bullets tore up the wall where he'd been. He took cover at the rear axle of one of the tanker trucks, went down on one knee.

Julia ran to him, slid to a stop. Put a hand on his shoulder to let him know she was there, her legs pressed up against him.

Mitch gestured rapidly with his support hand. "He's two trucks that way. Front of the truck. He's laying down behind the front axle of the tanker. You understand?"

Julia wasn't sure, but she nodded.

Mitch shifted so that his back was against the tanker. He gulped a few breaths, looked over his shoulder. "I'm gonna fire on him. You go prone right here at my feet, okay?"

"Okay."

"When he pops back up, you ice his ass."

"Okay."

This was combat. It was pure chaos. Everyone making it up as they went. They called it *adapting and overcoming*, but really it was just flying by the seat of your pants and hoping your fundamentals were better than the other guy's.

She dropped in place. The tires in front of her. And Mitch's boots.

Mitch shuffled to the left and shoved his rifle out, firing about ten rounds in the general direction of their target.

Julia leaned to her right so she could see past the tire.

Concrete stretched out like a desert basin. Black tires rose up like monoliths all across this terrain. There were several tanker trucks, all parked side by side next to each other. In the visual confusion, she had no idea where to look...

The target leaned out before she could figure it out.

She shifted her rifle in his direction.

He saw her. His muzzle swung and pointed right at her.

She fired.

She watched his muzzle bloom.

He collapsed.

She didn't.

She rolled back into cover, breathless, unbelieving, elated. "I got him," she wheezed.

Abe's voice over the comms: "My shooter's down."

Mitch responded. "Roger, ours too." He gave Julia a thumbs-up. "Julia got him."

"Everyone hold what you got," Abe transmitted. "Blake, can you hold our base of fire? We need Morrow to help clear the structure. Logan's down."

"I'm moving to you," Morrow responded.

Mitch grabbed Julia's arm and hauled her to her feet.

"Are you okay?" Julia asked him. "You got hit during entry."

He twisted to show the left side panel of his armor. There was a darkened, ragged hole in the nylon plate carrier, but the bullet hadn't penetrated the armor. "I'm good," Mitch said. "Just knocked my wind for a second. Go help Logan."

THIRTY-TWO

NUEVAS FRONTERAS

LEE MADE IT TO THE BOTTOM of the hill.

He saw the road leading into the airport through the trees ahead of him. He paused at a large tree, breathing hard. A coughing fit came on. He hacked into his arm. When he got his breath back, he keyed his comms.

"Julia, get me a casualty report as soon as you can."

"I copy," she answered. "I'm workin' on Logan now."

Lee was about to push off the tree when Deuce stiffened at his side and let out a low growl.

Lee snapped his rifle up in the direction that Deuce was facing, ears completely up, tail unmoving. He heard rustling in the brush. Lee stared at the forest, letting his eyes drift, trying to catch the movement.

Carl emerged. He stopped short as he saw Lee, and stood still for a moment until Lee ported his rifle. Deuce relaxed. Wagged his tail once.

Carl looked more exhausted than Lee, if that was possible.

He jerked his head towards the gates. "Let's go."

Lee caught up to him. "You good?"

"Yeah, I'm good."

They exited the woods about twenty yards from the gate. Lee saw Blake, kneeling at the front of the still-smoking truck, his SAW propped up on the ruined hood.

Lee's eyes went to Buildings One and Two. They hadn't cleared those yet. How many more hostiles were in those buildings? He hadn't seen anyone coming or going, but that didn't necessarily mean…

Carl halted in his tracks. Put an arm out to catch Lee.

"What?" Lee said.

Carl's head turned northward, away from the airport. Down the road to where it curved out of sight. "You hear that?"

Lee held his breath to listen. By the time the sound hit his brain and he identified it, Carl was already making for the woods again. Lee jumped after him, keying his comms as he went. "Blake! Vehicles incoming! From the road! Behind you!"

Lee bounded into the woods and spun around, sliding into a prone position behind some underbrush. Deuce was there, right on top of him.

Lee smacked the dog on the rump and snapped, "Go!"

It wasn't a learned command. Deuce simply knew he didn't want to be present, and he bolted into the woods like his tail was on fire. Lee knew that he wouldn't go far. He'd maintain a line of sight with Lee.

They'd cleared the road just in time.

Looking to his left, Lee saw the shapes of vehicles through the trees, coming around the bend in the road, now in the straightaway, their engines roaring as they accelerated for the gates.

Shit shit shit! Lee thought. *Who the fuck is this?*

"Blake, they're coming up quick!" he transmitted, then looked to his right, where he could see the soldier jumping up from his position and wheeling around to face the road, his machine gun at his hip. "Get cover!"

What Lee wanted was for Blake to sprint for Building Four and get his ass to safety.

What Blake did was raise the M249 to his shoulder and let off a sustained rattle of automatic fire, spraying the incoming vehicles.

There was the sound of bullets hitting sheet metal, hitting concrete, ricocheting, spattering through the woods.

The sound of tires screeching.

The lead vehicle took the brunt of Blake's spray. It veered off the road and hit a tree, ejecting a body through the windshield that crashed through the woods like it had been shot out of cannon.

The other vehicles skidded to a stop along the road directly in front of Lee, some of them angling sharply for the shoulders. They started shedding men. Out of doors. Out of truck beds. Armed men, shouting in a language Lee didn't know.

Nuevas Fronteras.

How did they know?

Blake ran for the back end of the blown-up pickup. He vaulted over the side of the bed as the first strings of return fire peppered the ground where he'd been. He shoved his SAW up onto the cab and started blind-firing to get heads down, to give him a tiny window to get up into his sights without catching a bullet to the dome.

Lee pressed himself into the dirt, thinking, *You stupid, ballsy fuck!*

Blake wasn't getting cover for himself. He was making a stand.

With his face pressed to the ground, Lee couldn't see Blake anymore. But he could hear the rhythm of the fight, and that told a story all its own. He heard the return fire from the intruders rapidly taper off in the face of a chattering machine gun, and then the machine gun's fire became more measured.

He's up, Lee knew. *He's in his sights. He's pacing his shots.*

A burst of five rounds.

A pause.

A burst of three.

Shouting, directly ahead of Lee.

Someone screaming, wounded.

A body thrashing through the brush.

A spray of leaves and dirt.

A boot skidded to a halt, inches from Lee's face.

Lee stared at the tread pattern.

Raised his head, just an inch, to see over the sole.
Legs.

A body.

A torso. A head. A rifle.

The man was alive.

He was completely focused down the road.

He had slid into concealment, right where Lee was, stopping short of being literally on top of Lee. And he never looked back. He kept staring through his rifle sights, his chest heaving.

Lee couldn't breathe. It would be too loud.

His heart hammered. Lungs ached.

He released his grip on his rifle.

Slowly slid his arm back to his plate carrier. To the knife.

Lee's foot shifted. Rustled leaves. Somehow, it managed to happen right in a space of dead air between Blake's bursts of machine gun fire.

The man inches in front of Lee jerked his head up, started to look over his shoulder.

Lee leapt. Took the man on the back. Hooked his left arm hard around the man's head, so that his forearm was planted over the man's mouth, muffling his scream of surprise.

Then he rolled.

Onto his back. The man on top of him. Lee wrapped his legs around the man's waist, hooked them, then thrust his hips, so that the man's body was splayed out wide and vulnerable, and he yanked back on the man's head as hard as he could, exposing the neck.

Lee put the knife into him. Into the side of his neck. And then a quick swipe out, severing the carotids, and the windpipe. Just the spine and about six inches of skin keeping the head on.

The man's body thrashed. Made an unearthly noise out of his severed windpipe.

Lee lay below him, holding tightly to him, while the blood spewed out, rained down, a waterfall of it. Lee turned his face away from it. He felt it, warm and horribly intimate on the side of his cheek. Pooling in his ear. Dripping towards his left eye so that he had to squint it closed.

With one eye open, he looked across the forest floor amid the shouting and the gunshots, and he saw Carl watching him, but there was no expression on Carl's face. He appeared to simply be waiting for Lee to be finished.

Carl's fingers squirmed up. Pointed further into the woods. He clearly mouthed the word: *Peel.*

Blood touched Lee's lips.

He nodded once in response.

The body on top of him shivered. Made a final, violent twitch. Then became dead weight.

Lee held it for a moment more, then gently let it roll to his left side.

He kept eye contact with Carl the whole time.

Carl's fingers, counting down.

Three.

Two.

One.

Carl came up onto one knee, sweeping his rifle up. He started firing and racking his bolt as fast as he could manage.

Lee stumbled out of the tangle of limbs, scooped up his rifle and sprinted for the woods. Everything was a rush of greens and browns. He found the thickest trunk that was within fifteen yards of him and dove behind it. He posted the rifle to the side and started firing.

Carl moved at the sound of Lee's rifle, jolting out of the brush and tearing through the woods. He ran past Lee, and Lee kept firing. He listened for the sound of Carl's rifle.

A clear and throaty *whu-BOOM*.

He turned and ran.

Bullets skipped after him through the woods. Leaves and small branches fell around him. The convoy was gaining their bearings to the surprise attack on their right flank and was shooting back.

Lee felt a hammer-blow square in the center of his back. He almost pitched forward, but managed to keep his feet. A second later a bullet zipped his right shoulder, ripping through the meat of it.

Lee posted behind another tree. His lungs were a ragged mess. He hacked as he turned and fired. Bullets shattered the side of the tree, spraying his face with splinters. He didn't have the wind to shout to Carl, but they were moving on command of each other's rifle reports now, a panicked sort of rhythm establishing itself.

Running back towards Lee, Carl's left leg bloomed red, and he stumbled, caught himself on the ground and scrambled on all fours behind a fallen log.

Lee wiped sweaty wood out of his face. Coughed. Got his bearings.

They were heading back up the hill.

He heard someone in his ear. It was Abe.

"The fuck's going on out there? Someone fucking answer back!"

Lee shot a glance towards the airport. He could no longer see Blake through the trees, but he could still hear the chatter of his machine gun.

But for how much longer? Blake had been maintaining a near-constant stream of fire. Had he reloaded yet? Blake only had one additional soft mag for the M249. A total of two hundred rounds. And when you were firing that constantly, two hundred rounds went fast.

Lee felt the urgency to coordinate with the rest of his team inside the airport. He looked over at Carl, laying on his back behind the log, sprays of woodchips erupting from the opposite side of it while Carl tried to check his leg wound.

"Carl!" Lee yelled to him. "Can you move?"

Carl didn't answer, just held out a thumbs-up.

The convoy was concentrating their fire on Lee and Carl's position now. Lee thought about making a run for it, but knew beyond a shadow of a doubt that they'd die if they did. They'd lost the initiative. They were pinned.

"Mitch!" Lee transmitted. "Mitch, are you free and do you have any more forties?"

Mitch came back, sounding strained. "Lee! I got forties! What do you need?"

Lee closed his eyes to the cacophony of death all around him. Tried to picture the layout of the airport in his mind. "Are you in Building Four? Near the side door?"

"Yes. Tell me what you need."

From that position, Mitch wouldn't be able to see the convoy through the trees. But Lee could.

"Mitch," Lee tried to speak clearly. "Standby one second. Blake, can you copy? I need you to copy me buddy."

It took four agonizing seconds for Blake to find the time to answer. The machine gun continued to fire in the background as Blake yelled into his mike to be heard: "I copy! I'm runnin' outta ammo here!"

"Blake, when Mitch starts firing grenades, you split from your position and get the fuck to Building Four, you copy?"

Blake tried to answer, then a scattering of rounds-on-metal were audible and Blake yelped. The machine gun fire came to a stop. "Fuck. Goddammit. I'm empty. I copy you. Get me the fuck out of here."

"Mitch," Lee commanded. "Arc a round over the trees, towards the road. You want to hit the road, about fifty yards out from the gate. I'll guide you in. How copy?"

"Copy. Ready."

"Carl!" Lee yelled. "Get ready to move!" Then he transmitted again. "Mitch, send one."

Distantly, Lee registered the heavy *KA-THUNK* of a launcher sending out a 40mm grenade.

Lee waited.

BOOM

He leaned out from cover for the quickest of peeks and heard a bullet buzz-whine past his ear.

A cloud of dirt and smoke, just inside the trees to the right flank of the convoy, but the distance was good—right smack dab in the middle of the convoy.

Lee hugged cover again. "Splash," he told Mitch. "Shift fire to *your right*, about fifteen yards."

Another distant thump of a report.

Another long second of flight-time.

BOOM

This time Lee heard men screaming, and their screams were terrible and beautiful to Lee. Immediately, the withering fire on Lee and Carl's position stopped. Lee managed another tiny peek, just to confirm. This time he saw the impact was right in the middle of the road.

"Mitch, you're right on! Send everything you got!" Then Lee shouldered his rifle and yelled, "Carl! Move!"

Out from cover, this time low on the base of the tree, Lee sighted through his rifle and found the shape of a man hiding at the rear-wheel of one of the vehicles. He fired and watched the man go down.

Behind him, Carl thrashed through the woods.

Mitch's rounds started hitting, one after the other, destructive blows shattering down on the middle of the convoy.

Lee turned and ran. This time Carl and Lee didn't stop. They pointed their faces for the top of the hill, and they ran until they couldn't run anymore, and then they jogged, and then they staggered, breathlessly, wounded, shot, desperate, to the crest of that hill.

Somewhere along the way, Deuce picked them up again, whining and then yapping, and then whining again, his ears flattened out and his tail between his legs. Lee hoped to God that it was just the hellacious gunfire, and not the scent of something else.

At the top of the hill, they collapsed at the sniper's hide that Lee had abandoned only ten minutes before. They heaved for air. Lee felt like he was hacking up a lung. But neither of them took the time to catch their breath. There was no time.

Carl ripped his small IFAK free of his rig, and hurriedly set to packing his leg wound.

Lee eyed the hole in his shoulder. It was starting to stiffen up, but the blood had only soaked the top part of his arm. Treating it was low priority in his mind.

Lee posted up on the downed pine tree once again, and scoped the convoy. He couldn't see all of it. He could only see the tops of a few of the vehicles. Some of the vehicles had made it into the compound, had skirted around the ruined truck where Blake had made his defense.

"Blake," Lee wheezed into the comms. "Did Blake get out?"

But Lee answered his own question before anyone else did.

Halfway between the ruined pickup truck and the corner of Building Four, Lee saw a shape on the ground. He felt his heart skip, drop, squirm. He brought his rifle up. Looked through the scope.

It was Blake.

Still alive.

He had no machine gun now. He'd abandoned it, empty, in the truck.

He was crawling for cover, his legs dragging behind him, a pistol in his right hand, firing blindly at the attackers that he was trying to get away from, while his left arm clawed across the pavement, gaining only inches when he needed yards.

When Lee opened both eyes, he saw the huddled shapes of his teammates at the corner of Building Four, but they couldn't get around the corner to help Blake. The side of the building was getting chewed up by a constant barrage of shots from the attackers.

Little puffs of concrete dust around Blake.

The pistol went dry. Locked back.

Blake put both hands into crawling.

Lee's original estimate of five vehicles had been off—there were almost a dozen. Two of them had already made it into the gate, and the men were stacked up behind them, using them as cover, while three more inched forward, the men shuffling alongside of them like infantry alongside a tank.

Everyone was either shooting at the corner of the building, or at Blake.

Too many targets.

Lee started firing. Aiming and firing.

He got two shots off and went empty.

"Motherfuck!" Lee shouted, then said to Carl, more out of ingrained habit, than any real need: "Reloading!"

Lee dropped the empty mag. Shucked a new one from his pouch. His eyes remained fixed on the airport the whole time, so that even as he reloaded as fast as his practiced hands could manage, he saw the moment when the bullets finally found Blake.

One found him, stopped his crawling. His hands still reached, but he didn't seem to have the strength to pull himself any further.

Lee seated the mag, sent the bolt forward in the same motion.

Another found Blake, and after that, Blake never moved. A third and fourth found him. Jolting his body. Puffing dust and blood off of him. Then a final barrage of four or five rounds skittered over him, and then the attackers turned their attention back to Building Four.

"I'm up," Lee breathed, like the fight had been punched out of him. But when you fight so much, and for so long, when it's all you've ever known, then even when it's punched out of you, you keep going by force of habit.

Lee slapped the rifle down, running on autopilot now.

What could he do?

Hammer nails. That's all there was *to* do.

They had four functioning teammates inside Building Four.

Two more on a hill outside the compound.

And—rough estimate here—about thirty armed men storming the gate.

There was nothing else to do but pick targets and pull triggers, until they either killed him or he ran out of ammo.

So that's what he started doing.

Carl tightened down his pressure dressing and immediately posted on his own rifle. Firing. And sighting. And firing. The fierceness gone out of it now, because they could feel it like the coming darkness as you're bleeding out. They could feel the momentum had shifted, and that this was not going to end well for them.

This was just a last stand.

They were little more than a stinging bee now. Doing as much damage as it could, knowing full well that it would die.

—

Logan was crying.

Not for himself.

Julia had to keep herself pressed down on top of him, because he was trying to get up and go to Blake. He would've been able to if he hadn't been shot through both legs.

Death huddled around them, seeming to darken the midday sun.

Mitch, Rudy, and Abe, pasted up against the side of the building, hunching and cringing as bullet impacts rattled all around them.

Beside Julia, Morrow held Logan by the back of the neck, telling him to chill out, telling him to calm the fuck down.

The stink of spent propellant was sharp.

Still practically laying on Logan, Julia pulled her head to the right and left, looked over her shoulder at the tall fencing, wondered if they could cut their way through, escape into the woods.

If they started cutting the fence now, they might get through before *Nuevas Fronteras* overran them. But then all of this was going to be for nothing.

You have to figure out a way to save your team. Save their lives, Julia. You have to figure it out.

Then she looked out, clear across the airport.

She saw the south gate of the complex.

Could they all get into a fuel truck and ram their way out of here?

Except for Lee and Carl. They would be left behind.

Would they be able to circle back and get them?

Not if the cartel guys swarmed the woods. Which they would do.

If they ran now in the trucks, she would never see Lee alive again.

She was stuck, mentally, in an impossible mire of circumstances.

She was still trying to think of a way for *all of them* to live through this.

But that wasn't going to happen, was it?

Still staring across at the south gate of the airport, she spotted something huge and tan speeding toward the gate. She looked at it in confusion, not knowing what the hell it was, until it hit the gate, and the gate appeared to simply disintegrate, and the roar and rumble of that massive dirt-colored object reached her ears.

She didn't have military experience, but she knew what it was.

She felt her heart wither inside of her.

None of them were getting out alive.

Nuevas Fronteras was now blocking their only viable escape with a tank.

THIRTY-THREE

REINFORCEMENTS

LEE STOPPED FIRING WHEN Carl elbowed him.

At about the same moment, Lee heard the sound, rumbling over the gunfire.

He opened both eyes. Looked up over the scope.

Over the top of Building Four, where his eyes were immediately drawn to the movement. The south gate of the airport hung open, battered to pieces, and through it was flowing a convoy of military hardware that made Lee's stomach turn to water.

In the lead was an M1 Abrams tank.

Lee was in shock at the sight of it, roaring across the field, flattening the bodies of the men that Lee had shot out there. His fingers moved without him thinking about it. He keyed his comms.

"They got a tank! Tank rolling in on top of you guys! Get the fuck out of there!"

Lee couldn't believe the words, even as he said them. A tank.

Was that the price that President Briggs had paid for the cartel's cooperation? Not to mention the three guntruck Humvees that tailed it...

"Give us cover!" Abe called over the squad comms. "Hold those boys at the gate down while we cut our way through the fence!"

So that was it. That was how this whole clusterfuck was going to end.

Lee put his cheek to his rifle stock and found the next target, splashed a round through the man's chest, then moved to the next target, all while the sound of the rumbling tank and the roaring of its jet-like turbine engines seemed to wash out all other noise.

"Reloading!" Carl called out. "Last mag!"

Lee fired another round. Jerked the trigger in the moment of tension and sent the shot wide. His bolt locked back. Empty. Lee swept down for another magazine, and realized that he'd already used his last.

"Up!" Carl said, and started firing again.

"I'm out!" Lee shouted, anger and disbelief turning his voice to rage.

He looked over his scope, feeling hollowed out, feeling the crushing defeat of his decisions bearing down on him, decisions that had cost lives, and would not produce anything. They had lost teammates for nothing—

One of the vehicles at the gate suddenly ceased to exist.

In one heartbeat, it was there, men with rifles huddled around it, shooting over the top of it, targeting the corner of Building Four, and with the next heartbeat it was just a gout of greasy black smoke.

The sound of the explosion hit Lee in the face, followed only a half-second after by the thunderous report of the Abram's main gun.

Lee instinctively ducked behind the pine tree. "Holy fuck!"

Then immediately looked back up.

Beside him, Carl had stopped shooting.

The two of them stared, goggle-eyed at the place where the cartel truck had been, a column of fire and smoke now guttering up from its remains. All around it, like revelers passed out around a bonfire, men lay, their bodies disassembled, wrecked, and left in a ragged circle by the blast.

Lee became aware of Abe's voice: "Are they firing on us? Where was that impact?"

Six hundred yards away, what remained of the cartel convoy became utter bedlam. The trucks at the gate were throwing themselves into reverse, squealing tires, ramming into each other, ramming into their own men, in a panic to get away. Inside the gate, the remaining two vehicles were trying to cut a tight turn, while their comrades flung themselves into the doors, and into the truck beds.

The Abrams tank pulled to a violent stop, right between the two sets of buildings, torn earth and concrete rolling out in front of its bulk like a wave. It rocked to a halt. The turret turned and this time Lee watched, unable to tear his eyes away.

The main gun sprouted a mushroom of flame.

One of the cartel trucks that was broadside to the tank shattered in fire and smoke. The truck's smoking shell tumbled, skidded to a stop, half-blocking the gate. Another truck hit it, then tried to back up and go around it.

The tank's M240 coaxial machine gun puffed smoke, and rattled in a long, devastating string of fire that lanced the truck trying to escape, shredding it and everything inside of it. Men tried to break cover and run through the woods, and the coaxial gun tracked them, ripped them apart before they could get to safety.

Four trucks managed to make the road and when they got their tires on pavement, the drivers inside weren't waiting for anybody. Their engines revved, their tires chirped, and they got the fuck out of there, trailing a gaggle of desperate men that knew there was no place they could go.

Lee watched a few of them throw down their weapons and try to surrender, but whoever was manning the coaxial gun didn't care. They went down like the rest. And in another time, in another life, this might have twisted in Lee's gut, but all he felt now was joy.

"Lee! You there?" Abe demanded. "What the fuck's going on?"

"Hold what you got!" Lee answered. "Just standby a minute. That tank is not cartel. Repeat, the tank is not cartel."

Beside Lee, Carl reached over and grabbed a hold of his arm, gave him a stern look. "That doesn't mean it's friendly."

Lee nodded back, tempering any enthusiasm before it could really take hold and make him feel hopeful.

The tank sat deathly still now. Like a giant predator that's gorged itself and now basks in the sun.

The three Humvees took positions, fanning out behind the tank, filling in gaps. But no one came out of the trucks. The gunners hunched behind their armored .50 caliber M2s and scanned the premises for any more threats, but there was only dead bodies for them now.

"Well," Lee mumbled. "What the fuck do we do now?"

An amplified voice shattered the ear-ringing silence. "This is Captain Lehy. Is there a Captain Lee Harden, or any other Coordinator from Project Hometown present?"

Lee felt a jolt go through him. He must have twitched, because Carl raised an eyebrow. "Friend of yours?"

"Maybe," was Lee's only answer. Then he remembered that Abe was down there, too. He touched his PTT. "Abe, don't you fucking move. You guys maintain cover until we figure this out. You copy?"

Abe responded that he did, but didn't sound pleased about it. With an Abrams breathing down their neck, "cover" didn't really exist.

Lee rose up onto his feet and looked at Carl. "How many rounds you got left?"

Carl shrugged. "Two or three."

Lee nodded. "Well. If shit goes sideways, make 'em count."

—

Lee walked along a road strewn with human wreckage.

Deuce trotted along beside him, sniffing at the dead as they passed their mangled corpses.

Smoke wafted across the roadway like swift-moving fog, occasionally obscuring the Abrams tank ahead of him. Fire licked from the inside of a vehicle that had caught one of Mitch's 40mm rounds—a panel van with charred limbs hanging out of its open doors.

Lee walked with his rifle slung, his hands loose at his sides.

The blood of the man he'd knifed felt stiff on his face. He wiped what he could off with his sleeve, but he could still feel it crusting around his hairline and his ears.

This is who I am, he thought, as he picked his way steadily through the colossal wreck of warfare that he'd orchestrated. And the sizzling fires around him seemed to whisper back, *this is what you do.*

And he felt no recrimination in it this time.

It was simply truth.

It was destiny.

The river had carried him here.

Would *always* carry him here.

His lungs felt wheezy and ragged, but he didn't feel sick. The hole in his shoulder was stiff and painful, and it leaked, but he thought he could still manage it for a while. The round he'd taken to his back, surprisingly enough, ached the worst. Like it had misaligned a few of his vertebrae when it hit.

At the gate, he stepped around the burning remains of the truck that had taken a tank round there. He thought he saw a fleshless skull in the driver's seat.

The wind was coming towards him, so that when he passed through the gate, he stepped through the pall of smoke like a curtain.

He stopped there, between the gate and the tank, and he stared at it.

One of the gunners atop a Humvee swiveled his M2 to point in Lee's direction.

Lee expected Captain Lehy to come out of the tank. But when Lee raised his hands to show they were empty and that he was compliant, it was the Humvee with the M2 pointed at him that opened its doors, and out stepped a man that Lee didn't think he'd ever see again in his lifetime.

Captain Terrance Lehy, Coordinator for Texas, was a tall man with sandy hair. He wore no cover, no helmet. Just a chest rig and a rifle. Multicam pants and shirt. The sleeves rolled up to reveal two arms coated in tattoos. A battered pair of Oakley M-frames shielded his eyes.

The two men surveyed each other at a distance.

Captain Lehy pulled the sunglasses from his eyes, pushed them up onto his head. He eyed Lee up and down, walking slowly towards him. Lee decided to meet him halfway. They stopped when they were about three paces from each other.

"Jesus, Lee," was Captain Lehy's greeting. He looked…concerned.

"Tex," Lee replied, his voice hoarse and quiet. Amid the crust of smoke and dirt and blood that coated his face, his eyes scanned off to the right. To where Blake's body lay on the concrete. Then back to the man in front of him. "What are you doing here?"

Terrance "Tex" Lehy's mouth twitched. Made a clucking noise. "Well…it's complicated."

"It always is, huh?" Lee worked his tongue. Realized he was parched. He looked at the military hardware arrayed before him. "How'd you know I was here?"

"I know you're suspicious. I would be too." Tex nodded. "I'll explain everything I can. But, first off, we're on the same side. Second, you and I both have a friend in Greeley. And third, you've got a leak at Fort Bragg that you need to plug, A-S-A-fucking-P."

Then Tex extended his hand to Lee.

Lee stared at it for a moment, like he didn't know what it was for. Like he wasn't sure about the point of civil gestures. But just as the moment started to grow taut, Lee stepped forward and took Tex's offered hand. Gave it one firm shake.

Tex smiled grimly. "We got a lot to talk about."

It was at that moment that Deuce turned his nose northward, back the way they'd come, and he let out a low growl that very suddenly built, and built, and ended with a snarling bark.

Tex twitched a bit when Deuce did this. Retracted his hand from Lee's. "What's he doing?"

Deuce was now backpedaling away from the burning, destroyed gates. Gates that would no longer be useful to keep anything out. His tail was low, not quite between his legs, but almost. He let out another bark, and this time looked at Lee as though to say, *You're fucking hearing me bark right?*

Lee looked out, and down the road where the destruction of war lay littered, the air shimmering from the heat of multiple fires. Was it just the air shimmering there, or had a shadow briefly flitted across the road?

"Means there's infected coming," Lee said to Tex. What he didn't say was the thought that skittered through his head: *After a thirty minute firefight like that, we've attracted every goddamn primal within five miles of us.*

Lee keyed his comms. "Carl, if you're not already on the way, you need to get a move on, brother. Primals are comin'."

"Roger that," Carl came back, sounding out of breath. "Already on the move."

He must have been closer than Lee thought, because he emerged from the woods a moment later, hobbling along on his wounded leg, toting his big sniper rifle with him. Almost to the smoking gates already.

Lee started moving towards Carl, but turned to look at Tex over his shoulder. "You need to get everyone inside and batten down the hatches."

"Now?" Tex asked, already beginning to step backwards towards his Humvee.

Between Deuce's own panicked barks, Lee thought he heard a scream, out beyond the fences, somewhere in the woods.

Lee called over his shoulder, "Cover us first."

He reached Carl and threw an arm around the other man's shoulder, and for once, Carl didn't hesitate to be helped. He leaned heavily on Lee as they jogged through the wreckage of the burning vehicles, back towards Building Four.

Behind them, no more screams came.

And Lee knew what that meant.

THIRTY-FOUR

SKELETONS

Colonel Staley finally located Angela in the Emergency Room of the Medical Center.

He was back in his Desert Digital Uniform. He entered the Emergency Room, which had become a madhouse since the lockdown had been lifted. There were only a few legitimate injuries, but the scare of infection seemed to be making people crazy. People were demanding to have their blood checked for infection, even though they hadn't come into contact with the primals.

There was a virulent rumor floating around that the primals that had attacked them had been one of the families from Fort Bragg. That they'd somehow been infected by something—food and water were two differing opinions—and that they'd been holed up in their house until they'd gone fully mad and went on a rampage.

It showed a shocking lack of understanding about how the FURY bacterium worked.

You would think that people who had survived this far would have more knowledge about what exactly they had survived.

But fear was potent, and it poisoned people's reason.

All they could do at this point was try to educate the people, and continue to calmly deny the ridiculous rumors. Though denial seemed only to incite more conspiracy theories. But what else could they do to stem people's panic?

Staley barged through the crowded emergency room, ignoring questions that were randomly lobbed at him. He found the room where Angela was holed up with Abby, Sam, Marie, and Kurt. Then he shut the door behind them.

The door quieted the rumble of the idiots on the other side.

Angela was sitting next to Abby's bed, looking like she was about to fall asleep. Her groggy eyes opened when he closed the door, and she stood up, as though attempting to look like she hadn't been falling asleep.

"Colonel," she said, exhaustion thick in her voice. "What's the word?"

"Just got my Marines out the gate," Staley answered. "They're hauling ass towards Alabama as we speak."

"Any word from Lee yet?"

Staley shook his head. "No, ma'am."

Angela nodded, her eyes unfocused. She frowned. "What about the primals? Did you find where they got in?"

"Yes." Staley took a troubled breath. "There was a culvert. It drains out of McFayden Pond. It has a gate over it. Carl Gilliard's boys have been aware of the culvert for some time. They said there was a large padlock that kept the gate secured. When it became apparent that the primals had gone into that tunnel, we sent a squad in after them. They found no primals, but they did find an open gate, and a padlock that looked like it had been cut through."

Angela's eyes widened. Then narrowed again. "Wait. You're not saying…"

Staley shook his head. "No, I don't think the primals cut it. The squad leader that found the lock reported that the cut was rusted over, and the lock was buried in a layer of silt. It was cut some time ago."

Angela looked over her shoulder at the others, then back to Staley and lowered her voice. "Sabotage?"

Staley shrugged. "No way to be sure."

"So that culvert gate has been unsecured for God-knows how long."

"Yes. Of course, we've re-secured it. Welded it shut, actually."

"Are there any other drain gates like that?" Angela asked. "Any other places we haven't thought about?"

"I've got people looking into it."

Angela nodded, but still looked troubled.

Staley looked past her at Abby. "How is she?"

Angela bowed her head. Lowered her voice even more. "Doctor Trent says...*cautiously optimistic*. Whatever the fuck that means. Pardon my French."

Staley waved off her apology.

"They say," Angela continued. "That at this point they would expect to see an elevated white blood cell count. If she was actually...you know...infected." Angela straightened some. Forced a smile. "But they don't. They say her white blood cells are good. So. We're not out of the woods, he says. But it's looking good."

"That's excellent news," Staley said. Then looked very seriously at Angela. "And it also raises some very interesting questions."

Angela had an expression that said she didn't want to get into it at that moment. "Just trying not to look the gift horse in the mouth, colonel."

Staley nodded curtly. "Of course." He gave her a platonic squeeze on her shoulder. "I'll leave you be for now. Lots to do. And you should rest, Angela. Fort Bragg is going to need you."

Angela promised that she would, and Staley left the room.

Back out into the mob of fearful sheep.

He got about halfway to the exit when he heard someone calling his name.

He chose to ignore it until it sounded like they were right behind him.

"Colonel Staley, sir!"

Finally, with a grumble under his breath he turned and found himself facing Lieutenant Derrick, the Watch Commander from last night. The man looked frazzled and about as tired as the rest of them.

"Yes, lieutenant?"

"I've been trying to find you, sir."

"Clearly. What is it?"

Derrick glanced around, shuffled closer to Staley. "Sir, I think you'd like to have this conversation in private."

Staley pursed his lips. "Alright then. Walk with me."

They shouldered through the rest of the crowd.

Exited the ER.

Out into bright, midday sunshine.

Staley kept walking. He'd walked to the Medical Center from his offices in the Soldier Support Center, and he intended to walk back. He kept a brisk pace, and said nothing until they were fully clear of the entrance to the hospital.

"Alright. Talk."

"Well, sir..." Derrick seemed hesitant. "I came across a...discrepancy. With the satphone."

"M-hm."

"The one we keep in the office."

"Yes?"

"Well, sir, I checked the call log. Just...on a whim. You know?"

Staley didn't answer. Kept walking.

"There was a number that was dialed last night. From our satphone. I didn't recognize it. So I cross-checked it with the numbers we have on file. And...well, it's not any of the stations in the UES. It's not a number we have on file."

Staley stopped walking. He faced Lieutenant Derrick. Looked the other man in the eye. "Did you call the number?"

"Yes, sir." Derrick's hesitancy had turned to something like nervousness.

Staley raised his eyebrows as if to say, *spit it out.*

"When I called, a man answered. I didn't recognize the voice. I asked him to identify himself, and he hung up."

Staley frowned deeply, feeling the first little primers of suspicion go off in his gut. Lee had advised them of a possible leak here at Fort Bragg. This could be their first evidence of that.

"Did you record the number?" Staley demanded.

Derrick nodded hastily and produced a slip of paper from his shirt pocket. He handed it to Staley, then stood there, looking unsure of himself. Looking pained.

Staley eyed the number. Then pocketed it. "Who was the last person to use the phone?"

Derrick swallowed. "Well. Angela used it to speak with Lee last night. But..." a deep breath. "That's why I came to you directly, sir. It was, uh, well..."

"Speak," Staley growled.

"It was Claire, sir. She returned the phone to me last night. She was the last person to have the phone."

The two men stood there in the warm sun for a long moment. Staley staring at the lieutenant in front of him like he was trying to turn him into stone. The lieutenant seemed to have run out of words. He didn't move. Didn't even sway on his feet. Maybe he *had* turned to stone.

It's a mistake, Staley thought. *Some sort of mistake. Claire will clear this up.*

Staley sniffed. "Did you tell anyone else about this?"

"No, sir. I came straight to you."

Staley nodded stiffly. Thought.

Thought hard.

Claire will clear this up.

"This conversation stays between me and you," Staley said. "I'll investigate it myself."

Derrick's eyes squirrelled around, like that answer troubled him, but he nodded crisply. "Of course, sir."

—

After Angela watched Colonel Staley leave the ER, she stood there in the room, peeking out at the hubbub of gathered people, and the woefully understaffed medical personnel flying about, doing their best to try to tell people that they weren't infected, and that there was no risk simply because primals had gotten inside the wire.

Some people accepted this. Others demanded to have their blood tested. But the medical staff knew there wasn't enough equipment to test everyone's blood. And if they allowed one person to have their blood tested, everyone would want theirs tested too.

Angela thought about stepping out and trying to address the people.

Then she thought perhaps she'd just make the situation worse.

Are you losing control of these people?

Did you ever have control of them in the first place?

In all the rushing around she spotted a bald, sweating head, worried eyes behind a pair of wire-framed glasses.

Doc Trent. Doing his best to be helpful.

She remembered that he'd been trying to get ahold of her before everything had gone to shit. It seemed that right now was just as poor a time to try to talk with him, but then again, after everything that happened, she wondered if there was ever going to be a *good* time again.

She turned back to the bed where Abby lay. She was going to tell Abby that she would be gone for a moment and come right back, but Abby was asleep now.

She left the room. Plunged through the crowded area beyond, keeping her head down and hoping people wouldn't bother her. She was lucky. Everyone was too concerned with their own problems to start haranguing her.

She angled around the nurses' station and caught up with Doc Trent as he was walking away. He was moving briskly, like he was trying to make a fast, discreet exit.

"Doctor Trent?" she called out after him.

She watched his shoulders slump as he heard his name.

She thought maybe he might continue to try and escape. But he turned.

And stiffened when he saw Angela.

"Oh. Angela." He looked frozen. Caught.

Angela stopped in front of him. "Sorry, I know you're busy right now."

He gave her a wavering smile. "It's like the world's ending. Again."

Angela nodded, but was focused on what she needed from him. "You've been trying to get a hold of me."

He blinked a few times. His countenance appeared to wither. Then his eyes darted about. "Right. Yeah. Uh..." His smallish hands wiggled in the air, like he was trying to feel his way through this. Then they clenched, and went to his sides. "Not here."

He turned, motioned with his head, and began walking again.

Angela kept pace behind him.

He led her out of the main ER, into a corridor beyond where there were no less than ten hospital beds with people sitting on them, waiting for blood tests that weren't going to happen. Some of these people looked up at Angela as Doc Trent led her past them.

Was that fear in their eyes?

Anger?

Resentment?

Did they blame her for this?

Doc Trent made an abrupt stop at the end of the hall, at a door with a plaque that said "X-RAY." He keyed a code into a push-button lock, then swung the door open and slipped in, holding the door for Angela. He peered out as though they were thieves breaking in, then quietly shut the door behind them.

The x-ray room was dark. Empty. The technician's station was partitioned off, and the only light in the room was coming from the overheads there, spilling through the observation window. The big hulk of the x-ray machine hung from the ceiling, still and unused.

Doc Trent faced her in this dim space, his hands now clasped together in front of him.

"The primal," Angela prompted. "The one that Lee brought back from Field Twenty-Nine. That's what this is about, right?"

Doc Trent wet his lips. Nodded.

Angela was torn between wanting to tell him to forget it, she didn't want to know, and a sort of morbid curiosity that gripped her. She didn't like the way that Doc Trent was acting about this. But...

She was the president.

She needed to know.

"I understand," she began again. "That you were trying to determine its age. Were you able to do that?"

Doc Trent shuffled his feet and adjusted his glasses. He seemed agitated. "Yeah. Sure." A long pause. "It's somewhere between two and sixteen."

Angela stared at him, trying to absorb what he'd said. She opened her mouth. Hesitated. Decided to go with, "Well, that's a pretty large range of years."

Doc Trent let out something like a mad giggle. He didn't seem to be aware of how ridiculous it sounded. His eyes were locked on Angela's. "This...this primal. It's..." He took a big breath. "The size of the creature suggests a juvenile of about eight. The muscle density suggests someone in their teens. The bone plates in its skull suggest a child of about two. And its dentition...its dentition is all over the place. The top and bottom canines are rooted.

Like adult teeth. But…no molars at all. The incisors are typical, unrooted baby teeth." He crossed his arms. "So, you ask me how old this thing is and I tell you: it's somewhere between two and sixteen."

Very suddenly, Doc Trent appeared to wilt. The tension left him, like voicing the words had turned his muscles to slag. He slouched in place, staring off to the right, eyes unfocused, looking at nothing in particular.

Angela felt her pulse in her head, but it was still steady. She heard her own respirations. They were steady too. Steady, like someone walking a tightrope. Steady, because that's what you had to do to keep from falling.

She swallowed. "How is that possible?"

Another weird titter came out of the older man. "Because it's not human?" he offered. "That wasn't a question. It's a statement. It's not human. *They* are not human. I don't know how such a divergence can happen in such a small amount of time. But it did. They're not just people that have gone insane anymore, Angela. They're a different species."

"That's not possible. Did you confirm this? Did you test the DNA?"

Doc Trent flapped his lips. "Pff. We don't have the equipment for DNA testing. I can't prove it. But it's the only thing that makes sense to me. So I guess…" he smiled unpleasantly. "I guess it's just a theory. Just like Jacob. I'm a fucking quack like Jacob now."

"They're outbreeding us."

"Who the hell knows?" Doc Trent snapped. Then looked ashamed. "Sorry. I didn't want Lee to be right. I didn't want to believe..." he trailed off. Took a sharp breath. "It's menstruating."

The statement was so oddball and out of place, that Angela twitched, and then blinked. "I'm sorry. What?"

"Lee was right," Doc Trent said. Heavy. Dreamy. "The thing was probably two years old. But it was menstruating. I could see it in the lining of its uterus. Two years old, Angela. And sexually mature. No natural predators. Top of the food chain." He raised a finger to his eyebrow, swiped a greasy bead of sweat away. "In another year, there's going to be more primals in this country than humans."

—

Nurse Sullivan walked stiffly down the sidewalk as the sun set at her back. She saw her shadow stretching out in front of her. Another shadow, to her right, was coming abreast of her.

She'd already spied Elsie Foster a block back. Elsie had been walking very deliberately toward Nurse Sullivan. Sullivan had hurried on, hoping in vain that she was not the target.

Her feet moved hurriedly across the sidewalk, all but speed-walking at this point. Like she was terribly late for something. The legs of her scrubs made little *swish-swish* noises.

Elsie Foster's shadow loomed to her right, and Sullivan realized that she wasn't going to speed-walk her way out of this.

She slowed to a more reasonable pace, her heart already thumping. Her breathing starting to quicken.

The nurse glanced to her right. Elsie walked along beside her, eyes forward, a stern expression on her lips.

"If I didn't know better, I'd say you were just trying to get away from me, Taylor."

Sullivan glanced around nervously, but there wasn't anyone around to overhear them. "We shouldn't be talking in the open like this." And then, to make it seem like she was worried about Elsie, she added, "It could be dangerous for you right now."

"You let me worry about who I talk to out in the open, okay?"

Sullivan clamped her lips down.

They went another three brisk paces.

Sullivan could see the house that she shared with another family, up ahead. Two blocks away.

What would they think if they saw her with Elsie Foster?

Sullivan was nearly overcome with the desire to be rid of Elsie.

At that moment, she would have consented to nearly anything if it meant that Elsie would peel off and leave her be.

The problem was, she'd already *given* her consent, hadn't she?

Yes. She'd already agreed to something terrible. Earlier that very morning, actually.

She just hadn't gone through with it.

"You know why I'm here, Taylor," Elsie prodded.

"We don't know yet," Sullivan snapped. "Okay? I didn't do it, because we don't know."

"Is she infected, or isn't she? That should be a pretty simple thing to determine."

"Well, it's not." Sullivan almost left it at that, but if she left it at that, she knew that Elsie was going to pursue her right up onto the front porch and smile and wave for Sullivan's house-mates. "She's still under observation. It might not manifest for another day or so. Sometimes the infection through bites can take a while. And…" Sullivan looked around again, feeling conspicuous. She lowered her voice. "I'm not going to do it if I don't have to!"

"If you wait too long, it's going to look suspicious."

"I won't wait too long," Sullivan assured her, and felt suddenly sick. Her mouth sweated violently, and she felt like the blood was draining out of her. Was she really saying this? They were talking about a little girl!

Sullivan almost had to dive for the gutter and puke.

But a deep breath managed to still her quaking guts.

"She is *going* to get sick," Elsie said, her voice icy and as immovable as a thousand-year-old glacier. "Either by natural causes, or by unnatural causes. And it needs to happen quickly, Sullivan, or we're going to have problems. You do understand that, don't you?"

Sullivan nodded. Felt clammy sweat on her palms. Limbs trembling.

"Tomorrow," Elsie said. "Tomorrow, I want to hear the news." She finally turned and fixed Taylor Sullivan with a firm and meaningful gaze. "Or people are going to find out about what Ben's been up to. And you don't want that, do you? Because a boy who rapes the neighbor's daughter, not to mention his mother who knew about it and didn't say anything...why, I don't think they'd be very welcome around here anymore. They'd get kicked out of the Safe Zone. Out of the UES in general. Out beyond the electric fences. Out with all the primals." Elsie smirked. "And don't kid yourself, Taylor. You and Ben wouldn't last a fucking day."

Sullivan realized she had stopped walking. She was standing, her face as white as a full moon, staring at the cracked sidewalk in front of her and the leaves and pine needles that cluttered the concrete and the curb.

"Don't think about Abby, Nurse Sullivan," Elsie advised, putting a familial hand on her shoulder. "Just think about Ben. And yourself, of course." She gave Sullivan's shoulder a squeeze. "Just get it done and everything will be okay."

Then she left Sullivan standing there.

After perhaps thirty seconds, which is a very long time to be standing stock-still in the middle of a sidewalk, Nurse Sullivan suddenly straightened, as though a switch had been flipped in her mind. Her expression went from the look of person staring at a torture rack for which they are bound, back to the look of someone who is simply walking home from work.

She walked the remaining block to her house, and only paused a moment before she opened the door. She fixed a tired smile on her face, and then pushed through.

—

Staley felt sick to his stomach as he stood in his daughter's room.

She was an adult. She deserved to live on her own. But that was not how the world worked anymore. People had to make do. They lived in tight quarters. And so she lived with her father. He didn't mind. Sometimes, he felt that she did.

He looked at the bed. The dresser. Cheap furnishings. Battered and reclaimed.

After everything she'd been through. After everything *they'd* been through. When she'd been taken by the Followers. And the desperation that he'd felt as he searched for her. The surreal elation that he'd felt when he'd finally found her again. The guilt. The wondering. About what they'd done to her.

She didn't say, but he knew. They all knew.

Oh, my little girl.

How could he possibly distrust her? After everything she'd been through?

Claire will clear this up.

But then why was he standing in the middle of her room?

He'd learned long ago not to ask questions when you didn't want to know the answer. But that didn't always work. When he'd searched for her, when he'd chased the Followers and their psychotic cult leader halfway across the state, he'd known that he might find her dead one day. But he still had to do it. He was *compelled*.

Just as he was compelled now.

He *had* to know.

He moved methodically through the room. He searched slowly, and with care. He put everything back where he found it.

His mind was in knots. Dealing with the lives of battalions of American Marines had never done this to him. Only when you were dealing with your own child did it turn your stomach like this.

Your own daughter.

He fervently hoped not to find anything.

But the universe rarely cared what he hoped for.

He found it in her dresser.

There was a small space, between the back of the bottom drawer, and the back of the dresser itself. When he gently pulled the drawer all the way out and laid it on the floor next to him, he saw it. Duct-taped to the fiberboard backing.

He didn't touch it for a while.

And then he did.

Why else was he there?

He pulled the satphone from its spot. Gently, so as not to mess up the tape. It was identical to the ones that they had been using between Fort Bragg and the other settlements. It was one of the one's from Lee Harden's bunkers. It was easy enough to imagine how she'd gotten ahold of one. When they were first getting established here at Fort Bragg, their inventory systems had been nonexistent.

He powered it on. Then he went into the call log.

There was only one number in that log. A number that had been called over and over again.

Staley didn't need to check the slip of paper, but he did anyway.

He prayed for just one digit to be off.

But every number matched.

He shut the satphone off.

Sat there for a long time, on his knees, on the carpet, not looking like a colonel at all. Certainly not feeling like one. Old, hard-assed devil dog. Laid out like this. Laid bare.

Claire will explain this, he told himself again.

But then, he had to ask himself, *How? How the fuck do you explain this?*

He went through many options at that point. He weighed them all. The courses of action. The consequences. Who to tell. Who not to tell. Whether to tell anyone at all.

Eventually, he put the slip of paper with the number back in his pocket. Taped the satphone to the back of the dresser again, and replaced the bottom drawer. Closed it. Stood. Brushed off his knees. Straightened his uniform. Looked around the room and saw that everything was how he had found it.

And then silently walked out.

ABOUT THE AUTHOR

D.J. Molles is the New York Times bestselling author of *The Remaining* series. He is also the author of *Wolves*, a 2016 winner in the Horror category for the Foreword INDIES Book Awards. His other works include the *Grower's War* series, and the Audible original, *Johnny*. When he's not writing, he's taking care of his property in North Carolina, and training to be at least half as hard to kill as Lee Harden. He also enjoys playing his guitar, his violin, drawing, painting, and lots of other artsy fartsy stuff.

You can follow and contact him at:
Facebook.com/DJMolles

Sign up for his monthly newsletter by using your smartphone camera to scan this QR code, or go to
http://eepurl.com/c3kfjD

Also By D. J. Molles

The Remaining series:

The Remaining (Book 1)
The Remaining: Aftermath (Book 2)
The Remaining: Refugees (Book 3)
The Remaining: Fractured (Book 4)
The Remaining: Allegiance (Book 5)
The Remaining: Extinction (Book 6)

A Grower's War series:

The Purge Of District 89 (Book 1)
Renegades (Book 2)
Rogue Cell (Book 3)

Stand Alone Books:

Wolves

Johnny (Audible Original)

Made in the USA
Columbia, SC
10 June 2019